# THE CURE
# OF SOULS

Phil Rickman

# THE CURE
# OF SOULS

MACMILLAN

First published 2001 by Macmillan
an imprint of Pan Macmillan Ltd
Pan Macmillan, 20 New Wharf Road, London N1 9RR
Basingstoke and Oxford
Associated companies throughout the world
www.panmacmillan.com

ISBN 0 333 90623 3

5 7 9 8 6 4

A CIP catalogue record for this book is available from
the British Library.

Typeset by Intype London Ltd
Printed and bound in Great Britain by
Mackays of Chatham plc, Chatham, Kent

# Contents

# CONTENTS

## Part Two

## Part Three

# CONTENTS

# The Cure of Souls

# Prologue

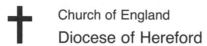 Church of England
Diocese of Hereford

# Ministry of Deliverance

email: deliverance@spiritec.co.uk

Click
⊃ Home Page
Hauntings
Possession
Cults
Psychic Abuse
Contacts
Prayers

If you've had a worrying experience of an unexplained or possibly paranormal nature, we may be able to help.

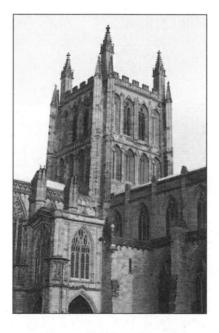

Many people troubled or frightened by the unknown are often embarrassed to discuss their problem or are scared of being laughed at or disbelieved.

The Deliverance Ministry is here to listen and advise – and we never make light of it.

# 1

# Special

It was really getting to Jane now, tormenting her nights, raiding her head as soon as she awoke in the mornings. The way things did when there was nobody – like, *nobody* – you could tell.

*I'm sixteen years old, and I'm . . .*

Feeling deeply isolated, she walked numbly out of the school, with its acrid anxiety-smell, and into the sun-splashed quadrangle, where Scott Eagles and Sigourney Jones were already into a full-blown, feely snog almost directly under the staffroom window.

The big statement. This was Jones and Eagles telling the sad old gits in the staffroom that the English Language GCSE that they and Jane and a bunch of other kids had just completed, was, like all the other GCSEs – the focus of their school-life for the past four or five years – of truly minuscule significance in comparison with their incredible obsession with one another.

Yes, having done their sleeping around, they were into something long-term and meaningful. Life-partners, possibly. An awesome thing.

Jane, however, felt like part of some other species. *Sixteen years old and . . .*

She closed her eyes on the superior, super-glued lovers. Walked away from the whole naff sixties edifice of concrete and washed-out brick sinking slowly into the pitted asphalt exercise yard, which the Head liked to call a quadrangle. She needed out of here, like *now*. And yet she kept wishing the term still had weeks to run.

'So, how was it for you Jane?'

'Huh?'

She spun round. The sun was a slap in the face. Candida Butler was shimmering alongside her, tall and cool, the words *head girl material* shining out of her sweatless forehead as they probably had since she was ten.

'The exam, Jane.' Candida wrinkled a sensible nose at the Jones-and-Eagles show. Her own boyfriend was at Cambridge, reading astrophysics. An older guy, natch. Candida – who was never going to be called Candy by anyone – was serene and focused, and knew it.

'Pity the essay titles were all so crap,' Jane said.

'Did you think so?' Candida looked mildly surprised. She'd have opted for the utterly safe and anodyne *My Grandmother's Attic*. 'Anyway, it's another one over, that's the main thing.' She looked down at Jane with that soft, mature smile. 'So what are you going to be doing with yourself this summer?'

The sun's reflection lasered out of the plate-glass doors of the new science block. Danny Gittoes and Dean Wall, who probably still couldn't get the letters 'GCSE' in the right order, came out of the toilets grinning and ripping off their school ties in preparation for another bid to get served in the Royal Oak, where the teachers drank. Went without saying that *they* wouldn't be coming back in the autumn.

Jane wished it was already winter. She wished she could spend the next seven weeks holed up in her own attic apartment, under the Mondrian walls, with a pile of comfort-reading.

*I am sixteen, and I'm an old maid.*

'I'm going on holiday for a couple of weeks,' she said miserably. 'With my boyfriend. At his family's holiday home.'

From the edge of the quad, where it met the secondary playing fields, you could see across miles of open countryside to the Black Mountains on the horizon.

On the other side of the mountains was Wales, another country. Eirion's country.

On the edge of Wales, probably nearly a hundred miles away, was the Pembrokeshire coast, where Eirion's family had their five-bedroom holiday 'cottage'. Where you could go surfing and walk the famous coastal path and lose your virginity. That kind of thing.

'Some people have all the luck,' said Candida. 'We're kind of

8

constrained this year, because Robert's got a holiday job at his cousin's software plant near Cheltenham.'

'Beats strangling poor bloody chickens at Sun Valley.'

'I suppose.' Candida's wealthy farming family probably had major shares in Sun Valley. 'Welsh, isn't he, your guy?'

'Not so's you'd notice.' Jane blushed. Then, furious with herself, she went over the top again. 'I mean, he doesn't shag *any* old sheep.'

Candida's eyes narrowed. 'Are you all right, Jane?'

'Yeah.' Jane sighed. 'Fine.'

Candida patted Jane's shoulder. 'See you next term, then. On the A level treadmill.'

'Sure.'

Jane watched Candida stride confidently across the quad towards the car park, where her mother would be waiting for her in the second-best Range Rover. Jane's own mum – ancient, clanking Volvo – would be a while yet. She'd had an early funeral to conduct: Alfred Rokes, who'd gone out at a hundred and two, having still been blacksmithing at ninety, so nothing too sorrowful there. And then – a little grief here, maybe – the Bishop was expected to call in.

With a good hour to kill, Jane could have strolled round the back for a cigarette. If she'd been into tobacco. But when your mum smoked like a chimney, what was the point?

Jane's nails dug into her palms.

An old maid who didn't even smoke. What kind of life *was* this?

OK, the problem. The problem was that Eirion was giving every impression of wanting to move them up to the Scott Eagles – Sigourney Jones relationship level.

Jane watched Jones and Eagles heading hand in hand for the students' car park. Scott had passed his test on his seventeenth birthday; he'd been driving Land Rovers since his feet could reach the pedals, which had probably been around the age of nine, because he was a tall guy, maybe fully grown now. Adult. Experienced.

Also, Eirion, himself – sexy enough, in his stocky, amiable way – had obviously been putting it about for years. *Well, you know, I was in this band*, he would say. Oh, Eirion had been around, no question.

And he *could* have had Jane, too, by now. She would have had sex with him, no arguments. In the back of the car or somewhere, anywhere; she just wanted the bloody thing cleared away, like dirty dishes – everybody said the first time was crap anyway, this messy chore to be undergone before you could start enjoying it.

But Eirion would gently detach her clammy little hand from his belt. *I want this to be proper*, he'd mumble. *Do you know what I'm saying?*

Proper? Like, what did *proper* have to do with it?

*I don't want this to be . . . ordinary, you know? Run-of-the-mill. Me and you, we're . . .* And then he'd go all embarrassed, looking out of the car window at the moon. Jesus.

*Ordinary?* Listen, 'ordinary' would have been just fine by Jane, who had no illusions, didn't expect rockets and Catherine wheels. 'Ordinary' would've been an enormous relief.

She found herself stomping across the playing field between the tennis courts, panting with anguish under the merciless sun. A torrid sun, guaranteed to turn the Pembrokeshire coast into Palm Beach. Did Eirion's fat-cat family have their *own* beach? Did they all sprawl around naked and uninhibited? Like, just because they were Welsh didn't mean they were all buttoned-up and chapel-whipped, necessarily. Probably the reverse: she and the Young Master would be assigned a double room and presented with a gross of condoms.

*Shit*. She shouldn't be feeling like this, because back in the exam room she'd probably done OK. You always sensed it. She'd get her ten GCSEs and then come back in September and do some A levels.

Come back as an adult, with a lover.

She swallowed.

So Eirion, at seventeen, was experienced and mature, had done the rounds, and had met Jane – who was sexually backward to what, in this day and age, was a frightening extent – and she had become like 'special' to him, maybe because when they'd first met she'd been physically hurt by someone she'd thought was a friend, and he'd felt protective and stuff . . . and that was OK, that was acceptable.

And '*special*'? . . . yeah, OK, that was flattering.

Or *would* have been flattering if she was ready to be 'special', which might have been the case if there'd been others – or least one other – before Eirion. But the first guy you actually did it with, at

10

the age of sixteen, really should not be 'special', should he? Not *long-term* special, not Jones-and-Eagles special. Not the very first guy.

Why the hell had she said she'd go there?

Jane began to blink back tears, seriously unravelled, not knowing what she wanted – except not to be a virgin. Not to be a virgin *now*. Not to have to take this useless lump of excess baggage with her to the Holiday Cottage.

In fact, if there'd been some not-over-acned sixth-former wandering towards her right now, she'd probably have been tempted to make him an offer he couldn't refuse, just to get IT out of the way.

Sure.

She was alone on the playing field. Somewhere in the distance she could hear howls of laughter – Walls and Gittoes on the loose, ready to crash the Royal Oak, pick a fight with a teacher. Their last week at school, the week they'd been dreaming of for five long years. They were adults now, too. Official. *Even Walls and Gittoes were adults!*

Panic seized Jane and she stood there, feeling exposed, the sun directly above her like a hot, baleful eye.

She was a child. Still a child.

Ahead of her was the groundsman's concrete shed, a square bunker standing out on its own. The groundsman was called Steve and he was about thirty and had big lips, like a horse, and this huge beer gut. He was a useful guy to know, however, because of this concrete shed: a safe house where card schools could meet, cigs and dope could be smoked, and Es and stuff exchanged. Steve would also deal the stuff himself, it was rumoured, but not with everybody; he was very careful and very selective.

Lower-sixth-formers Kirsty Ryan and Layla Riddock were less selective. They laughed openly at Steve but sometimes went into his shed with him after school. And what did slobbery Steve give them in return? Nobody knew, but it *was* rumoured that he could get actual cocaine for anyone who offered that kind of payment.

*School life. Sex and drugs and—*

Jane saw that the blinds were down over the window in the shed. There was absolutely no reason why a groundsman's hut should have blinds at all, but every window in the school was fitted with the same type, black and rubbery, so that educational videos could be shown at any time or the Net consulted.

There was no TV in here, obviously, no computer. The lowered blinds could only mean one thing: with the English Language GCSE not half an hour over, slobbery Steve was in there doing business.

You couldn't get away from it, could you? Jane shook her head wearily and was about to turn back across the field when the wooden door of the shed swung open.

She stiffened. The sun-flooded playing fields stretched away on three sides: everywhere to run, nowhere to hide.

'Well, come *on*,' a voice drawled from inside. 'Don't hang around.'

Jane didn't move. She imagined pills spread across Steve's work-bench – or maybe some really desperate sixth-former. Jane felt cocooned in heat and a sense of unreality.

She blinked.

Layla Riddock, large and ripe, stood there in the doorway of Steve's hut – in her microskirt, blouse open to the top of her bra. Like a hooker in the entrance to an alleyway.

'Well, well,' Layla said. 'The vicar's kid. We *are* honoured.'

# 2

# Little green apples

*Safety in numbers . . . spread the load . . . a problem shared.* The Bishop was heavy with clichés this morning, although what he was saying made sense when you accepted that the Church of England looked upon the supernatural like the Ministry of Defence regarded UFOs. Visitations? The blinding light on the road to Damascus? The softly glowing white figure in the grotto? God forbid.

The blinding sunlight over Ledwardine Vicarage was diffused by the thin venetian slats at the kitchen window. Bernie Dunmore's friar's tonsure was a fluffy halo. He topped up his glass with Scrumpy Jack from the can, beamed plumply at Merrily.

'They look at *you*, they see a symptom of escalating hysteria. They see the Church being dragged towards the threshold of a new medievalism simply to stay in business. Oh no.' Bernie shuddered. 'If the Third Millenium *does* witness the collapse of the Anglican Church, we'd rather go down quietly, with our passive dignity intact, leaving you out there waving your crosses at the sky and waiting for the angels.'

'That's not *me*, is it, Bernie?' Below the dog-collar, Merrily wore a dark grey cotton T-shirt and black jeans. Her hair was damp from the swift but crucial shower she'd managed to squeeze in between Alf Rokes's funeral and the arrival of the Bishop. 'They're saying that? Even after Ellis?'

But, OK, she knew what he meant. Nick Ellis had been a rampant evangelical who preached in a village hall plastered with CHRIST IS THE LIGHT posters and used the Holy Spirit like an oxyacetylene torch. Merrily Watkins was the crank who prayed for the release of earthbound spirits, currently setting up the first Hereford Deliverance Website to offer basic, on-line guidance to the psychically challenged. They hadn't liked each other, she and Ellis, but to a good half of the clergy they were out there on the same ledge.

And one of them was mad, and the other was a woman.

Bernie Dunmore was quite right, of course: she'd been putting it off too long.

She saw that he was blatantly inspecting her from head to feet – which wasn't far – as if looking for signs of depreciation.

'So you want to build a team, then, Bishop?'

'If Deliverance has its back to the wall, better it should be more than *one* back,' Bernie said sagely.

Well, fine. Most dioceses had one now: a Deliverance cluster, a posse of sympathetic priests as back-up for the exorcist. It was about spreading the load, fielding the flack, having people there to watch your back.

'OK, let's do it.' She came to sit down opposite him at the pine refectory table, where bars of yellow sunlight tiger-striped her bare arms. 'The problem is . . . who do we recruit?'

Bernie sank more cider. Merrily tried to think what his appearance suggested if not *Bishop*. You could almost think he'd been appointed simply because he looked so much like one – unlike his predecessor, Mick Hunter, who might have been a rising presenter from *Newsnight*. Previously, Bernie had been suffragan Bishop of Ludlow, the number two who rarely made it to the palace. But his formal acceptance by Downing Street as Bishop of Hereford had been a relief all round: a safe option.

'Anyone in particular you want to sound out, Merrily?'

Of course, she'd already been thinking about this a lot. But the members of the local clergy she most liked and trusted tended to be the ones who wouldn't touch Deliverance with coal-tongs and asbestos gloves. And the ones who actively sought involvement in what they imagined to be a hand-to-hand battle with Satan . . . well, Nick Ellis had wanted the job for himself; that told you all you needed to know.

'There must be any number of people out there better equipped spiritually than me.' Fighting off the urge to dig for a cigarette, she poured herself some spring water. 'I mean, so many people who seem to be living in what, seen from my miserable level, looks awfully like a state of grace.'

She glanced at him, worried he might think she was fishing for praise and reassurance. But there truly wasn't a day that went by without her feeling she wasn't up to this job, wondering if she wasn't any better than the mystical dabblers she was obliged to keep warning off.

'Then make me a list of these saintly buggers.' Bernie Dunmore would never have considered himself one of them either, but then saintliness had never been a prerequisite for bishops. 'Fax it across to the Palace or give it to Sophie. I'll make the approaches, if you like. Suppose we start with . . . what would you suggest . . . two?'

'Two clerics?'

'That's enough to begin with. Don't want Deliverance looking like a faction. And, ah, would they . . . pardon my ignorance, but would these two need to be, ah . . .?'

'What?' Merrily blinked.

'*You* know.'

'You mean psychic?'

He looked pained. 'What's that other word?'

'Sensitive?'

'Yes. Well . . . would they?'

'That's a good question.' She sipped some water.

'I mean, I never liked to ask, Merrily, but would you say that you yourself . . .?'

'Well, er . . .'

'This is not a witch-hunt, Watkins.'

'I don't honestly know,' she said. 'Maybe we all are, to a varying degree. And maybe just doing this job gives you . . . insights. That is, God—'

'All right,' Bernie said. 'Forget it. What else do we need?'

'A tame shrink. Sure, we can make a good guess at who's in genuine psychic torment and who's clinically paranoid, but a guess isn't good enough.'

'And how on earth do we go about finding one of *them*?' The

Bishop shook his cider can, but found it empty. Merrily rose to fetch him another from the fridge, but Bernie shook his head and put a hand over his glass. 'I mean, should we make a direct approach to the Health Authority, asking for nominations? And wouldn't a proper psychiatrist require some kind of retainer? Doctors don't like to do anything for nothing, in my experience, and the Archdeacon would be the first to query any kind of—'

'I don't know.' Merrily sat down again. 'There's a whole lot I don't know.'

'We're all feeling our way here,' said Bernie, whose official elevation had been confirmed only at the end of May. 'I mean, it's all hit-and-miss, isn't it? You get the wrong shrink, point him at some little old lady spouting the Lord's Prayer backwards in a rich baritone, and he'll still swear she's a paranoid schizophrenic.'

'Be hard to find one who won't always say that. And he – or she – also needs to be a Christian because, if we ever get someone with a malignant squatter inside them, the psychiatrist is going to have to be there for the showdown.'

Bernie winced at the terminology. 'I really can't help you much there, I'm afraid. I don't think I actually know any psychiatrists of *any* religious persuasion.'

'Me neither,' Merrily said. 'But I know a man who does.'

He looked at her with the interest he usually displayed when she mentioned she knew a man. She didn't elaborate. She was aching for a cigarette. Ethel, the black cat the vicarage had acquired from Lol Robinson, jumped onto her knee as if to prompt her, but Merrily kept quiet.

The Bishop got up and moved to the window. He was wearing his golfing clothes: pale green polo shirt over cream slacks and over what you didn't like to call a beer gut. If this had been Mick Hunter, the ensemble would have been mauve and purple-black: *episcopal chic*. But Mick Hunter wouldn't have played golf.

'What you said a few moments ago—' Bernie was looking out over the vicarage lawn, which Gomer Parry insisted on mowing twice a week '—about people living in a state of grace.'

The lawn ended at the old Powell orchard, which belonged now to the church. There were already tiny green apples on the trees, like individual grapes. Where *was* the year going to?

Merrily glanced at the clock. She was going to have to leave soon to pick up the kid after her English exam. No anxiety on that one, at least; English came naturally to Jane and it was the one GCSE that required no revision.

The Bishop coughed. 'There's something I've been meaning to say to you for a while.'

'Mmm?'

'You're still young.'

'Ish.'

'Young,' he said firmly. He had grandchildren Jane's age. He turned back into the room. 'And a very young widow.'

Merrily was about to remind him that if it hadn't been for a particular fatal car-crash on the M5 she might have been a not-so-young divorcee and therefore would never have made it into the priesthood. But she guessed they'd been into all that before.

Bernie said, 'We all know that when Tommy Dobbs was exorcist here he felt it incumbent upon him to develop a rather rigid, monastic way of life. Frugal. Steeped himself in prayer.'

'Yes,' she said. 'I think I can understand that fully now – why he did that.'

'However, he was an old man. You're a—'

'Whatever.' She stood up.

'Obviously, stepping into Dobbs's shoes, you were bound to feel you were walking on eggshells.'

'Well . . . that, and for other reasons, too.' She had a vague idea what was coming and clapped her hands together briskly. 'Look, Bernie, I'm afraid I've got to be off in a minute. Have to collect Jane from the school. GCSE-time? Once they finish an exam they can go home. I don't really want her heading down the pub.'

He nodded, not really taking it in. 'I . . . we've never minced words, you and I. Both accept that Hunter set you up to succeed Dobbs, to appear trendy . . . politically correct . . . all that tosh. And again, in my opinion, as I've told you on a number of occasions, in spite of all that it was probably one of Hunter's better moves. Not least because people who wouldn't dare go near that gruesome old bugger Dobbs will talk to you, as a human being. Young people, for instance. It's very important that we should help the young people.' He screwed up his face. 'What I'm trying to say, Merrily . . . I don't want you to be *scared* to be a human being.'

'Huh?'

'I mean, there must be times when you find yourself looking at young Jane – with all of it just beginning for her. Boyfriends, parties, you know what I mean. You must feel—'

'They're fairly human, too, in my experience.' Merrily raised an eyebrow. 'Nuns.'

There was a moment of silence, then the Bishop sighed softly. 'Well, you said it.'

'I was trying to help you out.'

'Bloody hell, Merrily!' He brought his left fist down on the back of a dining chair.

Well, what was she supposed to say? She hadn't exactly *applied* for the job down here on the coalface of Christianity: day-to-day confrontation with the intangible, the amorphous and the unproven, as experienced by the damaged, the vulnerable, the disturbed and the fraudulent.

Was the Bishop actually implying that she might find all this easier to cope with if she went out, got drunk, and got laid a time or two?

Probably not. He was probably just covering himself.

'All I'm saying—' Bernie thrust his left hand into his hip pocket, maybe to conceal the fact that he'd hurt it on the back of the chair '—is that Deliverance has started taking on a much higher profile than any of us imagined. I don't want you cracking up on me, or *tightening* up – building some kind of impenetrable spiritual shell around yourself, the way Dobbs did.'

'Oh, I doubt I'd have the personal strength for that, Bernie.'

'Didn't matter with Dobbs, because half the Hereford clergy didn't even know what he actually did. He could go his own way. All his pressures were . . . inner ones.'

'Yes.'

She noticed that a few of the little green apples had either fallen or been plucked from the orchard trees and now lay forlornly on new-mown grass that was already showing signs of sun-scorching.

She wondered if there was some sinister piece of local folklore about premature windfalls.

'Anyway,' the Bishop said, 'I'll want you to fax me that list by tomorrow night.'

'I will, I will.'

'And start helping yourself to a bit of ordinary life, Merrily. Before it gets eaten away.'

# Soiled place

It was like some illicit members' club for which she'd accidentally given the secret sign. One foot over the threshold, and she was pulled in and Layla Riddock had closed the door behind them. Then she heard a lock turn and Layla was pulling the key out of the door, sliding it into her skirt pocket.

*What?*

The two candles on the workbench made shadows rise and turned the metal handles of the oldest lawnmower into twin cobra-heads. One of the flames was reflected, magnified and distorted, in the bevelled side of a glass. It looked like one of the water glasses from the dining hall, upturned in the centre of the bench-top.

'Welcome,' Layla Riddock said.

If Candida Butler looked mature, Layla looked somehow *old*, as in seasoned, as in tainted, as in kind of corrupt – or maybe you just thought that because of what you knew about her and all the guys she'd had. Like, actual *guys*, not boys.

But there were no guys in here today, not even Steve the beer-gutted groundsman.

'Take a seat, then.' Layla pulled out some kind of oil drum, tapped on the top of it with her nails.

The other girls said nothing.

Only the chunky Kirsty Ryan, Layla's mate, turned her spiky red head towards Jane. Kirsty was sitting on the mower's grassbox turned on its side. The other girl, on a stool, kept on looking down at the bench-top where pieces of cardboard the size of playing cards were

20

arranged in a circle, the candles standing outside of it, in what looked like tobacco tins.

'Well, go *on*,' Layla said.

Jane sat down on the oil drum, next to Kirsty Ryan, because . . . well, because when Layla told you to do something, you somehow just did it. Layla was tall and good-looking in this kind of pouting, sexual way, and she somehow had this *forceful* thing about her, an aura of grim authority. Her father had been a gypsy – she liked to tell people that, liked hinting she had a long tradition of secret powers behind her. The gypsy must have moved on pretty quick, though, because Layla's mother was long-married to Allan Henry, the well-known builder and property developer – *ALLAN HENRY HOMES* – and they lived in this huge, crass, ranch-style bungalow, with a swimming pool and a snooker room, out near Canon Pyon. Riddock was presumably her mother's family name . . . or the gypsy's.

'It's Jane, right?' Layla sat down on a stool at the head of the bench, behind the candle tins. 'Kirsty you know, I assume. And that's Amy. Fourth-year.' She pushed the candles further apart, so that they were arranged either side of her and she looked like some sombre, smouldering idol in an Indian temple.

The card in front of Jane said **NO**. The letters were printed on white paper stuck to the card. Now she had an idea what this was.

Kirsty Ryan turned to her. 'You got the ten quid on you?'

Jane said nothing.

'She can bring it in tomorrow,' Layla said crisply, then looked at Jane without smiling. 'Cheap at the price, love, you'll find out.'

Kirsty smirked.

Jane thought she saw Amy stiffen. The kid was slight and fair-haired and was the only one in here wearing her school blazer, despite the heat. She was sitting directly opposite Jane. In front of her was the card that said **YES**.

Kirsty said to Jane, 'You come with a special question? Got a problem you want sorted?'

Jane shook her head.

'Lying little cow,' Kirsty said.

Jane said nothing. She had to get out of here, but it would be seriously unwise to let any of them know that.

'Told you there'd be another one along, didn't I?' Layla folded her arms in satisfaction.

'There was this other kid,' Kirsty explained, 'but she got shit-scared and backed out, and we were worried they wouldn't like it. There should be four.'

*They?* Jane cleared her throat. 'Why?'

''Cause we *started out* with four. So, like . . . your mother's a vicar, yeah?'

'So?'

'Oh, not just a vicar,' Layla said, 'is she, love?'

Jane shrugged, keeping her lips clamped. She didn't like talking about what Mum did, especially to someone like Layla Riddock.

'So what would she say to this, your old lady?'

Jane managed a nervous grin but still said nothing. Her old lady would probably have snatched up the glass, scattered the letters and called on God and all His angels to cleanse this soiled place like *now*.

Kirsty said, 'Who told you about this?'

'Nobody,' Jane said. 'I was just—'

'It doesn't matter.' Layla leaned forward, those big, heavy breasts straining to come bouncing out of her blouse. 'This is excellent. I think . . . I really do think that this is going to be a really good sitting.'

'Yeah,' said Kirsty, rebuked. 'Right.'

Jane had never actually done this before. It belonged to the realm of sad gits, people with no real hold on life. It was a joke. Unhealthy, maybe, but still a joke.

She had to keep thinking like that, because she knew there was no way she was going to get out of here until it was over. OK, she could leap up and demand the key and they probably wouldn't use violence to stop her. (Or would they?)

But that wouldn't be awfully cool, would it?

Besides, it might be, you know . . . kind of interesting.

The air in the groundsman's hut smelled of oil and sweat. The candlelight had found a little moisture in the cleft over Layla Riddock's upper lip as it curled at last into a sort of smile.

'Let's go for it, then,' Layla said.

It was terrifying.

And like . . . really addictive.

The glass made an eerie sound as it moved across the greasy surface of Steve's bench. Like a coffin sliding through the curtains of a crematorium, reflected Jane, who had never been inside a crematorium, not even when her dad had died.

The first time—

'Are you here?' Layla had asked calmly.

—the glass shot directly to **YES** with the snap precision of a fast cue ball on a snooker table, and the sudden movement made both candle-flames go almost horizontal, like in the wind created when someone suddenly slams a door. Jane was so shocked she almost jerked her finger away.

'Good,' Layla said.

Jane let out a fast breath. She hadn't expected that to happen. Nobody could be pushing; it just wasn't possible.

'Now, tell us your name,' Layla instructed.

*It*, Jane thought.

There couldn't be an *it*. Not on a summer afternoon in Slobbery Steve's filthy shed in the precincts of the dreary once-modernist Moorfield High School, Herefordshire.

It was a scam, that was all. There had to be a trick to it, a method of setting up momentum without appearing to apply pressure – an interesting end-of-term conundrum for the anoraks in the new science block.

Jane looked into Layla's face. Layla's eyes were shut, but her wide mouth was set into a closed-lips smile that seemed to shimmer in the moist light, and Jane felt sure that Layla could see her through those lowered lids, as—

The glass glided, dragging Jane's finger, then her hand across the oily bench-top towards the letter J.

OK, that was it. She was annoyed now. So, like, suppose *she* tried to manoeuvre it. Suppose she exerted a little deliberate pressure of her own next time. Suppose, with some really intense concentration, a blast of hyper-focused will-power, she could make it spell out *Jane* . . .

Will-power, yeah: thought-projection. She glanced up at Layla. Layla's eyes still didn't open.

All *right*. She located the letter **A**, halfway between Kirsty and the kid Amy, and she really, *really* concentrated on it, and when the glass began to move, she tried to—

The glass was dragged from under her forefinger, to slide unstoppably to the letter **U**.

Jane leaned back. She didn't like this. She really didn't like it.

She became aware that the girl opposite her, Amy of the fourth form, had begun panting. Her fair hair was pulled back tightly from her face and her skin seemed to be stretched taut. Now, Jane knew exactly who she was. She was the one who looked like one of those plaster mannequins in an old-fashioned school-outfitters: skirt always uncreased, blazer always buttoned, tie always straight, hair perfectly shoulder-length, perfectly brushed. Amy's ultimate role model would be Candida Butler.

What was *wrong* with her? If this scared her so much, what was she doing here?

Because it was addictive? Because it worked?

*Get me out of this.*

The glass moved under Jane's finger, slid back into the centre of the circle of letters and off again. The bloody thing seemed to know exactly where it was going, and she just let it happen now, watching the finger in motion, with the forefingers of the other three – all of them apparently just resting on the thick base of the glass – and all the time trying to *separate* herself from this, pretending that finger was no longer connected to her nervous system.

Watching the glass spelling out one word, before it stopped in the dead centre of the circle.

J-U-S-T-I-N-E

Amy drew in a long, ratchety kind of breath.

# Part One

## The Flavour in the Beer

*The hop belongs to the same family as hemp and cannabis and is a relative of the nettle. A hardy, long-lived climbing perennial, its shoots can reach 20 feet in length but die back to ground level every winter. It has no tendrils and climbs clockwise round its support. Although it will grow in the poorest soils, only optimum conditions will produce the quality needed for today's shrinking markets. As a result, hop-growing in Herefordshire is now concentrated in the sheltered valleys of the Frome and Lugg, where there are at least 18 inches of loamy soil.*

*A Pocketful of Hops* (Bromyard and District Local
History Society, 1988)

# Ministry of Deliverance

email: deliverance@spiritec.co.uk

**Click**

Home Page
Hauntings
Possession
Cults
⟳ Psychic Abuse
Contacts
Prayers

## Psychic Abuse

Psychic abilities, real or pretended, are often used to gain power and influence over groups and individuals. It is very easy to become intimidated by a person who claims to have access to super-normal forces, even though we may suspect these 'powers' amount to nothing more than a strong or dominant personality.

This kind of situation usually calls for some personal spiritual defence, beginning with prayer and then perhaps extending, if necessary, to support from a priest.

# ONE

# The Wires

In the warm, milky night, Lol was leaning against a five-barred gate, listening for the River Frome. It couldn't be more than six yards away, but you'd never know; this was the nature of the Frome.

Crossing the wooden bridge, he'd looked down and seen nothing. That was OK. It was a small and secretive river that, in places, didn't flow so much as seep, dark as beer, obscured by ground-hugging bushes and banks of willowherb. Already Lol felt a deep affinity with the Frome; he just didn't want to step into it in the dark, that was all.

'River?' Prof Levin had said vaguely this morning. 'That's a river? I thought it was some kind of sodding drainage ditch.'

Which had only made Lol more drawn it. Later, he'd sat down in the sun with his old Washburn guitar and started to assemble a wistful song.

> *Did you ever think you'd reach the sea,*
> *Aspiring to an estuary.*
> *But − hey − who could take that seriously . . .?*

Yeah, *who*? Like, wasn't he supposed to have turned his back on all this for good?

Now here was Prof Levin, forever on at him to give it another go. And Prof didn't give up easily, so Lol had gone wandering out into this milky night feeling guilty and confused, nerves quivering, jagged pieces of his past sticking out of him like shards of glass from a smashed mirror.

Seeking the unassuming tranquillity of the night-time river, nothing more than that. The modern countryside, Prof Levin had insisted this morning, was one big sham.

'Close to nature? Balls! This is heavy industrial, Laurence. Guys in baseball caps driving machinery you could build motorways with – six-speaker stereo in the cab, blasting jungle. These lanes ain't wide enough for the bastards any more.'

Grabbing hold of the bottom of Lol's T-shirt, Prof had towed him to the window, overlooking someone else's long meadow sloping to the bank of the River Frome.

'Week or two, they'll be out there haymaking . . . *techno*-hay-making. Come September they start on the hops over there – and *that*'s all mechanized. Take a look at the size of those tractors, tell me this ain't heavy industry. They don't even stop at night! Got lamps on them like frigging great searchlights – doing shift work now! Who ever hears the cock crow any more? This, Laurence . . . this is the new rural. And here's me padding out the frigging walls to double-thickness on account of I don't want to disturb *them*.'

Prof Levin grinning ruefully through his white nail-brush beard: a shaven-headed, wiry man of over sixty years old – precisely how far over nobody would know until he was dead and not necessarily even then. When Lol had first known him, Prof had been the world's most reliable recording engineer, always in work, and then, after forty years in the business, he'd emerged as a revered producer, an icon, an oracle.

And now a bucolic oracle. Disdainful of belated acclaim, Prof had quit the mainstream industry. He would produce only material that was worth producing, and only when he was in the mood. He would create for himself a bijou studio, a private centre of excellence in some deeply unfashionable corner of the sticks. Knight's Frome? Yeah, that sounded about right. Who the hell had ever heard of Knight's Frome?

Who indeed? Down south, there was at least one other River Frome, only much bigger. The Frome Valley here in east Hereford-shire had just the one small market town and a string of villages and hamlets – Bishop's Frome, Canon Frome, Halmond's Frome and little Knight's Frome, all sunk into rich, red loam and surrounded by orchards and vineyards and hopyards under the Malverns, Middle England's answer to mountains.

Not that Prof appeared to care about any of this; that it was obscure was enough. In fact, the real reason he was here, rather than the west of Ireland or somewhere, was that an old friend, a one-time professional bass-player and cellist, was currently vicar of Knight's Frome. It was this unquestionably honest guy who had identified for Prof a suitable property: a cottage with a stable block and pigsties but no land for either horses or pigs, therefore on sale at an unusually reasonable price. And Prof had shrugged: *Whatever.* He had no basic desire to communicate with the landscape – or with people, for that matter, except through headphones.

Unless, of course, he needed help. Arriving out here, marooned among crates of equipment, Prof had put out an SOS to every muso and sparks he knew within a fifty-mile radius – only to find that most of them had moved on, some to the next life.

In the end, it was only Simon, the vicar, and Lol Robinson, formerly songwriter and second guitar with the long-defunct band Hazey Jane, now on holiday from his college course in psychotherapy. Not that Lol was any good with wiring, but that wasn't important; it was mainly about making the tea and listening to Prof grouch and taking the blame for malfunctions. This afternoon they'd installed the final wall-panels, and tested the new acoustics by recording – in the absence of anything more challenging – some of Lol's more recent numbers.

This had continued into the night when, at some point, Prof had stopped cursing and wrenching out leads and replacing mikes . . . and sat back for a while behind the exposed skeleton of his mixing board, just listening to the music.

And then had stood up and stomped across the studio floor, positioning himself menacingly in the doorway of the booth where Lol sat with the old Washburn on his knees.

'Laurence! You little *bastard*, stop right there.'

Lol looking up timidly.

'Listen to me.' Prof glowered. 'How long, for fuck's sake, have you been *sitting* on this stuff?'

It was past eleven now, but the night was still awash with pale light, forming long lakes in the northern sky. To the south, a plane tracked across the starscape like a slow pulse on a monitor.

In the middle distance was a round tower, like some story-book castle, except that the tip of its conical hat was oddly skewed. There was a window-glow visible in the tower, unsteady like lantern light. Lol was stilled by the unreality of the moment, half feeling that if he were to climb over the farm gate and walk towards that tower, the entire edifice would begin to dissolve magically into the grey-black woodland behind.

It was, he concluded, one of those nights for nothing being entirely real.

From the shadowed field beyond the gate, he heard the slow, seismic night-breathing of cattle, so loud and full and resonant that it might have been the respiration system of the whole valley. The air was dense with pollen and sweet with warm manure, and Lol experienced a long moment of calm and the nearness of something that was vast and enfolding and brought him close to weeping.

At which point he cut the fantasy. The fairy-tale castle hardened into a not-so-ancient hop kiln. There were dozens of them around the valley, most of them converted into homes.

Sad. Not some rich, mystical experience, just another bog-standard memory of the womb.

. . . *Because therapy, Laurence, is the religion of the new millennium. And we're the priests.*

Lol gripped the top rail of the gate until his hands hurt. Prof was exaggerating, of course. His material wasn't that strong.

Anyway, Lol was too long out of it. The most he'd done in years had been occasional demos, for the purpose of flogging a few songs to better-known artists – makeweight stuff for albums, nothing special. It was an income-trickle but it wasn't a career, it wasn't a life, and he thought he'd accepted the reality of that a long time ago.

Back in January, he'd enrolled on this course for trainee psychotherapists, the only one he could find still with any available places, up in Wolverhampton. It made a surreal kind of sense to Lol, though he didn't share the irony of it with any of the other students, certainly not with the tutors.

Without actually saying *therapy, shmerapy*, Prof had managed to convey a scepticism well over the threshold of contempt.

'I can't believe you waste your time on this! You want to take money for persuading the gullible to remember how they were abused by their daddies, then they go home and slash their wrists? It's like I say to Simon: you're just being a vicar for *you*, not for them. Who gets married any more? Who wants to hear a sermon, sip lemonade at the vicarage fête? If you want to reach people, cure people, calm people, and you have it in you to give them beautiful music, from the heart . . . then, Jesus, *this* is the real therapy, the real spirituality. Forget this counselling bullshit! Who're you really gonna change?'

Of course, Prof knew all about Lol's history on the other side of psychiatry, brought about by early exposure to the music business – the blurred fairground ride ending in half-lit caverns with drifting, white-coated ghosts and gliding trolleys, syringes, pills.

Medication: the stripped-down NHS was a sick system, drug-dependent. It made sense to Lol that he should be using his own experience to help keep other vulnerable people *out* of the system. Otherwise, the medication years were just a damp, rotten hole in his life.

Prof knew all about this, just didn't accept the logic.

'Listen to me, boy, I have strong contacts these days . . . people who trust me, who tend to act on what I say, and I'm telling you, you gotta take these songs into the market place.'

'Well, sure,' Lol said obligingly. 'Anybody who wants one—'

'No! They'll want *you*! Listen to me. I can get you a good tour—'

Lol had been backing away into the booth at this point, the guitar held in front of him like a riot shield, Prof pursuing him, hands spread wide.

'Laurence, you're older now, you know the score, you know all the traps. I'm telling you honestly: you don't do this now, you'll be a very embittered old man one day. Jesus, what am I saying, *one day*? How long you been out of it now – ten years, fifteen? That's three whole generations in this business! How much time you really got left? How long now before the looks start to fade, before the winsome little-boy-lost turns into some sad, wrinkled—? *Listen* to me!'

'I can't . . . I can't tour.' Face it: he couldn't even *play* all that well any more.

'Right, let's see, now.' Prof went on like he hadn't heard. 'It would have to be as support, the first time. But supporting somebody *tasteful* – don't worry about that, it can be arranged. REM, Radiohead . . . all these guys admit to being influenced by your work. You're a cult . . . OK, a minor cult. But a cult is still a cult . . .'

'Prof?' Lol was resting the guitar on his trainers, his fingers among its machine-heads. 'Be honest – you don't even know that's true, do you?'

'The hell does that matter? Laurence, I apologize in advance if this sounds immodest, but if I'm the one spreading it around, everyone is going to believe it, therefore it *becomes* the truth.'

'I can't tour.' Lol stood with his back against the partition wall again, his breathing becoming harder at the very thought of *on the road*.

'You *can* tour! You *need* to tour . . . this will kick-start your confidence. You're just using this therapy shit as some kind of buffer against the real world. You're institutionalized and you don't even know it. It's like . . . like so many schoolteachers are really just kids who were afraid to leave school. Believe me, Laurence.'

And part of Lol did believe him, because Kenneth 'Prof' Levin had been down in the half-lit caverns, too – in his case alcoholism, the destruction of a good marriage.

Lol recalled the buzz he'd felt when he'd had the message to call Prof, a couple of weeks ago – around the same time he was concluding that knowing the difference between cognitive therapy and human-istic therapy didn't make either of them any more effective. In fact, the day after his senior tutor had told him, not with irony but with something approaching pride: '*Therapy, Laurence, is the religion of the new millennium. And we're the priests*' – the voice slick with self-belief, after a few glasses in the wine bar down the road from the college. '*Everybody needs a church. A confessional. Forgiveness.*' This senior tutor, this high priest, was younger than Lol, maybe thirty-four.

'All right!' Prof Levin had finally backed off. 'Enough. We'll talk about this again. For starters, we just do the album.'

'*Album?*'

Prof had spread his arms magnanimously. With his own studio set up, he was at last able to make these decisions without consulting anyone in a suit.

And Lol had thanked him for the offer – very profusely, obviously, because having Prof Levin produce an album for you was kind of like having Spielberg take on your screenplay – but then pointed out, reasonably enough, that he had only four songs: not quite *half* an album.

Prof had smiled beatifically through his white, nail-brush beard.

'You have the whole summer, my son. This summer . . . is yours.'

And he had shambled smugly away to his room in the adjacent cottage, leaving Lol to switch everything off before climbing to his own camp bed in one of the old haylofts.

Like he was really going to sleep after this?

Instead, he'd stumbled out, bemused, into the warm night, to commune with the Frome. But the river was already asleep and that was how he ended up following the track running down a line of poplars and out the other side, close to where the hop-kilns stood. The sky was now obscured by a tangle of trees, and he was aware of a high, piercing hum that somehow translated itself into *Everybody needs a church. A confessional. Forgiveness.*

Not exactly the wisest analogy to hang on Lol who, in his late teens, had seen his parents find religion, watched them being swept away on waves of foaming fundamentalist madness, causing them to reject the Godless kid playing the devil's music – the kid who would always remember coming home one weekend to find that those two small mantelpiece photos of himself as a toddler had been replaced by framed postcards of Jesus. Which was probably how it had started – the alienation.

And then – in just this last year – a surprise development. Lol's fear and resentment of the Church had been fatally compromised by encounters with a priest called Merrily Watkins who lived and worked, as it happened, less than twenty miles from here . . . but if this was another reason for coming back to Herefordshire he wasn't going to admit it, least of all to himself. Their last meeting had followed events so dark that maybe she wouldn't want to be reminded.

He felt a sharp pain below his knee and stopped, feeling suddenly out of breath. He realized he'd been running, like he sometimes did to try and overtake a dilemma, to put an impending decision behind him. He must have veered from the path and now he was in the middle of an unknown wood and there were brambles tangled around his legs.

Wrong turning, somehow. It was easy enough to do, even in the daytime, even in countryside you thought you knew. In the middle of this unknown, unmanaged wood, snagged with hawthorn, he heard his T-shirt rip, and he stood there, shaking his head.

Lost again. Story of his life.

Knight's Frome was a scattered hamlet with no real centre, so it wasn't as if he could look around for a cluster of lights. Or even listen for the river. All he could hear was the humming: a plaintive sound that rose and fell and pulsed as if a melody was trying to escape.

Lol turned, walked back the way he'd come, putting a hand up to his glasses, pushing them tight onto the bridge of his nose; losing your specs was not something you did in a wood at night. When he took his hand away, he saw the trees and bushes had fallen away and there was now a clear space up ahead. A small yellow light appeared, not too bright, a little unsteady, with a black cone above it: a witch's hat. The kiln tower again.

When the sky was clear of branches, a trailing scarf of brightness told him which direction was north . . . and then it was suddenly split by something black and rigid that made him reel back, startled. He slipped and stumbled, went down on one knee before it – waiting for the thing to move, bend down, snatch him up, hit him.

Nothing moved. Even the humming had stopped. Lol scrambled warily to his feet.

It was only a pole, half as thick as a telegraph pole, but not tall enough to carry telegraph wires or electricity cables – although it did support wires of some kind. To avoid it, he took a couple of steps to the right. No trees or bushes stood in the way and the ground was level.

A second black pole appeared, rearing hard against the northern sky, and this one had a short crosspiece like – his first thought – a gibbet. From it hung something limp and shrivelled, the skeletal spine of a dead garland; when he passed between the two poles, his bare elbow brushed against the remains with a dry, papery crackle.

Now he could see the extent of it: dozens of black poles against the pale night, in lines to either side of him across the barren ground, most of them with crosspieces, some connected by dark wires over-head. It was like a site laid out for a mass crucifixion. Between the wires, he could still see the yellow kiln-house light, perhaps two hundred yards away. And the nearness of the kiln told him what this was . . . or *should* have been.

It was high summer and these poles should be loaded with foliage, the ripening bines high on the wires, rippling with soft green hop-cones. But this whole scene was in black and white and grey, and there was an awning of silence: no owls, no scurryings in the under-growth. No undergrowth, in fact.

The silence, Lol thought, was like a studio silence: soft, dry, flat and localized. The air seemed cooler now, and he could feel goose bumps prickling on his bare arms as he ventured tentatively into a hop-yard where no hops grew, along an alley of winter-bleak, naked hop-poles, a place as desolate as the stripped-back bed of someone recently dead. He felt a little scared now. There was no contented cattle-breath around this place – it felt less like a memory of the womb than a premonition of the grave.

No reason to stay. Lol started to turn away. Afterwards, he couldn't remember whether these thoughts of death had occurred in the moment before the humming began again, or whether it was the combination of the sound and the stark setting that conveyed the sense of mourning, loss, lamentation. The bleak keening seemed to be around and above him, as if it was travelling along those black wires, as if they were vibrating with some kind of plangent sorrow.

And then, as he turned, there was another noise – a crispy swishing, like dried leaves in a tentative breeze, like the noise when he'd touched the remains of the dead hop-bine, only continuous –

and a pale smear blurred the periphery of his vision like petroleum jelly spread on a camera lens.

Lol saw her.

It was like she was swimming through the night towards him, from the far end of the corridor of crosses.

No sense of unreality here, that was the worst of it. It was not dreamlike, not hallucinatory.

She stopped between the poles, legs apart, leaning back, one moment all shadows, and then shining under the northern sky: a thin, white woman garlanded with pale foliage. Rustling and crackling like something dead and dusty, moved by the wind.

But there *was* no wind.

Lol backed into a pole, felt it juddering against his spine and the back of his head, as he gasped and twisted away, semi-stunned and reeling, into a parallel hop-corridor, the poles rushing past him like black railings seen from a train.

Between them, he saw the woman moving. A long, dried-out, bobbled bine was wound around her like a boa, around her neck, under her arms, over her shoulders, pulled up between her legs – the cones crackling and crumbling on her skin, throwing off a spray of flakes, an ashy aura of dead vegetation.

As she drew level with him, he could see, under the winding bine, black droplets beading her breasts, streaks down her forearms, as though the bine was thorned.

She turned to Lol and the bine fell away as she extended her hands towards him.

Lol very nearly took them in his own.

*Very* nearly.

# TWO

# In the Old-fashioned Sense

It was like she'd told the Bishop: anything iffy, out came the coal-tongs and the asbestos gloves, and it made you wonder whatever happened to that old job-description: *The cure of souls.*

'I'd just said "The blood of Christ keep you in eternal life," and that was when the girl went slightly crazy,' Canon Dennis Beckett explained on the phone.

To be fair, he had good reason to feel this wasn't really his problem. He was retired now, and lived on the other side of the county. He only came across to Dilwyn to take the Sunday services for two weeks a year, when Jeff Kimball, his godson, was away on holiday. Which was a diversion for Dennis, too, and a nice place to drive out to: this neat black and white haven with its village green.

But at the end of it, the thing was, other than on a superficial, hand-shaking level, he didn't really *know* these people, did he? And in this case there was a young girl involved – always dicey. Also, for extra tension, a touch of drama, it had happened during Holy Communion.

'We've all had situations of people becoming ill, of course,' Dennis said, 'even dying in their pews on two occasions that *I* can recall. But . . . well, it's usually elderly people, isn't it?'

'Mmm.' Since coming to Ledwardine less than two years ago, Merrily had seen a stroke, a blackout, an epileptic fit and a birth. 'Not invariably.'

She wasn't yet seeing this as a deliverance issue. She'd met Canon Beckett two or three times at local clergy gatherings, remembered him as grey-bearded, vague, affable. She wondered why, if this incident had occurred last Sunday, it had taken him five clear days to decide he should tell her about it.

It was the first morning of Jane's school holidays. Friday the thirteenth, as it happened.

'It was embarrassing rather than anything else, at the time,' Dennis said. 'The mother appeared to be affected the most – essentially such a good family, you see, in the old-fashioned sense; a family, in fact, to whom the term *God-fearing* might once have applied. And I'm afraid you can't say that of very many of them nowadays, can you?'

'No.' Merrily tucked the phone under her chin, leaning forward through a sunbeam to pull over her sermon pad and a felt pen. 'I suppose not. So, what *did* happen, exactly?'

'She dashed – that's the only word for it – *dashed* the chalice from my hands. And then she was sick.'

'She actually—?'

'Threw up. Copiously. Tossed her cookies, as my grandson would say. In the chancel. On everything. On me.'

'Oh.'

'Rather a mess. And the smell soured everything. Hard to continue afterwards.'

'I can imagine.'

'Everyone was extremely understanding and trying not to react. Someone said, *Oh dear*, very quietly, and then they all discreetly moved out of the way. The mother was absolutely white with the shame of it, poor woman. She's one of Jeffrey's regulars – cleans the church, arranges the flowers. There she was, dragging the child away down the aisle, followed by the father, and I was starting to go after them when this elderly lady suddenly began clutching her chest. I thought, *Oh Lord, that's all we* . . . Anyway, as it turned out, the old dear wasn't in the throes of some cardiac crisis, which was a mercy, but by the time I reached the door, the whole family had vanished. So . . . we simply cleaned everywhere up and . . . resumed. At the time it seemed—'

'The best thing?' Merrily said.

'Luckily, I managed to find a fresh surplice. There were only about five communicants left by then. A few had walked away in . . . the wake of it.'

Dennis Beckett paused. Through the scullery door, Merrily heard impatient footsteps across the flags in the kitchen.

'Look, I'm aware this doesn't sound like much, Merrily,' Dennis said. 'Certainly didn't seem so to me, at the time, but I thought I ought to reassure the parents, so I got their number and when I arrived home I gave them a call. No answer. I made a note to try again the following day, but I'm afraid it got mislaid and other things cropped up, and it wasn't until this morning that I finally got through to them.'

'Mum?' Behind Merrily, the scullery door opened. Jane stood there in jeans and a yellow sleeveless top, summery but somehow waiflike, a bit forlorn. 'Look, I'm going to get the bus into Hereford, OK?'

Merrily held up a hand, signalling for the kid to hang on until she was off the phone. 'Sorry, Dennis . . .'

Dennis Beckett lowered his voice.

'It was still quite a long time before anyone answered. I was about to hang up when the mother came on, rather abrupt until she realized who I was. Whereupon she simply burst into tears. An erup-tion. As if she'd been holding it back for days. You know . . . *"Thank God you've called. Thank God. I didn't know what to do. I don't know what"* . . . No, in fact, her actual words were: *"I don't dare to think what's got into her."* ' He paused.

Jane scowled, threw up her arms in exasperation and walked out.

' "Got into her"?' Merrily said cautiously.

'Her own words. The child's being generally . . . not herself. She's normally a quiet, studious, demure sort of girl. A *nice* girl. Been taken to church every week since she was about seven. Suddenly, she's exhibiting signs of a distinct . . . aversion. Claiming she's not well on Sunday mornings – headaches, this sort of thing.'

Merrily thought about Jane. 'Being generally difficult? Mood swings? Emotional?'

'I gather.'

'How old?'

'Fourteen.'

'Well . . .' Merrily tapped her pencil on the desk, remembering similar phases. 'No need to get too carried away about that. Unless—' An obvious thought had struck her. 'Could she be pregnant?'

'*What?* Oh . . . I see what you mean.' He was silent for a moment, thinking it over. 'Well, she . . . seemed to me to be a very *young* fourteen. She was wearing her school uniform, which in itself is a rather uncommon sight these days, out of school hours.'

'True.' Half of Jane's school clothes seemed to have vanished by the time she reached home.

'Let me tell you the main thing,' Dennis said. 'It seems Amy had been brought along to Holy Communion precisely because her parents were getting worried about her spiritual health. In the old-fashioned sense.'

'Meaning what, exactly?'

Dennis hesitated and then sighed. 'Meaning they're now asking for something I would not personally be happy to undertake,' he replied eventually.

As Merrily went into the kitchen, Ethel the cat looked up at her from a sun-pool on a deep windowsill. No sign of Jane; the kid must have gone back up to her apartment in the attic. Merrily went back into the scullery, stared at the phone for a few seconds and then picked it up and rang Sophie at the Gatehouse.

'I'm just following procedure here, Soph.'

'Do we *have* a procedure?' The Bishop's lay secretary, servant of the Cathedral and posher than the Queen, would be in her office next to the Deliverance room, from where she also dealt with the admin side of Merrily's business.

'We have a rule. There's only one situation where we have a rule,' Merrily said, 'and this is it.'

'I see.' A tiny pause, a vacuum snap – Sophie uncapping her Gold Cross fountain pen. 'What would you like me to tell the Bishop? We're talking *major* exorcism?'

'Won't be an exorcism at all, if I can help it. I suspect they don't know quite what they want, apart from some reassurance. I'm just informing the Bishop, according to the *rule*.'

Jane appeared in the doorway. 'What?' She saw the phone at Merrily's ear and rolled her eyes.

'Sorry, Sophie, I've just got to ask Jane something before her very limited patience snaps.'

'I am sixteen,' Jane muttered. 'As you keep telling me, I have all the bloody time in the world.'

'You know a kid called Amy Shelbone?'

Jane blinked. 'Know the name. Probably.'

'I think she goes to your school.'

'She does?'

'Not in your class, then?'

'No, she . . . I guess she's probably in the fourth . . . or the third year. Something like that.'

'OK.' Merrily nodded. 'Thanks, flower.' Worth a try, but kids in a lower form were pond life. 'Sorry, Sophie.'

Jane didn't leave. Merrily frowned at her. 'You'll miss the bus.'

'So like, what's this Amy Shel . . . thing done?'

'Go,' said Merrily.

She waited until she heard the front door slam. Her dog-collar lay in the centre of the pale blue blotter, glowing in the sunbeam. Sophie would disapprove of her discarding it simply because of the heat. The women's ministry had been hard-won; it was like some ex-suffragette not turning out for the polls because it was raining.

'Sorry about that.'

'I think you can assume she's gone now,' Sophie said. 'But you may wish to check the room for listening devices.'

Sophie would also disapprove of Merrily asking the kid about Amy Shelbone, but Merrily knew it would go no further. It had reached the stage, with Jane, where there was a certain trust, forged out of experience. Jane was sixteen; there wasn't such a huge age-gap between them. They told each other almost everything. Didn't they?

She sat for a while at her desk, looking down the garden towards the apple trees. She was thinking about Father Nicholas Ellis, the fundamentalist zealot who had interpreted the term '*cure of souls*' all too freely, administering exorcism like doctors prescribed antibiotics, without ever consulting the Bishop.

But at least Ellis had certainty, a complete faith not only in God and all His angels, but in himself as the approved wielder of an archangel's broadsword. How he must have despised her.

Merrily put on her dog collar.

Ellis had crossed the line, big-time. She was never going to do that, God help her. Nor was it up to the priest to decide who was genuine, who was misguided, and who was trying it on.

She knelt by the side of the desk, under the window, put her hands together, the backs of her thumbs against the centre of her forehead. She closed her eyes, let her thoughts fall away. The sunshine through her eyelids made her feel washed in a warm orange glow. It felt good.

*Too* good. Merrily moved into shadow, facing the white-painted wall of four-hundred-year-old wattle and daub, and prayed for perception.

Since Dennis Beckett had first told her about Amy Shelbone, she'd been thinking, on and off, about the occasion she'd thrown up in church herself – her own church, on the fraught night of her installation as priest in charge. Churches were powerful places; they sometimes amplified emotions, might well have an emetic effect on stored-up stress. It didn't necessarily mean any kind of *invasion*.

However, this was at Holy Communion, and a dramatically adverse reaction to the presence of the sacrament was . . . something that needed to be looked into.

After a few minutes, Merrily picked up the phone and called the number Dennis Beckett had given her for the Shelbones, in Dilwyn.

There was no answer.

THREE

# Stock

The first time Lol saw Gerard Stock, he thought the bloke must have some kind of status here, that maybe he was the original owner of the whole place, including the stables and the pigsties.

This was perhaps because Gerard Stock kind of *swaggered*.

It was not a word Lol recalled ever mentally applying to anyone before. Stock walked like he was shouldering his way through a crowd of people who didn't matter, to get to somebody who did. This looked odd, because he was all alone on the track which crossed the hay meadow. No bushes, no banks of nettles, no cows; nothing but lush, knee-high grass in a valley smouldering with summer.

It was eleven-thirty in the morning, and Stock was heading their way.

Prof was not glad to see him. 'The sodding countryside. You get more privacy in Notting Hill. He wants to know who you are. He always has to know who everybody is, the bastard. He's obviously seen you walking around here and he thinks you might be someone of significance.'

'Obviously hasn't noticed my car, then.'

Lol was standing, with a mug of tea and a slice of toast, at the window of the studio anteroom-cum-kitchen, which had once been a pigsty and now possibly looked even more of one.

'This guy . . .' Prof drained his mug, added it to a pile of unwashed crockery beside the sink. 'I ask myself, should I have to cope with guys like this any more, my time of life? The business is top-heavy with the bastards, always has been. They know *everybody* –

shared spliffs with Jerry Garcia, toured with Dylan, played jew's harp on the cut that never made it onto *Blood on the Tracks* . . . which, of course, is how come their name was tragically omitted from the sleeve. These guys . . .' Prof palmed his stubbly white chin. 'These guys are losers the likes of which I hoped that by moving out here I should never have to encounter again.'

'So who exactly is he, Prof?' Lol saw a man who was not that taller than he was, but wide and powerful. A man swaggering like he owned the place, but not hurrying. A man wanting them to know he was coming.

Prof snorted. 'For my sins, my nearest neighbour. He lives, with his distressingly younger wife, in a converted hop-kiln somewhere over there where I've never been. He walks over here two, three times a week, in case maybe I got Knopfler or Sting hanging out.'

'A . . . hop-kiln.' Lol had fallen asleep thinking of a woman in a hop-yard near a kiln, then had dreamed of her, and then had awoken this morning thinking *Did that really happen?*

'Very sought-after, these old kilns, apparently. So how come such a loser is able to buy one? Answer: he didn't. It was an inheritance, and not even his own. His wife's uncle left it to them. What kind of man *was* this uncle to bequeath this leeching bastard to the community?'

'Nice guy, actually,' said the man who was sitting on the floor below the window, his back against the whitewashed bricks, mug between his knees. 'Though he went a little strange, I suppose, before his death.'

Prof turned on him. 'And you . . . when you were selling me on this place, did you mention the proximity of this freeloader, this *ligger*, even once?'

'You weren't interested in the neighbours.' Simon St John, bass-player, cellist and vicar, had known Prof for many more years than Lol had. 'As long as they don't have noisy kids or barbecues, you're never remotely interested in your neighbours.'

'Life's too short for neighbours,' Prof said gruffly. 'Whatever time I got left, I want to spend it laying down good music in my own place, at my own pace. Is that too much to ask?' He glared down at Simon. 'You knew him well, this uncle?'

'Prof, I buried him.' Simon lifted pale hair out of his eyes. 'But before that, he used to come and see us periodically. He was interested in the history of the church. He was interested in most things local.' He turned to Lol. 'You'll see his books in various shops in Bromyard. Local books, full of pictures – photos. Old ones and new ones he took himself, but he did them in sepia, so they looked like old ones. *An Illustrated Guide to the Frome Valley, Past and Present* and *The Hop-grower's Year*. They're still selling very well. I think Gerard's quite annoyed because the income from those books was left to another niece.'

'And all they got was the house,' said Prof. 'Poor little bleeders.'

'Stewart Ash was his name – the uncle,' Simon said. 'Good bloke. What happened to him seemed really shocking, obviously, especially in a close community like this. But in my own defence, Prof, I have to say that when I first told you about this place I hadn't yet met friend Gerard.'

Prof snorted.

'Both times I called at the kiln – making my initial pastoral visit, as we do – he appeared not to have heard me knocking.' Simon flicked a wrist. 'Naturally, I assumed he was of a reclusive disposition. And not exactly a Christian.'

'Reclusive? Jesus, nah, you were wearing your bloody uniform – no wonder he wasn't answering the door. The bastard thinks you're collecting for the organ fund, and he doesn't have any money, and of course that's the very last thing these hustlers are ever going to admit – their private capital's always tied up in some big-deal pro-motion they can't tell you about just yet.'

Lol wanted to ask what had happened to the uncle that had so shocked the community, but there wasn't going to be time for that. He saw Gerard Stock push through the gate, leaving it open behind him, and cross the yard. Stock's thinning hair was slicked straight back and he had a beard that was red and gold, fading to grey where it was trimmed to a small, thrusting wedge.

And Lol was still not sure what the bloke actually did.

'See, if there was a whole *bunch* of neighbours—' Prof spread his hands '—it might not be so bad. But this guy on his own, with the wife at work all day – oh yeah, it might be *her* inheritance, but *she* goes to work while he hangs around here, supposedly engaged in renovation but actually pissing the time away and getting in what remains of my hair. I tell you, if you live in the sticks and you have just the one neighbour, it's like I would imagine being in prison and sharing a cell. As you'll find out when I go.'

Lol smiled. Prof kept saying *when I go* like he was expecting imminent death. In fact, he was going to Abbey Road studio to produce the long-awaited fourth solo album by his old friend, the blues-guitar legend Tom Storey. Lol had agreed to mind the studio while Prof was away – knowing this was Prof's way of forcing him to work on his own solo album, which was *not* long-awaited, not by anybody.

There was a knock on the back door. Just the one. Prof jabbed his thumb towards the passage.

'And if you ever do let Stock in here when I'm gone, you don't permit him to play a chord or touch a knob on that board, that clear? Not for my benefit I'm saying this, but for yours, because if your album eventually starts to sell in any quantity, he's gonna swear blind he co-produced it. Am I right, Simon?'

Simon rose languidly to his feet. He wore well-faded jeans and a collarless white shirt. 'You know me, Prof. I must never allow myself to think the worst of people.'

Prof turned to Lol. 'If it reaches court, this man will be your principal witness. He don't play bass so good any more, but his God loves him increasingly.'

Simon St John smiled but didn't reply. Nothing Prof said ever seemed to offend him; he would bend with it, like a willow. Simon had probably not changed much, or put on a pound in weight, in twenty years. He seemed to know exactly who he was and to feel comfortable with that. He made Lol feel unstable and directionless.

'Aw, just let the bastard in,' Prof said, resigned. Then he grinned at Lol. 'I'll do you the favour of ensuring that he develops no interest in you from the start.'

As good as his word, Prof handed Gerard Stock a mug of lukewarm tea and jerked a thumb at Lol.

'Gerry, this little guy is Laurence Robinson. He used to be in a minor band, way back. Now he's a psychotherapist.'

Lol sighed. He was polishing his glasses on the hem of his T-shirt, so Gerard Stock was just a blue-denim blur, but he could feel the guy's lazy gaze like a damp towel as Stock cranked out a laugh.

'Guess we've all been down that road at some time.'

Lol put his glasses back on. Stock's voice had surprised him: underneath the vague mid-Atlantic slur, it was educated, upper-middle-class, like Simon's. He saw that the bloke had intelligent, canny eyes, a wet little rosebud mouth inside the oval of the beard and moustache.

'I was in therapy for six months, in the States,' Stock said. 'It really fucked me up.' He laughed again, eyes glinting with challenge.

Lol nodded. 'It can happen. It isn't right for everybody.'

Stock drank some tea. 'And what kind of person isn't it right for?'

'Don't get him going,' Prof snapped. 'He'll bore the arse off you with his psycho-babble. What can we do for you, Gerry? I hate to hurry you, but we need to have this rig up and running. Time is money in this business, I don't need to tell you that.'

'You most certainly don't, Prof,' Stock said. 'Actually, I wanted a word with the vicar.'

Prof said nothing, clearly thrown by this.

'Me?' Simon said, also thrown, obviously.

'If you have a few minutes.'

'Sure.' Simon shrugged. 'I was just leaving anyway. I should be out there ministering to my flock, but Prof's still a novelty, made me self-indulgent. Would you excuse me one minute, while I pop off and have a wee? Then I'll walk back with you,'

When Simon vanished into the passage, Lol went over to the sink and filled it with hot water for the washing-up. When he turned round to find a teacloth, he saw that Gerard Stock was contemplating him, eyes screwed up like he was trying to figure out the species of a bird in the garden.

'You were in a band? Laurence . . . Robertson . . .?'

'Robinson,' Lol said. 'Lol, usually. But you probably wouldn't—'

'Ah,' Stock said triumphantly. 'Hazey *Jane*.'

Lol's turn to be surprised. Maybe it took one loser to recognize another.

'You did this Nick Drake-y thing,' Stock recalled, 'long before the man was rediscovered. All sensitive and fingerpicking, when everybody else was crashing about on synths. Brave of you.'

'Didn't get us anywhere,' Lol said lightly.

'If ten years too early.' Stock's teeth were very white and even – Hollywood teeth. He couldn't always have been a loser. 'And now everybody's discovered Drake, it's probably too late. A hard and ungrateful business, my friend. You're probably better off, even in psychotherapy.'

'Unfortunately, everybody's discovered that, too,' Lol said. 'Story of my life.'

'Sad,' said Gerard Stock, as Simon returned.

Prof and Lol followed the other two men down the passage and out through the back door, Prof seeming much happier now that he was seeing Stock's back. The sun was a big white spotlamp, tracking them, and all around the countryside was surging with summer, the meadow lavishly splattered with wild flowers – Mother Nature flaunting herself, happy to be a whore.

Prof stopped in the yard, and sat a Panama hat on his bald head. 'He piss you off, Laurence?' he asked hopefully.

'Not particularly.'

'Give him time.' Prof rubbed his beard. His baggy American T-shirt carried the merry message *BABES IS ALL*. 'What's he want with Simon, that's what I would like to know. He strike you as a man who feels himself in need of spiritual absolution?'

Lol smiled. 'You jealous?'

'I shall treat that with the contempt it deserves,' Prof said.

'What does Mr Stock actually do? You never said.'

'Nothing! Strolls about like the squire while the poor wife's at work, temping for some agency in Hereford. She inherits the house, now she earns the money for them to live there. All right, he *was* some kind of a freelance publicist, a term that can mean whatever he wants it to mean on any particular day. He offers to handle my PR. I say, Gerard, watch my lips: I do not want any relations with the public.'

Lol watched Stock and the vicar crossing the river bridge at the bottom of the meadow, where the line of poplars began. Where he'd walked last night. He told Prof about the hop-kiln he'd seen, with its fairy-tale tower. Prof nodded.

'Yeah, I expect that would be his place. It's not a prime location, Stock maintains, on account of being blocked in on either side by these two enormous great metal barns. Same situation as this, with the land all around it owned by someone else. He should moan – like he paid a penny for it.'

'They still grow hops there?'

'Used to.'

'Only there was this kind of hop-yard with no hops – well, a few shrivelled bits of bine hanging from the wires. I mean, hops had obviously been grown at one time, in quantity, but it was all barren now. Scorched earth and just these poles. It was . . . depressing.'

'Hmm,' Prof said. 'This would be the wilt, I expect.'

'What?'

'Verticulum Wilt . . . nah, that's wrong, but some word like that. It's this voracious hop disease – no known cure. Wipes out your whole crop, contaminates your land like anthrax or something, throwing hop-farmers out of business. You want to know about this stuff, take a walk down to the hop museum by the main road.' Prof smiled slyly. 'You'll like it there – check out the back room.'

'Why?'

Prof winked. 'Anyway,' he said, 'apparently that's how these stables got split off from the farm. The owner has hard times, maybe from the wilt, sells his land bit by bit, flogs off what buildings he can, for conversion. Maybe that's also how Stock's wife's uncle got his kiln, I forget. It's an ill wind, Laurence.'

It was noon, the time of no shadows, but the sun was momentarily weakened by a trailer of muslin cloud.

'What's the, er . . . what's the wife like?' Lol asked.

Prof gave him a curious look. Prof had sensitive, multi-track hearing – sometimes even picking up tracks you hadn't recorded.

'Never met her, Laurence. Quiet, I'm told. Often the case with a guy like that – wants a listener.'

'And what happened to the uncle?'

'Ha! I'm detecting – forgive me – a burgeoning interest here?'

'Well, not—'

'The moment I mention hop-kilns! After our discussion, am I to conclude you went for one of your little strolls and you came back with – dare I suggest – the seed of an idea? I'm thinking of the song you did a year or two back for Norma Waterson – "The Baker's Tune"?'

' "The Baker's Lament".'

'About the slow fading of the old village fabric – a good one. Well, I'm not pushing it, but there are strong themes here, too. Change and decay. Visit the Hop Museum – in fact, I'm going to set that up for you.'

'Prof, there's no—'

'Check it out. Reject it, if you want, but check it out first.'

Lol gave up. In an avalanche, lie down.

'So what *did* happen to the uncle?'

'Aha.' Prof sat on an old rustic bench against the stable wall, tilting his Panama over his eyes. 'Well, that, Laurence, was a *very* sick wind.'

Lol waited. Prof seemed to have a remarkably extensive knowledge of people he claimed he hadn't ever wanted to meet.

He talked from under his hat, stretching out his legs. 'I think what Simon didn't mention about this Stewart Ash was his interest – as an author, a chronicler of social history – in our travelling friends. Not the New Age travellers – the old kind.'

'Gypsies?'

Prof nodded. 'Romanies. Used to come here in force every autumn for the hop-picking. Enormous work in those days before the machines. Some of them even travelling over from Europe in their *vardos*, year after year. A colourful spectacle – you'll find all this in the hop museum, as well. The Romanies were a little community inside a community, and of course Ash very much wanted to record their memories, for his book – what they thought of the hop-masters, how well they were treated. A man with a social conscience. Well, there's a few Romany families, not many, still coming back, to help the machinery do the work – though whether they'll be back this year, after what happened, is anyone's guess. Anyway, off goes our

Mr Ash to talk to them. Only gypsies, by tradition, don't like to talk. It's their history, why should the *gaujos* profit from it?'

Prof tilted up his hat, looking for Lol's reaction.

'That's a point,' Lol said cautiously.

'I have sympathy for the Romanies,' Prof said. 'A persecuted race, big victims of the Holocaust.'

Prof rarely talked about this; he liked to call himself a 'lapsed Jew', but Lol knew from other sources that his family had been considerably depleted by Hitler. Aunts and uncles, certainly, if not his parents. It would explain why Prof, who was accustomed to ignoring his immediate neighbourhood, had taken a certain interest in this story.

'But Ash, you see, was by all accounts a generous man, and he didn't expect the stuff for nothing. He established what you might call a *rapport* with a few of the gypsies. What *he* might have called a rapport, though they would probably have had a different name for it.'

'Like, they got more out of him than he got out of them?'

'They haven't survived, the Romanies, by passing up on oppor-tunities, though it was probably a little more complicated than ripping off the guy for a bunch of made-up stories. Complicated, for one thing, by Ash being representative of *another* significant minority.'

'Oh?'

'Did he form too *close* a rapport with certain of his travelling friends? Did they take his money for services rendered? None of this ever came out in court when the case was heard earlier this year. It amounted to two little bleeders breaking in one night. Gypsy boys, brothers. Old man comes down in the night, catches them messing with his cameras and stuff – this was how it was put in the papers. They beat the poor bugger to death.'

'Christ,' said Lol.

'Last year, this would be, late summer. There you go: ain't what it was, the countryside.' Prof laughed hoarsely. 'Bear this in mind, Laurence. Make sure you always lock up at night, when I've gone.'

# FOUR

# The Reservoir

St Mary the Virgin guarded Dilwyn like a mother hen: a good, solid medieval parish church with a squat steeple on the tower. But it was always going to be the village below that got the attention: bijou black-and-white cottages around the green – a movie set, birthday card, timber-framed heaven.

In fact, you only really noticed the church on the way out of the village. And if she hadn't been leaving the village, Merrily might also have missed seeing the woman, coming down from the porch past ancient gravestones – just a few of them, selectively spaced as if the less-sightly stones had been removed.

She seemed as timeless as the cottages themselves: a big woman, comfortably overweight, walking with her head high, a shopping basket over her arm. You expected there to be big, rosy apples in it, maybe some fresh, brown eggs.

*It could be her, couldn't it?* Merrily slowed the car and then reversed, turning on the forecourt of the Crown Inn, and parking next to the village green.

The Shelbones' bungalow had been easy enough to find, sunk into a lane leading out of the village in the general direction of Stretford whose church of St Cosmas and St Damien – once desecrated with a pool of urine and a gutted crow – had been the scene of Merrily's first, humiliating exorcism-of-place. The bungalow had lace curtains and flower beds with bright clusters of bedding plants. It was traditional – no barbecue, no water-feature. And no one had answered the door.

But this woman looked promising. She was about the right age – mid-fifties. With her dark green linen skirt and her grey-brown hair loosely permed, you had the impression she didn't care overmuch if she did resemble her mother at that same age.

Merrily switched off the engine, wound down the window and waited for the woman to reach the green. Late afternoon had brought on the first overcast sky of the week, dense with white heat. Droplets of birdsong were sprinkled over the distant buzz of invisible traffic on the main road above the village.

The woman had stopped to check something in her basket. Wearily, Merrily levered herself out of the car, leaned against the door. She was wearing a blue cotton jacket, a white silk scarf over her dog collar in case the Shelbones didn't want the neighbours knowing they were having visits from strange clergy. She hadn't bought any new summer clothes last year, and there'd be no need for any this year either. She wasn't planning to go anywhere. This would be the first summer she'd stayed behind while Jane went off on holiday – joining another family in a big farmhouse in Pembrokeshire where there was sea and surfing.

Not that the kid seemed especially excited. She just slumped around, sluggish and grumpy. Maybe it was the weight of the exams and the weather. Or some unknown burden? Something they needed to discuss? Perhaps there'd be a violent thunderstorm tonight, with the electricity cut off, as it usually was: a time for candlelight confidences to be swapped across the kitchen table, maybe their last chance for a meaningful discussion before Jane went away for a month, leaving Merrily alone in the seven-bedroom vicarage.

The woman was now crossing the road towards the green. Merrily stepped away from the car.

'Mrs Shelbone?'

'Good afternoon.' She looked neither surprised nor curious – in a village this size a stranger would swiftly have rounded up a dozen people who could have pointed her out.

'I had a call from Canon Beckett, this morning,' Merrily said. 'I'm Merrily Watkins. I rang—'

'I know. It wasn't convenient to talk to you then. I'm sorry.' Mrs

Shelbone spoke briskly, local accent. 'I was intending to call you back tonight when we could speak freely.'

Dennis must have told her to expect a call from the deliverance consultant, but the girl, Amy, had been in the house, Merrily guessed, at the time she rang. She suddenly felt wrong-footed, because this woman already knew exactly who she was and what she was doing here, and now she was getting that familiar, dismayed look that said: *You're the wrong sex, you're too young, you're too small.*

She slipped a hand defensively to her scarf. Mrs Hazel Shelbone shifted her shopping basket from one hand to the other. In the basket were two tins of polish and some yellow dusters, neatly folded. No apples, no eggs.

'Well, my dear,' Mrs Shelbone said, 'this isn't really a good place to leave your car. I should take it a little way down that lane over there. Perhaps we could meet in the church in about five minutes?' She produced a smile that was wry and resigned. 'The scene of the crime, as it were.'

In the long church porch with its glassless, iron-barred Gothic windows, Merrily took a few long breaths, whispered a rather feverish prayer.

Jane had once asked, insouciantly, *So when do they issue you with the black medical bag and the rubber apron for the green bile?*

The truth was that Merrily had never exorcized a person. Deliverance Consultant might be an unsatisfactory title, but it was a more accurate job description than Diocesan Exorcist. Heavy spiritual cleansing had never been more than an infrequent last-resort.

*Tell me if it's real,* Merrily mumbled to God. *Don't let me get this wrong.*

It was only a few steps down from the porch, but the body of the church had a subterranean feel – a cool, grey cavern. Hazel Shelbone was alone there, waiting in a front pew, a few yards from the pulpit and the entrance to the chancel where her daughter had – in the phraseology of Dennis Beckett's grandson – tossed her cookies.

She half rose. 'I'm sorry, Mrs Watkins, if I was abrupt. It's been very difficult.'

'Yes.'

'I . . . would like you to understand about me from the outset. I am a Christian. *And* a mother.' She said this almost defiantly, her wide face shining in the white light from the leaded windows.

Merrily nodded. 'Me, too.'

'You've got children?'

'Just the one. A girl. Sixteen.'

Mrs Shelbone's brown eyes widened. 'A child bride, were you?'

'Sort of. My husband was killed in a car accident. Long time ago.'

The body of the church seemed fairly colourless. There was no stained glass in the nave, but behind the altar was a crucifixion window with blood-red predominant.

'And you remarried?'

'No, I . . .'

'Found the Church instead.' A deep nod of understanding from Mrs Shelbone. 'It's important to know where your destiny lies, isn't it? I knew from a very early age that I was destined to be a mother, that this was to be my *task* in life. My occupation. Do you see?'

Merrily smiled. Hazel Shelbone's expression rebuked her.

'But we couldn't have children, Mrs Watkins! Couldn't *have* them. Imagine that. It was enough to shatter my faith. How terribly cruel of God, I thought.'

'So—'

'But after a while I began to understand. He intended for me to be a reservoir, do you see? A reservoir of maternal love for little children who were starved of it. When I came to that understanding it was a moment of great joy.'

'So you—'

'Foster-parents we were, for a number of years. And then we took on Amy as an infant, and God, in his wisdom, decided that she was to stay and become our daughter. We had a big, decrepit old house, up in Leominster in those days, with lots of bedrooms, so we sold that and we moved out here. This was when Amy was five and we knew she was going to be staying.'

'I didn't realize she was adopted.' Merrily was wondering what basic difference this might make. As a foster-parent, Hazel Shelbone would probably already have had considerable experience of kids from dysfunctional families, kids with emotional problems. She wouldn't easily be fooled by them. 'What does your husband do?'

'David's a listed-buildings officer with the Hereford Council. He looks after the old places, makes sure nobody knocks them down or tampers with them. They offered him early retirement last year, but he said he wouldn't know what to do with himself.' Her eyes grew anxious. 'I wish he'd taken it, now. He's not been in the best of health recently, and now . . .'

She looked ahead, through the opening in the oak screen, towards the altar, and then suddenly turned, leaning urgently sideways in the pew, towards Merrily.

'We never *pushed* the Church on her. We never forced religion on any of our children. We just made sure they knew that God was waiting for them, if and when they were ready. There's a great difference between indoctrination and bringing up children in a home which is full of God's love.'

Merrily nodded again. 'That's sensible.'

'And Amy responded better than anyone could have wished. A daughter to be proud of – respected her parents, her teachers and her God.' Hazel Shelbone paused, looking Merrily straight in the eyes. 'You understand I'm only talking like this to you now because you're a woman of God. I don't make a practice of scattering the Lord's name willy-nilly on barren ground. The Social Services people one has to deal with in fostering and adoption, many of those people are *very* left-wing and atheistic, and they'll automatically take against you if they think you're some sort of religious fanatic. Well, we're *far* from fanatics, Mrs Watkins. We just maintain a Christian household. Which you always think will . . . will . . .'

She bit her lip.

'Will be a protection to them?' Merrily said softly.

Hazel Shelbone leaned back and breathed in deeply as if accepting an infusion of strength from God for what she was about to say. 'Sometimes, when I come home and she's been alone in the house . . . it seems so cold. There's a *sense* of cold. The sort of cold you can feel in your bones.'

Merrily said nothing. Once something started gnawing at your mind, it could produce its own phenomena.

'Last Sunday, when she was . . . sick, and we took her *from* here, I don't think she even realized where she was. Her eyes were absolutely vacant, as though her mind had gone off somewhere else. Vacant and cold. Like a doll's eyes. Do you know what I mean?'

'Yes.'

'It was only when we got her home that she began to cry, and even then it was like tears of . . . defiance. I'd never seen that before, not in Amy. We've had other children, for short periods, who were resentful and troublesome, but not Amy. Amy became our *own*.'

Merrily asked carefully, 'Have you consulted a doctor?'

Hazel Shelbone blinked. 'You mean a psychiatrist?'

'Well, not—'

'We are a Christian household, Mrs Watkins. We seek Christian solutions.'

'Well, yes, I understand that, but . . .'

'You may say we've become complacent in our middle years, having a daughter who was always conscientious with her school work, who'd been going happily to church from the age of seven . . . and was, by the way, confirmed into the Church in March this year by Bishop Dunmore. A girl who even—' she looked at Merrily, whose silk scarf had come loose, revealing the dog collar '—who even talked of one day becoming a minister.'

Merrily thought of Jane who once, in a heated moment, had said she'd rather clean public lavatories.

'She always kept her Bible on her bedside table – until it went missing and I found it wedged under the wardrobe in the spare room. The Holy Bible wedged there, face down, like some old telephone directory! This was the child who always wanted to be assured, before the light went out, that Jesus was watching over her. Now she doesn't want go to church any more, she looks down at her feet every time she has to even *pass* the church . . .'

'Since when?'

'Five weeks? Six weeks? The first time she wouldn't go, she claimed she was feeling ill, with a bad stomach. Well, she's always been truthful, never tried to get a day off school, so of course I sent her back to bed at once. The second time . . . Oh, it was some essay she had to write for school – she's always been *very* assiduous about her school work, as I say. Very well, her dad said, you must decide what's most important, and she promised she would go to evensong that night instead, on her own. And, sure enough, she got changed and off she went. But I know she didn't turn up. I *know* that.'

Her voice had become loud enough to cause an echo, and Merrily glanced quickly around to make sure they were still alone.

'Another time, she made the excuse of having a particularly severe period pain. But when she gave me the same excuse again last Sunday, I counted up the days and I can tell you there's nothing wrong with my arithmetic. "*Oh no*," I said, "*up you get, my girl. Now!*" And I made her come with us to the early Eucharist.'

'Did she make a fuss?'

'She was sulky. Distant. That glazed look.'

'Has she got a boyfriend?'

'What does that—? No. She hasn't got a boyfriend. But she's only fourteen.'

'You sure about that?' What could be better guaranteed to undermine the piety of a starchy fourteen-year-old girl than a sudden, blinding crush on some cool, mean kid who despised religion? 'For instance . . . where did she *really* go, do you think, when she claimed she was off to evensong?'

'I know what you're thinking, Mrs Watkins! And *yes*, I've had her to the doctor this week, and *no*, he couldn't find anything wrong with her. But . . . well, I can tell you there certainly has been illness in the house as a result of all this. David's had migraines again, and my . . . Anyway, everything has seemed under a cloud. Unhealthy. A darkness, even in the height of summer. And you may say this is subjective, but I know that it isn't. The child's become a receptacle for evil.'

Hazel Shelbone stood up, her back against a stone pillar by the pew's end. Defensive, Merrily thought. *If she's so certain, then there's something else.*

Mrs Shelbone walked into the chancel and faced the altar.

'I come here, and I polish and polish the bit of rail where she was sick, and I pray for her to be redeemed, and I get down on my knees and ask God what our family could have done to deserve this.'

Merrily went to join her. 'You seriously believe Amy is possessed by evil.'

'By an evil spirit.'

'And you want her to be exorcized.'

'I feel it's not something we can ignore.'

'Yeah, but it's . . . it's not something we undertake without a lot of . . . There's a procedure, OK? I'm afraid it would involve bringing in a psychiatrist, initially.'

Hazel Shelbone didn't turn around. Her whole body had stiffened.

'We need to be sure.' Merrily put a hand on her arm. 'What might at first appear to you or me to be demonic possession could be some form of mental breakdown.'

'Reverend Watkins . . .' Hazel Shelbone stared up at the cruci-fied Jesus in the window above the altar. 'We've had our share of problem children, David and I. We've had children from broken homes . . . children whose parents have been admitted to psychiatric institutions . . . disturbed children, a child who ran away after smashing up our living room. There's really not a lot anyone can tell me about child psychology.'

'We have to be sure,' Merrily said, and took a step back as the big woman spun round at her.

'Is *this* what it's come to? Has the Church become a branch of the Social Services now? Do I have to sign forms? Mrs Watkins, it's quite simple – I would like the darkness to be driven out, so that God may be readmitted into the heart of my daughter. Is that too much to ask of a priest?'

'No. No, it shouldn't be.'

'Then?'

Then, Merrily needed advice. This sounded like a simple and sudden adolescent rejection of parental values, but you could never be sure. Before taking this any further, she needed at least to talk to Huw Owen over in Wales.

Who, of course, would warn her not to leave the village without praying for and – if possible – *with* this girl.

'Mrs Shelbone,' Merrily said softly, 'is there something you haven't told me?'

'I don't know what you mean.' It came back too quickly.

'It's just that for you to want to put your daughter through the stress of a spiritual cleansing—'

'She knows things,' Hazel Shelbone mumbled.

'What?'

'She knows things she shouldn't know. Things she *couldn't* know.'

'Like . . . what?'

Mrs Shelbone bowed her head once, and moved away from the altar. 'She will look into my eyes sometimes and tell me things she could not possibly know.'

She started to walk quickly back towards the nave, where her homely shopping basket sat on the raised wooden floor at the foot of the front pew.

'All right.' Merrily moved behind her. 'Where is she now?'

'At home, I assume, in her room. She spends most of her time in her room. I'd better go now. Her father will be home in an hour.'

'Why don't we both go and have a chat with her?' Merrily suggested.

# FIVE

# Al and Sally

*Like a fine-boned girl,* he thought: *pale and graceful and slim-hipped.*

Lol was suddenly besotted. Since coming into the museum he'd been aware of little else. His gaze kept returning to this shadowed alcove, overhung with tumbling bines.

The man standing by the counter covered with books and leaflets was watching him, smiling. He wore a white linen jacket, of Edwardian length, and looked about sixty-five. He had long white hair and a pointed chin, goblinesque, and there were tiny gold rings in both his ears. He gestured towards the alcove. 'Go ahead.'

Lol moved closer but didn't touch.

Mother-of-pearl was inlaid around the soundhole but the soft-wood top was otherwise plain, with a dull sheen but no lacquer, no polish. There was an orange line of yew in the neck. She was like one of those old parlour instruments from the late nineteenth century.

A holy relic. What was it doing *here*?

Lol said reverently. 'She's a Boswell.'

'Mother of God!' The man with long white hair strode out from behind the counter. 'She's a guitar!' Carelessly plucking the instrument from its stand, handing it to Lol. 'Go on, take her. But no plectrum, if you don't mind. I'd hate to need a scratchboard.'

'I'm no good with a plec, anyway.' Lol accepted the guitar, one hand under its sleek butt.

'Quite right, lad.' The man clapped his hands, two rings tinking. 'Plectrums, thumb-picks – condoms for the fingers. Why would God have given us nails?' His sharp rural accent, with flat northern vowels, was unplaceable, the kind sometimes affected by traditional folk singers.

The guitar was unexpectedly lightweight.

'Yours?'

The man smiled. '*Check out the back room,*' Prof had said earlier, winking. Back room?

'Ah, you're embarrassed,' the goblin man said. 'All right. I'll leave you alone with her for a while.' From behind the counter, he pulled a wooden stool for Lol to sit on. 'I'll give you just one tip – don't be too delicate with her. She won't repay you.' He wagged a finger. 'Remember now, Lol, she's not sacred. She's only a guitar.'

Lol looked up at him, unsure whether he'd fallen on his feet or into a trap.

'The Prof.' The goblin smiled – a couple of gold teeth on show. 'The Prof said you'd be around sooner or later.' He unlatched the door. 'I shall be back in about ten minutes. Enjoy!'

The Hop Museum was set back from the main road to Bromyard, about fifty yards from the turning to Knight's Frome. Like Prof's place, it was the remains of farm buildings, but in this case with a few acres around it. There were two ponies and a donkey in the field in front, and a pond with ducks. Also, a gypsy caravan in green and gold.

The River Frome passed unobtrusively under the access drive, through what looked like a culvert.

Earlier, Lol had played the Frome song for Prof, as far as it went. The chorus had written itself, but sounded a bit trite.

> *The River Frome goes nowhere in particular*
> *It isn't very wide*
> *There's nothin' on the other side . . .*

Pity it was pronounced *froom*, to rhyme with *doom and gloom*. Lol had decided he'd still have it sounding in the song like *home* and *loam* so as to carry the vowel in that first line: *Frome goes nowhere*. He was, after all, a stranger.

'You don't know enough about the place to finish this song,'

Prof had said flatly. 'It might be about what a complete loser you are, but you still need some images to carry it. What do you really know about this sodding river except its name and that it isn't very wide? You ask me, Laurence, it's time you went to talk to Sally, down at the hop museum. The river, the hills, the woods, the people – Sally knows everything about them all.'

'Sally?' Lol had stared at him. 'You actually know this woman? I thought you had a policy of not knowing local people unless they could play something useful?'

'It was an accident,' Prof said.

It was about five-thirty when Lol had set off to walk the half-mile or so from the studio. The white-haired man had been closing the gates at the foot of the drive but had beckoned Lol in anyway. The only visitor they'd had all afternoon, he said. Admission was a pound, and there were a few items on sale inside.

But not, presumably, the Boswell guitar, handmade by the great Alfonso Boswell who had given all his guitars women's names. The same instrument on which Lol now played the slow and ghostly Celtic instrumental he called *Moon's Tune* . . . knowing it was going to remind him of the abandoned hop-yard, the place of the wilt, and the woman he'd seen there. He'd dreamed of her since, twice in one night. Not pleasant, though, as dreams went.

*Are you all right? Then letting her approach to within a few inches before he slunk bashfully away. Registering by the rhythm of her movements and her blurred smile that she was not hurt, bar the scratches, and had not been attacked or forcibly stripped . . . was more likely some stoned moonbather who'd assumed she was alone but didn't really care.*

The low-beamed room, one of three linking up to accommodate the museum, was dim and crowded with annonated exhibits that looked at first like junk. These included the hop-cribs – hammocks in frames, in which the cones were separated from the bines; the giant sausage sacks called hop-pockets, in which they were collected; a huge cast-iron furnace, rescued from some subsequently converted kiln.

On the walls were blown-up black-and-white photographs of kilns like Gerard Stock's, in which the harvest had been dried on platforms over the furnace. The atmosphere in the museum was humid and laden with a mellow, musky aroma that could only be the hops themselves. And because hops were used to flavour and preserve beer it was easy to find the smell intoxicating. It seemed to soften Lol's senses, made it easier to accept the curious turn events had taken.

He pulled the Boswell guitar comfortably into his solar plexus. The soundboxes of Boswells had curved backs long before Ovations became ubiquitous but, while Ovations were fibreglass, the back of the hand-crafted Boswell was like a mandolin's. There were probably fewer than a hundred of these instruments, so it had to be worth more than anything else in the museum. But what was it doing here – and did it have anything to do with hops?

Lol played the opening chords of the River Frome song: B-minor, F-sharp. The tone was entirely distinctive: deep but sharp, a bit like the voice of the man with the long, white hair.

He stopped playing. *No* . . . No, really, it couldn't be. Because he was dead, wasn't he? He would surely have to be dead, after all this time.

'Al,' he said, jabbing a thumb at his own chest. 'And this is Sally, my wife.'

They stood together in the doorway, looking strangely like a period couple from a sepia photograph. Sally's hair was ash-grey, fine and shoulder-length. She was tall and slim and, at surely close to the same age as Al himself, still startlingly beautiful. She wore a long, dark blue dress and half-glasses on a chain.

But her handshake was businesslike and her accent clipped and cultured. 'I know,' she said, 'you thought he was dead. Everybody thinks he's dead. Which is absolutely no handicap at all when we have one to sell. It gives it a certain patina of antiquity.'

'You like her, then?' Al Boswell asked him. 'You like my baby?'

He meant the guitar.

*Al.*

Alfonso Boswell: virtuoso blues and ragtime guitarist and perhaps the most revered, if eccentric, guitar-maker of the past half-century.

'Can't believe this,' Lol mumbled.

'He's a little older than he looks.' Sally Boswell flicked at her husband's snowy hair. 'But also he's been making guitars and things since he was just in his teens, so that rather confuses people.'

'I *wanted* to stop,' Al Boswell said, 'but after I finished the last one, I awoke in the night with what seemed very like the first twinges of arthritis. Well, I'm a superstitious man, from a long line of supersitious men, so I started work again the very next morning.'

Lol thought of the gypsy caravan outside. According to the legend, Alfonso Boswell would travel the country lanes, selecting and cutting his own wood and then set up his workshop in some forest clearing – each instrument growing organically in the open air, under the sun, under the stars. There would be no more than three or four guitars a year; it was never a full-time job, and he'd also be doing seasonal work on the farms: fruit-picking and . . . hop-picking?

Looked like Al Boswell had uncoupled his caravan and settled down.

'And if you didn't know already,' Sally Boswell said dryly, 'the Rom are renowned for their outrageous lies. Proud of it, too, for reasons that still escape me after all these years.'

'Non-confrontational is all we are,' Al said. His face carried very few lines and his skin was lighter-toned than you'd imagine on a pure-bred gypsy. 'Amazing, it is, how much conflict can be avoided by a well-timed fib. The truth can be hurtful and dangerous sometimes. Come on, lad, what do you *really* think of the instrument?'

Lol thought this was getting increasingly unreal. He thought, Why should Alfonso Boswell care what the hell I think?

'We heard your playing,' Sally said. 'We were listening outside the door, I'm afraid.'

'So you'll know why I'm not worthy even to tune it.' Lol was embarrassed. He was still holding the guitar but careful to keep his fingers well away from the strings.

'How long you been playing?' Al Boswell asked him.

'Oh . . .' Lol blinked nervously. 'Since I was a kid with a plastic one. Sad, isn't it?'

'It's not the technique, lad. It's the *heart*, the relationship. You know that.' Al tapped the body of the guitar. 'This one – she's very young, you see. She's the first this year. And she'll probably be the last, I reckon. What she needs is a good playing-in. I never let one go until she's been played-in. What do you think, now? Is she worth it?'

'Oh, Al!' Sally frowned. 'You can hardly expect a snap judgement. Why don't you let Mr Robinson take the thing away for a couple of weeks?'

Al stared at her, then he threw up his arms. 'Well, damn it, why didn't I think of that? Aye, you take her away, lad. Break her in. Bring her back in – what shall we say? – September? Unless you want to buy her, of course. In which case we can discuss terms.'

Lol was shocked. He put the guitar carefully back on the stand, stepped away from it.

'Now what's that mean?' Al said. 'Is it some form of *gaujo* insult?'

Sally closed her eyes, shaking her head.

'This is all moving too fast,' Lol said. 'I just walk in here, you don't know a thing about me . . . I can't just walk out with six thousand quid's worth of—'

'Mother of God!' Al cried. 'Is that what they're fetching now? I've never had more than two and a half!'

Sally smiled tiredly at Lol. 'Mr Robinson, a short time ago, Mr Levin rang us to say you were on your way. Al has known him for many, many years. Mr Levin feels you could use a little inspiration.' She looked at him over her half-glasses. 'Don't, as they say, knock it.'

Al Boswell laughed loudly, threw up his arms and walked out of the museum.


'He loves his little games,' Sally explained. 'They're mischievous sometimes, like elves. He's just gone to find you a guitar case.'

She bent to adjust the guitar on its stand. When she straightened up she stood taller than Lol. Where Al Boswell was volatile, Sally seemed watchful and serene.

'Al owes Prof Levin some favours from way back and wanted him to have a guitar, but Mr Levin insisted that a Boswell should never go to someone who couldn't play. This is the guitar he was promised. Consider yourself an intermediary in this. Play it while you're there, if it agrees with you, and then perhaps forget to take it with you when you leave. In a few years, I suppose, it'll be worth ten or twelve thousand to a collector.'

Lol was still bemused. 'He recorded with Prof?'

'Mr Levin would always find Al session work when we needed money. He's a kind man, and he's very fond of you. He doesn't want you to fall by the wayside.'

'The wayside's OK, sometimes,' Lol said awkwardly.

She arched an eyebrow. 'That's the sort of thing Al says. But we are not Romanies, you and I. When *we* fall, we don't just roll over and land on our feet again, grinning all over our faces.'

Lol was curious. 'Did Prof know Al was going to be here when he bought the stables?' *I have sympathy for the Romanies*, Prof had said.

'Pure coincidence, actually, although Al knew Simon St John, of course. We're all parts of interlinked circles, aren't we?'

Lol wondered how this very English woman had come to link up with Al Boswell, pure-bred Romany, apparently luring him off the road for good.

'But, according to the Prof, you want to know about the Frome Valley,' Sally Boswell said. 'Therefore I want to tell you . . . because there are aspects of life here which *do* need to be recorded, and nothing keeps memories flowing onwards like songs. And the Frome flows through that guitar – the vein of yew in it came from prunings from a thousand-year-old tree in Simon's churchyard and there's also a little willow from a tree which bends over the river itself. The Romany is ever a discreet scavenger. He lives lightly on the earth.'

She led him into the next room. Hop-bines were intertwined along the beams (silent, but as soon as he saw them he could almost hear them crackling and rustling, and he felt a small shiver). More blown-up photographs were spotlit on the walls: men in flat caps, women in print dresses, berets and headscarves. People laughing. The strange sadness of frozen merriment.

'Until mechanization began to take over in the sixties, hop-picking was very much a multicultural phenomenon,' Sally Boswell explained. 'Well . . . four cultures, really: the indigenous locals, the Welsh Valleys, the Dudleys, as we called them, from the Black Country, and the gypsies.'

She told him how, at picking time, in September, the local population would expand eight- or tenfold – perhaps a good thing, leaving the locals far less insular than in other rural areas. The hop-masters would have huge barrack blocks for the pickers, and the pubs were always overflowing – the police constantly back and forth, breaking up the fights.

Lol studied a photo in which the smiles seemed more inhibited and there were scowls among the caravans and the cooking pots.

'Ah, yes,' said Sally, 'when did the travellers *ever* like to be photographed? They were always a settlement apart, but usually very honest and faithful to their particular employers. They liked being able to return to the same establishment year after year.'

'Al was here, too?'

'For a while.'

'That was how you met?'

'Romanies can be charming.' She didn't smile. 'Also infuriating.'

Lol peered at a picture showing a girl lying in one of the hop-cribs, laughing and helpless, men standing around.

'Cribbing,' Sally said. 'When the picking was almost over, an unmarried girl would be seized and tossed into the crib with the last of the hops. The unspoken implication was that she, too, might be picked before next year's bines were high on the poles.' She looked solemn. 'Al and I met when I was . . . drawn to the Romany ways. I've been planning to write a book. Well, I *was* planning to. In the end, I gave all my material to Mr Ash, for *his* book. I suppose this place is better than a book, in the end. More interactive, as they say. And Al, like most Romanies, is suspicious of the written word.'

'Doesn't seem to have done Mr Ash much good either,' Lol said hesitantly, 'in the end.'

She looked at him thoughtfully, as if deciding how much to say. 'No,' she agreed eventually. 'Stewart was the last casualty – we all hope – in an unhappy chain of events at Knight's Frome.' She nodded towards the next doorway. 'Go through.'

No hop-bines hung in the third and smallest room. It was also the darkest, with no windows and few lights. A long panel in a corner was spotlit. It was a painting on board, in flat oils, or acrylics, of a stark and naked hop-yard at night, with pole-alleys black against a moonlit sky, a tattered bine hanging from one of the frames. Halfway down the central row, hovering above the bare ground, was a woman in a long dark dress, like Sally's, billowing in the wind. The caption read: *The Lady of the Bines: a ghost story.*

If Sally noticed he'd gone quiet, she didn't comment on it.

'The hop-farmer's angel of death,' she said with a curator's jollity. There was a half-smile on the face of the woman in the picture.

'Who painted it?'

'I did,' Sally said.

'It's really good. It's as if—'

'As if I've actually seen her?' She laughed lightly. 'Perhaps I have. Sometimes I can imagine I have.'

Lol was glad it was dark in here. This was unreal – the sequel to a dream.

'I expect there's a story,' he said.

'She was the wife of some local lord or knight – maybe the original knight of Knight's Frome, for all I know. And she couldn't give him a son. So he sent her away.'

'Like you do.'

'Like you *did*, apparently. What was the point of having the king give you a few hundred acres of stolen land if you couldn't found a dynasty? Anyway, he threw her out. Gave her some money to go away, and then settled down with his mistress. But the poor, spurned lady pined for the valley. Pined all night long in the fields and the hop-yards.'

'Is this true?' It sounded like the theme of a traditional folk song.

'Until one morning, one beautiful midsummer morning, with the hops ripening on the bines—' her voice hardened '—they found the poor bitch hanging from one of the frames.'

'When was this?'

'Don't know. No one does. It's a legend. I suppose, if it had any basis in fact, the story couldn't have dated back earlier than the sixteenth century because hops weren't grown for brewing in this country until 1520. The postscript is that, from the night she died, the knight's hops began to wither on the bines and his yard was barren for many years. And if you see her ghost, then your crop will also wither . . . or someone's will.'

Lol recalled the shrivelled old hop-garland hanging from the gibbet-like arrangement of poles. He didn't want to think about the naked woman in the hop-yard. He found himself wanting her to have been a ghost. Ghosts were simpler.

'She's become a metaphor for Verticillium Wilt,' Sally said. 'And, before that, for red spiders, aphids, white-mould . . . all the scourges of the hop. Wilt, particularly, renders a hop-yard virtually sterile for a number of years. Perhaps you should write a song about her, Lol.'

'It's a thought,' he said uncertainly – although he knew he could. If he knew what he was writing about.

'Perhaps we could have it playing softly in this room.' Sally Boswell laughed. Lol thought she didn't seem to have much sympathy for either the knight or the Lady of the Bines.

'She still seen?'

'Depends who you believe. It's certainly said she was widely observed in the sixties.' She nodded towards a black-and-white photograph of a man with a heavy moustache, who looked a bit like Lord Lucan. 'But then, people would say that – in the last days of the Emperor of Frome, when all was darkness and chaos.'

She was poised to go on, but for Lol, the darkness and chaos could wait.

He hadn't planned to ask it. He just did. 'Does she always have a dress on?'

Sally Boswell's face was gaunt with shadows. From two rooms away, there was a skimming of strings: the legendary Al stowing away his creation.

'What an extraordinary question,' she said coldly.

# SIX

# Full of Dead People

Muffled sobbing gave way to those time-honoured battle-cries from the generation war.

'*Leave me alone! Just go away! It's nothing to do with you!*'

The clouds were a deep luminous mauve now, and the sky looked like a taut, well-beaten drum-skin through the long window pane in the front door.

It was stifling in the small, rectangular hall with its beige woodchip and wall-lights with peeling coppery shades. Merrily stood under a print in a chipped gilt frame: Christ on the Mount of Olives. Opposite her was a cream door with a little pottery plaque on it.

*Amy's Room*

The door was closed, but its plywood panels were not exactly soundproof. Merrily thought David Shelbone, historic-buildings officer, was unlikely ever to see his own home listed, except as a classic example of 1970s Utility. How did the Shelbones spend their money? Probably on their adopted child? Perhaps long, educational holidays.

'*Amy. Please.*'

'*I . . . am . . . not . . . going . . . anywhere! Do you understand? There is nothing wrong with me! And . . . and if there is, it's nothing to do with you. It's nothing to do with her. Just get her out of the house. Please. This is . . . disgraceful.*'

*Please? Disgraceful?* Comparatively speaking, this was a restrained, almost polite response. In extreme situations, kids were rarely able to

73

contain extreme language. *You sad old bitch* had sometimes been Jane's starting point, before things got heated.

Hazel Shelbone murmured something Merrily didn't catch.

'*No!*' Amy screamed. '*You . . . How dare you make out there's something wrong with me?*'

'*Amy, do you really think you'd be in any position to judge, if there was?*'

'*What do* you *know? What do you know about the way I feel? How can you understand? You're not even—*'

Merrily willed her not to say it. This was not the time to say it.

'*—my moth—*'

Then the unmistakable and always-shocking sound of a slap. Merrily closed her eyes.

An abyss of silence. Jane would have been composing a response involving the European Court of Human Rights.

Amy just started to cry again, long hollow sobs, close to retching.

But this was surely not the first time she'd thrown out the not-my-mother line. There had to be something additional to have provoked Hazel, the seasoned foster-mother, the reservoir. *And when I look into her eyes . . .*

With no windows you could open, it was hard to breathe in here. Merrily ran a finger around the inside of her dog-collar, walked away towards the front door. She felt like an intruder. She felt this was becoming futile. She looked across into the placidly glowing face of Jesus in the picture, and Jesus smiled, in His knowing way.

Merrily closed her eyes again, let her arms fall to her sides, stilled her thoughts.

Mrs Shelbone was saying, '*Oh, my darling, I'm so sorry, but you—*'

'*Go away. Just go away.*'

'*We only want to—*'

'*You can't help me. Nobody can help me.*'

'*The Good Lord can help you, Amy.*'

Another silence. No sniffles, no whimpers. Then, as Merrily straightened up, Amy said,

'*There's no such thing as a Good Lord, you stupid woman.*'

'*Amy!*'

'*It's all just a sick, horrible joke! There's nobody out there who can*

*protect us. Or if . . . if God exists, he just totally hates us. He watches us*
*suffer and die and he doesn't do a thing to help us. He doesn't help*
*us, ever, ever, ever! He enjoys watching us suffer. You can plead and*
*plead and plead, and you can say your prayers till you're b—blue in the*
*face and nobody's going to ever save you. It's all a horrible sick lie! And*
*the Church is just a big . . . a big cover-up. It's all smelly and musty*
*and horrible and it's full of dead people, and I don't . . . I don't want*
*to die in—'*

Merrily leaned back against the wall. Christ gave her a sad smile.
The door of Amy's Room opened. Hazel Shelbone stood there,
stone-faced. 'Mrs Watkins? Would you mind—?'

*'Don't you dare bring her in here! I'm not talking to her, do you*
*understand?'*

Merrily took a step back along the hall. Something *had* happened
to this kid. If not a sneering boyfriend, what about some cool, com-
pelling atheistic teacher?

She whispered, 'Hazel, I . . . think, on the whole, it might be
better if Amy came out, and—'

*'I'm warning you, if she comes in here I'll smash the window. Do*
*you hear me? I'll smash the window and I'll get out of here for good!*
*I'll throw the chair through the window. Can you hear—?'*

'I'm sorry.' Mrs Shelbone pulled the door closed behind her, new
lines and hollows showing in her wide, honest face. 'I don't know
what to do. She's never been quite like this before, I swear to you.'

*'You just keep lying to me. Lies, lies, lies!'*

Merrily opened the front door and stepped down to the flagged
garden path, followed by Amy's mother.

The bungalow was detached but fairly small, with a bay window
each side of the door. There were other houses and bungalows either
side of the country lane, well separated, with high hedges and gardens
crowded with trees and bushes.

The sky was the colour of a cemetery. In contrast, a small yellow
sports car, parked half up on the grass verge, looked indecently lurid.

'Hazel, what does she mean by lies?'

'I don't know. I've told you, this is not my Amy. I don't know
how she can say these things about God.'

But she looked away as she spoke, and Merrily thought perhaps she *did* know . . . knew *something*, anyway.

'What's she been like at school?'

'Well behaved, always well behaved. Her teachers have nothing but praise for her.'

'Do you know her teachers?'

'Most of them. We've always made it our business to know them. As good parents.'

'What about her friends?'

'She's . . .' A sigh. 'She's never had many friends. She's very conscientious, she studies hard. She's always felt she had to, because . . . well, she's bright, but she's no genius. Because she's adopted, I think she feels she has to make it up to us. Make us proud, do you see? Good children, children who study hard, they aren't always very popular at school these days, are they?'

'Has she been bullied, do you think? Picked on?'

But after that one small confidence, Mrs Shelbone had tightened up again. 'Look, Reverend Watkins, this isn't what I expected at all. I think she needs an infusion of God's love, not all sorts of questions.'

Merrily sighed. 'I'll be honest with you. I'm not really sure how to handle this. Can't take it any further without talking to her, and if I go in there, it's likely to cause a scene, isn't it? The last thing I want is to upset her any more. I mean . . . I suppose I could start by taking off the dog-collar.'

Mrs Shelbone's brown eyes hardened. 'What's the point of *that*? You're a priest. Aren't you?'

Merrily stared hopelessly at the close-mown lawn, at the well-weeded flowerbeds. Demonic evil was something you could sense, like a disgusting smell – sometimes precisely that. The only identifiable odour in this house had been floor-cleaner wafting from the kitchen. All she'd sensed in there were confusion, distress . . . and perhaps something else she couldn't yet isolate. But it wasn't evil.

In the end, all she had – the only universally accepted symptom of spiritual or diabolic possession – was the mother's suggestion of a sudden, startling clairvoyance.

'You said she knew things. Things she couldn't have known.'

'I'm sorry I said that, now.' A nervous glance back at the house, as though a chair might come crashing through the window. 'It's nothing I can prove.'

'*What* things?'

'This isn't the time, Mrs Watkins.'

'What kind of . . . intrusion do you think might be affecting her?'

'Isn't that for you to find out? Isn't that what you're supposed to—'

'Help me,' Merrily said.

Amy's mother stared over the low hedge, across the lane. 'The spirit of a dead person.'

Merrily didn't blink. 'Specifically?'

There was a movement at the window of a room to the left of the door. The child stood there, not six feet away. She wore a white, sleeveless top. Her fair hair hung limply to her shoulders. She looked maybe twelve. She looked stiff and waxen. The room behind her was all featureless dark, like the background to a portrait. '*It's so cold now. There's a sense of cold. The cold you can feel in your bones.*'

Merrily tried to attract Amy's gaze, but the kid was looking beyond her.

She turned. Nothing. Nothing had changed in the lane. There was nobody about; even the yellow sports car was pulling away.

It began to rain – big, warm, slow drops. When she looked back at the bungalow, the girl had vanished.

Hazel Shelbone walked back to the door. 'My husband will be home presently. I don't really want him to know you've been here. He's under enough pressure.'

'I'll take advice,' Merrily promised. 'I'll be back. I'll leave you my number but I'll call you tomorrow, anyway, if that's all right.'

'Just pray for her,' Mrs Shelbone said limply. 'I expect you can do that, at least.'

No thunder, yet, but the rain was hard and relentless, clanking on the bonnet of the old Volvo like nuts and bolts, turning the windscreen into bubblewrap. Both wipers needed new blades. After a few miles, Merrily was forced into the forecourt of a derelict petrol station where she sat and smoked a Silk Cut rapidly, filling up the car with smoke because she couldn't open the window in this downpour.

Nothing was ever straightforward, nothing ever textbook.

In the car, behind the streaming windows, she prayed for Amy Shelbone. She prayed for communication to be reopened between Amy and her mother. She prayed for any psychic blockage or interference to be removed. She prayed for the healing of whatever kind of wound had been opened up, by the puncturing of what the kid now evidently believed to be the central lie of her upbringing.

She prayed, all too vaguely, for a whole bunch of *whatevers*.

With hindsight, if she couldn't work with Amy, it ought to have been her mother. With *extra*-hindsight, she and Hazel Shelbone ought to have prayed together before they left the church. Except at that stage, Merrily hadn't been convinced. She'd needed to see Amy.

And, having seen Amy, having heard her, she still wasn't convinced.

She could perhaps have persuaded Mrs Shelbone to let her stay until Amy's dad got home. Perhaps the three of them could have returned to the church this evening and, with Dennis Beckett's permission, conducted a small Eucharist. Just in case.

In case *what*?

Six p.m., and she was back in the scullery-office, with the window open and the dregs of the rain dripping from the ivy on the wall. A Silk Cut smouldered in the ashtray. Jane was not yet back from Hereford.

Merrily felt like a cartoon person flattened in the road, watching a departing steamroller.

The phone was life support.

'It's the old dilemma,' she said. 'Don't know whether I'm making too much of it, or not enough.'

'When do we ever?' said the Rev Huw Owen. 'You should know that by now.'

'Did I tell you? – Bernie wants me to set up a deliverance group.'

'Never liked committees, focus-group crap. But in this case – traps everywhere, folk always looking for some poor bugger to blame when it all goes down the toilet. Do it, I would. Just don't co-opt a social worker.'

She could picture him in his study in the Brecon Beacons, his legs stretched out, his ancient trainers wearing another hole in the rug. The old wolfhound, her Deliverance mentor, technical adviser to half the exorcists in Wales and the West Midlands.

'Tell me that last bit again, lass. You asked the mother what she reckoned had got into the girl. And she said . . .'

'The spirit of a dead person,' Merrily said. 'That was what she said.'

'Anybody in particular?'

'That's what I asked her next, but she didn't reply. Then she started to backtrack on what she'd said earlier about Amy telling them things she couldn't possibly have known without—'

'If they don't cooperate, you're buggered.'

'Mmm.'

'Basically, you want to know whether they need you or a child-psychiatrist.'

'Mmm.'

Huw was silent for about a minute. She knew he was still there because she could hear his trainer tapping the fender. No matter how hot it was, he always kept a small fire going. Not that it could ever get over-hot in a rectory well above the snowline.

Outside a late sun was blearily pushing aside the blankets of cloud.

'Got a favourite coin?' Huw said at last.

Merrily's heart sank.

'Well?' said Huw.

'When you told us about this on the first course, I thought you were kidding. Then I read Martin Israel on exorcism, but I still think—'

'Stop shaking your head, lass. I've done it a few times. It's always worked – far as I could tell. It either tells you what you already knew or it tells you to think again. And once you start thinking again, you find some new angle you hadn't noticed and that's the way ahead.'

'I wouldn't have the bottle.'

'Aye, you would. Take an owd coin and bless it and explain to God what you're doing. I use this old half-crown. Not legal tender any more, therefore not filthy lucre. I keep it in the bottom of a candleholder on the altar.'

Merrily imagined some hapless parishioner wandering in and witnessing the Rev Owen apparently settling some vexed spiritual issue on the toss of a coin. It could overturn your entire belief-structure.

'Course, it's nowt to do with the coin,' Huw said.

'Any more than the Tarot is to do with the cards.'

'Don't go fundamentalist on me, lass.'

Merrily laughed.

'Look at Israel – a scientist, a distinguished pathologist. And they made him exorcist for the City of London. What d'you want? Oh aye, I know what *you* want. You want summat foolproof. You want a solution on a plate.'

'A second opinion would do.'

'If you don't like the cold, come out of the mortuary.'

'Thanks a bunch.'

'Any time,' said Huw.

Merrily sighed.

'Look, luv, give yourself some credit, eh? I'd've kicked you out of the bloody ring meself if I didn't think you were a contender.'

'You *tried*.'

'That were only before you got your little feet under t'table. Listen, trust your feelings and your common sense. If you want a second opinion, ask Him, not me. Like the song says, make a deal with God.'

'You're a complete bastard, Huw.'

Then she remembered that he actually was: born in a little *bwthyn* halfway up Pen-y-fan and then his mother escaped to Sheffield where he was raised, after a fashion.

'Sorry,' Merrily said.

Huw laughed.

At least Jane looked happier when she came into the kitchen. She'd been saving up the money she'd earned working two Saturdays a month at the eight-till-late shop, and she was loaded with parcels: clothes for the holiday. No alluring nightwear, Merrily hoped – though, from what she'd heard about Eirion's father's extended family, nocturnal recreational opportunities were likely to be seriously limited.

A small carrier bag landed in her lap.

'What's this?'

'It's a top. It's for you. You never get yourself any new clothes.'

'Gosh, flower . . . that's very . . .' Merrily pulled it out of the bag. It was pale orange, cotton, very skimpy. 'It's going to be, er, how can I put this . . . slightly low-cut, isn't it?'

'Won't go with the dog-collar, if that's what you mean,' Jane said smugly.

'Well . . . thank you.' Merrily put the top back in its bag. 'Thank you very much. It was very thoughtful.'

'If you don't wear it, I'll be seriously offended,' Jane said. 'It's going to be a long, hot summer.'

'That's what we always say, and it never is.'

'Yeah.' Jane sat down, stretched her bare arms. 'I expect Lol'll be taking a summer break from his course about now. You do *remember* Lol?'

'Ye-es.'

'The greatest living writer of gentle, lo-fi, reflective songs and also a cool, sensitive person in himself.'

'Yes, flower, I think I remember.'

'No, all I was thinking was, if you found me an inhibiting presence, this would be a good opportunity—'

'Thank you, flower, for considering my emotional welfare.'

'Any time,' Jane said. 'Oh, that Amy Shelbone – I remembered – she does go to our school.'

'I know.'

'I suddenly realized who you meant. Kind of old-fashioned. Always tidy. Bit of a pain, basically.'

Merrily nodded. 'Mm-mm.'

'So, is there, like, anything I can help you with?'

'I don't think so,' Merrily said, 'at this stage.'

'Because, like—'

'Sure,' Merrily said. 'What time's Eirion picking you up?'

'Half-nine.'

'You looking forward to this?'

'Sure,' Jane said.

With the kid upstairs, Merrily went into the hall and ran a hand along the top of the tallest bookcase. It was still there, in all the dust, where she'd popped it hurriedly after they'd found it under the bath when they were having – the year's big luxury – a new shower installed.

It was thick and misshapen, the head of the monarch obscured but Britannia distinct on the other side, also the date: 1797 – over a century after the death of Wil Williams the martyr, Ledwardine's most famous vicar.

Feeling faintly ridiculous, she slipped the coin into a pocket of her denim skirt.

# SEVEN

# Stealing the Light

In the early evening, a sinister, ochre light flared over the Frome Valley before the storm crashed in, driving like a ram-raider down the western flank of the Malverns.

Although there wasn't much thunder, every light on the mixing board went out at 7.02 p.m., leaving only Prof Levin incandescent.

'Some farmer guy comes on to me in the post office in Bishop's Frome: "Ah, you want to get yourself a little petrol generator, Mr Levin." These *hayseeds!* You imagine recording music with a bloody generator grinding away out there?'

'But think of the amazing effects,' Lol said innocently. 'The lights flicker . . . the tape stutters. Elemental scratching?'

'Fah! You're just being flippant because you got a new toy.'

'It's your toy. I'm just minding it.' Lol had been trying to identify the different fragments of tree involved in the Boswell guitar. Here in the studio, its range and depth were incredible.

'He's getting it back,' Prof said. 'I don't know how, I don't know when, but he's getting it back. They pulled a fast one on me. I said to Sally, "Help the boy if you can. Inspire him." That's all I said. So they palm you off with this ridiculous, overpriced—' He pulled up the master switch so that everything wouldn't happen at once if the power ever returned. 'Still . . . you at least know where you are now, geographically, I would guess.'

'Well,' said Lol, 'I know why Knight's Frome's all in pieces.'

Prof sniffed. 'The Great Lake,' he said.

'Conrad Lake?'

'A moral tale.' Prof went back to his swivel chair, behind the board. 'The Fall of the Emperor of Frome – that's what they called Conrad, behind his back at first, but they say he grew to like it. She told you how the gods turned against him? His problems with the wilt?'

'Actually, it wasn't the wilt as such. It seems that Verticillium Wilt only—'

'Verticillium! *That's* the word.'

'—Only really hit these parts in the seventies. It started in Kent, and took a long time, decades, to reach Herefordshire. But there were other scourges before that: red spiders, aphids, white mould. He got them all, like the Seven Plagues of Egypt.'

They were both talking in epic terms, Lol realized, because it *had* seemed epic: the bountiful legacy of four generations of hop-masters wiped out in about seven years. Conrad Lake was, in effect, the last – and for a while the biggest and wealthiest – hop-master in Herefordshire. His poles and frames had surrounded Knight's Frome like a great creosoted barrier. Looking like Belsen, Sally Boswell had said disdainfully, like Auschwitz. The estate was big enough when he inherited it, and twice as big when the first disaster struck.

Lol recalled the portrait photograph of Conrad Lake in the third and smallest room at The Hop Museum, his smile submerged in a heavy moustache. A difficult, greedy and obsessive man, Sally had said, referred to by the locals, behind his back, as The Emperor of Frome. Twice married and both wives had left him, the second taking his infant son. They never divorced; the boy, Adam, was raised by his mother and grandparents in Warwickshire – never again saw his father, who stayed in Knight's Frome and fought all through the 1970s against the aphids, the red spiders and the white mould. And against the banks, who kept squeezing him, forcing him to sell off his estate piece by piece.

'Big drama,' said Prof laconically.

The land had then been bought by various farmers, most of them from outside Knight's Frome, which explained why there was no real community any more, why so many of the scattered houses were now owned by incomers like Prof. A few of the old hop-yards had been reinstated, but demand was no longer so great, with so many breweries importing cheaper hops from Germany and the USA. Most of it was grazed now. A pity, in a way, Sally Boswell had said, because the deep river loam in the valleys of the Frome and the Lugg was so perfect for hops. And yet, in a way, not a pity at all; it was no accident that the third room in the museum was the darkest, a sober coda to the song of the hop.

But not everyone, it seemed, believed it was over. Least of all Adam Lake, son of the Emperor.

Though the storm had passed and the evening fields were left steaming under a bashful sun, the power failed to return, and Prof announced in disgust that he was going to bed.

'You give me a call when it's dark, Laurence . . . *if* we've got the bleeding juice back. I always work better after dark, as you know.'

Lol watched him stumping across the yard to the cottage, then went back and sat for a while in the studio, trying the River Frome song again on the Boswell, and then, because he felt bad about deserting it, on his faithful old Washburn.

But the song still lacked direction, and after a while he gave up and went out into the luminous, storm-washed evening. As the trees dripped and the air glistened with birdsong, Lol made his first real foray into what remained of the community of Knight's Frome.

A soggy rug of slurry unrolled from a farm entrance towards the edge of what passed for the centre of the hamlet. Big old trees, oak and sycamore and horse chestnut, were still dripping onto the roofs of stone and timber-framed cottages that sprouted like wild mushrooms. A humpback bridge straddled the Frome, and on the other side of it was the church, sunken and settled as an old barn, and next to it the white-painted vicarage where Simon St John lived.

There was no shop here any more, but a pub survived – a pub created sixty years ago, Lol had learned, out of a row of terraced cottages, to cater for the hop-picking hordes. It hadn't changed much. There were no friendly signs promising food or coffee, no rustic fort for the kids, just a rotting bench beside the porch.

The pub was called the Hop Devil; on its sign, nothing more demonic than a red and smoking brazier. The sign was hanging from a gibbet at the road end of the dirt forecourt.

It was reassuring to see places like this still in business, but that didn't necessarily mean you had to go inside. Lol, the sometime folk singer, the traditionalist, was actually wary of country pubs – often the haunts of old men in worn tweeds and young men in stained denims, bruising you with their stares until you finished your drink too quickly and slid away.

As he padded cautiously past the pub, its scuffed and rust-studded oak door creaked open, releasing a richly brackish old-beer smell and also a man in a checked shirt with the sleeves rolled up, moleskin trousers stuffed into high tan boots. He came loping angrily over the puddles in the forecourt, a tall bloke with mutton-chop whiskers, swallowing his scowl when he saw he wasn't alone, glancing briefly over Lol's head.

'Evening.'

Lol took a step back into the slurry to avoid having the guy knock him down and walk over him.

'Needed that storm, I suppose,' the man called back over his shoulder. He was about thirty-five, with a lean face and a wide, beer-drinker's mouth. He gave the sky a dismissive glance. 'Getting too muggy.'

Lol nodded. 'Was a bit.'

But the big guy appeared to have finished with him, was climbing into a mud-scabbed Land Rover Defender on the edge of the forecourt, and now another voice was curling lazily out of the pub porch.

'Lol *Robinson*.'

Prof's unwelcome neighbour, Gerard Stock, was leaning against the door frame, a whisky glass in his right hand, a roll-up smouldering in his left.

Lol walked over – like he had a choice. The Defender crunched and clattered away through the trees and into the lane, while Stock stood watching it go.

'Wanker,' he said. 'Arsehole.'

Lol realized he was drunk.

'Wanker strolls in—' Stock tossed his cigarette into a puddle. '— and here's Gerard Stock sidding at the bar, minding his own. Wanker barks out cursory greeting, then drifts off to the dark end of the bar, engaging Derek, the landlord, in some trivial chat. And all the time, liddle sidelong glances, corner of an eye, wondering whether this is the day to make his move. And Gerard Stock's just smiling into his glass and saying nothing. And the wanker knows that Gerard Stock *knows* he's a phoney liddle arsehole.'

'I don't really know too many people around here,' Lol said. 'Who was he?'

Stock swallowed some whisky. There was a powerful fug of mixed fumes around him, like, if you struck a match, the air would flare and sizzle.

'See, I don't have to talk to people if I don't want to. It's a rare skill and I'm good at it, man. I can be *very* relaxed, *very* cool, sidding quietly, saying nothing. Liddle-known trick of the trade – people think PR men talk all the time, talk any old shite, but a good publicist has *control*. Tells you what he wants you to know, when he wants you to know it. Timing. And Gerard Stock, 'case you were wondering, is still a *fucking* good operator. You coming in, Lol?'

'Well, I don't think—'

'Come 'n have a drink. I'd offer you some spliff, and we could sit out here, chill out, reminisce, but poor old Derek's very timid, for a country landlord.' Stock grinned. 'See, I've made you curious. You thought you were supposed to know who the wanker was, and now you want to. You really want to. Technique: I can turn it on, man.'

They were inside the Hop Devil now, small and square and dark as a chapel. The landlord peered out from the shadows around the bar. 'Sorry, gents, only bottled and shorts. Power's off, see.'

'Put your glasses on, Derek, it's me again,' said Stock. 'With a friend. What are we having, Lol Robinson?'

Lol said a half of shandy would be good and Stock groaned. 'Jesus Christ, no wonder you got yourself out of music.'

'Have to pay for a pint shandy, I'm afraid,' the shadowy Derek said. 'Got to open a bottle of beer, see, and they don't come in quarter-pints.'

'And another Macallan,' Stock said. 'How long've I been here, Derek?'

'Since just before lunch.' Derek sighed. 'On and off.'

After they collected their drinks, Stock steered Lol to a table by the biggest window. The only other customer appeared to be an elderly man with a bottle of Guinness and a copy of the Worcester *Evening News* he surely couldn't see to read. Lol made out an inglenook fireplace with a brazier like the one on the sign outside.

'What's a hop devil?'

'Thing they burned coke in. Hop-pickers used to cook their meals over it. You wanna know all this rustic shite, there's a dear old couple run a hop museum out on the main road. Sold me a hop-pillow.'

He obviously hadn't discovered who Al Boswell actually was.

'Supposed to give you a good night's sleep. *Sleep?*' Stock brayed. 'Fucking hops work like rhino horn. Fact, man. Me and Steph, we're living in this old kiln, walls impregnated with as much essence of hop as . . . as the beer poor old Derek can't pump. My wife—' Stock swallowed whisky, shook his head and growled. '—leaves scratches a foot long down my back. You wan' see?'

'I'll take your word.' Lol avoided Stock's eyes, wondering how he could find out what the guy's wife looked like.

'Could *use* some bloody sleep.' Stock bawled out, 'Can I sleep here, Derek?'

'Thought you always did, Gerry,' said Derek.

'Ger*ard*, you fucking peasant!'

The old man looked up from the paper he couldn't see to read.

'Language, sir,' said Derek.

'Derek goes to church, Lol.' Stock had lowered his voice but not much. 'Derek listens to Saint Simon's sermons. Can't be so pissed, can I, if I can say that? *Shaint* . . . Did I tell you I was briefly head of publicity for TMM? For whom *Saint Shimon* used to record as a young man? Wasn't so fucking saintly in those days, by all accounts. Shaint Shimon the shirtlifter—Jesus, that's an even better one. *Shaint Shimon the shirt—*'

'I'm going to have to ask you to leave in a minute, Mr Stock.'

Stock waved an arm in the direction of the bar. 'I'll be quiet. Don't send me home, landlord, I'm too shagged out.'

'You were going to tell me who that guy was,' Lol said. 'The guy with the . . .' Putting a hand either side of his face to signify side-whiskers.

Stock beamed. 'I said, didn' I? Said I could still do it. You're curious, yeah?'

Lol sighed. 'I'm curious.'

'Liddle shit annoyed the piss out of me, following me in here like that.'

'You'd already been here about six hours,' Derek said quietly, 'before Mr Lake came in.'

'As if he thought *I* was going to make the move – that I'd ask him to make me an offer. No chance. *No* frigging chance.'

'I'm sorry,' Lol said. 'I'm not getting this.'

''Course you aren't. I'm about to tell you. Wanker's Adam Lake. His old man *owned* Knight's Frome, more or less. Then lost it. The lot – several farms, this pub, finally even my place, that clapped-out old kiln. Died in penury, well-deserved, by all accounts. And now Adam, the boy—'

'That was him? With the—?'

'—The young squire . . . the wanker . . . wants it all back . . . roots, birthright – the whole, sprawling Lake estate.'

'Right,' said Lol. Some of this he'd already had, if less colourfully, from Sally Boswell.

'Field by field, barn by barn. He's approaching the buggers who bought land off his old man, one by one, making 'em offers only a complete idiot would refuse. His heritage, geddit? Buying back his heritage. The young Emperor of Frome.'

'He can afford?'

'Oh, yeah. Big irony is the liddle shit can *well* afford. He's a dot . . . com . . . fucking . . . millionaire.' Stock spat out the words like cherry stones. 'Or whatever else they called them 'fore someone coined the term. Adam, we've since learned, invested some of his ma's money, few years ago, in what might've appeared at the time to be an off-the-wall software concept proposed by an old university friend . . . which in fact created the world's fastest search-engine . . . at the time. Probably be like a bloody steamroller these days. Sold it off for some obscene sum, and then . . . Oh, this is boring, it's not bloody important how the cunt got his millions.'

Lol sipped at his shandy, which was warm. 'I'm sorry about your wife's uncle.'

'Poor old bugger,' Stock said viciously. 'Wonder how well *he* knew the fucking vicar.'

'That's it,' said Derek softly, coming out of the shadows, a bald, middle-aged man with serviceable fists. 'Out you go, Mr Stock.'

'Shimon shirtlifter,' Stock said and giggled into his glass.

Lol couldn't avoid walking back with him, and for most of the way Stock was talking about his career as a publicist, at TMM and other recording and management companies, and then working solo for book publishers and film and TV companies: outfits that hadn't known how badly they needed him until they had him on board.

'*And* I could do it for Levin, too, man. Doesn't see it yet, but he will. Poor old guy thinks he's being cool and enigmatic getting out of London, downsizing, all that shite. Doesn't realize how soon he'll be forgotten.'

'Actually, I think he *wants* to be—'

'I could make that hovel of a studio world-famous in six months. A hint here, a line there. I could get Levin on *The South Bank Show*. Got a good friend at LWT.'

'Maybe, you—' Lol gave up. Stock wasn't the kind of bloke to whom you said: *You don't really know Prof very well, do you?*

They left the lane and walked down the track, past Prof's stables towards the concealed river, under a sky like beaten copper. Gerard Stock raised his face to the sun and it reddened his beard. He looked wide and powerful and ruthless – and yet somehow, Lol thought, unsure of himself, like a Viking on a strange shore.

'And you, Lol Robinson. Shy boy with the liddle glasses. Very cute, to a certain kind of woman. *You* were marketable, man. Once.'

Lol said nothing. Stock was talking, the way he had earlier, as if it was all too late for a career which Prof seemed to see as still salvageable. Maybe this was deliberate, to sound him out – or put Prof down.

'And let us not forget—' Stock grinned slyly '—all those years in and out of the loony bin. Marketable, *plus*.' Lol shot him a sidelong glance. 'Oh, yeah, I know your history. Checked you out soon's I got home. My business is to know everything about everybody. I am The Man.'

Stock kicked a stone down the track, and then he looked directly into the sinking sun and his voice suddenly sagged.

'And now – all right – I'm broke. Only cash flow, of course, as we say.'

'You've got the house – the kiln.'

'Yeah, stroke of luck, there, 'cause we'd been reduced to living in a bloody trailer at the time. Poor old Stewart. Perhaps he should've taken the Wanker's offer when he had the chance. You see, buying the kiln back – very, very important to Adam, because *that* was the site of the original ancestral home.'

'Conrad Lake's mansion?'

'Lord, no, that came later. But this was the original family farm. Twice the size it is now – but not big enough for Conrad, once he was on the up. Built the new place for the new wife, 'bout a mile over the hill there – where Adam lives. All there was left to bequeath to the boy. The old man'd already knocked down half the farmhouse – this is late sixties, when you could still get away with flattening history – just kept the kiln. When he died and the bank or whoever flogged it off, Stewart picks it up for a song.'

They crossed the river bridge, passed between the poplars. And then suddenly the kiln was in view, halfway up a hill – or, rather, part of a conical tower was visible, the tip of its cowl pointing at an angle.

Lol stopped, shocked.

A wall of bright blue corrugated metal concealed the rest of it – the side of some huge industrial building, rising almost as high as the kiln itself. It hadn't been apparent the other night, except as a patch of shadow that might have been trees or part of the hill. Now, in an area where most of the farms and cottages looked almost organic, its brashness was savage.

Stock watched Lol's reaction, half-smiling. 'You like Adam Lake's barn? There's another one the other side, even higher. About ten yards away. Man, we're living in a barn sandwich.'

'*He* did that?'

'Wanker's land surrounds us. Had the first one put in place after Stewart refused to sell him the kiln.'

'Can he do that?' Stock's fury made sudden sense.

'Done it, hasn't he? Yeah, sure he can. Country landowners can throw up whatever kind of monstrosity they want, long as it's an agricultural building and they can show a need for it. *Need.* Jesus. You know what those barns are used for? Nothing. They're empty – great, echoing, empty shells.'

'He did it just to—'

'Steal the light.' Stock was sweating, but he seemed sober now. 'It's about stealing the light. You see, this was particularly cruel – though whether Lake was subtle enough to realize that is anybody's guess – because the old boy was a photographer.'

'Light being his medium.'

'Yeah.' Stock took out his tin to roll a smoke. 'He loved light. 'Course, Lake wasn't trying to force him to sell. He just needed some extra storage facilities for hay and sundry fodder at the extremity of his estate. That's what he tells you. The cunt.'

'Didn't . . . Stewart make any kind of protest?'

'Didn't live long enough, thanks to his good friends, the gypos – those lithe and slippery gypo boys, dear, oh dear. But, yeah, he did make a last, meaningful gesture.'

The path forked – Lol thought this was probably the point at which he'd lost his way the other night – and Stock went to the left and climbed over a stile.

The kiln house was in front of them now. It was built of red brick and was smaller than it had looked by night, and now the full horror of the barn sandwich became apparent. The actual kiln tower, with just one window, was at the front, but most of the other windows seemed to be on the sides, permanently shadowed by industrial metal.

Lol climbed over the stile and found Stock standing on the edge of the field, lighting his roll-up.

'If you hadn't guessed, Uncle Stewart's final gesture was Gerard Stock. Stephie was Stewart's—' he coughed out smoke '—favourite niece. Always close to her after her parents split. How's she repay him? Marries Gerard Stock. Steph's sweet eighteen, this guy's twenny years older, smokes a lot of dope, gets both of them busted one time, dear oh dear. And, oh yeah, the clincher: one night Stephie falls downstairs and loses her baby and there's some internal messiness so there aren't gonna be any *more* babies. And this is all Gerard Stock's fault, naturally. And Stephie, once beloved, gets sliced out of Stewart's will. We thought.'

They both looked up at the kiln house.

'Now why,' said Stock, 'would the dear old turd-burglar let his beloved home fall into the hands of a man he couldn't stand the fucking sight of? You're right. He didn't bequeath his house to Gerard Stock. He bequeathed Gerard Stock to Adam Lake.'

Stock coughed, then laughed. The sun was sinking fast, and the side of the kiln house facing the nearest barn was already almost black in its shadow.

'When Lake finds out who inherited, we get a letter from his agent, making an offer. We refuse. That's when the second barn goes up.' He nodded at the house. 'There you go – power's back on.'

Lights had appeared in two of the windows in the shadowed wall. None of them seemed to be very big windows, Lol noticed, and the Stocks wouldn't even be allowed to enlarge them because the kiln house would be on the historic-buildings list. Living there couldn't be easy; it would look like deepest winter all year round.

'You have to keep lights on all day?'

'Some. Yeah, we live like moles, but it's a liddle better than the trailer.'

'What, even though—?' Lol broke off. He couldn't say it.

Stock could. 'Even though we have our dining table resting on the flagstones where the nice gypsy boys spread Uncle Stewart's brains?'

He burst out laughing again, but it was shallower this time and soon tailed off. The light that Lol remembered from the other night came on palely below the conical roof of the kiln.

'Spooky.' Stock's cigarette lit up in his rosebud lips, like a spark from the setting sun. He stood with his legs apart, looking like some kind of psychotic troll. 'It's a spooky place. You believe in ghosts, Lol?'

Lol thought of the naked woman in the naked hop-yard who, for one icy moment—

'Yeah,' he said. 'I suppose I do.'

'I don't.' Stock squeezed out his cigarette between finger and thumb and winced. 'But something needs dealing with.'

# EIGHT

# Mercury Retrograde

Late Saturday afternoon, the vicarage seemed more still and vast than Merrily had ever known it. One woman, seven bedrooms. Even the kitchen was as quiet as a crypt.

Wearing Jane's old unofficial Radiohead T-shirt, dumped in disgust after the *Kid A* album, she sat down at the table, took out the lumpy old penny from a hip pocket of her jeans, and stared at the blurred woman with the trident. Some broads had all the backbone.

In the dawn-lit chancel, she'd blessed the coin on the altar – and then been unable to go through with the rest, spending the next half-hour on her knees, concluding that she was not a natural psychic and could never imagine herself approaching a state of grace.

And then it had been time to go home and finish the last bits of Jane's packing and help carry her bags out to the boot of Eirion's stepmother's silver BMW, where Eirion stowed it as carefully as if it was the kid's trousseau and kept looking over his shoulder at Jane, as if to make sure she was still there, his guileless face breaking into the kind of smile that told you everything you didn't really want to know.

Merrily caught herself thinking he was the sort of guy Jane ought to meet in about ten years' time, when she'd . . . been around?

God, it was always so hard. Sometimes you wished they could have some kind of life-experience cell implanted in their brains as soon as they hit puberty.

Jane was being practical, methodical, counting off on her fingers all the things she needed to take – and avoiding Eirion's eyes, Merrily noticed. Eirion she thought she could understand; Jane was more complex. Jane, she suspected, would always be complex.

Last night, the power hadn't gone off. They hadn't managed a proper talk, but what was she supposed to have said, anyway: *Don't do anything I wouldn't do?* At about three and a half years older than Jane, she'd been pregnant.

'You will be OK, won't you, Mum?' The kid wore a high-necked lemon-and-white striped top and white jeans. She'd looked about nine.

'Yes, flower, I'll avoid junk food, I won't drink to excess, I'll observe speed limits and I'll try to be home before midnight.' The kid was still looking too serious; her mood clearly did not match Eirion's. 'And, erm . . . I expect you'll ring occasionally from Pembrokeshire?'

''Course.'

'Got enough money?'

'I won't flash the plastic unless things get really tight, if that's—'

'Whatever,' Merrily said. 'Do you want to take the mobile?'

They still only had one between them.

'Your need's far greater than mine. Besides, it's supposed to be a holiday.' Jane picked up Ethel, the black cat, and nuzzled her. 'A whole month. She won't remember me.'

'Of course she will.'

'Anyway, I can borrow Irene's phone.'

'Ring any time. Any time at all.'

'It's all in.' Eirion had closed the boot and stood with his back to the car, his baseball cap hanging from both hands at waist level, obviously trying to control his smile, contain a youthful glee that might be viewed as uncool.

'Off you go, then, flower.' Merrily accepted Ethel, popping her down on the lawn, where she lifted a paw and began to lick it, unconcerned. Cats.

Hugging them at the gate, Eirion had felt reassuringly stocky and trustworthy. Jane's face had felt hot.

Now, Merrily laid the coin on the table, her eyes suddenly filling up, a hollow feeling in her chest.

She was thirty-seven years old.

She wondered sometimes if the kid's dead father, the faithless Sean, could ever see them. She tried to remember if Sean had ever been remotely like Eirion, but the only image she could conjure up was the range of emotions – dismay, anger, resignation and a final apologetic tenderness – warping his twenty-year-old face on the night she'd told him that something that would turn out to be Jane had been detected.

She walked aimlessly into the echoey hall, looked at herself in the mirror, a good two inches shorter than Jane now. On her, the one-size, once-venerated, Radiohead T-shirt looked as baggy as a surplice.

She thought about taking the coin to the church again. But it wasn't long after five p.m., and there'd probably still be the odd tourist about. Or worse, a local. The vicar tossing a coin at the altar? It'd be all round the village before closing time at the Black Swan.

On impulse, she went out to the Volvo.

Unfinished business: a surprise visit to the Shelbones in the cool of a Saturday evening. Just happening to be passing.

In the churchyard at Dilwyn, the yews threw big shadows across three women leaving the porch. None of them was Hazel Shelbone, and when Merrily reached the bungalow, there was no car in the drive and the garage doors were open – no vehicle inside.

Family outing?

But as Merrily drove slowly past, she caught a flicker of movement at the end of a path running alongside the garage.

She drove on for about two hundred yards, past the last house in the lane, and parked the Volvo next to a metal field-gate. With no animals in the field, she figured it was safe to leave the car there for a while. She got out and walked back to the Shelbones' bungalow, where she pressed the bell and waited.

No answer. OK. Round the back.

The flagged path dividing the bungalow and the concrete garage ended at a small black wrought-iron gate. As Merrily went quietly through it she heard a handle turning, like a door opening at the rear of the house. Around the corner of the bungalow, she came face to face with Amy Shelbone, emerging from a glassed-in back porch.

The girl jumped back in alarm, her face red and ruched-up, thin, bare arms down by her sides, stiff as dead twigs, fists clenched tight.

'Sorry, Amy. I rang the bell, but—'

Amy was blinking, breathing hard. She had on a sleeveless yellow dress. Her thin, fair hair was pulled back into a ponytail. She wore white gymshoes, not trainers.

'They're not here.'

Merrily turned and closed the metal gate behind her, as if the girl might bolt like a feral kitten. 'Well,' she said, 'perhaps—' Moving slowly to the edge of the path, taking a step on to the lawn.

'No!' The kid backed away towards a small greenhouse in which the sun's reflection hung like a lamp. '*No!* You just keep away from me!'

Recognition at last, then.

'It's OK, I'll stay here.' Merrily looked down at her T-shirt. 'It's my day off. See – no cross, no dog-collar.'

'Go away.'

Merrily shook her head. 'Not this time.'

'You're trespassing! It's disgraceful. I'll call the police.'

'OK.'

Amy backed against the greenhouse, then sprang away from it and started to cry, her shoulders shaking – a gawky, stick-limbed adolescent in a large, plain, rectangular garden.

'I only want to talk,' Merrily said. 'Or, better still, listen.'

'Go away.'

'What would be the point? I'd just have to keep coming back.'

'People like you make me sick,' Amy said.

'So I heard.'

'Ha ha,' Amy cawed.

'I was sick in church once. It's no big deal.'

Amy looked down at her white shoes in silence.

'And sometimes I've felt God's let me down,' Merrily said. 'You think he's watching you suffer and not lifting a finger. You think maybe God's not . . . not a very nice person. And then sometimes you wake up in the night and you think there's nobody out there at all. That everybody's been lying to you – even your own parents. And that's the loneliest thing.'

Amy didn't look at her. She walked to the middle of the half-shadowed lawn. The garden, severely bushless and flowerless, backed on to open fields that looked more interesting. Amy stopped and mumbled at her shoes, 'They *did* lie.'

'Your mum and dad?'

'They're not—'

'Yes, they are. They wanted you. Not just any baby . . . *you*. That's a pretty special kind of mum and dad.'

Amy didn't reply. She was intertwining her fingers in front of her, kneading them, and seemed determined to keep at least six yards between herself and Merrily. With feral cats, you put down food and kept moving the bowl closer to the house. It might take weeks, months before you could touch them.

'Where are they – your mum and dad?'

Amy produced a handkerchief from a pocket of her frock. A real handkerchief, white and folded. She shook it out, revealing an embroidered *A* in one corner, and wiped her eyes and blew her nose.

'Shopping,' she said dully, crumpling the hanky. 'They go shopping every second Saturday. In Hereford. She can't drive.'

'How long have they been gone?'

'Why do *you* want to know?' Amy hacked a heel sulkily into the grass. Then she said, 'They went off about nine. They always go off at nine. They'll be back soon, I expect.'

'And you stayed home.'

'There was no point.'

It wasn't clear what she meant. At first, she hadn't seemed much like the teacher's-pet type of girl described by either her mother or – more significantly – Jane. Yet there was something that kept pulling her back from the edge of open rebellion, making her answer Merrily's questions in spite of herself.

'Could we go in the house, do you think?'

'*No!*'

Merrily nodded. 'OK.'

'I don't have to talk to you.'

'Of course you don't. Nobody has to talk to anybody. But you often feel glad afterwards that you did.'

Amy shook her head.

'You used to talk to God, didn't you?' Merrily said. 'I bet you used to talk to God *quite* a lot.'

The girl's intertwined fingers tightened as if they'd suddenly been set in cement.

'But you don't do that any more. Because you think God betrayed you. Do you want to tell me how he did that, Amy? How you were betrayed?'

'No.'

'Have you told your mum and dad?'

Amy nodded.

'And what did they—?' Merrily broke off, because Amy was looking directly at her now. Her plain, pale face was wedge-shaped and her cheeks seemed concave. She did not look well. Anorexics looked like this.

'I don't need to talk to *God*.' Sneering out the word. 'God doesn't tell you anything. God's a waste of time. If I want to talk, I can talk . . . I can talk to *her*.'

Her voice was suddenly soft and reverent. For a moment, Merrily thought of the Virgin Mary.

'Her?'

Over Amy's shoulder, the lamp of the sun glowed in the greenhouse.

'*Justine*,' Amy whispered.

'Justine?'

In the softening heat of early evening, Amy's lips parted and she shivered. This shiver was particularly shocking because it seemed to ripple very slowly through her. Because it seemed almost a sexual reaction.

Merrily went still. 'Who's Justine, Amy?'

Amy's body tightened up. 'No!'

'Amy?'

'Get out!' Amy screamed. 'Just get *out*, you horrible, lying thing! It's nothing to *do* with you!'

As if she'd been planning this for some minutes, she suddenly hurled herself across the lawn, passing within a couple of feet of Merrily, and into the glazed porch, slamming the door, shooting a bolt and glaring in defiance from the other side of the glass, poor kid.

Three times that evening, Merrily tried to call Hazel Shelbone. Twice it was engaged, the third time there was no answer.

When she'd got home, there'd been a message from Jane on the answering machine. Merrily replayed it twice, trying to detect the subtext.

'*Well, we got here. All of us. The whole family. It's quite a big place, an old whitewashed farmhouse about half a mile from the sea, near an old quarry, but you can see the sea from it, of course. So it's . . . yeah . . . cool. And the whole family's here. Everybody. So . . . Well, I'll call you. Look after Ethel and, like . . . your little self. Night, night, Mum.*'

Hmm. The whole family, huh?

The shadows of apple trees meshed across the vicarage garden. In the scullery, Merrily switched on the computer, rewrote her notes for tomorrow's sermon and printed them out. It was to be the first one in – well, quite a long time – that she'd given around the familiar theme of *Suffer little children to come unto me.* A complex issue: how *should* we bring kids to Christ? Or was it better, in the long term, to let them find their own way?

Merrily deleted a reference to Jane's maxim: *Any kind of spirituality has to be better than none at all.* Dangerous ground.

'*We never pressed the Church on her, David and I,*' Hazel Shelbone had said. '*Never forced religion on any of our children.*'

*Bet you did, really*, Merrily thought, gazing out at the deepening blue, *whether you intended to or not.*

She recalled Hazel saying, in answer to her question about what might have got into Amy, '*The spirit of a dead person*', in a voice that was firm and intense and quite convinced.

Now she had a question for Hazel: *who is Justine?*

She reached out for the telephone and, as often happened, it rang under her hand.

He said his name was Fred Potter. It was a middle-aged kind of name, somehow, but he sounded as if he was in his early twenties, max.

He said he worked for the Three Counties News Service, a freelance agency based in Worcester, supplying news stories to national papers. He said he was sorry to trouble her, but he understood she was the county exorcist.

'More or less,' Merrily admitted.

'Just that we put a story round earlier,' Fred said, 'but a couple of the Sundays have come back, asking for a quote from you or the Bishop, and the Bishop seems to be unavailable.'

'Let's see . . . Saturday night? Probably out clubbing.'

'*What*? Oh.' He laughed. 'Listen, Mrs Watkins, if I lay this thing out for you very briefly, perhaps you could see if you have any comments. I've got to be really quick, because the editions go to bed pretty early on a Saturday.'

'Go on, then.'

'Right. This chap's convinced his house is badly . . . haunted. He and his wife are losing a lot of sleep over this. It's an old hop-kiln, a man was murdered there. Now they say they're getting these, you know, phenomena.'

'I see.'

'Wow,' said Fred, 'it always amazes me when you people say "I see" and "Sure", like it's everyday stuff.'

'Isn't it?'

'Wow,' Fred said. 'Brrrr.'

'Is this person living in the diocese?'

'Of course.'

'Just I haven't heard about it.'

'Well, this is the point,' Fred said. 'Our friend gets on to his local vicar and asks him if he can do something about this problem. And the local vicar refuses.'

'Just like that?'

'More or less.'

'What did the vicar say to you?'

'He said, "No comment".'

*Odd*.

'So what do *you* think? Do you think it's a genuine case of psychic disturbance?'

'Hey, that's not for me to say, is it? What I wanted to ask you was, what is the official policy of the diocese on dealing with alleged cases of, you know, ghostly infestation, whatever you want to call it. Like, if you get something reported to you—'

'We help where we can,' Merrily said.

'And how common is it for you to refuse?'

'I didn't refuse. It's never been referred to me.'

'No, I mean—'

'Let me tell you the normal procedure with Deliverance, which is the umbrella term for what we do. A person with a psychic or spiritual problem goes to his or her local priest and explains the situation, then the priest decides whether to handle it personally or pass it on to someone like me, right?'

'Do they have to tell you about it?'

'No. I'm here if they need me. Sometimes they'll just ring up and ask for a bit of advice, and if it's something I can tell them I do . . . or maybe *I'll* need to seek advice from somebody who knows more about a particular type of . . . phenomenon than I do.'

'So, if I say to you now, have you had a call or a report from the Reverend Simon St John, at Knight's Frome, about a plea for help he's received from a Mr Stock . . .?'

'No, not a word. But the vicar doesn't have to refer anything to me.'

'Even if he's refusing to take any action?'

'Even if he's refusing to take any action.'

'Doesn't it worry you that there's someone in the diocese who's plagued by ghosts and can't get any help from the Church?'

Merrily had dealt with the media often enough to recognize the point where she was going to be quoted verbatim.

'Erm . . . If I was aware of someone in genuine need of spiritual support, I would want to see they received whatever help we were able to give them. But I'd need to know more about the circumstances before I could comment on this particular case. I'm sure the Rev St John has a good reason for taking the line he's taken.'

There was a pause, then Fred Potter said, 'Yep. That'll do me fine. Thanks very much, Mrs Watkins.'

'Whoa . . . hang on. Aren't you going to give me this guy's address, phone number . . .?'

'Mr Stock? You going to look into it yourself?'

'Just for the record, Fred.'

'Oh, all right. Hang on a sec.'

She wrote down Mr Stock's address. Afterwards, she looked up the number of the Rev Simon St John. She didn't know the man, but she thought she ought at least to warn him.

No answer.

Lately, everywhere she tried, there was no answer. Jane would explain this astrologically, suggesting Mercury was retrograde, thus delaying or blocking all forms of communication.

Bollocks.

'. . . *Always amazes me when you people say "I see" and "sure", like it's everyday stuff.'*

Merrily gathered up the printed notes for her sermon and walked into the lonely, darkening kitchen.

# NINE

# God and Music

They'd turned Stock's kiln-house into Dracula's castle, rearing against the light, looking to Lol very much as it had on that first, milky night, only darker, more brooding.

    . . . *BLACK HELL*

It shrieked at him from the pile of newspapers in the shop, the top copy folded back to page five. Two other customers bought copies while he was still staring.

*You believe in ghosts, Lol?*

Christ, he hadn't seen this one coming, had he? Nobody had, judging from the comments in the shop. 'I've heard of this feller,' a woman in sweatpants told the newsagent. 'He's an alcoholic.'

'On bloody drugs, more like,' an elderly man said.

The newsagent nodded. 'Need to be one or the other to live in that place.'

Whichever, it was a development Prof Levin did not need to know about, Lol decided, driving back from Bishop's Frome with a bunch of papers on the passenger seat. It was eight-thirty, the sun already high: another hot one. Prof was due to leave for London before ten, his cases already stowed in the back of his rotting Range Rover – Abbey Road beckoning. The unstable virtuoso Tom Storey would already be pacing the floor with his old Telecaster strapped on, spraying nervy riffs into the sacred space.

Lol considered leaving the *People* in the Astra until after Prof had gone. Not as if he'd notice; all the time he'd been staying here, Lol had never once seen him open a newspaper; it was only Lol himself who was insecure enough to need to know the planet was still in motion.

In the end, he gathered the papers into a fat stack, with the *Observer* on top, and walked into the stables with it under his arm. He found Prof in the kitchen, connected to his life-support cappuccino machine, froth on his beard.

'Two things, Laurence. One: when I return, I expect to hear demos of five new songs. No excuses. You get St John over to help. If he don't want to come, you get his wife to kick him up the behind – metaphorically speaking, in her case, as you'll find out.'

'The vicar's married?'

Prof gave him a narrow look. 'Why do you ask?'

'No particular—'

Prof frowned. 'Robinson, I can read you like the *Sun*. Who's been talking about the vicar?'

'What was the second thing? You said two things . . .'

'The second thing – maybe I mentioned this before – is you keep that bastard Stock out of here. Bad enough he shows up when I'm around, I don't want him— *What?* What's going down? What's wrong?'

Lol sighed. He didn't want to pass on Stock's innuendo about Simon. He unrolled the newspapers: *Observer, Sunday Times, People*. He handed the tabloid to Prof.

'What's this crap?' Prof held up the paper, squinting down through his bifocals. 'What am I looking at?'

Lol said nothing.

After about half a minute, Prof peered over the page at him, looking uncharacteristically bewildered, glassy-eyed, as if he'd been winded by a punch from nowhere to the stomach. He put down the paper on the upturned packing case he was still using as a breakfast bar.

'This man,' he said at last, 'is the most unbelievable piece of walking shit it was ever my misfortune to encounter. Is there *nothing* in his life he won't exploit?'

There were two pictures, one of them tall and narrow, running alongside the story. This was the Dracula's Castle shot of the kiln-house, doctored for dramatic effect. The other, near the foot of the page, showed an unsmiling Gerard Stock, holding a candle in a holder, his arm around a younger woman with curly hair.

## OUR BLACK HELL IN THE HOUSE OF HORROR
*by Dave Lang*

**A terrified couple spoke last night of their haunted hell in the grim old house where a relative was brutally murdered.**

*And they claimed that a 'rural mafia' had condemned them to face the horror alone.*

Gerard and Stephanie Stock say their six-month ordeal in the remote converted hop-kiln has driven them to the edge of nervous breakdowns.

But when they asked the local vicar to perform an exorcism, he refused even to enter the house, which is so dark they need lights on all day, even in summer.

The couple inherited the 19th century kiln house near Bromyard in Herefordshire from Mrs Stock's uncle, Stewart Ash, the author and photographer who was beaten to death there by burglars less than a year ago.

Since they moved in at the end of last January, the Stocks say they have endured:

- creeping footsteps on the stairs at night.

- strange glowing lights in an abandoned hop-field at the front of the house.

- furniture moving around a blood-stain that won't go away.

- an apparition of a hazy figure which walks out of solid brick walls.

'It's become a complete nightmare,' said Mr Stock, a 52-year-old public relations consultant. 'Everybody locally knows there's something wrong in this place, but it's as if there's a conspiracy of silence. It's a rural Mafia around here. And now it looks as if even the vicar has been "got at".'

**Turn to page 2**

Prof shook his head slowly.

'Madness, Laurence.'

'You reckon?'

'Nah.' Prof turned over the page and creased the spine of the paper, laid it back on the packing cases next to his coffee cup, contemptuously punched the crease flat with the heel of a fist. 'Not in a million frigging years. Let me finish this, and then we'll talk.'

Lol read the story over Prof's shoulder.

Mr Stock and his thirty-four-year-old wife say the house has proved impossible to heat, and they've built up massive electricity bills, running to hundreds of pounds.

And the already gloomy house was made even darker when neighbouring landowner Adam Lake built two massive barns either side of it, blocking light from all the side windows.

Mr Lake has claimed the buildings were necessary for his farming operation.

But Mr Stock claimed the landowner was furious because both they and Stewart Ash had refused to sell him the house and had the giant barns built to make the haunted kiln impossible to live in.

'Lake showed up here once,' Prof said. 'Made me an offer for this place even though it wasn't part of his old man's original estate. Crazy. The guy's as mad and arrogant as Stock. Dresses like some old-style squire twice his age. Campaigns for fox-hunting. Jesus!'

'I saw him the other night.'

'He's a buffoon. And he don't fully realize the kind of desperate bastard he's up against – though maybe he does now.'

'You really think Stock's making all this up, to try and publicly shame Lake into moving those barns?'

'Look,' Prof said, 'Stock's on his uppers, right? Suddenly he gets a break; he wins a house. With problems attached, sure, but it's a wonderfully unexpected gift, and he's determined to capitalize. He wants the very maximum he can get. He's gonna use whatever skills he's got, whatever contacts. What's he got to lose? Nothing, not even his credibility. What's he got to *gain*? Jesus, those barns go, you can add seventy, eighty thousand to the market value of that place.'

'Why doesn't he just sell to Lake for some inflated price and walk away?'

Prof opened out his hands in exasperation. 'Because he is *Gerard Stock.*'

'That first barn made poor Stewart's life into a black hell,' Gerard Stock says. 'But he was a stubborn man and refused to give in.'

But Mr Ash's determined stand was ended the night he surprised two young burglars.

**They beat the sixty-six-year-old author to death on the stone floor of his kitchen.**

'I did not believe in ghosts or hauntings, but I've often felt Uncle Stewart's presence in the kitchen,' says Mrs Stock. 'I feel his spirit has been somehow trapped in the darkness of this place.'

The Stocks approached the local vicar, the Rev Simon St John, asking him to exorcize their home.

'But he didn't want to know,' said Mr Stock. 'He implied that we ought to be looking for psychiatric help. When something like this happens, you become aware of a rural mafia at work. Stewart Ash fell foul of it, and it looks as if we have too.

'*Nobody in the village speaks to us, except other outsiders. I've even been refused service in the pub.*'

Lol shook his head. 'He only got thrown out because he was completely pissed and insulting people.'

Prof's beard jutted. 'Who was he insulting, Laurence?'

'Well . . . Simon. Called him Saint Simon. And other things. Stock said he used to work for TMM when Simon was in a band recording with them.'

'The Philosopher's Stone,' Prof said tonelessly. 'For your own information, Simon was a classical musician. A session cellist, if you like, and he was brought into this band about twenty years ago. Tom Storey was in it, too, for his sins. I worked with them for a while – for all our sins. It didn't last.'

'I think I remember something.'

Prof looked hard at Lol. 'Whatever you heard, it was probably crap. Whatever Stock said about Simon, you can put it to the back of your mind. For a while, God and music were fighting over Simon, but it was never really a contest. He's a good man, he loves his music, but he needs his God. *And* his wife. And whatever else you hear . . . Simon and Isabel – this is a marriage to die for. You understand?'

'Whatever you say,' said Lol, bemused.

'Of course, he refuses to exorcize the house of this despicable scheming bastard! He knows as well as I do that there's no conceivable basis for this garbage.'

'Stock asked me if I believed in ghosts,' Lol said.

Mr Stock added: 'I never believed in ghosts but after what we've witnessed here, it seems to me that the spirit of Stewart Ash cannot rest, even though two young men have been convicted of his murder. **'I can't help feeling that the whole truth has not yet come out and perhaps someone in the area knows more than they're saying.** 'We feel very isolated, but we feel we owe it to the memory of Steph's murdered uncle to see this through.'

The Rev Simon St John refused to comment about what he said was 'a private matter'.

But Hereford's diocesan exorcist, the Rev Merrily Watkins, said last night that she would be looking into the case.

'If I was aware of someone in genuine need of spiritual support, I would want to see they received whatever help we were able to give them,' she said.

'Pah.' Prof tossed the paper to the stained stone flags on the floor. 'He's trying to stir the shit. It's what he does. Now they have to try to shore up this nonsensical crap by calling in some stupid woman who doesn't know Stock from Adam. And then they wonder why— What's the matter *now*, Laurence? What is the *matter* with you this morning?'

'Nothing,' Lol said. 'That is . . . I know her, that's all.'

'The exorcist?'

'We lived in the same village – when I was with Alison. And then . . . not with Alison.'

Prof squinted curiously over his bifocals. 'You know this exorcist, this woman priest? I thought you couldn't stand priests.'

Lol shrugged.

'Except for this one, eh? Nice-looking?'

'She's . . .' Lol thought he was too old to be blushing; Prof's little smile indicated that perhaps he wasn't yet. 'I haven't seen her in some months. She's become a friend.'

'A friend.'

'We can all change,' said Lol. He had a mental image of a small woman in a too-long duffel coat borrowed from her daughter, wind-blown on the edge of an Iron Age hill fort overlooking the city of Hereford. *Requiem*.

'My, my.' Prof stood up and went to rinse his coffee cup at the sink. 'And see, by the way, that you keep this place in such a condition that we don't have visits from the jobsworths at the Environmental Health.' He placed the cup on a narrow shelf matted with dust and grease. He started to whistle lightly.

'What?' said Lol.

'Hmmm. They got room for a mere man, with God in the bed? I don't think so. Women priests, women rabbis? You ask me, it's the Catholics got it right on this one.'

'Not that you're an old reactionary or anything?'

'Plus, exorcism, that isn't a game.' Underneath the cynicism and bluster, Prof was some kind of believer. Lol had always known this. 'This Stock crap – *this* is a game . . .'

'You're entirely sure of that, Prof?'

Lol had kept staring at the picture, of Gerard Stock and Stephanie Stock but, like the shot of the kiln. it was printed for effect, her face two-dimensional in the candlelight. It *could* be, but he couldn't be sure. And if it was, what did that say about Stock and his alleged haunting?

'Listen, don't get involved.' Prof unplugged his capuccino machine, began to roll up the flex. 'You let Stock and Lake get on with destroying each other. Warn the woman priest to keep out of it as well.'

'You're taking that thing with you?'

'Just work on your songs,' Prof said. 'Don't let any of those people into this place – when I'm gone.'

TEN

# Bad Penny

'I'm just calling to apologize,' Merrily said to the vicar of Knight's Frome. 'I wasn't exactly misquoted, I just wasn't *fully* quoted. They didn't use where I explained that I couldn't really comment on a case I knew nothing about and I was sure you must have had good reason for refusing to deal with this guy. So I'm sorry.'

'Yeah, sure. I mean, that's fine,' the Rev Simon St John said. There was a pause on the line. 'Sorry . . . which paper did you say it was in?'

*What?*

It was gone three in the afternoon. It had been before nine this morning when she'd called into the Eight-till-Late in Ledwardine, on her way back from Holy Communion, to ask if she might have a quick flip through the tabloids – actually missing the story first time, never expecting a spread this size.

'You mean . . .' Merrily sat up at the scullery desk. 'You mean you haven't read it?'

'I don't see the papers much,' Simon St John said in his placid, middle-England voice.

'But you must have known they were going to publish it?'

'I suppose I had an idea, yes.'

'Had a—?' The mind boggled. She tried another direction. 'Erm . . . the feeling I get is that this Mr Stock is trying to . . . get back . . . at the landowner. Mr Lake.'

'And also his wife's uncle, I'd guess,' St John said.

'The one who's dead?'

'It's rather complicated.' He didn't seem unfriendly, but neither did he seem inclined to explain anything.

Last try: 'You've also been accused of being part of a rural mafia,' Merrily said.

Simon St John laughed. There was laid-back, Merrily thought, and there was indifferent. 'I've been accused of far worse things than that,' he said eventually. 'But thanks for letting me know.'

'That's . . . OK.'

'I expect we'll get to meet sooner or later.'

'Yes.'

'Goodbye, then,' he said.

It was another of those days: Mercury still retrograde, evidently.

She tried the Shelbones again and let the phone ring for at least a couple of minutes before hanging up and calling back and getting, as she'd half expected, the engaged tone. The implication of this was that someone was dialling 1471 to see who'd called. So maybe they would phone her back.

But they didn't, and Hazel Shelbone's excuse that she didn't want to talk to Merrily while Amy was in the house was wearing thin. Most people now had a mobile, especially senior council officials. Behind that old-fashioned, God-fearing Christianity, deep at the bottom of the reservoir of maternal love, there was something suspicious about this family.

So how was she supposed to proceed? The request for a spiritual cleansing was still on the table. Merrily didn't think she could just turn away, like Simon St John. Besides, she was curious.

She was finishing her evening meal of Malvern ewe's cheese and salad when Fred Potter, the freelance journalist, rang again.

'Before you say anything,' Merrily said, 'who alerted you to this story? I mean originally.'

'Ah, well.' He laughed nervously. 'You know how it goes, with news sources.'

'Yeah, down a one-way street. If someone like me doesn't disclose something, we're accused of covering up the truth, while you're protecting your sources.' She paused. 'How about off the record?'

'Oh, Mrs Watkins . . .'

'You know,' Merrily said thoughtfully, 'something tells me this won't necessarily be the last time our paths cross. I do tend to get mixed up in all kinds of things that could make good stories. Who knows when you might—'

'You're a very devious woman.'

'I'm a minister of God,' she said primly.

The scullery's white walls were aflame with sunset. She lit a cigarette.

'All right,' Fred Potter said. 'Off the record, it was brought in by our boss, Malcolm Millar. He knows Stock from way back. Stock was in PR.'

'When was all this? When did you learn about it?'

'Couple of days ago. Malcolm sent me out to see the Stocks yesterday morning.'

'So it's likely they cooked it up between them?'

'Oh *no*. I don't think so. I mean, a ghost story – that's not something you can verify, is it? I can tell you it's dead right about how dark it is in there. *I* couldn't live in that place. It's a scandal that this guy, Lake, can just block off someone's daylight to that extent.'

'There are laws on ancient lights. It's one for Stock's solicitor.'

'But the press don't charge a hundred pounds an hour, do we?'

'What I'm getting at, that's not *our* problem, is it? I mean the Church's. We just come in on the haunting. And if *that* turns out to be made up—'

'Please, Mrs Watkins.'

'I'm not making notes, Fred. I'm just . . . covering myself.'

'It's like asking if I believe in ghosts,' he said. 'Maybe *I* don't, but a lot of people do, don't they? Presumably *you* must.'

'Sometimes.'

'OK . . .' A pause, as if he was looking round to make sure he was alone. 'He's a bit of an operator.'

'Stock?'

'He's been in PR a long time. A lot of PR involves making up stories that sound plausible. If he did want to make up a story, he'd know how to go about it and he obviously knew where to take it. It's only people close to the media who know that if you want to make a big impact very quickly, you don't go to a paper and offer them an exclusive, you go to an agency like ours because we can send it all round . . . national papers, TV, radio . . .'

'And the more outlets you send it to, the more money you collect.'

'Sure, news is a business. But it's in our interest, at the end of the day, to make sure the story's sound – or at least, you know, stands up – or else various outlets are gonna stop coming back to us. If you get a reputation for being a bent agency, it's not good, long-term.'

'But, bottom line, this probably *is* a scam.'

Fred hesitated. 'I don't know. He's a bombastic kind of bloke – comes over like big mates soon as he meets you – but underneath . . . I reckon there *was* something worrying him. He was really shaky. I mean, when people are quivering and telling you how terrified they are, it could be an act. But when somebody's got this veneer of cockiness, and something else – call it fear – shows through, that's harder to fake, isn't it? Or it could mean he's got a drink problem or something, I really wouldn't like to say. You're not gonna drop me in it, are you? I mean, I'd love to work for the *Independent* or something, but you've got to take what you can get.'

'Life's such a bitch, Fred. What did you ring for, anyway?'

'A follow-up, I suppose, a new line on the story. I mean, you said you were going to look into it . . .'

'I didn't really, though, did I? What I said—'

'Give me a break, Merrily. I think you'll find a few papers'll pick up on this again tomorrow.'

'Meaning you'll try and persuade them to.'

'It's . . .' Fred Potter whistled thinly. 'It's a business, like I said.'

'All right – off the record?'

He sighed. 'Yeah, OK.'

'I'm in a difficult position,' Merrily said. 'It's hard for me to move on anything unless the local minister requests assistance. In this case, it strikes me that the local guy, St John, knows exactly what Mr Stock's up to. So I don't think we're going to want to get involved.'

'But if you do take it any further . . .'

'I'll let you know, promise.'

'That's what they all say.'

'Yeah, but I'm a minister of the Church, Fred.'

'Hmm,' Fred Potter said.

Merrily washed up her solitary dinner plate, went back into the scullery and called the Shelbones yet again.

The phone rang and rang, and she just knew the bungalow wasn't empty. She imagined all three Shelbones standing in the narrow hall, silently watching the base unit quivering. These Shelbones were wearing starched Puritan dress, like the Pilgrim Fathers, and the phone was a dangerous conduit to a bad, modern world that they believed could only do them harm.

She put back the receiver, picked up her cigarettes and lighter and took them into the kitchen, where she put the kettle on. She stood at the west window, waiting for the water to boil, looking out on the twilit garden and the scrum of shadows in the apple orchard where, in 1670, the Rev Wil Williams, of this parish, was said to have hanged himself to escape a charge of witchcraft. It was claimed Wil had frolicked here with sylphs and fauns. Except it probably hadn't been so simple.

Merrily recalled Amy Shelbone's thin body surrendering to that eerie shiver.

*Who's Justine, Amy?*

She slid a cigarette between her lips and flicked at the lighter. Nothing happened. Several more flicks raised nothing more than sparks. Merrily took her shoulder bag to the kitchen table and felt inside for matches. Something rolled heavily across the table and fell to the floor.

The room was sinking into the dregs of the day. She put on lights and finally found a book of matches with the logo of the Black Swan Hotel. Its timber-pillared porch stood across the cobbled village square from the vicarage under a welcoming lantern, and she briefly thought how pleasant it would be to wander across there in the dusk and sit in the new beer garden at the back with a glass of white wine.

She sat down at the kitchen table, lit her cigarette and saw, through the smoke, an image of Jane at the front gate yesterday morning. Merrily bit her lip, leaned back out of the smoke, and finally

**115**

bent and picked up the misshapen penny dated 1797. It must have rolled from her bag, though she didn't remember putting it in there.

It just kept turning up. Like a bad penny.

'*If you don't like the cold, come out of the mortuary,*' Huw Owen had said mercilessly.

Merrily sat for a while, with Ethel the black cat winding around her ankles, and smoked another cigarette before she left the vicarage.

It was that luminous period, well beyond sunset, when the northern sky had kindled its own cool light show above the timbered eaves of Ledwardine and the wooded hills beyond. The village lights were subdued between mullions, behind diamond panes.

Wearing her light cotton alb, ankle-length, tied loosely at the waist with white cord, Merrily crossed the cobbles and slipped quietly through the lych-gate.

The church looked monolithic, rising out of a black tangle of gravestones and apple trees into a sky streaked with salmon and green. In a summer concession to trickle-tourism, the oak door was still unlocked, but she assumed she'd be alone in here; since evensong had been discontinued, Sunday night was the quietest time.

She didn't put on the church lights, finding her way up the central aisle by the muddy lustre left by dulled stained glass on shiny pew-ends and sandstone pillars. It was cool in the nave, but not cold.

In the chancel, behind the screen of oaken apples, she took out her book of matches and lit two candles on the altar, creating woolly, white-gold globes which brought the sandstone softly to life.

She placed the old penny on the altar, blessing it again.

'*As I use it in faith, forgive my sins . . .*'

It was, she realized now, not a game of chance but a simple act of faith. Of trust. Most priests, in times of crisis, would open the Bible at random, trusting that meaningful lines would leap out, telling them which way to jump.

How different was that to one of Jane's New Age gurus cutting the Tarot pack?

The difference was Christian faith. There was a huge difference. Wasn't there?

The candles had hollowed out for her a sanctum of light, with the nave falling away into greyness, along with the organ pipes and the Bull Chapel with its seventeenth-century tomb. The atmosphere was calm and absorbent, the church's recharging time just beginning. As Jane would point out smugly, this was a site of worship long-predating Christianity. *'You're employing some ancient energy there, Mum.'*

Predating Jesus Christ perhaps, she'd reply swiftly – but not predating God.

*'Gods.'* Jane grinning like an elf. *'And goddesses.'*

Merrily let the kid's image fade, like the Cheshire cat, into the flickering air, with its compatible scents of polish and hot beeswax. She knelt before the altar, her covered knees at the edge of the carpet, just within the globes of light.

*OK.*

She closed her eyes and whispered The Lord's Prayer and then knelt in silence for several minutes, feeling the soft light around her like an aura. She remembered, as always, those deep and silent moments in the little Celtic chapel where her spiritual journey had begun: the moments of the blue and the gold and the lamplit path.

Her breathing slowed. She felt warm with anticipation and dismissed the sensation immediately.

Then she summoned Amy Shelbone.

More minutes passed before she was able to visualize the child: Amy wearing her school uniform, clean and crisp, tie straight, hair brushed, complexion almost translucently white and clear. Amy kneeling at the altar, as she'd been on the Sunday she was sick.

*I don't know anything about her,* Merrily confessed to God. *I don't know what her problem is. I don't know if she's in need of spiritual help or psychological help or just love. I don't know. I want to help her, but I don't want to interfere if that's going to harm her.*

Her lips unmoving. The words forming in her heart.

Her heart *chakra*, Jane would insist: the body's main emotional conduit.

Without irritation, she sent Jane away again and put Amy at the periphery of her consciousness, at the entrance to her candlelit sanctuary. She knelt for some more minutes, losing all sense of herself, opening her heart to . . .

She'd long ago given up trying to visualize God. There was no He or She. This was a Presence higher than gender, race or religion, transcending identity. All she would ever hope to do was follow the lamplit path into a place within and yet beyond her own heart and stay there and wait, patient and passive and without forced piety.

When – if – the time came, she would ask if Amy might join them in the sanctuary.

Amy and . . .

*Justine?*

Three questions hovered, three possibilities: *Is the problem psychological, or demonic, or connected with the unquiet spirit of a dead person?*

Merrily let the questions rise like vapour, and prayed calmly for an answer. More minutes passed; she was only dimly aware of where she was and yet there was a fluid feeling of focus and, at the same time, a separation . . . a sublime sense of the diminution of herself . . . the aching purity and beauty of submission to something ineffably higher.

At one stage – although, somehow, she didn't remember any of this until it was over – she'd felt an intrusion, a discomfort. And for a long moment there was no candlelight and the chancel was as dark – darker – than the rest of the church and bitterly cold and heavy with hurt, incomprehension, bitterness and finally an all-encompassing sorrow.

She didn't move, the moment was gone and so, it seemed, was Amy Shelbone. And Merrily's cheeks were wet with tears, and she was aware of a fourth question:

*What shall I do?*

*Please, what shall I do?*

She tossed the heavy old coin and it fell with an emphatic thump to the carpet in the chancel. She had to bring one of the candlesticks from the altar to see which side up it was. But it didn't matter, she knew anyway. This was only proof, only confirmation.

She held the candle close to the coin. The candle was so much shorter now, the candlestick bubbled with hot wax.

Tails.

*Nothing demonic.*

She tossed again.

Tails.

*No possession by an unquiet spirit.*

She nodded, held the coin tightly in her right hand, snuffed out the candles, bowed her head to the altar and walked down the aisle and out of the church.

In the porch, it was chilly. The goose bumps came up on her arms.

In the churchyard, it was raining finely out of a grey sky that was light though moonless. Clouds rose like steam above the orchard beyond the graves. It had been a warm, summer evening when she went in, and now—

Now a figure appeared from around the side of the porch, carrying an axe.

ELEVEN

# One Girl in Particular

The dew on the tombstone was soaking through the cotton alb to her thighs. She had her arms wrapped around herself, one hand still clutching her coin, and she was shivering.

Disoriented, she looked up, following the steeple to the starless sky, puzzled because it was so bright up there, yet she couldn't see a moon.

'Oughter get home, vicar,' Gomer Parry said. 'Don't bugger about n'more.'

He was leaning on his spade. It was an ordinary garden spade, not an axe, but could be nearly as deadly, she imagined, in the hands of the wiry little warrior in the flat cap and the bomber jacket. So glad it was Gomer, Merrily tried to smile, but her lips took a while to respond. She felt insubstantial, weightless as a butterfly, and just as transient. She gripped the rounded rim of the tombstone, needing gravity.

'Wanner get some hot tea down you, girl.' Gomer's fingers were rolling a ciggy on the T-handle of the spade.

Now in semi-retirement from his long-time business of digging field drains and cesspits, Gomer saw to the graveyard, where his Minnie lay, and kept the church orchard pruned and tidy. Also, without making much of a thing out of it, he reckoned it was part of his function to look out for the vicar. This vicar, anyway. Been through some situations together, she and Gomer. But still she couldn't tell him why she'd been in the church tonight or what had happened in there.

The colour of the sky alarmed her. It was streaked with orange cream, laying a strange glare on Gomer's bottle glasses. Merrily pushed her fingers through her hair. It felt matted with dried sweat.

'Time . . . time *is* it, Gomer?'

'Time?' He looked up at the sky behind the steeple. 'All but five now, sure t'be.'

'Five in the *morning*?'

Her knees felt numb. Strips of . . . of *sun* were alight between layers of cloud like Venetian blinds over the hills.

Gomer struck a match on a headstone. 'That Mrs Griffiths, it was, phoned me. Her don't sleep much n'more since her ole man snuffed it. Reckoned there was some bugger in the church, ennit? Bit of a glow up the east window, see. *Vicar? What's wrong – ?*'

'It can't be.' Merrily was shaking her head, frenziedly. Her face felt stiff. 'It *can't* be. I've only been— Gomer, I . . .' She clutched his arm. 'I went in there . . . maybe an hour ago. An hour and a half at the most. It was about ten o'clock . . . ten-thirty.'

*And then the earth turned.*

The molten copper of the dawn sent terrifying pulses into Merrily's head.

Gomer patted her hand.

'Young Jane . . . Her's gone away, then?'

'Huh?'

'First time you been alone yere, I reckon, vicar.'

'It was ten-thirty,' she said faintly. 'I swear to God, ten-thirty at the latest.'

She remembered then how far the candles had burned down. *It couldn't be.*

*Six hours?* Those few minutes had become . . . hours?

Her hands were trembling. The penny dropped out of one and fell onto the tombstone where she'd been sitting.

She recalled a blurred Britannia on the coin. *Tails.*

Gomer lit his ciggy. 'Needs a bit of a holiday yourself, you ask me, vicar. Pack a case, bugger off somewhere nobody knows you, or what you do. Don't say no prayers for nobody for a week, I wouldn't.'

She bent to pick up the coin. 'I'm sorry. I'm really sorry for dragging you out, Gomer. I really . . . Maybe I fell asleep or some-thing.'

'Sure t'be.' Gomer Parry stood there nodding sagely, patient as a donkey.

She met his eyes. Both of them knew she didn't believe she'd been asleep in the church, not for one minute of those six hours.

She invited Gomer back to the vicarage, but he wouldn't come with her. 'Strikes me you don't need no chat, vicar,' he said perceptively. ''Sides which, me and Nev got a pond to dig out, over at Almeley. Get an early start. Makes us look efficient, ennit?'

She walked back to the vicarage lucidly aware of every step, the warming of the air, the shapes of the cobbles on the square, the tension of the ancient black timbers holding Ledwardine together.

Back in the kitchen, she looked around the painted walls, as if walking into the room for the first time. Yes, she'd been away for a while, a night had passed. She put the kettle on and some food out for Ethel. The little black cat didn't start to eat for quite a while, just sat on the kitchen flags and stared at her, olive-eyed, while she drank her tea.

'I look different or something, puss?'

Ethel didn't blink. Merrily went upstairs and had a shower hot enough to hurt. She was aching, but she wasn't tired. She still felt light and unsteady, slightly drunk. But also strengthened, aware of a core of something flat and firm and quiet in her abdomen. Afterwards, she stood at the landing window, wrapped in a bath towel like some-one out of a Badedas ad, and watched the morning sun shining like a new penny.

Lifted up or cracking up? State of grace or a state of crisis?

If she'd been seriously stressed-out last night, she could have understood what had happened: the collapse into the arms of God, the acceleration of time, the flooding of the senses.

*Like being abducted by aliens.*

She started to laugh and went to get dressed.

It wasn't about stress. It was about the decision to toss a coin.

She put on the grey T-shirt and the dog-collar and an off-white skirt. It was Monday, usually a quiet day in the parish. Meetings with the Bishop in Hereford were on Tuesdays.

With the decision to toss the coin she'd broken through something – probably her own resistance. She went quickly down the stairs and into the kitchen, its walls cross-hatched now with summer-morning light. The kitchen clock said nearly eight. Time still seemed to be moving faster than usual. She needed to ground herself. She needed another tombstone to sit on.

She went on into the scullery and sat behind the desk of scuffed and scratched mahogany. She didn't plan to wait too long before she phoned the Shelbones. She'd ring just once, and if there was no answer she'd drive over there.

Knowing that this time she would get some straight answers.

She'd make the call at 8.45. She went back into the kitchen to make some breakfast, then decided she wasn't hungry and cleaned the sink instead, scrubbing feverishly. She had energy to spare. *Don't question it. Don't question anything about this.*

Just after 8.35, as she was drying her hands, the phone summoned her back into the scullery.

'Merrily,' Sophie said quietly. 'Can you come in, please – as early as possible.'

Not a question.

'Problem?'

'Yes,' Sophie said. 'I'm afraid there is.'

Merrily lit her first cigarette of the new day.

It was the usual battle getting into Hereford, with the hundreds of drivers who just wanted to get *through* Hereford . . . and the inevitable roadworks. Not half a mile from the Belmont roundabout, southern gateway to the city, lorries were feeding pre-cast concrete into what used to be Green Belt and would, when completed, apparently be known as the Barnchurch Trading Estate.

Merrily found herself winding up the car window in response to a sudden sensation of the air itself being polluted by human greed, like poison gas.

*Don't let's get carried away, vicar . . .*

The traffic started to move again, and this time she made it all the way to Greyfriars Bridge without a hold-up.

Hereford Cathedral sat at the bottom of Broad Street, snug rather than soaring. Behind it, the medieval Bishop's Palace was concealed by an eighteenth-century and Victorian façade that made it look like a red-brick secondary school with Regency and Romanesque pretensions.

This was Administration; it brought you down to earth.

The morning had dulled rapidly and a fine rain was falling as Merrily parked the old Volvo next to the Bishop's firewood pile close to the stone and timbered gatehouse, the quaintest corner of the complex. The view under its arch was back into Broad Street; you went through a door in the side of the arch and up some narrow stone steps and came out at the Deliverance office, with the Bishop's secretary's room next door, from where Merrily could hear people talking – two male voices. She didn't know what this was about, hadn't liked to ask on the phone because it had been clear that Sophie was not alone.

Now Sophie appeared in her doorway. She wore a silky, dark green sleeveless dress and pearls. Always pearls. And also, this morning, a matching pale smile. She slipped out of the room, to let Merrily go in.

'Ah,' said the Bishop.

The other man, elderly with grey and white hair, didn't say anything, and Merrily didn't recognize him at first.

'We'll have tea later, Sophie,' Bernie Dunmore called out, and then lowered his voice. 'We shall probably need it. Come in, Merrily, take a seat. You know Dennis, don't you?'

Oh God, it was, too. Since she'd last seen him, Canon Beckett had shed some weight and his beard. He looked crumpled and unhappy.

'Dennis?' Merrily went to sit in Sophie's chair by the window, overlooking the Cathedral green and the traffic on Broad Street.

'I, ah . . . imagine you can guess was this is about,' the Bishop said. He sat across the desk in the swivel chair he used for dictating letters to Sophie, his episcopal purple shirt stretched uncomfortably tight over his stomach. The bishop was looking generally uneasy.

Canon Beckett just looked gloomy, sitting on a straight chair a few feet away, with his back to the wall.

'Dennis's presence offers a clue,' Merrily said.

'Merrily, did you go to see this girl Amy Shelbone on Saturday evening, when her parents were out?'

'Well, I . . .' Merrily glanced across at Dennis, who was inspecting his hands. 'I went over with the intention of talking to her parents, actually. They were – as you say – out. But I met Amy in the garden. I tried to talk to her about – obviously you know what about, Bishop. I mean, Dennis has presumably filled you in on the background?'

'The child behaved in a disturbed fashion during the Eucharist, as well as exhibiting symptoms of what appeared to be clairvoyance, plus personality changes . . . enough to convince her parents she was being, ah, visited by an outside influence. You, however, seem *un*convinced.'

Merrily nodded. 'She did seem to have turned away from God, but it seemed to me more like disillusion. Or, if there was an influence, then it was an earthly influence.'

'You didn't offer the parents any suggestions as to how she might have become susceptible to whatever was influencing her?'

'I wondered about a teacher, or a boyfriend.'

'Boyfriend?'

'But her mother insisted she didn't *have* a boyfriend.'

'Quite immature for her age,' Canon Beckett mumbled.

'The girl went to church with her parents yesterday,' said the Bishop. 'Did you know that?'

Merrily raised an eyebrow. 'No.'

'Not to Holy Communion this time. To the morning service.'

'She was all right, then?'

'Dennis . . .?' The Bishop swivelled his chair towards the Canon.

'She was fine, as far as I could see,' Dennis said. 'I kept a close eye on her, obviously. She was a little quiet, sang the hymns somewhat half-heartedly. It seems she and her parents had had a long talk the previous night. After . . . Mrs Watkins's visit.'

The Bishop swivelled back to face Merrily across the desk. 'The child admitted to her parents that she'd been caught up in certain activities involving other pupils from her school. One girl in particular.'

'Activities?' Merrily tilted her head.

'You don't know about this?'

'Am I supposed to?' Was she being naive?

'Spiritualism,' the Bishop said. 'The ouija board. Making contact with . . . the spirits.'

'Amy?'

'Seems unlikely to you?'

'It would have, at first. She really didn't seem the sort. Far too prissy. But then—'

'Prissy?'

'Inhibited, strait-laced, unimaginative, if you like. But then, on Saturday night, she said – fairly contemptuously – that she didn't see any point in trying to talk to God, but if she did want to talk she could talk to someone called Justine.'

'Her mother,' Dennis Beckett said.

'What?'

'Her real mother. She was adopted by these people. Her real mother was called Justine.'

Merrily closed her eyes, bit her lower lip.

'The apparent opportunity to talk to one's dead mother,' said the Bishop, 'would, I suppose, be sufficient bait to lure even a *prissy* child into spiritually dangerous terrain.'

Merrily had come down with a bump that was almost audible to her. 'I've been stupid.' She felt herself sag in Sophie's chair.

'Have you?' the Bishop said.

'I should have made the connection.'

'Why?' asked the Bishop, a lilt in his voice. '*Why?*'

She felt like crying. Driving into Hereford, she'd still felt high, swollen with . . . what? Faith? Certainty? Arrogance? She'd cast aside her scepticism, opened her heart, broken through – six hours passing like minutes.

*Tails.* The coin kept coming up tails. She'd been given her answer.

And it wasn't the answer. It wasn't any kind of answer. The inspiring and apparently mystical circumstances had obscured the fact that little had been revealed to her. It might even have been misleading.

'Where did this happen? These ouija board sessions?'

'You don't know?'

'You don't have to rub it in, Bernie. I *don't* know. The kid wouldn't talk to me.'

The rain was coming harder, rivulets on the window blurring Broad Street into an Impressionist painting. She felt a pricking of tears and looked down into her lap.

'I really don't think you do know, do you?' The Bishop's voice had softened. She shook her head. 'Or the identity of the girl who led Amy into these spiritualist games?'

She looked up into his fat, kindly face. His eyes were full of pity. The room tilted.

'What are you saying, Bishop?' She turned on Dennis Beckett. 'What are *you* saying?'

Bernie Dunmore shuffled uncomfortably. 'Your daughter Jane goes to the same school, doesn't she?'

'Yes, she—' It was as if her mouth were full of cardboard. '*No!*'

'After the service, Merrily, Mr and Mrs Shelbone invited Dennis back to their house, where Amy admitted to Dennis that she'd been lured into what had become quite a craze at Moorfield High School for attempting to make contact with the dead. She said— You'd better relay the rest of it, Dennis, I don't want to get anything wrong.'

Dennis Beckett cleared his throat. He didn't look directly at Merrily.

'Amy told her parents, in my presence, that a Jane Watkins had approached her one day in the playground and told her that a group of them had been receiving messages from a certain . . . spirit . . . who kept asking for a girl called Amy. Amy gave this – this Jane short shrift, until the girl told her the woman had identified herself as Amy's mother, from whom Amy had been parted as an infant. Amy, of course, had always known that she was adopted.'

'And she was then persuaded to attend one of these, ah, sessions, was she?' said the Bishop.

'Which, it seems, proved somewhat convincing – and immensely traumatic, apparently. The child claims she was able to communicate with the spirit of her mother – who gave her some very frightening information. Mr and Mrs Shelbone, however, declined to tell me what this information was.' Dennis leaned back, as if exhausted, his head against the wall. 'For which, to be quite honest, I was grateful. Suffice to say that Amy asked the Shelbones certain questions about her birth-mother and then proceeded to give them information about things which they did know but had never revealed to the child. Beginning with the significant disclosure of the mother's name.'

'*Justine,*' Merrily whispered. 'Oh God.'

'They were so shocked to hear her saying these things that Amy could tell at once, from their reactions, that she must be in possession of the truth. All of which was quite enough to reduce both the girl and the parents to a state of absolute dread.'

*The spirit of a dead person.*

The Bishop said, 'Did she tell them *then*, Dennis, about the ouija board sessions? Because—'

'No, she didn't. This initial exchange took place immediately following Amy's . . . upset, during the Eucharist. When they got home, there was an attempt at a family discussion, which ended rather abruptly when Amy realized that her adoptive parents had concealed this – whatever it was – disturbing information from her. She became resentful and spiteful. She told them she was in contact with her *real* mother, but she didn't explain how this had come about. She was, I would guess, behaving in a rather sly way: playing her parents off against her natural mother.'

'Pretty *un*natural mother, if you ask me,' Bernie Dunmore spluttered. 'So this, presumably, is what led to the adoptive mother's request for an exorcism.'

'Hazel Shelbone didn't tell me about any of this,' Merrily said tonelessly. 'And as for Jane's—'

'It was only after Mrs Watkins's latest visit that Amy explained, somewhat reluctantly, about the ouija board,' Dennis Beckett said. 'Which I would imagine carries less kudos than direct personal contact with one's late mother.'

'Do we know when the mother died?' Bernie asked.

'No.'

'Not in childbirth, then.'

'I don't know, I'm sorry.'

'Are they still asking for this exorcism?'

'I was able to pray with the child,' Dennis said.

Merrily felt the Bishop's glare this time. *More than you were able to do.*

'I think it was sufficient,' Dennis said. 'But I'm prepared to go back.'

'Look . . .' Merrily fumbled for words. 'I . . . I accept that I probably mishandled this from the beginning. And maybe I shouldn't even have attempted to talk to Amy when her parents weren't there. But I can't accept that Jane's in any way involved in this.'

'Merrily,' the Bishop said, quite gently, 'I think I'm correct in saying that it wouldn't be the first time Jane's exhibited curiosity about things that—'

'She would not do *this.*'

There was silence, the two men looking anywhere but at Merrily. The door was open; Sophie, presumably in the Deliverance office next door, would have heard everything.

'She's my daughter,' Merrily said. 'I would know.'

Bernie Dunmore pulled out a tissue, blotted something on his beach ball of a forehead. 'You'd better tell us the rest, Dennis.'

'Amy . . .' Dennis Beckett half turned to face the Bishop. 'I'm afraid that Amy maintains that Mrs Watkins was fully . . . *fully* aware of her daughter's involvement.'

Merrily shut her eyes, shaking her head.

'And when Mrs Watkins came to see Amy on Saturday evening – when her parents were out – she warned the child very forcibly—'

'*What?*' When her eyes reopened, Dennis Beckett was finally staring directly at her, perhaps to show how much he wasn't enjoying this.

'—That she'd better keep quiet about Jane Watkins—'

Merrily sprang up. 'That's a complete and total—'

'—If she knew what was good for her,' Dennis said.

'It's a lie,' Merrily said.

Bernie Dunmore breathed heavily down his nose. 'Sit down, Merrily,' he said. 'Please.'

# Part Two

*When I am involved in the work of deliverance I admit my own ignorance . . .*

Martin Israel: *Exorcism – The Removal of Evil Influences*

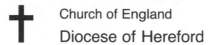

Church of England
Diocese of Hereford

# Ministry of Deliverance

email: deliverance@spiritec.co.uk

Click
Home Page
⌐ Hauntings
Possession
Cults
Psychic Abuse
Contacts
Prayers

## Hauntings

Haunting or spiritual infestation of property is a complex problem which constitutes most of the work of the Deliverance Service. It falls into a number of clear categories and each case needs careful investigation before a particular course of action is undertaken.

The following pages will attempt to explain the difference between the most common types of haunting: poltergeist activity, 'imprints' and 'the unquiet dead' and why each demands different treatment.

TWELVE

# Everybody Lies

'The Lady of the Bines in person?' The Rev Simon St John was slumped like a tired choirboy on a hard chair he'd pulled into the centre of the studio floor, his cello case open beside him. 'Scary.'

He hauled the cello out of its case. It was every bit as dented and scratched as a much-toured guitar. Simon drove the bow over the cello strings, and the sound went up Lol's spine, like a wire.

'It *was* scary at the time.' He'd decided he had to tell somebody. It wasn't so long ago that a vicar would have been the very last person he'd have opened up to, but there were aspects of Simon St John that made him more – or maybe less – than what you thought of as a normal clergyman.

Lol had spent the night, as usual, alone in the stables. Prof had said he should move over into the cottage, but he felt more comfortable in the loft room above the studio. All last evening he'd been somehow expecting Stock to turn up, with an explanation of the newspaper story, but Stock hadn't shown. And then, this morning, when the footsteps sounded in the yard, it had been Simon St John in jeans and trainers, carrying his cello case, looking like a refined version of Tom Petty.

Prof had mentioned that Simon would often drop in on a Monday, to unwind after an entire day of being polite and cheerful to his parishioners. Before moving to Knight's Frome, he'd been in some bleak sheep-farming parish in the Black Mountains, which thrived on threats and feuds and general hatred and where the vicar was expected to be hard-nosed and cynical.

135

'But – am I right? – you didn't know the story of the Lady of the Bines at the time you saw this woman,' Simon said.

Lol sat a few feet away, on the hardwood top of an old Guild acoustic amp he'd picked up in Hereford last year. 'No.'

'That *is* quite spooky.' Simon's bow skittered eerily across the strings. He winced. 'And naked, hmm?'

'And bleeding from superficial cuts, like she'd just run through some spiny bushes or brambles or—'

'It's how ghost stories are born,' Simon said. 'Give me your chord sequence again. B-minor, F-sharp . . .?'

'Then down to E-minor for the intro to the verse.' This was the River Frome song, for which there were still some lyrics to write.

'And you made a careful exit,' Simon said. 'Wise.'

'I was thinking drugs, I was thinking witchcraft. I was wondering, should I call the police in case she's been . . . you know? But she was . . . smiling. She seemed relaxed. Have *you* ever met Stephanie Stock?'

Simon pushed the bow over the strings of the cello in a raw minor key, recoiled. '*Ouch.* I'm just so bloody atrocious these days. No . . . when he comes to Church – and he's actually been a time or two recently, the cunning bugger – he comes on his own. She's a mouse, they say – quiet, goes off to work in Hereford in her little Nissan. Making the best of the dismal place, presumably, when she gets home, because she never goes to the pub with him.'

'So, what do you reckon?'

'Dunno, is the short answer. I don't know *what* you saw. Why don't you ring her one night while he's out? *Why were you naked in the old hop-yard, Mrs Stock?* Simon lifted his bow. 'No, wouldn't be such a good idea. Anyway, it doesn't change my view of the situation. He's a lying git. "*I need an exorcism, Si, soon as you can.*" Jesus!'

'That was what he was asking for when he came here? And you said no.'

'Damn right. An Anglican exorcism, sanctioned by the Bishop of Hereford, would put God and the Church of England firmly on Stock's side. Comes to a civil court case, I get called as a witness. Stuff that.'

'But why would he then go to the papers? Why would he expose himself to public ridicule?'

'You think that bothers him? He's a PR man. He knows how transient it all is. News today, chip-paper tomorrow . . . except in Knight's Frome. Here, it might send a slow ripple up the river . . . Still, what's he got to lose?'

Lol persisted. 'OK . . . Prof suggests Stock's making up the haunting bit to put pressure on Adam Lake to dismantle his big barns and stick them somewhere else. But that still doesn't quite add up. Getting rid of the barns might put a few thousand on the value of the place. But when you think how many people'd want to live in a house well known as a murder site – and now even better known – at the end of the day, Lake's going to be the only person really interested in buying it.'

'All right.' Simon leaned forward, letting his arms droop over the body of his cello. 'I'll tell you what I think, why I think Stock wouldn't talk to Lake's lawyer when the first approach was made. I think, in normal circumstances, he'd sell that place tomorrow. He's a townie, an *arch*-townie. He hates it here. But I don't think he *can* sell. Not to Lake, not to anybody. What did Stock say to you about the reason Stewart Ash left them his house?'

'He said Ash didn't bequeath his house to Gerard Stock, he bequeathed Stock to Adam Lake. He wanted to be sure there was someone in that house who wasn't going to do Lake any favours.'

'Yeah, but Stock doesn't do *anyone* any favours. Especially not someone who's both dead and stupid enough to leave him a house.'

'But it was his wife's inheritance.'

'His wife does what she's told. She's a mouse. What other kind of woman would Stock marry? What I'm trying to suggest to you is that Stewart Ash would never leave his house in the hands of someone like Stock to make sure it didn't fall into Lake's hands . . . if he hadn't already taken steps to make sure Stock *couldn't* sell it, anyway.'

'You mean some kind of – I don't know the legal term . . .'

'Restrictive covenant. Stock wants us to think he doesn't want to sell the kiln, when in fact he *can't*. I'd put money on it.'

'It makes sense,' Lol admitted.

'It's the only explanation that does. He's buying time until he can find some way – legal or otherwise – around it. Maybe the place is going to mysteriously catch fire one night, maybe one of the extra candles he needs to combat the awful darkness topples over. Oh, there are lots of things he could do.'

'And still emerge looking clean and innocent?'

'He doesn't care, Lol, long as he stays out of jail. Look . . . he wants – ostensibly – to get back at Lake for what he did to the house and to Stewart Ash. He also wants – perversely, it might seem, but not when you get to know him – to get back at Ash for saddling him with a saleable country property that he can't sell. Which means he's almost certainly looking at a way of turning the situation into money – maybe even now selling the story, a book, a TV documentary. Something . . .' Simon stood up, leaned his cello against the chair seat.

Lol stood up, too. 'What if you're wrong? What if he really has got problems in that place?'

'Why are *you* so bothered?'

Lol shrugged.

'Anything to do with your forlorn and possibly unrequited love for the Reverend Watkins?'

Lol sighed. 'Good old Prof.'

'Yeah, yeah, he called in at the vicarage before he left for London. And then, lo, she rang me herself. Apologetic, in case she'd said something to the press that might have offended me.'

Lol went still. 'Merrily?'

'I truly hope your friend has the sense not to get involved. You don't have any influence there, I suppose?'

'I'm a songwriter, Simon. I write songs.'

'And don't *you* go making any silly connections between some doped-up woman and the Lady of the Bines.'

'Am I allowed to write a song about it?'

Simon made a thoughtful, sibilant sound through his teeth. 'All right,' he said, 'I'm going to tell you the truth about the Lady of the Bines, OK?'

Lol sat down again.

'According to the legend,' Simon said, 'if you see her, your hops will start to wither before the season's out. Right?'

'Uh huh.'

'Once the Wilt hits somebody's yards, the old codgers in the pub will start muttering about the Lady. You'll have seen the signs: *Keep Out. Danger of Infection.* Most big yards have them. The Wilt's voracious and it can be carried by people just walking in and out of a field. Most people observe the restrictions. Kids, though, are another matter. Always been a problem keeping kids out. And I guess that's why they made up the story.'

'Made it up? Who made it up?'

'*They* did. I don't know who, but it's bollocks, Lol!' Simon threw out his arms; you could almost see the bat wings of a surplice. 'The story was made up to scare kids away from the hop-yards. The history of hops in Herefordshire doesn't go back as far as the days of knights and ladies.'

'Sally Boswell was spinning me a line?'

'Maybe *she* made it up. She's a clever lady; she's been around long enough.' Simon had picked up his bow and was tapping it against his leg like a riding crop. 'This is the country, Lol. In the country, in certain situations, everybody lies.'

## THIRTEEN

# Question of Diplomacy

Although she worked for the Bishop and the Church of England, in essence Sophie Hill served the Cathedral. If you confided in her, only God and those medieval stones would ever know.

She was not exactly a mother-figure – just that little bit too austere – and certainly not an older sister. Agony aunt would probably get closer. Merrily wondered how many perplexed priests in a crisis of faith, or facing divorce or the prospect of being outed as gay had, over the years, consulted Sophie before – or instead of – bishops and deans and archdeacons.

'Except, I should have done *something*,' Merrily insisted. 'From the start, Huw Owen always used to stress that, regardless of our own opinions, we should never leave the premises without—'

'Merrily – seriously – how could you?' Sophie handed her tea in a white china cup. 'If the girl herself wouldn't have anything to do with you, and if the mother felt unable to take you completely into her confidence—'

'She took bloody Dennis into her confidence.'

'Only because the girl had accused you of threatening her – transparent nonsense which, in my view, throws immediate doubt on her casting of Jane as the instigator.'

Merrily paused, with the cup at her lips. '*You* don't see Jane involved in this?'

'There was a time, not too long ago,' Sophie conceded, 'when there was very little of which I would have acquitted Jane without a number of serious questions. But no. There's an element of . . .

140

malevolence here. Not that I think she *was* ever malevolent but, with younger children, mischief and maliciousness can be horribly interwoven, and I rather think she's grown beyond that stage.'

'Well, thank you.'

'All the same, you do need to speak to her without delay. Where is she now?'

'On holiday, with her boyfriend's— with Eirion's family. In Pembrokeshire.'

'Can you contact her on the phone?'

'If I can't,' Merrily said, 'I'll be driving down there tonight.'

'*Don't* overreact.'

'Sophie, I've just been accused of menacing a juvenile!'

'Accused *by* the juvenile.'

'I wasn't aware of Dennis Beckett immediately springing to my defence.'

'No. But then, Canon Beckett was hardly vociferous in support of the ordination of women.'

'I didn't know that.'

'I'll make you a list sometime.' Sophie pushed the phone across the desk to her.


'Merrily!' Gwennan squealed. 'How marvellous it is to hear from you again!'

They'd spoken twice on the phone but never actually met. She hadn't met Eirion's father, either, the Cardiff-based business consultant, fixer, member of many quangos and chairman of the Broadcasting Council for Wales. Gwennan was his second wife.

'Erm . . . I just wanted a very quick word with Jane, please,' Merrily said. 'Something she might have forgotten to tell me before she left.'

'Oh dear,' said Gwennan. 'You've just missed her. She's just this minute taken the children to the beach.'

'What time will she be back?'

'Oh heavens . . . I don't know really. The problem is, Merrily, that Dafydd and I have a lunch appointment in Haverfordwest, so we won't be seeing Eirion and Jane until tonight. They've taken the children out for the day. Isn't she *marvellous* with children?'

Merrily blinked. 'She is?'

'What I'll do, I'll leave a note in case they come back earlier. Though, knowing Jane, she'll have too much planned for them all. But she'll definitely call you tonight, I'll make sure of it.'

'If you would. It's nothing vital, just something I need to check. She's actually looking after the children, then? Young children?'

'Eight and eleven,' Gwennan said. 'She's wonderful with them. You don't have any other children of your own, do you? I expect that's what it is.'

Merrily put down the phone to the sound of heavy footsteps and puffing on the stairs: the Bishop returning, after seeing Dennis Beckett to his car. He came in and closed the door.

'I've told him to keep this to himself, naturally.'

'Don't feel you have to protect *me*,' Merrily said bitterly. 'If it turns out to be remotely true about Jane, I'll be out of here before you can say Deuteronomy.'

'Merrily, the very last—' The Bishop glanced around to make sure the door was firmly shut, then sat down opposite her at Sophie's desk. 'The very last thing I want is to lose you from Deliverance because of something—'

'Bernie, if this *is* true, I'll have to leave the parish, the diocese . . . everything, probably.'

'That's ridiculous.'

'I've told her she has to *speak* to Jane.' Sophie placed a cup and saucer in front of the Bishop, poured his tea.

'It looks like it'll be tonight before I get through to her,' Merrily told him. 'I'll also need to speak to the Shelbones, of course, but not until after I speak to Jane.'

'No!' The Bishop dislodged his cup, splashing hot tea on his cuff. 'Out of the question. You stay well away from that family. Dennis has prayed with the girl, and that's enough for the present, as far as I'm concerned.'

'You can't say that. Now it's out in the open, I'm going to have to find out about this ouija-board stuff. If that's not part of the Deliverance Agenda, what is?'

'What this whole business is, my girl, is a pretty firm pointer to why we need a Deliverance support group, without delay. Jobs like this, it's like the damned police – you need to go out in pairs to give yourself a witness. Have you even provided me with a list of possibles yet?'

'Well, at least I've eliminated Dennis.' She took out her cigarettes. 'Would you mind?'

Sophie frowned, but Bernie Dunmore waved a hand. 'Go ahead, if it'll make you think clearer.'

'Suppose I have a word with the headmaster at Moorfield?'

'Do you *know* the headmaster?'

'Bernie, Jane goes there.'

He coughed. 'Yes. What's his name?'

'Robert Morrell.'

'I don't think I've met him yet.'

'You probably won't.' Merrily lit a cigarette. 'He's an atheist.'

'Aren't they all? But, sure, go and see him, by all means. Go and see him in your capacity as a concerned parent – if he isn't already in the Algarve or somewhere.'

'Thanks.'

'I'll call him for you,' Sophie said.

'In a moment, Sophie. Merrily, there's something else we need to look at, on the other side of the county, as it happens. Sophie, could you get that e-mail? You'll be glad to know, Merrily, that you're not the only minister in this diocese facing, ah, flak.'

'I know.' Merrily took one more puff on the cigarette and then stubbed it out in the empty powder compact she used as a portable ashtray. 'That was all I needed, thanks. This would be the vicar of Knight's Frome?'

'You've read the Sunday paper, then.'

'I was quoted in it, Bernie.'

'Yes. Of course you were.' He wiped a hand across his forehead. 'I think I need a holiday.'

'And Sunday wouldn't be Sunday, at Ledwardine Vicarage, without the *People* and the *News of the World*. Anyway, I thought I ought to ring him. He certainly didn't seem over-worried, and he didn't ask for any help. I've also spoken to the guy who – well, let's just say a journalist. The inference is that the story was engineered by Mr Stock, for reasons of his own. So my feeling is that Simon St John probably knew exactly what he was doing when he said no.'

Bernie Dunmore's dog-collar disappeared under his chins. 'Just as *you* did when you said no to Mrs Shelbone on that first occasion?'

Merrily was silent.

When the Bishop had gone, she stood up to let Sophie repossess her desk.

'He obviously just wants to keep me well away from Dilwyn.'

'Oh, more than that, I think.' Sophie scoured her blotter for traces of ash. 'If it was anyone other than the Reverend St John, he might have let it go. But I don't think *any* of us are entirely sure about Mr St John.'

'Tell me.' Merrily sat in the chair vacated by the Bishop.

'And it's *not* simply that he used to be in some sort of rock-and-roll group in the eighties, if that's what you were thinking.'

'I wasn't aware of that. Would it be a band I've heard of?'

'You probably would, but I don't even recall the name. Nor is it the fact that St John isn't known for his diplomacy . . . or the delicacy of his language.' Sophie's eyes narrowed under her compact coiffure. 'Even more profane than you, Merrily, by all accounts.'

'A Quentin Tarantino priest?'

'Certainly a troubled priest. Or was. I believe he's come very close to leaving the Church more than once. He seems to have what you might call an attitude problem. Came to us from Gwent, newly married. His wife's quite seriously disabled. The vicarage at Knight's Frome had to be considerably modified before they could move in.'

'How does that affect his ministry?'

'Not at all – except by eliciting sympathy from the parishioners. Not that Mrs St John appears to welcome sympathy. I think, in the end, it probably does mainly come back to that question of diplomacy. He tends to be volatile and arbitrary. For instance – and this is the instance the Bishop's no doubt recalling – he once refused to marry a member of a very well-established local farming family, someone with family graves in the churchyard going back at least two centuries, because he said it was a marriage of convenience and the couple clearly didn't love one another. He told them to . . . "Eff off to a registry office".'

Merrily rolled her eyes. 'The times I've wanted to say *that*.'

'But you didn't, did you?'

'Only because *a*, I didn't have the bottle and *b*, Uncle Ted the churchwarden would've had me on toast. Come to think of it, that comes down to bottle, too, doesn't it?'

'It's simply a matter of tempering one's responses,' Sophie said. 'The Reverend St John tends to form personal opinions about people and act on them. Which is why the Bishop feels it might be advisable in this instance to have a second opinion. There's also this message – probably the first serious response to your Deliverance website.'

Sophie laid in front of her an e-mail printout.

Rev. Watkins,

I am grateful that you were less quick to dismiss my appeal for spiritual assistance than was my local minister. I am assuming you were not misquoted in saying that if you were aware of someone in genuine need of spiritual support, you would wish to see they received whatever help you were able to give them. May I therefore appeal to you as a Christian to at least investigate the situation here before my wife and I are driven to the edge of sanity. May I stress that this is not a 'wind-up'.

    Yours very sincerely,
    Gerard Stock.

'Note where it indicates copies,' Sophie said.

Merrily read:

Copies: Bishop of Hereford, C of E Press Office, The People, BBC Midlands Today, BBC Hereford and Worcester.

'That explains everything. So, it's on TV tonight, is it?'

'They haven't approached us yet, but I suppose they will. What do you want me to say?'

'Better say we'll be talking to Mr Stock. What choice have we got?'

'You want me to reply to him, too?'

'I'll do that.'

'I don't envy you any of this.' Sophie began to put the cups and saucers back on a tray. 'Your biggest problem's always going to be sorting out what's genuine from what's—'

'Complete bollocks,' Merrily said, unsmiling.

'One can only hope you don't get on *too* well with the Reverend St John.' Sophie started to carry the tray to the sink in the corner opposite the door and then she put the tray down again. 'If you don't mind me saying . . . you seem different.'

'I do?'

'This is none of my business, but has something happened in your personal life?'

'I don't have much of a personal life, Sophie.' Merrily looked out of the window, over Broad Street. The rain had stopped, but the sky was still mainly overcast, layer upon layer of cloud, fading to amber rather than blue. 'Actually, something odd did happen, but you wouldn't thank me for pouring it out right now.'

Sophie nodded and picked up the tray. 'Whenever you want to talk, I'm here.'

'Thanks. Really.'

She picked up the e-mail, went into the Deliverance office and switched on the computer to reply to Mr Stock, whose copies list alone revealed his media know-how. Was it still conceivable this man could have a genuine psychic problem?

She wondered if Simon St John had tossed a coin.

# FOURTEEN

# Thankless

The headmaster said it had to be considered heartening to hear of any fourteen-year-old girl who was communicating at all with a parent. Even if the parent was dead.

'Well, there we are.' Merrily smiled warmly. 'Everyone was saying what a complete unbeliever and a rationalist you were. But I had faith – I just knew you'd take it seriously.'

The staffroom had been updated to resemble a kind of scaled-down airport lounge with fitted recliner seats around the walls. There were two computers, a TV set and a video – maybe the teachers played stress-management tapes in their lunch hour. Robert Morrell looked health-club fit in his polo shirt and sweatpants. He'd reacted to hair loss by shaving what was left to within a millimetre of his skull.

'Put it this way . . .' There was a faint smile on his face, but she could tell he was annoyed by her attitude. 'I'd rate it considerably lower down the scale of antisocial behaviour than marketing drugs in the cloakrooms.'

Morrell was going on holiday with his family tomorrow, which was why the meeting had been arranged for this afternoon, before Merrily would've had a chance to talk to Jane. It was clear he would also rather have put it off – probably until next term, when it all might have blown over – but Sophie had enviable ways of dealing with authority figures.

'However,' he said, 'to forestall any accusations of being anti-Christian, I took the liberty of inviting our chairman of governors to sit in. A regular churchgoer, Mrs Watkins.' He inclined his head to her, patronizing bastard. 'And, as it happens, a golfing companion of your Bishop's.'

'Listen—' she must have looked pained; like everybody else, he was covering his back '—I'm not here to make a big deal out of it, Mr Morrell, I'm just trying to find out what's happening, who's involved and if any other kids have been damaged by it.'

'Damaged?' A corner of his mouth twisted up; not quite a sneer. 'Damaged *how*? Physically? Emotionally? Psychologically?'

She shrugged, reluctant to use a word he *would* sneer at. Jane despised him for teaching maths, playing electronic Krautrock in his car and joining the older boys for rugby training – his way, the kid reckoned, of getting around the ban on corporal punishment.

Thoughts of Jane made Merrily tense. Maybe she'd still been high from the time-lapse experience, or lack of sleep, but so far she'd managed not to think too hard about the kid's possible involvement. Now, in this deserted school, with its hostile head teacher, she felt insecure and it seemed altogether less unlikely that Jane had been into some psychic scam.

'And do *you* accept the idea of communication with the dead?' Morrell asked, as heavy footsteps echoed in the corridor outside, like the dead themselves walking in, on cue. Merrily jumped, but Morrell looked relieved. 'We're in here, Charlie!'

'Rob, so sorry I'm—' The chairman of governors came into the room like someone used to having people wait for him. 'Oh.' A leathery face registered unexpected pleasure. 'I was expecting old Dennis – whatshisname?'

'This is Mrs Watkins, Charlie. She's—'

'I *know* who she is. She's the reason Bernie Dunmore spends so much time in Hereford these days instead of walking off some of that weight on the golf course.' His right hand flashed. 'Charlie Howe.'

'Hullo.' Merrily was letting him squeeze her fingers when she suddenly realized who he was. 'I think I . . . may have encountered your daughter.'

'Yes indeed!' He beamed. 'We're all very proud of Anne.' His local accent was as mellow as old cider. He wore a light suit and a broad, loose tie. He was in his sixties, had wide shoulders and strong, stiff, white hair in what, in his young days, would have been called a crew-cut.

Charlie Howe: one-time head of Hereford CID, father of its current chief, DCI Annie Howe, the steel angel. Icy blonde with a serious humour deficiency. Merrily searched for family resemblance, could find none at all.

'She's done well, Mr Howe.'

'Youngest head of CID we've ever had. She'll have outranked her old man before she's finished. Can't hold you girls down, these days.' Charlie Howe took a step back to have a proper look at Merrily. 'My Lord, when I think of your predecessor, old Tommy Dobbs, what a— well, God rest his poor old soul, but what a bloody *improvement!*'

And she had to smile, not least because this was the kind of sexist remark guaranteed to turn Annie Howe white.

Morrell said, 'Mrs Watkins believes there's reason to suspect the school's become infested with the Powers of Darkness, Charlie.'

Merrily sighed.

They sat at a circular table from which Morrell had discreetly removed a pack of playing cards. 'You must know,' he said, 'that even as the chief executive of this establishment, there isn't much I can do without knowing the name of either the victim or the instigator.'

Merrily hadn't felt empowered to name Amy, had revealed only that it involved a girl with a dead mother. She didn't think Morrell would be able to narrow it down, especially with no staff to consult.

'Look,' she said. 'You asked how the child had been damaged. What you had here was a well-behaved, considerate, hard-working, honest and possibly slightly dull kid who's turned into someone who is secretive, remote, resentful . . . and seems to have rejected God while embracing what some people like to call the spirit world. In effect, it seems the dead mother's become her private support mechanism, to the exclusion of . . . anyone else.'

'The way children sometimes find an imaginary friend,' Morrell said smoothly. 'To fill a gap in their lonely lives.'

Merrily shook her head. 'Not really.'

Charlie Howe leaned back on an elbow. 'Can *you* believe this young girl might *actually* be in contact with her mother, Merrily?'

'I *could* believe it. But I think it's more likely to be a contact with . . . something else.'

'Like *what*?' Morrell's chair jerked back with a squeak that amplified his outrage.

'Poor Rob,' said Charlie Howe, 'this en't your world at all, is it?'

Merrily said, 'When a group of people get together, in a circle – like we are now – with a particular objective in mind, then perhaps that focus of group consciousness could result in – well, it could be like a radio picking up signals. Or maybe like a computer network, and one of the group goes home with a virus attached.'

'That's based on science, is it?' said Robert Morrell.

Merrily shrugged. 'I'm just telling you it can have harmful effects.'

'You're talking about possession?' said Charlie Howe.

Merrily wrinkled her nose. 'It's not my favourite word.'

Morrell said, 'Mrs Watkins . . . when I was teaching in Bristol, I used to pass, every day, on my way to work, a former warehouse that sported a large sign proclaiming it to be a Spiritualist Church. A church. Like your own, but less grand. And presumably some of the members of this church had children or grandchildren attending local schools, where the teaching staff were obliged to respect all the various forms of religion, whether Islam or Sikhism or Hinduism or . . . Voodoo, for all I know.'

'We're not talking about *religion*, Mr Morrell, we're talking about a bunch of kids hunched up in a cloakroom with an upturned glass and a set of Scrabble letters!'

'And frankly, as I've made clear, Mrs Watkins, I'd have to find something like that a good deal less disturbing than if they were trading their pocket money for pills and then, when the pocket money ran out, clobbering some elderly lady for her pension.'

'Whoa!' Charlie Howe put up his hands. 'Let's get this into proportion, shall we, folks? I was a copper for nigh on forty years. Sure, I know what drugs can do and I know what some kids'll do to keep supplied. But I also know, Rob, what . . . what religion can do. Well, not religion, so much as . . . well, I don't know what you'd call it. But I think I know what Merrily's warning us about, and in my experience it can sometimes lead to offences a sight worse than mugging.'

Morrell's lips clamped shut. He looked affronted.

'For instance,' Charlie Howe said, 'some years back, I was on the fringe of a very big murder hunt – one that I'm sure we all know about – where the murderer, when he was finally nicked, insisted he'd been told by "voices" to kill a particular kind of woman.'

'Charlie, that's—'

'Give me an hour or two and I could find you a dozen or more other cases in the past ten years where killings, serious assaults and God knows what else, with someone acting entirely out of character, have been put down to—'

'But Charlie, this is—'

'This is a juvenile. Certainly. But aren't youngsters more prone to this kind of thing than adults because their imaginations are that much bigger? I'm going to use the word "delusion", Merrily, for Robert's sake. And, anyway, we all know that a delusion can be just as real to the person involved. Now if this child's become antisocial and starts taking advice from what she reckons is her dead mother, then who knows what her so-called mother's going to advise her to do next? No, I'd be the last to dismiss this kind of problem out of hand.'

Merrily felt like filling the silence with applause. Morrell spread his hands on the table, looked down between them for a moment.

'All right,' he said, 'but what do you suggest we do about it now? The summer holidays have just started. The students are no longer under my jurisdiction. Chances are that, by September, there'll be some new fad.'

'The truth of it is,' Merrily said apologetically, 'this was supposed to be an informal inquiry.'

'Nothing formal about me, my dear,' said Charlie Howe.

'I was hoping somebody might have some idea about what was going on – like if there were certain kids known to be particularly fascinated by the occult . . . maybe encouraging or even pressurizing other kids into getting involved. Teachers usually have their noses to the ground.'

'Tell me,' said Morrell, 'have you asked your daughter about this?'

'She's . . . away on holiday.'

'You see, I'm afraid I really can't help you. I don't know anything about any ouija-board sessions. They could very well be happening outside school hours, outside the campus. If you want to give me this girl's name, we can probably arrange some counselling for her next term.'

'Or,' said Charlie Howe, 'why don't you ask Merrily to come and give a talk to the sixth-formers? We still have religious education, don't we?'

'Social and cultural studies. I'd have to discuss it with my team.'

Merrily pushed back her chair. 'Well . . . thanks for listening to me. Although I suspect I've wasted your time.'

'Absolutely not.' Charlie Howe placed a hand over hers. '*Emphatically* not. Anything that's affecting the lives of our young people, we want to know about it.'

'Of course,' Morrell said.


The car park had a view of playing fields and the distant Black Mountains. Moorfield High, serving scattered villages in north and central Herefordshire, was half a mile from the nearest one and not a church steeple in sight – which wouldn't displease Morrell, Merrily thought.

Watching the head driving away, the chairman shook his head.

'It's his one blind spot, Merrily. He's a good headmaster in most respects. Knows about discipline. Doesn't let the little beggars run wild. But he's an unbeliever. Don't mind me calling you Merrily, do you, Reverend? I feel I know you, after talking to Bernie.'

'Whatever's he been saying?'

'He just gets anxious about you, poor old devil.'

'Ah, but he handles anxiety very well,' said Merrily. 'It's part of being a bishop.'

'You're not wrong.' He patted her shoulder, then consulted his watch. 'Half-four. Fancy nipping over to Weobley for a coffee?'

'I'd like to, Mr Howe, but I've got to . . . talk to someone.'

'*Charlie*. If I can't be Chief Super any more, I'll just be Charlie. Least you didn't call me *Councillor* Howe.' He looked sad for a moment, as though his useful life had ended when he retired from the police, which it clearly hadn't.

'You're Chairman of the Education Committee now, aren't you?'

'Vice-chairman.' He put his head on one side, winked at her. 'As yet. Tell you what, why don't you come and talk to one of our sub-committees? Tell the beggars a few things they didn't know.'

'You think they'd want that?'

'They never know what they want these days. Think they know what goes on, but they bloody well don't. I know you've got a pretty thankless job. Got to deal with some weird customers.'

'You'd know all about that.'

'What, thankless jobs?'

'I meant weird—'

'Oh, aye,' Charlie said. 'Getting more thankless all the time, policing. I don't know how they keep going, today's coppers, with all the restrictions and the human-rights legislation – known criminals laughing at you from behind their slippery lawyers.'

He gazed across the fields towards Wales, sucking air through his teeth. A pillow of cloud lay over the Black Mountains.

'Your daughter seems to be coping,' Merrily said.

'You reckon?' He looked up at the sky for a moment, as if deciding whether it would be disloyal to take this any further. Then he turned to her. 'I'll tell you, Merrily, it was the shock of my life when Anne joined the force. Never told me, you know. Never said a word. Leaves university with a very respectable law degree, moves away, next thing there she is on the doorstep in her uniform.'

'Not for very long, I imagine.'

'Oh no. Fast-track, now. Doing undercover work while she was still a PC, out of uniform altogether within a couple of years. Detective-sergeant at twenty-five.'

'Chief Constable material, then.'

'Aye,' Charlie said. His eyes narrowed shrewdly. 'Don't get on too well with her, do you?'

'She tell you that?'

'No need. When it comes to religion, Anne stands shoulder to shoulder with Brother Morrell. Always been her blind spot.'

'Hasn't held her back. Not even in a cathedral city.'

'No.' Charlie Howe stood with his legs apart, his back to the horizon. He must have cut an intimidating figure as a detective, framed in the doorway of the interview room. 'Not as a copper, no.'

Merrily, who'd had two encounters with Charlie's daughter, didn't know what to say. She wasn't sure she could have got on with Annie Howe if the woman had been Mary Magdalene with a warrant card.

Charlie took out his car keys and tossed them from one hand to the other. 'Didn't tell Brother Morrell everything, did you?'

'I doubt it would have helped. What do you think?'

'Oh no, you're quite right, it wouldn't've helped at all. But you wouldn't have brought him out here in the school holidays if there wasn't something about this issue that had you particularly worried – now, would you?'

Merrily met his eyes: they were deep-sunk but glittery, playing with her.

'Well,' she said, 'I don't really like this kind of thing. New Age stuff I can put up with – a bit of fortune-telling, astrology, meditation. Trying to contact the dead, that's unhealthy. Let them go, I say.'

'And where *do* the dead go, young Merrily? Heaven? Hell? Purgatory?'

'Leominster, Charlie. Everybody knows that.'

He grinned. 'Well, you have a think about talking to my subcommittee. I'll give you a call in a week or two.'

She stood by the old Volvo and watched him drive away in his dusty Jaguar. She thought she liked him but she wasn't sure if she could trust him – he *was* a councillor.

Back in the vicarage, she paused under the picture in the hall: a goodquality print of Holman-Hunt's *The Light of the World*. It had been a gift from Uncle Ted, who knew nothing of the lamplit path, and showed Jesus Christ at his most sorrowfully benign. A middle-aged Jesus, laden with experience of humanity at its most depressing.

*What am I learning from this?* she asked him. *Because it seems to me I'm just muddling around, getting up everybody's noses and not helping a soul.*

Summer had never been her favourite season. People expected it to be a time of pleasure: new feathers, cares dropping away like rags.

But too often the old feathers refused to fall, and the rags still clung, clammy with sweat.

Inside the house, tiredness came down on Merrily like a tarpaulin. She checked the answering machine – nothing pressing, no Jane – drank half a glass of water and fell asleep on the big old sofa in the drawing room, with Ethel the cat on her stomach.

And dreamed she was back in the church.

It was evening. The sandstone walls were sunset-vivid and the apple glowed hot and red in the hand of Eve in the huge west-facing stained-glass window, and Merrily was standing in a column of lurid crimson light and she could hear her own thoughts as she prayed.

*Oh God, please tell me. Is Jane involved in the summoning of the dead? Please tell me. Heads for yes. Tails for no.*

Her thumb flicked against old copper; it hurt. The coin rose up sluggishly into the dense air, rose no more than three or four inches and she had to jump back to avoid catching it as it fell. She didn't see it fall but she saw it land because it appeared dimly on the flags, rolling onto one of the flat tombstones in the floor at the top of the nave, into the gaping, time-ravaged mouth of the skull at its centre.

She peered down, couldn't make out whether it was heads or tails. She bent over double and the shadows deepened. She went down on her knees and all she could see was a void.

She started to weep in frustration and found she was scrabbling in her bag, buried in the shadows beside the sofa, like a great cata-falque in the dreary brown light.

'Yes . . .'

'Mum . . .?'

'Jane!' She struggled to sit up, clutching the mobile phone to an ear.

'You OK?'

'I . . . yeah. Of course I'm OK.'

'Good.' Jane's voice was as light and hollow as bamboo.

'Are *you* OK?' Merrily sat on the edge of the sofa, hunched up. The room was dim and felt stagnant The dull day, deprived of any summer glory, was refusing to go gently and seemed to be sucking out the last of the light like a vacuum pump. The feeling she had was that Jane was *not* OK.

## FIFTEEN

# From Hell

Jane lay on Eirion's single bed, watching the last of the light in the sky over the sea. All kinds of emotions were pressing down on her – guilt, regret, some bitterness. But mainly she was furious, and not only at herself.

'So what did you tell her?' Eirion whispered.

'Everything. What *could* I tell her?'

Eirion had claimed the only bedroom as yet converted from the attic. It had white walls and the smell of new plaster, and even he could only just stand up in here. But the views towards Porthgain and the old mine workings were incredible.

If would be OK, brilliant even, if it was just Eirion and the views and this amazing moist, translucent feel you got in Pembrokeshire, the mystical *otherness* of the countryside.

*Oh, no*, she'd been about to say to Mum, *the house is top, it's the family that's from hell.* But she'd wound up playing that down, in the end, because of the guilt. And the fury.

Eirion stroked Jane's bare arm. 'You didn't tell me about any of this.'

'What was to tell? All kinds of shit happens at school. You put it behind you, don't you? And when you get back after the holidays it's all forgotten and there's a new kind of shit waiting.'

'So this Layla . . . is she a genuine medium?'

'Dunno. She *claims* to have psychic powers, gypsy ancestry, all that. And she's certainly got this . . . *charisma*'s not the word, it's more threatening than that. Can there be like negative charisma? I

156

mean, she lays it on, obviously – she's clearly found that being threatening, looking brooding, that works . . . gets you stuff. Even the
teachers don't mess with her – I've noticed this. Teachers are *very*
polite to her, especially the men. Arm's-length situation. They are . . .
kind of scared.'

'You know what that means, don't you?'

Jane rolled over. 'Enlighten me, O Experienced One, Mr Been
Around, Mr Done All That.'

'Yeah, OK,' Eirion said wearily, 'you've made your point.'

'So what's it mean? Half the male staff are shagging Layla
Riddock?'

'It only needs one,' Eirion said. 'Or maybe she set one of them
up and he was just that bit slow saying, "How dare you, young lady?"
They're only human, aren't they? And then they start gossiping in
the staffroom as well, warn each other of the traps – "Let's be careful
out there".'

'She's certainly got Steve on a string, the groundsman guy.'

'There you go.'

'But this kid, this Amy . . . I didn't realize how far it went, you
know? I mean, how could I? Like, OK, she's Miss Prim, fourteen
going on forty-five-year-old spinster, stiff enough to snap any time.'
Jane turned over, leaned across him and clicked on the bedside table-
lamp. 'And she set me up. She's scared shitless of Riddock so she set
*me* up. All it was, I just happened to be *there* . . . and virtually dragged
in anyway. I was nothing to *do* with it. This Amy's more or less
claiming I organized it! And I told Mum the truth, but all the time
I'm thinking, why should she believe me *this* time?'

'You should've told her in the first place, shouldn't you? You
knew that stuff was right in her ballpark.'

'Oh, come on, Irene, you *don't*, do you? You just bloody don't.
Even if it's somebody you don't particularly like, unless it's life and
death, you just don't grass them up. And now Mum could be in
some deep trouble over this.' She sank back, rolling her head on her
bit of pillow. 'She was really pissed off with me. More than she was
saying, because *whatever* I'd done she wouldn't want to louse up my
holiday – she's cool that way. But I could tell she thought I was
going to say it was all total crap, that I didn't know a thing about it,

that somebody had obviously fitted me up, et cetera. She was like totally shattered to find out there was some truth in it.'

'Sorry,' Eirion said. 'I'm not being very helpful, am I?'

'It's not your crisis. Maybe I should have noticed how it was with Amy and Layla Riddock. We've all been there, haven't we?'

'Bullying? Intimidation?'

'You ever have days you were so scared to go to school you were faking stupid symptoms? Hasn't happened to me since I was like really young . . . eleven, twelve. I was quite small then, for my age. Thought I was going to wind up looking like Mum.'

'Little and cute?'

'Little is not cute at school.'

'Always the ones who are just a *bit* bigger who go for you, isn't it?' Eirion said. 'The ones who've maybe been bullied a bit themselves. They do much worse stuff and they get away with it because nobody suspects them.'

'And you're just so scared at the time. Adults are like, "Oh, you should stick up for yourself." But *you* know they can do anything to you at school, right under the noses of the staff. Like, even if you *die*, it's only going to look like an accident! They're completely outside the law. Nobody out there realizes how totally evil kids can be. It's like some false-memory thing sets in with adults, and all kids become cute and need protecting. And that's how you wind up with teenage psychos like Riddock.'

'When you're nine—' Eirion lay on his back, gazing into the darkness of the room '—there are eleven-year-olds who're like . . . like Charles Manson.'

'Who?'

'This weird American guy who got people to kill for him. Murdered this movie star and all these rich people, just went into their homes and ripped them to pieces. Manson was claiming to be receiving these psychic messages. And the people who killed for him – who included women – they wrote "pigs" and stuff on the wall in the victims' blood.'

'You're right,' Jane said. 'You're really not being very helpful.'

She wondered if he'd grown up thinking of this guy, Manson as the ultimate bogeyman because his own family was so damn rich.

There was a knock on the bedroom door.

'Shiiiiiiiiiiiiiiit!' Jane reached up and snapped off the lamp. Did they never, never, *never* go to sleep?

'Eirion?' That hated tripping, lilting, little-girly voice.

'What?' Eirion called out hoarsely.

'*Ydy Jane yno?*

'Er . . . no,' Eirion replied.

'*Wel, ble mae Jane?*

'Probably gone to the shop.'

'*Aw, Eirion . . . ma'r siop ar gau!*

'That does it!' Jane swung her legs off the bed. She was wearing her jeans and her lemon-yellow top. She moved across the bare boards to the door.

Eirion was looking anxious. 'Look, don't,' he whispered. 'Can't you just let it go?'

Jane stopped at the door and thought for a moment, then smiled. She crept back and lay on the bed. Eirion was sitting on the side of the bed by now, shoving his bare feet into his trainers.

'Sioned?' Jane called out in this foggy, slurry voice.

'*Jane!*

'Look, would you mind giving us a few more minutes. We're having sex, OK? *Ni'n*, er, *yn shaggio.*'

A wonderfully awed silence.

Eirion kind of crumpled.

'*Again!*' Jane breathed loudly. '*Harder! Deeper! Oh God . . .!*'


From hell? Oh yeah.

See, most of the ordinary Welsh people she'd met, Jane liked. This might seem like generalized and simplistic, but they seemed kind of classless, no side to them. Contrary to what everybody said, you could have a laugh with them. Look at Gomer Parry.

Look at Eirion, for that matter: chunky, honest, self-depre-cating . . . and this incredible smile that was (as she'd written in a poem she was never going to show him in a million years) like all the birds starting to sing at once on a soft spring morning.

The poor sod. Raised among the *crachach*.

This was what they were called – the Welsh aristocracy, the top

families. A few of them had titles, but most of them were contemptuous of English honours, although – being sharp business
people – they were usually incredibly polite to the English people
they encountered.

Eirion said his dad, Dafydd Sion Lewis, was some kind of Welsh
quango king. He 'served' on the Welsh Development Agency, the
Welsh Arts Council, the Wales Tourist Board, the Broadcasting
Council for Wales. And he was a major executive shareholder in
whatever Welsh Water and Welsh Electricity were calling themselves
this week. There was a bunch of them like his dad, Eirion said. The
names of the organizations and businesses might change but it was
always the same people in control.

Dafydd Sion Lewis was plump and beaming and hearty and,
according to Eirion in his darker moments, majorly corrupt.

Gwennan was his second wife, about fifteen years younger. She
was a former secondary-school teacher of the Welsh language and
now – as a result of being married to the quango king – a key member
of the Welsh Language Board, which existed to keep the native
tongue alive and thriving.

Not that Jane had a problem with this. She was all for having
more languages around: Gaelic, Cornish . . . anything to keep people
different from each other, to create a sense of *otherness*.

At first, she'd thought that Gwennan, with her two cars and her
movie-star wardrobe, was a fairly cool person.

It had taken only one day of the holiday for her to realize what
Eirion had already kind of implied: that everything had gone to
Gwennan's head – the wealth, the status, the establishment of the
Welsh Assembly. She was now a warrior queen of the New Wales,
wielding the language like a spear.

'Except it isn't a new Wales at all,' Eirion had said morosely. 'It's
the same old place, run by the same old iffy councillors, except they're
now known as Assembly Members, supported by the same old bent
financiers, but with this new sense of superiority. Suddenly, they're
looking *down* on everybody . . .'

'Especially the English?' Jane had suggested.

'*Especially* the English because the English don't have Wales's
unique identity.'

Actually, Eirion said, most of the time he found Gwennan quite amusing. She was essentially superficial and quite naive. And she could be very kind sometimes. When she noticed you.

Unfortunately, Gwennan had come with baggage: Sioned and Lowri, eleven and eight, the little princesses. Bilingual through and through. Pocket evangelists for the language and the culture.

'No, Jane,' Sioned would say, wagging her little forefinger until Jane wanted to snap it off. 'I've told you and told you, I'm not doing it unless you ask me *yn Cymreig*.'

'You know what I'm really doing here, don't you?' Jane said to Eirion when Sioned had gone, presumably to wait for her mother and Dafydd to return to receive the shocking facts. (*Was* there such a verb as *shaggio*? They seemed to have converted every other English term coined since about 1750.) 'You know what I *am*?'

'If she says anything, we'll just simply tell her you were joking,' Eirion said uncomfortably. 'Kind of a risqué joke to make to an eleven-year-old, mind, but . . .'

'I'm the first English *au pair* in Wales, that's what I am. Do you realize that?'

Behind the door in the farmhouse kitchen Gwennan had hung an appointments calendar. Every day this week displayed a lunch date for her and Dafydd. Every evening they went out for dinner in St David's or Haverfordwest, because several of their friends also had cottages in the area. Because the Pembrokeshire coast was becoming like some kind of Welsh Tuscany.

And who had to look after the bloody kids, meanwhile?

'It's *exactly* like being an *au pair*,' Jane said with acidic triumph, 'because I work my butt off for the privilege of *learning the fucking language!*'

She began to beat the pillow with her fists.

'I'm sorry!' Eirion almost sobbed. 'I genuinely didn't realize she'd be quite so . . .'

'Opportunistic?'

Eirion was too honest to reply.

It was a big old farmhouse. The first floor had been divided into two sections. There was a separate staircase to Dafydd and Gwennan's suite; the other staircase led to three small bedrooms: Sioned, Lowri . . . and Jane in the middle. Most nights the kids fell asleep with their respective boom-boxes still pumping Welsh-language rock through the plasterboard walls either side of Jane's bed.

Come to think of it, Gwennan and Dafydd were unlikely to be at all put out by the thought of the young master giving one to the English *au pair*.

Not that he *had*, yet. The daily and nightly presence of the evil little stepsisters seemed to be intimidating him more than whoever had been his school's version of Charles Manson.

Stepfamilies: a nightmare.

She'd made the kids' supper. She'd made them tidy their rooms. She'd made them go to bed at ten p.m. She'd made them go *back* to bed at ten-fifteen. And in the course of this endlessly crappy evening, she'd been grilled by Mum over the phone and made to feel like shit. At eleven-thirty, probably looking like some totally knackered housewife, she'd followed Eirion up to his attic bedroom and collapsed, fully clothed, onto his bed and poured it all out.

'Let's go over it again,' Eirion said. 'This Layla and this . . .'

'Kirsty.' Jane moved closer to him, which wasn't difficult on a single bed.

' . . . Find that by staging little seances, or whatever you want to call them, they can wield enormous power over certain kids.'

'It's addictive, I reckon. You keep going back, even though you're terrified. I mean, *I'm* not terrified – OK, maybe a little scared – but I'm, like, somebody who's attracted to all this stuff anyway. As you know.'

'Yeah,' Eirion said grimly.

'But this is a buttoned-up kid from some fiercely Christian household, who's been taught that spiritualism is, like, firmly in the devil's domain, and her immortal soul is at risk – and she *still* keeps going back because something about it has . . . grabbed her.' Jane gripped what she thought was going to be Eirion's arm but turned out to be his thigh. 'Sorry.'

'Go . . . go on.'

'Kid knows she's like *doomed*. She's totally beyond the pale. I mean, I've listened behind the door when Mum's been counselling individual parishioners – which is, like, her version of confession. You get some people who are really, really scared that they've thrown it all away because of some really piffling sin.'

'Gets blown up out of all proportion.' Eirion tentatively slid an arm under her waist.

'You'd think it was only a Catholic thing, or hellfire Nonconformism or something, but I don't think it's anything to do with what denomination you are, or even what religion. It's a psychological condition. A kind of dependency. A terrible fear of getting on the wrong side of God. I mean . . . no wonder she threw up in church. Holy Communion? The Eucharist? You're kneeling there with a mouthful of the blood of Christ, knowing you've as good as sold your soul to the other guy? It's all gonna come down on you in a big way, isn't it?'

'Layla would have known about this girl's background?'

'Oh *yeah*, Riddock knew exactly what she was doing. Must have been giving her a major buzz, a cruelty high. But you can't help wondering how shocked *she* was when it really started to happen. When this Justine started coming through and turned out to be Amy's real mother.'

'Would heighten the power trip no end.'

'Mind-blowing. She wouldn't want to let Amy go after *that*.'

Eirion pushed a hand through her hair. 'You've got this pretty well sussed, haven't you, Jane?'

'I don't know. It's all guesswork, isn't it?'

'You tell your mum all this?'

'Not the theoretical stuff. But she'll have worked that out for herself by now. She's not thick.'

Eirion drew her to him, the length of his body the length of hers, toe to toe, faces almost touching. 'You haven't told me how it ended.'

Jane closed her eyes, saw the circle of letters, the glass with a mind of its own.

J-U-S-T-I-N-E.

'How it ended? We got raided, didn't we? Pretty ludicrous. The shed door just like crashed open and they burst in. The drug squad – the deputy head and the caretaker. All very dramatic. "*Nobody move!*

*Hands on the table!"* Like one of us might pull a gun. Of course they didn't expect it would be so dark. Layla just blew out the candles, and it was probably Kirsty gathered up the letter-cards. I don't know where she put them – down her front, I expect; they certainly weren't there by the time the caretaker found the lights. The glass was knocked off the table and smashed. It was just a glass. They were expecting . . . I don't know – Es or worse.'

'They search you?'

'Nah. Layla had her cigs out by then. Plain old Rothmans scattered across the table, like she was sharing them out. Smart bitch. You could see the relief on the deputy head's face, now it was clearly no longer a police matter. "Now, girls, because it's the end of the term, apart from confiscating these disgusting things, I'm not going to take this any further. However . . ." '

'That *was* smart of her.'

'Yeah.'

'What will she do now, your mum? Go and tell the girl's parents, try and patch things up?'

'Dunno.'

'Or go after this Layla?'

'Yeah,' Jane said soberly. 'I'm afraid that's exactly what she's going to do – having not the *slightest* idea of just how massively evil that bitch can be. And if I try to warn her, it'll look like there's something else I don't want her to find out. I . . . I'm like . . . feeling pretty pissed-off, Irene. On every front.'

He kissed her gently on the lips.

'OK,' Jane said, 'except maybe that one.'

She put a hand behind his head, opened her mouth to his tongue and moulded her body into his. One of Eirion's hands seemed to be trapped against her left breast.

Jane was feeling less and less like a knackered housewife when they heard the doors of Dafydd Lewis's new Jaguar slamming down in the yard, then laughter. And then something about Eirion, the great lover, Mr Experience, began to kind of shrink.

Soon afterwards, Jane crept back to her own room and lay glowering at the ceiling. She'd been set up; she'd been framed; she'd been used to damage her own mother. She couldn't live with this.

164

# SIXTEEN

# Mafia

Lol gently shook the hand of the vicar's wife.

'I won't get up,' she said.

Simon St John said, '*You* might think she says that every time.'

'Just go and get me a drink, you bugger.' Isabel's accent was Valleys Welsh. She was plump and had light brown hair, with tufts of gold, and warm eyes. 'No hurry. Give me time to get to know this boy.'

'I'll get these,' Lol offered.

Isabel glared at him. 'Sit *down*, you!'

Simon headed for the bar, still in plain clothes – the jeans, the crumpled collarless shirt. Vicar's night off. It was gone nine p.m., the Hop Devil three-quarters full. Lol sat down.

Isabel's black top was low-cut and glittery. Over one shoulder strap and a handle of the wheelchair, he caught a glimpse of Gerard Stock, sitting in the shadow of the bellying chimney breast. So the landlord had let him back in.

Stock was on his own, except for a pint of Guinness and a big whisky. He was leaning back against the wooden settle, with an empty smile and an arm extended along the top of the back rest like he was claiming an invisible girlfriend. Lol thought suddenly of the Lady of the Bines and felt uneasy for a moment.

'You a Catholic, Lol?' Isabel inquired loudly. 'Only I've decided it's time I went to Lourdes, but you've gotta go with a Catholic, isn't it, or it doesn't work.'

'Is that true?'

'What?'

'That you need to be accompanied by a Catholic?'

'Well, *he* won't take me, anyway. And his lot's rubbish at healing.' Isabel pouted. Then she laughed. 'I fell off a high wall, Lol, is what it was. A long time ago. So, that gets *that* out of the way. Now – what's a nice-looking boy like you doing all on his own?'

Simon had said he and his wife had made a practice of going to the pub on Monday nights, making it known that this was when the parishioners could get to them without making an official visit out of it – and therefore when delicate issues could be raised informally.

He'd asked Lol to join them, explaining that Isabel liked to meet new people; she didn't get out much.

So Lol had back-burnered his usual reservations about country pubs. Tonight, he felt he owed Simon several drinks. The first recording they'd made of the River Frome song – Lol humming the bits where the lyrics were incomplete – had been so much stronger, more atmospheric, more ethereal than the demo playing in his head. And this was all down to the cello, of course. The cello – dark, low-lying, sinuous – had become the spirit of the Frome.

Simon had sat there, listening to the playback with his arms folded, wincing at the cello parts and then remarking shrewdly, 'Somehow, you can't settle anywhere, can you, Lol? You're the kind of guy who really needs a proper home, but you don't know where it's safe for you to be.'

'Huh?'

'Rejected by the born-again parents, shafted by the shrinks, dumped by the girlfriend in Ledwardine. You want to trust, but you're scared to trust people. And then you fetch up here, and the first thing you latch on to is a sad little river.'

'Very perceptive of you, vicar,' Lol told him. 'But I've learned how to psych myself now, thanks.'

Isabel leaned her head close enough for Lol to smell her shampoo. 'Expecting trouble, he is,' she murmured.

'Simon?' Lol wiped condensation from his glasses.

'Needs you for back-up,' Isabel confided.

'*Me?*

'And me. Who's going to assault a clergyman minding a short-sighted songwriter and a cripple?'

Lol grinned. He loved the way she said *crip*-pel and *troub*-el. Now Isabel had turned away and was loudly advising a woman who didn't look pregnant to get the christening booked before she missed the boat. The woman looked alarmed for a moment, then dissolved into giggles and tossed Isabel an *oh you* kind of gesture on her way into the toilets. Lol thought that maybe the vicar's wife had already become more a part of this community than the vicar was ever going to be.

'There's a reason someone would want to assault him?'

'Oh, always *someone* who'd like to.' Isabel grimaced. 'Some people here, they'd do anything for Simon. Others . . . well . . . Trouble is, he doesn't care, see. Doesn't give a toss, not about himself nor who he offends. One reason I had to marry him. Give him a reason to keep himself alive.'

'Sorry?'

'You're not one of those men who says "sorry" all the time, are you?'

'Sor— no.'

'Good. Play well for you today, did he?'

'It was almost spooky.'

'You want to hear him on electric bass. Always be a fallback for him, when they chuck him out of the Church.'

'There's a danger of that?'

'He tries,' Isabel said.

Lol stood up to help Simon with the drinks: lagers and something golden-brown for Isabel. The atmosphere in the pub was like in the days before ventilators and smoking restrictions. Thin fluorescent bars glowed mauve between the beams, as Isabel jogged her neckline to and fro to fan the air on to her breasts. Lol tried not to look.

'Stock's over there,' he remarked.

Isabel pushed her wheelchair back to see. 'On his own, too, poor dab. She's a funny one, his wife. Adapted to that dreary hole like a bloody barn owl. Invite him over, shall I?'

'This woman is a liability,' Simon said to Lol, then he turned to

167

his wife, and spoke as to a child. 'Isabel, Stock has probably been in here three hours, at least. Do you know how drunk that makes him?'

Lol said, 'Why exactly are you expecting trouble?'

'After a while, you learn never to ask him that,' Isabel said. 'Never tempt fate.'

Trouble came, just the same. It came with the arrival of Adam Lake and a lovely young woman with a wide, sulky mouth and short hair the colour of champagne.

'His wife?' Lol wondered.

'Fiancée,' said Isabel. 'Amanda Rae. She's got a discreet little chain of tiny fashion shops in Cheltenham and Worcester, places like that. Not Hereford, mind – they wouldn't pay those prices for that tat in Hereford.' She sipped her drink. 'Don't much in Cheltenham, either, I reckon. That's why she'll always need someone like him. Shallow, pointless people, they are, supporting each other's public façades.'

'My wife the social analyst,' Simon murmured.

'They'll've come out for the first time today, I reckon,' Isabel told Lol. 'All these press people about the place, see, and the wrong *kind* of press. Rip off all their clothes for a centrefold in *Horse and Hound*, but the buggers'll lie low till this one's over.' She smiled slyly at Simon. 'Bit like him. Taking off before ten in the morning with his cello case.'

Simon glanced uncomfortably at Lol. Lol thought about the magical enhancement of the River Frome song. It was an ill wind.

It was getting very warm in the bar. He noticed that all the tables had been taken except for the one in front of Stock, who sat there motionless, still smiling. *See, I don't have to talk to people, if I don't want to. It's a rare skill and I'm good at it, man. I can be very relaxed, very cool, sidding quietly, saying nothing.* The level of Stock's pint had gone down a couple of inches, though, like he was taking it intravenously.

'Lake usually come in on a Monday night, too?' Lol asked Simon.

'More often than not. Meets his friends from the hunt. He's taken up the cause – a crucial part of the salvation of his birthright.

Just become local organizer for the Countryside Alliance, so *called*. Leads demonstrations to London.'

'Hypocritical bastards, they are,' Isabel growled. 'Still the Norman overlords, isn't it? All the countryside's their hunting ground. It *is* a class thing, whatever anyone says. But they also grow to enjoy killing. I've seen it. Doesn't have to be like that.'

'She means that, in the country, sometimes things do have to be killed, if they're preying on stock,' Simon explained. 'But there has to be something questionable about people who simply love to do it.'

'He said that in the pulpit one week,' Isabel said proudly. '*That* old bugger complained to the Bishop.' Lol followed her eyes to a fat man, seventyish, in a khaki shirt, at the centre of a group at the bar.

'Oliver Perry-Jones,' Simon said. 'Former master of the hunt. Failed politician. Almost made it into Parliament once, until the true nature of his politics became apparent, thanks largely to revelations by Paul Foot in *Private Eye*.' He swallowed some lager, leaned back and scanned the room. 'Knight's Frome's like all rural communities: scratch the surface and you come away with all kinds of crap under your—'

'Shhhh.' Isabel's warning hand on his wrist.

'Good for you, vicar,' Adam Lake said.

'I'm sorry?' Simon looked slowly up at him. Lake wore a light tweed jacket. His mutton-chop sideburns had been pruned and razored to sharp points. The whole style looked too old for him, too old for anyone of his generation, Lol thought. Lake was like a gangly mature student playing a spoof squire in the college review.

'It won't be forgotten,' Lake said, and Simon was on his feet.

'Oh shit,' said Isabel.

'*What* won't be forgotten?' Simon said quietly.

'Your support,' Lake said. He was taller than Simon, taller than anybody here. 'Your support for the community, against potentially disruptive influences.'

'Right, listen!' The bar noise sank around Simon like it was being faded by a slide control on some hidden mixing board. 'I *support* what my particular faith tells me is right. And you, Adam – you don't represent the fucking community.'

Dead silence. Adam Lake smiled nervously, his girlfriend looked annoyed. 'Fine language for a so-called minister,' Oliver Perry-Jones muttered.

'OK,' Simon said. 'As Adam's raised the issue, is there anything anyone thinks I ought to know about?'

And Lol realized what this was about: the vicar making himself available for questioning about the Stock affair. Most clergy might have saved it for the pulpit, but that would leave no opportunity for argument. In pubs, though, arguments never lasted long before they turned into rows, and rows turned into fights.

This was Simon St John opening his arms to the accumulating shit.

Which was admirable, Lol thought. Also a little crazy.

Simon looked around, raised his voice. 'Anyone here who thinks I'm under the thumb of what Gerard Stock likes to call the rural mafia? Anyone thinks I declined to assist Mr Stock purely for the purpose of currying favour with The Man Who Would Be Squire?'

Silence. No sign of anyone rising to the bait. Maybe it wasn't so crazy.

Simon shook back his hair. Isabel had a hand around her glass as if she was expecting someone to knock it to the floor. Eddies of tobacco smoke fuzzed the lights.

And then a slow handclap began.

*Pock . . . pock . . . pock . . .*

Heads started turning, cautiously.

Stock didn't lift his head, just went on clapping. His pint glass was down to its final quarter. His whisky glass was empty. The space in front of his table soon grew bigger, people instinctively edging away, until there appeared a meaningful emptiness between Stock's table and the one Lol was sharing with Simon and Isabel. Although no one was looking at him, Lol, who hated an audience, felt exposed.

'*I can get you a nationwide tour,*' Prof Levin promised in his head.

*Pock . . . pock . . . pock*

'What's the problem, Gerard?' Simon said.

Stock stopped clapping. His eyes were like smoked glass.

'You're a hypocritical bassard, vicar.'

Simon shrugged.

'But thas how the Church survives, isn't it? Never take sides.'

Isabel shouted, 'That's ridic—' Simon put his hand on her shoulder and she gripped her glass tighter, clammed up.

'Thas right,' Stock said. 'Keep the liddle woman out of it.'

Oliver Perry-Jones called from the bar, 'Why don't you just clear out, Stock?' His voice was high and drawly – like a hunting horn, Lol thought. 'Take your money from the gutter press and your drink-sodden fantasies, go back where you came from. People like you don't have a place heah.'

Stock stared into his beer for a moment and produced a leisurely burp before turning his head slowly. He was clearly very drunk. He peered in the general direction of Perry-Jones.

'Jus' like old Stewart, me, eh? Din' fit in either, did he, the old gypo-loving arse-bandit?'

'Take your foul mouth somewhere else,' Perry-Jones said predictably. 'There are ladies here.'

Isabel smiled.

'I bet . . .' Stock pointed unsteadily at Perry-Jones. 'I bet *you* were so fuckin' *delighted* when Stewart got topped. Served the bassard right. And, hey, it also took a couple of dirty liddle gypos out of circulation.'

No reaction. Stock's rosebud lips fashioned a blurred smile. Lol caught sight of Al Boswell with his wife, at the end of the bar. Expressionless. *Non-confrontational is all we are.*

'Din' like the gypos, did you, you old fascist? Gypos and the Jews. You and old man Lake, eh? Fuckin' blackshirts. Still got your armbands?'

Lol wondered if Derek, the landlord might intervene at this point, but Derek was looking down at the glass he was polishing; he'd know there were enough people here to deal with Stock – and enough people who would want to watch it happening.

Perry-Jones had started to vibrate with fury, but Lake's tanned face was like a polished wooden mask. His girlfriend, Amanda, had her mobile out. 'I'm calling the police.'

'Go 'head, darling,' Stock said mildly, not looking at her. 'Lezz have the coppers in. Whole wagonful of the bassards. Swell the audience. Lezz get the fuckin' press back.' He shouted out, 'Any hacks in the house?

Amanda clutched the phone but didn't put in a number.

'Where's the Lake boy gone? Where're you, you liddle arsehole? Tell me one thing: what you gonna do if the Smith boys geddout? Appeal's gotta come up soon. Case'll be wide open again, the Smith boys geddoff.'

If Stock was expecting a reaction from Lake, he didn't get it. He searched out Simon again.

'*You* think they did it, vicar? Maybe the police were a liddle hasty, there, whaddaya think, man? You're a *liberal* sorta guy. You think the Smith boys really did it? You ever wondered who *else* wanted poor ole shirtlifting Stewart out the picture?'

Lol sat up. A new agenda was forming like invisible ink appearing between the lines of the old one. He heard Lake's girlfriend saying, 'Right. I *am* calling them,' but felt nobody was really listening to her.

Adam Lake finally spoke. 'Put it away,' he told Amanda. 'Let him finish himself. Plenty of witnesses here. We can talk to my solicitor tomorrow.' He walked out into the space between Simon and Stock. 'Spell it out, Stock. What exactly are you saying? You think someone else killed Ash, rather than the convicted men? That it?'

'There's a turn-up,' Isabel murmured.

Lake said coolly, '*Well?*' He was either hugely arrogant or he really had nothing to hide.

Stock picked up his beer glass and drained it calmly.

'Come *on!*' Lake suddenly roared. 'Scared to say it, are you? Scared to say it in front of witnesses?' He put both big hands flat on Stock's table. 'Stock, for Christ's sake, how much do you really think I *care* about that place? You really think I'd . . . you think anyone would *kill* for it? For a broken-down bloody hop-kiln? Have you *seen* my place? Have you seen where I *live?* You really think I'm now going to offer you some ridiculous sum for that hovel, is that it? Just to get you out of my hair? Are you mad? Are you *sick?*'

Stock stared at him, froth on his beard, set the glass down hard, about an inch from one of Lake's hands. He said nothing. He'd got what he wanted: Lake was losing it.

'Let me tell you . . . *Gerard*. Let me tell everybody . . .' Lake looked around wildly, and Lol saw emotional immaturity twitching and flickering in his big angular frame like a forty-watt bulb in a street lamp. 'You picked the wrong man.' Lake levered in towards Stock. 'You couldn't have done it to my father and you won't do it to me.' His face inches from Stock's, exposed to the booze and the sour breath. 'You can stay in that dump for as long as you like, you and your imaginary ghosts, you stupid, pathetic little turd.'

Like some soiled Buddha, Stock gazed blandly into the bared teeth and the glaring eyes for maybe a couple of seconds before his own eyes seemed to slide up into his head and his body wobbled.

Lol knew what was coming and so did Lake, but too late.

Simon stood with Lol on the forecourt under a night sky like deep blue silk shot with rays of green.

His white shirt was dark and foul with brown vomit. The good shepherd. It was Simon who'd guided Gerard Stock outside. In his life of ducking and diving, bartering and bullshit, Stock had probably come close many times to getting beaten up; Lol reckoned maybe he was now so physically attuned to the proximity of a kicking that his metabolism automatically came up with the most effective defence.

After it happened, Adam Lake could have battered him, drunk or sober, into the stone flags without blinking. But it was clear that all Lake wanted – women and some men shrinking away from both of them with cries of abhorrence and disgust – was to get into the men's toilets and wash Stock away. On his way, he'd collided blindly with Simon.

Now Simon stank of Stock's vomit, too, but Stock was clean and dry, leaning casually against the pub wall, the calm in the eye of the storm.

'You are a piece of work, Gerard,' Simon said. 'It just drips off you, doesn't it?'

'I'm a survivor, Simon,' Stock said.

'You'd better go home. Lake's going to be out in a minute, in search of a change of clothes. He sees you out here, he – he's a big boy, Gerard. And not a happy boy.'

Stock made a contemptuous noise.

'You as good as accused him of murdering Stewart. You accused him in front of a score of witnesses.'

'Oh no.' Stock straightened up. Apart from the sheen on his face, caught in the blue light from the window, he looked almost sober. 'You don't listen, Simon. I asked a question, was all. I asked who else might have done for Stewart if it wasn't the Smiths. No libel in a question. Didn't even ask *him*, either, I asked *you*. He doesn't get me that easy. Nobody gets me that easy.'

Simon walked over to the pub door and pulled it until the latch caught. 'Where did you get that idea, anyway, Gerard?'

Stock tapped a meaningful finger on the side of his nose: not telling. 'But what a reaction, vicar. What a beautiful, instantaneous reaction . . . *and* – ' inclining his head to Simon ' – in front of witnesses.'

Lol wondered precisely how drunk Stock had really been in there. How pissed did you have to be to throw up on cue?

*A good publicist has control, tells you what he wants you to know, when he wants you to know it. Timing.*

What was happening here? Lol felt on the edge of something from which he could still, if he wanted to, turn away. 'You OK to walk home?' he said to Stock. 'Or you want Simon or me to—?'

Stock looked down at the dirt and cindered surface of the fore-court. 'Not going home, yet, Lol, thank you. Gonna take a walk, clear my head. Time is it?'

'Nearly closing time,' Simon said, 'in case you were thinking of going back inside, to attempt to get served.'

'Actually, I think this may finally call for a change of hostelry.' Stock produced a hawking laugh. 'What d'you think, vicar?'

'I think you're walking a narrow ledge,' Simon said.

'Reason I need a clear head,' Stock said, 'is I've got your lady exorcist coming to visit. Tomorrow, we lay Stewart, as it were.'

Lol froze, as the latch of the pub door clacked. 'Thanks very much,' Isabel said to someone, and wheeled herself out. Then she saw Stock. 'Bloody hell, you still here?'

'You're going to ask this woman to exorcize your place, then, are you?' Simon said quietly. 'It isn't that simple, you know, Gerard. It isn't just a formality.'

Stock sniffed. 'Goodnight, boys. Goodnight, Mrs St John.'

He began to walk away towards the lane. Above him rose the broad-leaf woods that enclosed the village, the pinnacles of occasional pines piercing the green-washed sky, stars beginning to show.

'Gerard,' Simon called out, 'it's not something you fart about with.'

Stock stopped about fifteen feet beyond him and turned round. He was quite steady. He pointed a finger at Simon.

'Don't *you*,' he said, 'presume to patronize me, sunshine. I came to you with an honest request and you told me to piss off. Whatever happens with this woman, it's down to *you*. Remember that.'

Lol thought the pointing finger quivered; he thought he saw a smear of something cross Stock's half-shaded face, and then Stock stiffened and turned and walked away. At some point before the shadows took him, Lol thought the walk became a swagger.

Lol walked back to the vicarage with the St Johns, Simon pushing Isabel's chair, lights blinking up on the Malverns.

'Bloody hell,' Isabel said. 'Stink rotten, you do, Simon.'

They crossed the humpback bridge over the silent Frome, hop-yards either side, the bines high on the poles. Simon looked over to the church, about fifty yards from the river bank, small and incon-spicuous among trees risen higher than its stubby tower.

'Maybe the stink around Stock is subtler.'

'I'm not sure he's right about Lake,' Lol said. 'The way he claimed he just threw out a question and Lake dived on it, like this was a sign of some kind of guilt. I don't think—'

'Be nice, it would, to think he did have a hand in it.' Isabel looked up at Lol. 'But it didn't feel right to me either. Boy was clever enough to realize smartish where Stock was going, but not intelli-gent enough to control his reactions – *if* he had something to hide. Does that make sense?'

Lol nodded. 'Lots of money, well educated, but nowhere near as clever as Stock. And yet . . .' He turned to Simon, took a breath. 'Look, what you said about exorcism . . .'

They came to the vicarage; against dark woods and hills and the lines of foliate poles in the hop-yards, its whiteness seemed symbolic.

There were no lights on in the front rooms, but a soft glow seeped through to most of the windows from some inner core.

'Is there something you're not telling me?' Lol said.

Simon didn't reply, went to open the gate. Isabel reached up and squeezed Lol's arm. 'Listen, love, he *gets* things he can't put into words, sometimes. You know what I mean?'

Lol looked up over the wheelchair to a broken necklace of moving lights rising up into the Malverns, to a band of black below the stars.

## SEVENTEEN

# Comfort and Joy

Sod it. Not a question of keeping confidences, not any more. Merrily switched on the anglepoise in the scullery, picked up the phone. At 10.45 p.m., this wasn't going to make her very popular.

However, the situation had altered. She hadn't been in a position to give away any names before, when all her information had come from Hazel Shelbone. But now there was another and possibly more reliable source.

*Reliable?* Merrily sat in the circle of light and prodded in Robert Morrell's home number. *Really?*

Little Jane Watkins, now learning that there was no such thing as a free holiday, had done it again. While she hadn't actually initiated the spirit sessions, she *had* been involved, albeit peripherally.

*Peripherally?* She'd had a finger on the damned glass!

The phone was ringing out at the other end. Morrell was going to be in bed getting a pre-holiday early night, sleeping the sleep of the self-righteous. The phone would also awaken his wife and kids – always hard to get kids off to sleep on the eve of a holiday.

Merrily wondered how easily Jane would sleep tonight. Getting it into proportion, she couldn't really imagine herself at sixteen – the black-clad, black-lipsticked Siouxie and the Banshees fan – standing up and warning her mates that their ouija game was actually a form of psychic Russian roulette, then walking primly away, to communal jeering.

Not even if she'd been a vicar's daughter.

'Yes?' The woman's voice wasn't sleepy, but it wasn't exactly accommodating either.

'Mrs Morrell? Could I speak to your husband? I'm sorry it's so late. My name's Merrily Watkins.'

'One moment.' Resentful now.

Merrily waited. The fact remained that Jane hadn't even mentioned the incident afterwards, even knowing it would be in confidence. This hurt; she'd thought they'd got beyond secrets, beyond concealment. She'd thought there wasn't anything they couldn't discuss any more. She'd thought they were friends, for God's sake.

The phone was snatched up. 'Mrs Watkins, I have to tell you that in just under seven hours, we're leaving for the airport with three small children.'

'Look, I'm really sorry. But this is something I need to know and if I left it until tomorrow I'd be doing it behind your back, which—'

'If this is about what I think it's about, I'd be immensely glad if you *did* look into it behind my—' Morrell calmed down. 'All right, I'm sorry. It's been a difficult year. I need a holiday. Go on.'

'I'll be very quick. I understand the organizer of – what we were talking about – is a girl called Layla Riddock.'

He breathed heavily into the phone. 'And you're asking if I'm surprised?'

'I can tell that you're not – which is interesting.'

'Before we take it any further,' Morrell said, 'anything I tell you has got to be absolutely unattributable. And I *mean*—'

'Of course.'

'Because normally I'd only discuss any of my students in this way with the police, and only then if there was some suspicion of—'

'Sure.'

'All right,' Morrell said. 'Layla Riddock . . . God almighty, do I really need this? Layla is . . . a dominant kind of girl. Stepdaughter of Allan Henry, yes?'

'Allan Henry of Allan Henry—?'

'Homes. With all the baggage that implies, and more. Obviously, I don't have an overview of their domestic situation, but if I had to guess, I'd say that, like a lot of wealthy men with potentially problematical stepchildren, he's been throwing money at her for years. Buying her compliance, until such time as she leaves home. She's driving around, for instance, in the kind of car *I* couldn't afford. Well . . . I probably could, but you know what I'm saying . . .'

'Mmm.'

'She's an intelligent girl, but she's got away with too much at home, which is why she expects to get away with the minimum of work at school. Swans around the place under this thin veneer of disdain at having to spend her days with children. You getting the picture?'

'A bully, would you say?'

'Not in the physical sense, far as I know. To be honest, I don't think she'd lower herself. I think she can be intimidating enough, without resorting to physical violence. I mean, she's quite . . .'

The line went quiet. Jane's word had been 'sinister.'

'Something you're thinking about, particularly?' Merrily pulled her sermon-pad into the lamplight, reached for a fibre-tip. 'Something which might save us both some time?'

She heard him breathe down his nose. 'I'm thinking, inevitably, about the Christmas Fair we held at the school last year. Did you come?'

'No, I was . . . a bit busy before Christmas. And Jane was off school, she wasn't very— No, we didn't come.'

'Well,' he said. 'I can tell you we were all quite surprised, to say the least, when Ms Riddock volunteered to take part in the fund-raising – a Christmas Fair being something she might normally consider well beneath her. What she did, she approached the teacher in charge of the event and volunteered to set up a fortune-telling stall.'

'Oh, did she?'

'Yeah,' he said ruefully. 'I thought that might get you. Made a few of the staff sit up when she appeared on the day in full gypsy costume. *Very* exotic – and very expensive, too, according to my wife. Long, low-cut black dress, big gold earrings – gold, not brass. Black hat with a dark veil. All very mature, very mysterious, just a bit sinister, I suppose – but that may be hindsight.'

'*She always looks . . . tainted, somehow,*' Jane had said. Merrily lit a cigarette.

'Some of the staff had reservations from the start,' Morrell said. 'But as it was the first time in anyone's memory that Layla Riddock'd shown any enthusiasm for anything apart from burning rubber outside the gates, they weren't inclined to push it. So they set her up in the hall, back of the stage, behind a curtain. Somebody painted a sign – *Gypsy Layla* – and, as all the other stalls were fairly routine, people were queuing up to cross her palm with silver. Men, too, once they'd seen her.'

'She's *very* attractive?'

'I suppose you would say she exudes a certain hormonal something. Something you don't often find at school Christmas fairs, anyway.'

'And was she good at telling fortunes?'

'She was bloody good at frightening people,' Robert Morrell said bitterly. 'Wouldn't have frightened *me*, as you probably realize by now. But I accept that a lot of people are taken in by that kind of rubbish, against all their better instincts. Anyway, I don't know much about this sort of thing, but I gather that the usual routine is to tell the customers they're going to cross the water, or come into some money, live long and happy lives, have lots of children.'

'What was she using? Crystal ball?'

'I wouldn't know. She was certainly reading palms at some stage. Anyway, the staff started to notice that very few people were coming out actually smiling. And the ones who did, their smiles tended to be rather strained. Then some granny emerges very white-faced and almost fainting. One of the female staff sits her down, brings her a cup of tea, learns that Layla's looked at her palm and advised her to start getting her affairs in order because she *ain't . . . got . . . long.*'

'Oh.'

'Quite. There were several others, we found out later. One pregnant woman, for instance, had been told to prepare for the worst. Or, as Layla apparently put it, "I see a withering in your womb."'

'You found this out on the night?'

'Not all of it. Some of the stories came out over a period of days. But, I suppose, the atmosphere on the night itself . . . well, as Christmas Fairs go, it's fair to say there was gradually less of an ambience of comfort and joy than one might have wished for.'

'She wasn't stopped?'

'Oh, she *was* stopped. Eventually. One of the parents had been kicking up about it long before it became widely known that she was taking people's money for predicting death and sickness. The guy was objecting on religious grounds. Eventually, to my shame, we had to use that as a way of bringing it to a close.'

'Anyone talk to Layla afterwards – ask her why she was doing this to people?'

'I had Sandra – the deputy head – haul her in on the Monday morning. Waste of time. The girl pretended she couldn't understand what the fuss was about – she was simply passing on the information she was picking up. Psychically. She claimed there was a long line of gypsies on her father's side – her real father. I wanted to make her an appointment with the schools psychiatrist—'

Merrily wrote down: *Gypsies – ask J.*

'—But Sandra talked me out of taking it any further. Let it go. Just make bloody sure Gypsy Layla and her crystal ball don't get invited back.'

'Any of the kids, the other students, go in to get their fortunes told?'

'I don't know.'

'Who was the parent who complained?'

'A religious nutter. I'm sorry, I *should* say, one of our churchgoing parents, appalled that such a thing should be allowed to go on in an educational establishment, was threatening to take it up with the Director of Education. I was a bit short with him at first.'

'What was his name?'

'Is that important?'

'Might be.'

'Shelbone.' A thoughtful pause. 'David Shelbone. Father of – a fourth-year girl. And unfortunately he works for the council. He actually *knows* the Director of Education.'

Merrily kept her voice steady. 'Layla know about this?'

'Well, yes, of course, everybody did. I . . . the way we played it – and I'm not proud of this, but it seemed expedient at the time – Shelbone was still around, in another part of the school, so we had someone tip him off that people had been upset by the girl's predictions. Sure enough, he comes rushing back. *In God's name, stop this wickedness!* Embarrassing, really.' Morrell chuckled. 'But I don't think anybody else went to have their fortune told after that. After a few minutes, Gypsy Layla walks away through the hall, head held high, grim little smile on her face. Crisis over.'

'You thought.' Merrily sat in the circle of lamplight and tried to remember if Jane had ever mentioned the incident. But she hadn't gone back to school until the January term; probably all blown over by then.

'And that's all I can tell you,' Morrell said. 'However, if you *are* planning to take this any further, I'd offer two suggestions – one, if you're going to take on Layla Riddock, remember you're taking on Allan Henry, too, and he's a man with unlimited money and with friends in high places.'

'Not as high as mine, I always like to think.' Merrily was starting to feel light-headed. How peevishly simple this could all turn out to be: Shelbone terminates Layla's power-trip; Layla puts the frighteners on Shelbone's daughter.

Morrell said, 'My other advice is, leave Shelbone alone.'

'You think he might try to convert me to Christianity?'

'If you want to know about David Shelbone, talk to our friend Charlie Howe. He'll tell you what kind of fanatic you're dealing with – and I don't just mean religion, which would probably never seem like fanaticism to you. The other reason not to bother Shelbone is that I'm afraid the poor guy has personal problems at the moment. I . . . I had a call about it earlier this evening. His daughter attempted suicide this afternoon.'

Merrily froze, the cigarette at her lips.

'Less uncommon, I'm afraid, than it used to be,' Morrell said, 'especially at this time of year – children thinking they've done badly in their GCSEs, therefore their lives must be over. Maybe nothing at all to do with us, so I'm not going to theorize at this stage. Summer can be a stressful time for some kids.'

'What did she do to herself?' Half an inch of ash fell to the desk.

'Friend of . . . Jane's – is she?'

'What did she *do*?'

'Overdose, I believe. Taken to the County Hospital. They got to her in time, I *gather*.'

Merrily closed her eyes. The penny started spinning.

'Always sad,' Morrell said. Just like Merrily, he must have been putting two and two together from the moment the name Shelbone left his lips.

But he *did* have to be at the airport by seven.

'So . . . if that's all, I'll get off to bed,' he said.

She called Dennis Beckett; he knew nothing about Amy and an overdose. He couldn't seem to absorb the significance. 'But I *prayed* with her,' he said querulously. 'We prayed *together*.' And then he added vaguely, 'Perhaps she should have seen a doctor.'

'Her parents wouldn't.'

'Well,' he said, 'when *I* left her, she was spiritually calm.'

*And how could you possibly know that?*

Merrily asked him if he'd be visiting the parents tomorrow. 'You are still minding the parish, aren't you?'

'Why *did* this have to happen?' Dennis said plaintively.

Meaning, why did it have to happen while Jeff Kimball was on holiday.

'What is it you want me to try and find out?' he asked her at last, with resignation. He clearly didn't want to have anything more to do with this case.

'Could you find out if they'll talk to me?' Merrily said. 'Both of them?'

She switched off the anglepoise and sat in the dark, watching the red light on the answering machine, wondering how she would have handled this if she'd known from the beginning about Layla Riddock.

When she switched the light back on, nothing seemed any clearer and it was eleven-thirty. She called Huw Owen, who never seemed to sleep.

'I tossed the coin,' she told him eventually. 'It came up tails. Twice tails: no spiritual interference, no unquiet spirit.'

'And how did you feel, lass?'

'Weird.'

'Come on, talk grown-up, eh?'

'Sorry. I felt separation. Transcendence. Little me, big God. Plus, I was in there all night, but it felt like . . . not so long.'

'How long?'

'Six hours felt like – I don't know – less than two. And you don't fall asleep on your knees, do you?'

'Contraction of time, eh?'

'And it was . . . profound, moving, exalting – all that stuff. But I'm trying not to get carried away, because somehow it didn't tally with what happened afterwards, out here in the material world. It's not been a great day for me, Huw.'

'Bugger me.' She heard him drawing in a thin breath, like the wind through a keyhole. 'You're still expecting God to make it *easy*?'

'I should scourge myself, put Brillo pads in my underwear?'

'What I'm thinking, Merrily,' Huw said reasonably, 'is if you were in the church all last night, you should be getting some sleep. Just a thought.'

'I grabbed an hour or so earlier. Look, I've got a kid who tried to kill herself. What can I do?'

'Nowt. Let this Dennis pick up the mucky end of the stick for a change. Hang back, see what transpires.'

'What *transpires*? Hasn't enough bloody transpired?'

'The girl'll be safe in hospital for the time being.'

'And what about Layla Riddock?'

'Aye,' he said, 'there's your problem, looks like. But we're not the police. And even if we were, what's she done wrong?'

'Apart from terrifying old ladies and driving a little girl to the point of suicide as an act of pure vengeance?'

'All right, it's a tough one,' he admitted. 'Needs thought, prayer.'

'Or the toss of a coin?'

'Get off to bed, Merrily,' Huw growled.


She lay in bed, with Ethel the cat in the cleft in the duvet between her knees. She slept eventually. She dreamed, over and over, that the phone was ringing. She dreamed of a withering foetus inside her and awoke, sweating, and then closed her eyes, visualizing a golden cross in blue air above her, and slept again and awoke – something coming back to her from the night in the church. And she thought, *Justine?*

Awakening, stickily, into blindingly mature sunlight and the echoey squeak-and-clang of the cast-iron knocker on the front door.

Panic. Jane would be late for— Stumbling halfway downstairs, dragging on her towelling robe before she realized there was no Jane to worry about. The knocking had long stopped; she didn't know how long it had been going on, and now the phone was shrilling. She dragged open the front door, and found nobody there. She ran through to the scullery, saw she'd left the anglepoise lamp on all night, and grabbed the phone.

'Oh. I was begining to think you'd left already.'

'Sophie—? Oh God, what time is it?'

'It's just gone eight. Are you all right?'

'Er – yeh. Sorry, I . . . Late night.'

'You haven't forgotten Mr Stock?'

'Mr S—?'

'The haunted hop-kiln,' Sophie said. 'You're due there by nine, remember? I made an appointment for you?'

'Oh *shit* . . .'

'Merrily, I was ringing to warn you that we've had more calls from the press. The *People* asked if they could be there – exclusively – for the exorcism. We said on *no* account. We also declined to confirm that there was going to *be* an exorcism. Also, more alarming as far as the Bishop was concerned, the religious affairs correspondent of the *Daily Telegraph*—'

'Did you know Amy Shelbone had tried to kill herself?'

'*What?*'

'Consequently, I need to speak to both the Shelbones. I think I've finally got some idea of what it's about. Now, obviously they're not going to want to speak to me, after what—'

'Is the child all right?'

'I think so. I don't know. I haven't had—'

'I'll talk to them. I'll arrange something if I can. Merrily. Meanwhile . . . I hate to do this over the phone, and I did try to reach you last night but you were constantly engaged . . . I have to tell you the Bishop would like you to expedite this hop-kiln thing with the minimum fuss and the minimum publicity. He doesn't want it dragged out. He doesn't want to see you walking out of there into a circus of flashbulbs and TV lights.'

'Sophie, it's not that big a story.'

'His exact words, as I recall, were . . . "Tell her to throw some holy water around and then leave by the back door." '

'Put a bottle in the post and do the rest down the phone, shall I?'

'He's nervous, Merrily. Since the Ellis affair, where Deliverance is concerned, he's been like the proverbial cat on hot bricks. Rarely a day goes by when he doesn't ask me if we have a shortlist yet, for the panel.'

'Meaning he doesn't quite trust me.'

'He's nervous,' Sophie repeated. 'And once he finds out about this attempted suicide, he's going to be very nervous indeed. Fortunately, he's leaving at ten for a three-day conference in Gloucester. Transsexuality in the clergy. Should absorb his attention for a while.'

'Three *days*?'

'This year alone, surgery has increased the number of female clergy in Britain by four,' Sophie said dryly.

'I need to speak to Simon St John, obviously. I trust *he*'s not in the operating theatre.'

Sophie made a small noise indicating it wouldn't surprise her unduly. '*I* shall call him and tell him you're on your way. Just . . . go.'

'I'll call you when it's over,' Merrily said. 'Whatever the hell *it* turns out to be.'

# EIGHTEEN

# Lightform

'And this is where . . .?'

'You're standing on it,' Mr Stock said.

Although a despicable shiver had started somewhere below her knees, Merrily made a point of not moving.

'The police, it seems, don't operate a cleaning service,' he said. 'So we could hardly avoid knowing precisely where it was.'

They were standing, just the two of them, on stone flags in the circular kitchen at the base of the kiln-tower. The place had a churchy feel, because of its shape and its shadows. The light was compressed into three small windows, like square portholes, above head height – above Merrily's, anyway. And it was *cold*. Outside, July; in here, November – what was that about?

*It's about doing your job, isn't it? It's about not prejudging the issue on second-hand evidence.*

She let the shiver run its course, let it sharpen her focus.

She'd driven over here with a head full of Amy Shelbone and Layla Riddock and Jane – everybody but Gerard Stock, whose problem had been devalued because he was allegedly a professional conman, a manipulator, a spin-doctor.

And then you walked out of a summer morning into this temple of perpetual gloom, and it came home to you, in hard tabloid flashes, that a man had actually been beaten to death, in cold blood, right here where you were standing, his face, his skull repeatedly crunched into these same stone flags.

Violent death would often have psychic repercussions; you knew that.

Then there was Gerard Stock himself – *bombastic, bit of an operator, possible drink problem.* This morning Gerard Stock was wearing a clean white shirt and cream-coloured slacks. His hair was slicked down and his beard trimmed. The impression you had was that Mr Stock had bathed this morning in the hope of washing away the weariness in his bones, changed into clothes that would make him feel crisp and fresh. But the weariness remained in his bleary eyes and the sag of his shoulders.

If this was an act, he was good.

'There are . . . two different versions of the story.' He was standing with his back to the cold Rayburn stove that sat on a concrete plinth, probably where the old furnace had once been. His voice was as arid as cinders. 'The prosecution's submission was that Stewart had been in bed upstairs – alone – when the boys broke in.'

'Boys?'

'Glen and Jerome Smith, nineteen and seventeen. Travellers. Members of their family had been helping Stewart with his research into the links between the gypsies and the Frome Valley hop farms. He'd bought the boys drinks in the Hop Devil, paid them also in cash for their "research assistance" – mainly a question of finding Romanies who were willing to talk to him. But, according to the prosecution, the Smiths got greedy, and they came to believe he had a fair bit of money on the premises.'

Merrily looked around. No indications of wealth and no obvious hiding places in a circular room that didn't seem to have altered much from its days as the lower chamber of a hop-kiln. Its walls were of old, bare brick, hung with shadowy implements, non-culinary.

Romantic, maybe, but not an easy place to live.

'In their defence,' Mr Stock said, 'the Smith brothers told a different story which, to me, has more than a ring of truth. It certainly didn't do their reputation any favours. Basically, they admitted visiting poor old Stewart on a number of occasions at night to . . . administer to his needs.'

'You mean sexual,' Merrily said. 'For money.'

Next to her was a dark wood rectangular tabletop on a crossed frame which looked as if it had once been something else. A large-format book called *The Hop Grower's Year* lay face down on it. On the back of the book was a photograph of the author – small features under grey-white hair so dense it was like a turban. The photo was one of those old-fashioned studio portraits with a pastel backcloth like the sky of another world, and the face brought home to her the reality – and the unreality – of why she was here. For this was him: the kiln-house ghost.

Her first task: to determine whether it was reasonable to believe that some wisp, some essence of this person was still here. Madness. Even half the clergy thought it was madness.

'. . . Agreed they'd accepted money several times,' Gerard Stock was saying, 'for research and for giving him . . . hand relief, as it was described to the court. All rather sordid, but gypsies aren't squeamish about sex. As Stewart pointed out in his book, their society might be closed to the outside world, but it's very open and liberal when you're on the inside. Gypsy kids tend to get their first carnal knowledge at the hands of siblings, if not parents. Prudish, they're not, which is healthy in a way, I suppose – you won't find many Romanies in need of counselling.'

He inspected Merrily, as if checking how prudish *she* might be. No way could she align this Stock with the slick PR man described by Fred Potter, the reporter, and hinted at by Simon St John. He was just someone trying to rationalize the irrational, more scared by it than he'd ever imagined he could be. He'd told her frankly that Stewart Ash and he had never got on – Ash always blaming him for leading his niece into a world of ducking, diving and periodic penury.

*People will talk to you, as a human being*, the Bishop had said, meaning she came over as small and harmless – no black bag.

'Look . . . if you want to sit down over there . . .' Mr Stock indicated a chair pulled out from the table. 'I'm afraid Stewart really *was* found lying with his head almost exactly where your feet are.'

'I'm OK. Go on.'

'Well, he was wearing pyjamas. There was a lot of blood. His face was almost unrecognizable. We've scrubbed and scrubbed at the flag, but when the sun's in the right position you can still see the stains distinctly.'

Merrily made a point of not looking down, inspecting the upper part of the room instead. She'd been in hop-kilns before, and couldn't help noticing how basic this restoration had been – rough boarding fitted where once thin laths would have been spaced out across the rafters, supporting a cloth to hold the hops for drying over the furnace.

'The Smiths always fiercely denied killing him, insisting, at first, to the police that someone must have followed them in and done it after they'd left.'

'Any evidence of that?'

'Of sexual activity? Apparently not. When there was nothing in the forensic evidence, nothing from the post-mortem, to suggest Stewart had recently had sex, they panicked and one of them changed his story – claiming they'd come here to do the business and found him already dead.'

'That couldn't have helped them,' Merrily said.

'Finished them completely, far as the jury was concerned. Found guilty, sent down for life. They've appealed now – everyone appeals. Couple of civil-liberties groups assisting. Probably won't succeed, but I imagine one or two people in the area are getting a touch jittery about it. We certainly are.' He laughed nervously. 'If *they* didn't do it, who did? It's one thing to live in a place where a murder was committed; something else to live with the possibility that the murderer's still out there.'

'You think that's a real possibility?'

'Oh yes.'

He walked over to the wall, pulled down a wooden pole with a slender sickle on one end. Unexpectedly, the crescent blade flashed in the shaft of sunlight from the middle window. Merrily stayed very still as he hefted it from hand to hand.

'They used these things for cutting down bines. *I* sharpened it. I thought, they're not going to get me like they got Stewart. Ridiculous.' He shuddered, replaced the tool. 'I just don't trust the countryside.'

So why hadn't the Stocks sold the place and got out?

'I don't understand. Why would anyone want to get to *you?*'

'I—' He looked at her, as if he was about to say something, then

190

he hung his head. 'I don't really know. I just don't feel safe here. Never have. Lie awake sometimes, listening for noises. Hearing them, too. The country is—'

'What sort of noises?'

'Oh – creaks, knocking. Birds and bats and squirrels.' He shrugged uncomfortably. 'I don't know. Nothing alarming, I suppose. Except for the footsteps. I do know what a footstep sounds like.'

'You've actually heard footsteps?'

'Not loud crashing footsteps echoing all over the place, like in the movies. These are little creeping steps. Always come when you're half asleep. It's like they're walking into your head. You think you've heard them, though you're never sure. But in the middle of the night, thinking is . . . quite enough, really.'

It wasn't quite enough for Merrily. 'What about the furniture being moved?'

He looked up sharply. 'Oh, we didn't *hear* that happen. We had the table over the bloodstained flag – to cover it, keep it out of sight. We'd come down in the morning and find it was back where . . . where it is now. This happened twice. But we never heard anything.'

'And you talked about a figure? You said in the paper you'd seen a figure coming out—'

'Yeah.' He walked over to the part of the wall opposite the door. 'Coming out . . . just here. I said "a figure" because you've got to make it simple for these crass hacks – my working life's been about avoiding big words. But actually it was simply a . . . a lightform. Do you know what I mean?'

'A moving light?'

'A luminescence. Something that isn't actually shining but is lighter than the wall. And roughly the shape of a person. We'd finished supper . . . a very late supper; it was our wedding anniversary. And sudenly the room went cold – now *that* happened, that's one cliché that *did* happen. It's a funny sort of cold, you can't confuse it with the normal . . . goes right into your spine . . . do you know what I mean?'

'Yes, I do.' This was, on the whole, convincing. When you thought of all the embellishments he might have added – the familiar smell of Stewart's aftershave, that kind of stuff . . .

Merrily shivered again, glad she'd put a jacket on – to hide the Radiohead T-shirt, actually. She'd left the vicarage in a hurry – no breakfast, just a half-glass of water – throwing her vestment bag into the boot. Usually, she'd spend an hour or so in the church before a Deliverance job, but there'd been no time for that either.

'Mind you, it's so often like a morgue in here.' Gerard Stock folded his arms. 'And dark in itself creates a sense of cold, doesn't it? The living room through there's no better. That was formerly the part where the dried hops were bagged up, put into sacks.'

'Hop-pockets,' Merrily said.

'Oh, you know about hops?'

'A bit.'

'Stewart had absolutely steeped himself in the mythology of hops – not that there's much of one. He got quite obsessed over something that— I mean, it's just an ingredient in beer, isn't it? A not very interesting plant that you have to prop up on poles.'

'There was a hop-yard at the back here?'

'*Was*. The wilt got it.'

'Is that still happening?'

'I believe there are new varieties of hop, so far resistant to it. But it happened here.'

'You said you saw lights out in the hop-yard.'

'My wife. My wife saw them. I never have. That was the first thing that happened. It was soon after we moved in. Winter. Just after dusk. We'd brought in some logs for the stove, and she was standing in the doorway looking down the hill towards the hop-yard and she said she saw this light. A moving light. Not like a torch – more of a glow than a beam. Hovering and moving up and down among the hop-frames – appearing in one place and then another, faster than a human being could move. She wasn't scared, though. She said it was rather beautiful.'

'Just that once?'

'No. I suppose not. After a while we didn't— This might sound unlikely to you, but we stopped even mentioning those lights. When far worse things were happening in the house itself, I suppose unexplained lights in the old hop-yard seemed comparatively unimportant.'

'Hops,' Merrily said. 'When you say Stewart was obsessed by hops, you mean from an historical point of view, or what?'

'Well, that too, obviously. But also hops themselves. I wouldn't claim to understand what he saw in them. To me, they're messy, flakey things, not even particularly attractive to look at. But when we first took possession of the house, the walls and the ceiling were a mass of them: all these dusty, crumbling hop-bines – twelve, fifteen feet long – and the whole place stank of hops. I mean, I like a glass or two of beer as much as anyone, but the constant smell of hops . . . no, thank you. And when you opened a door, they'd all start rustling. It was like—' He shook his head roughly.

'Go on.'

'Like a lot of people whispering, I suppose. Anyway, we cleared out the bines. It felt as though they were keeping even more light out of the place. Some of them were straggling over the windows. The windows in the living room back there once looked out down the valley. Apparently.'

Through the central window in here she could see blue sky. Through the other two, blue paint. It probably hadn't even been this dark when it was a functioning kiln with a brick furnace in the centre.

'The barns,' she said.

He nodded.

'That's awful,' Merrily agreed, 'but I'm afraid it's not—'

'Your problem. No.'

'Have you talked to a solicitor?'

'I've talked to a lot of people,' Mr Stock said.

'Erm – that aroma of hops.' Merrily breathed in slowly, through her nose. 'I almost expected you to say you'd been smelling it again.'

She thought his eyes flickered, but it was too dim to be sure. He shook his head. 'No, nothing like that.'

'So . . . what about your wife?'

He was silent. His face seemed to have stiffened.

'I mean, how badly has she been affected? She saw the . . . light-form?'

'My wife . . .' He turned away, shoulders hunched. 'Won't talk much about it. When the hacks were here, we had to virtually manufacture some suitable quotes for her. Maybe she thinks it'll all just go away.'

'You mean she's not so scared . . .?'

'As me? Probably not. Obviously, neither of us likes the darkness – it's the kind of darkness you have to *fight*. And you lose. In here, a two-hundred-watt bulb's like a forty. Bills've been horrendous. But Stephie – perhaps she just doesn't believe Stewart would harm her. Also, more of a religious background than me. Catholic, lapsed. But it doesn't go away. Not like . . .'

Merrily smiled.

'I'm sorry, didn't mean to be insulting. I was raised in the C of E.'

'All I meant about your wife,' Merrily said, 'is that I think she should be here too, when we do whatever we do. As a blood relative of Mr Ash.'

'Well, she will be . . . She'll be here tonight.'

'Mr Stock,' Merrily said, 'if I could just make a point here. Unless you really think that for some reason it's important for this to be done at night, I don't necessarily think that's a good idea. I think it might be better for all of us' – *better for the Bishop, too* – 'if we said some initial prayers, perhaps a small requiem service for Mr Ash. Without delay.'

'*Now?*' He didn't quite back away.

'By daylight, anyway. Personally, I always think there's an inherent danger in making this all too—'

'Serious?' Almost snapping.

'Sinister. I'll probably need the book, but we can dispense with the bell and the candle.'

She could almost see his thoughts racing, something almost feverish in his eyes. *Did* he have plans to involve the media? Had something already been arranged for tonight?

He unfolded his arms. 'All right. I can call Stephie at work. Maybe she can take time off. How long will the exorcism take?'

'That might be too big a word for what we do. Not very long, I shouldn't think. Best to keep things simple. Oh – and I'd also want to ask the vicar if he'd like to join us. Two ministers are better than one in this kind of situation and it's usual to involve the local guy when possible.'

'St John?' Hint of a sneer. 'He won't want to know, tell you that now.'

'I'd like to ask him, anyway, if that's all right with you.'

He shrugged. 'Your show.'

'Yours, actually. And your wife's. And it would actually be helpful to have a few other people who knew your wife's uncle. Is there anyone you think—?'

'Oh no!' Both hands went up. '*Definitely* not! I don't want local people in here, I'm sorry. We don't exactly have any close friends in the area. I'd rather this wasn't talked about.'

'But you went to the *press*.'

'I was desperate. I've told you, I felt threatened. I didn't know who I could trust, especially after the vicar refused to help us. Bottom line is I don't want any of those people in here. All right?'

'OK. Erm, another point – at a service of this kind, we need to draw a line under the past. A big element is forgiveness. I think that means we're looking for some kind of reconciliation between you and Stewart, which of course has to be initiated by you.'

He laughed. 'I'd guess that for Stewart one of the best things about death would be never having to see Gerard Stock again. But . . . you know best.'

'Well, I don't really know anything for sure,' Merrily said. 'We're assuming Mr Ash is what you might call an unquiet spirit.' Huw Owen would call it an *insomniac*. 'Our fundamental purpose has to be to guide him away from whatever's holding him down here towards a state of—'

'Look!' He put his hands on his hips, faced her. 'Is this going to, you know, tell us anything?'

'I'm not a medium, Mr Stock.'

'What if Stewart's . . . spirit, whatever you want to call it, is unable to rest because it wants to get a message across? Like, for instance, that his killer's still out there.'

'Ah.' Merrily looked down at the flags. Around her shoes she could now make out the outline of what might have been a stain.

*Hidden agenda coming out at last?* 'Who's the killer, then, in your view?'

'I can't tell you that,' he said.

'Because you don't know. Or maybe you've got ideas?'

'I've got ideas. However, I might be open to legal action were I to share them with you, Mrs Watkins.'

'OK. What's the actual time now? I'm afraid I came out without my watch.'

He held his wrist up to the light. 'Just after ten minutes to ten.'

God, was that all? She needed breathing space, prayer space.

'Look, I'll call her now,' he said. Something seemed to have lifted inside him. 'Daytime. Yes. I should've thought of that. Daytime's much better.'

'And meanwhile I'll go down to the church, talk to the vicar and change. See you back here in . . . an hour, or less?'

'Yes. Fine. Thank you.'

They went back through the living room, the former hop-store, where any extra light not blocked off by the barns was absorbed by drab leathery furniture – Stewart's, probably. By the back door, Merrily turned, looked up at Stock.

'Could I just ask you – what do want this to achieve? I mean you personally?'

He wasn't ready for this one, didn't meet her eyes. Instead, he went to open the door for her, and the day came in like a golden cavalry of angels.

'I want things to be normal,' he said. 'That's all.'

She drove up to the minor road leading to Knight's Frome and was almost through the village before she realized that it *was* the village. The church was out on the edge, the other side of the river; the white house nearby could only be the vicarage. No car outside.

She pulled on to the verge, about fifty yards away from the church, took off her jacket, threw it over the passenger seat, lit a cigarette and checked her mobile for messages.

Just the one. *'Merrily. Sophie. I'm afraid I can't raise the vicar, but Bernard says go ahead without him. He'll clear up any political debris. Which I suppose means I shall.'*

Right, then. Merrily switched off the phone and put out her cigarette. As she was climbing out of the Volvo, she saw, through the wing mirror, a rusting white Astra pulling in about twenty yards behind.

It was already hot, and not yet ten fifteen. A single cloud powdered the sky over the church, which was low and comfortably sunken, with a part-timbered bell tower. Pigeons clattered in what had once been a hedge surrounding the vicarage.

From the car boot, Merrily pulled her vestment bag and a blue-and-gold airline case containing two flasks of holy water. She'd knock on the vicarage door, on the off chance someone was home. If not, she'd change in the church, always assuming it was open. Slinging the bags over her shoulder, she bent to lock the car. As she pulled out the key, there were footsteps behind her, a quiet padding on the grass. She turned quickly, wishing she hadn't locked the car.

She froze.

The mirage was wearing a black T-shirt, jeans and those same round, brass-rimmed glasses. She was aware of the birdsong and the laboured chunter of a distant tractor as they stood and stared at one another for two long seconds.

He shuffled a little, nodded at the Radiohead motif on her chest. 'So, er . . . what *did* you think of *Kid A*?'

'Erm . . .' Stunned, she put down the vestment bag, adjusted the plastic strap of the airline case. She swallowed. 'Well . . . you know . . . Jane was disappointed, but it kind of grew on me. Parts of it.'

'Uh huh.' He nodded. Then he said rapidly, 'Merrily, I'm sorry to, you know, spring out at you like this. I did come round to the vicarage quite early this morning, but—'

'That – that was you knocking?'

'But there was no answer, so I went to buy a Mars Bar and a paper at the shop, and then I ran into Gomer Parry and we talked for a few minutes and then . . . when I got back your car had gone.'

'I . . . overslept.' Merrily saw flecks of grey in his hair. It was shorter now; the ponytail hadn't come back. She bit down on her smile, shaking her head. 'You really choose your times, Lol.'

'Because you're working.'

'Yeah. I mean, could we . . .? I mean . . .'

'Gerard Stock, right?'

She felt the smile die completely.

'As . . . as you know,' Lol said hesitantly 'I'm about the last person to try and tell you anything about your job. But . . . don't do this.'

'What?'

'Put him off – could you do that? Stall him? Please?'

'I . . . No. No, I can't do that.'

'Then at least come and talk to the vicar,' Lol said.

# NINETEEN

# And then . . . peace

The vestry at Knight's Frome was about the size of a double wardrobe and didn't have a proper door, never mind a lock. She had Lol stand guard just inside the church porch while she changed.

This was getting crazy, too much to take.

She unpacked the bag: full kit plus pectoral cross.

Jane, of course – Jane would love this situation, wouldn't she just? All the times in the past six months the kid had asked innocently, '*Have you heard from Lol? Has Lol been in touch? Does Lol spend* all *his weekends in Wolverhampton . . .?*'

Merrily took off her skirt and T-shirt, got into the cassock that she never wore except for services, since a certain incident.

Laurence Robinson: palely sensitive singer-songwriter – in downbeat, low-key, minor chords. Unlucky in love, survivor of a nervous breakdown and some years of psychiatric treatment. '*Might well have become the next Nick Drake*' – *Q* magazine. If, like poor Nick, he'd killed himself, the less satisfactory route to immortality.

But Lol had survived to become droll, self-deprecating and, from Jane's point of view, dangerously cool. The stepfather to die for. And flirt with, obviously.

Merrily did up all the fabric-covered buttons of the cassock. Fortunately the kid was away. Her own feelings she could control, up to the present.

The last time she'd seen Lol Robinson had been on Dinedor Hill, above Hereford, where a few days earlier a young woman's death had been shatteringly avenged – leaving Lol in the middle of steaming wreckage with two people dead and one dying. Heavy trauma. In a still December dusk, before Christmas, the two of them had stood next to a fallen beech tree on the edge of the Celtic hill fort and looked down over the city, where steeples and the Cathedral tower were aligned under a shadow of cloud and the distant Black Mountains.

A prayer, a meditation, in remembrance of the victims and then they'd walked back down the hill, hand in hand. And then Lol, no big fan of organized religion, had told her he was wondering if there wasn't some middle way between spiritual guidance and psychotherapy . . . a new path, maybe. And they'd walked away to their separate cars and she'd known in her heart that they *would* meet again sometime, at least as friends, but that this wasn't the moment to allow things to go further.

Lol Robinson. Just about the last person she'd expected to meet today, materializing in a heat-haze at the roadside. And, more confusingly, revealed as one of the anti-Stock contingent warning her to back off.

Like she had a choice.

Abandoning attempts to contact Merrily, Lol had been on the road by seven a.m., knowing that if he didn't catch her before she went out, she could be anywhere in the diocese and there'd be no chance of talking to her until she arrived at Stock's tonight – by which time it would be too late.

'*I truly hope your friend has the sense not to get involved,*' Simon had said. And then, last night, Isabel: '*He gets things he can't put into words.*'

When he found Merrily had left the vicarage, he'd gone into Hereford, checked the Bishop's Palace parking area, then called the office to make sure she wasn't there. Mrs Hill remembered him but wouldn't tell him where Merrily had gone. She'd offered to pass on a message; Lol said it was OK, no problem. He'd decided to stake out the entrance to Stock's place, all day if necessary, to catch her before she could go in.

But he'd arrived back in Knight's Frome to find she was already there. Shoved the car into some bushes, gone running down the gravel track by the kiln, about to go and hammer on the door, disrupt whatever was happening . . . when the door had opened and she'd walked out—

—Followed by Stock: Merrily and Stock together. The first time he'd seen her in six months and here she was with Stock, who was looking, from this distance, as pristine as the husband in some old soap-powder ad, a man on the side of the angels. Merrily had been nodding to him – conveying understanding and sympathy – and at one point seemed about to take his hand. But then she'd turned and walked towards her car and Lol had sidled along the bushes, back to the Astra, to follow the Volvo.

When she'd parked close to Simon's church, it had seemed *meant*. He'd made his move. Shock value. It hadn't even been too difficult to persuade her to walk with him the few yards to the white vicarage.

Where it had all seized up like an overwound clock.

The door had been opened by a woman of about sixty-five, in a pinny, who told them the vicar and Mrs St John had gone shopping in Hereford. They always went on a Tuesday, see, because it was a slack day in the city, between the weekend rush and the Wednesday market. Easier for Isabel to get around town, the housekeeper had explained. Easier for Hereford if Isabel was in a good mood, she'd implied.

Blank wall. How could he persuade Merrily to back away from this when he couldn't tell her any more than she already knew?

Like, what was the *real* reason Simon had refused to exorcize Gerard Stock's kiln? It was becoming clear that there was more to it than the vicar's declared belief that Stock was fabricating the whole thing either to screw Lake or milk some money out of an inheritance he couldn't sell.

Isabel had implied, *Trust him*. Lol *didn't* trust him – too many suggestions of instability there. And if anybody could spot instability, it was Lol.

He stood gazing down the aisle of Simon's very basic little parish church – no fancy carving, no stained glass – towards the altar. The truth was he had no reason to trust anyone in the clergy, except—

He turned at the swish of the velvet curtain, and she emerged from the vestry like she was stepping out of a dress-shop cubicle.

Apparently, some men were kinky for women priests, like with nurses and meter maids, because of the uniform. But when Lol watched Merrily stepping into the nave, in her cassock and white surplice, it only made him scared.

Stock was very bad news. Simon knew more than he was saying.

Lol . . . was just a guy who wrote songs.

She gave him a small smile. She looked like a child playing dressing-up – the silly-vicar outfit. Then he saw the lines at the corners of her eyes. New lines.

'Don't look so worried,' Merrily said. 'It's what I do.'

Walking back to the car, she sensed his discomfort. She didn't think he'd ever seen her in the full gear before. Now she was a priest, with an aura of black-and-white sanctity; not a woman any more. There was even a new stiffness, a formality, in the way he spoke to her.

'I just think,' Lol said, 'that perhaps you should ask him why he can't sell the kiln – just to see what he says.'

'Lol, that's . . .' It was childish, but she did it: pushed herself onto the bonnet of the Volvo, with the surplice fanning out around her. 'That's irrelevant, isn't it? I've heard all about him, I know what kind of man he's been, I realize he probably went to the papers for the express purpose of stirring it for this guy Lake, or capitalizing on it in some other way. But it – it doesn't change the fact that I do think he's got some trouble here. If I had to like and admire all the people I was asked to help, then . . . well, I'd be having a lot of days off, you know?'

Lol kept peering up the road and Merrily knew he was hoping to delay things until Simon St John got back from Hereford.

'If you're thinking about me . . .' She felt suddenly edgy and embarrassed and delved in her bag for cigarettes. 'I'm protected. From above, by the Bishop. And . . . from further above. I mean . . . you know . . . come in with me, if you want.'

'In?'

'When we do it. I don't imagine Mr Stock would mind. I wouldn't.'

Merrily bit her lip. She hadn't thought about that, she'd just said it. She thought about it now. The standard advice to Deliverance ministers was to have a few good Christians around at an exorcism, including a second minister, if possible. Back-up. What kind of Christian you could call Lol she had no idea, but he was actually *living* here, he actually *knew* Gerard Stock . . . and, however he felt about dogma and the clergy generally, she knew by now that she could trust him. All the way.

The car bonnet was warm under her cassock. She looked at the fragmented cloud over the little church of Knight's Frome and then back at Lol. He was coincidence. Charismatic Christians, like the infamous Nick Ellis, saw every small coincidence as a pointer from God.

'Look, there are two ways of looking at an exorcism of place,' she explained.' It's not waste disposal, pest control, Rentokil, whatever . . . it's helping a dislocated essence . . . spirit . . . soul back on to the path. What I mean is, maybe we're doing this less for Gerard Stock than for Stewart Ash.'

'Whom neither of us knew.'

'Every day, in crematoria all over the country,' Merrily said sadly, 'duty clergy conduct funerals for people they never knew, in front of grieving relatives they've only just met. Maybe we'll meet him today.'

Lol looked up, startled.

'It's been known for the subject of an exorcism to make one final appearance,' she said. 'And then . . . peace.'

'*Hi!*' Stephanie Stock sprang up from the old leather sofa. 'It's really, *really* nice to meet you at last.'

A central ceiling light-bowl and two lamps were on in the living room at the kiln-house. It still didn't get close to summer daylight. The walls had been painted white, but the furniture was old and dull. Unexpectedly, the brightest thing in the room was not the white-shirted Stock, but his wife. She squeezed Lol's hand, lingering over it, smiling into his eyes.

'I've kept on saying to Gerard, hey, bring him over! I had the first Hazey Jane album years ago, when I was at school, and I'm just *dying* to know what you've been up to since. It's not as if . . . I mean, you're looking *good!*'

Lol blinked. Stephie Stock wore a short white summer dress, like a low-cut tennis frock. She was considerably younger, conspicuously more animated than her husband who, close up, was looking as worn and grey as you might expect after last night in the Hop Devil. *She's a mouse*, Simon St John had said dismissively. *What other kind of woman would Stock marry?*

'Steph, this is Merrily Watkins,' Stock said. This was a different Stock, sober and withdrawn. He had raised no objections to Lol being here, expressed no particular surprise that Lol and Merrily were acquainted. The feeling Lol had was that Stock was just relieved it wasn't Simon.

Stephanie slowly let go of Lol's hand, running her warm, slender fingers to the tips of his. She looked at Merrily and her wide mouth flexed into a one-sided grin. 'You know, it's still really strange to see a woman with the full—'

'Steph was brought up a Catholic,' Stock said quickly. 'Convent girl.'

'And, let me tell you, you don't escape *that* easily,' Stephanie said ruefully.

Lol was studying her. He still couldn't be sure. He remembered that his Lady of the Bines had had darkish hair, stringy. Or maybe just wet. Stephanie's hair was golden brown, shorter, looked altogether healthier. As did the woman herself: smiling, confident, in essence not the keening banshee wreathed in dead bines. But then nor was this the Stephanie Stock he'd been told about.

'Coffee?' Stephie offered. 'Beer? Wine?'

Merrily shook her head. 'Maybe afterwards.'

'*Afterwards!* Wow. This is really going to happen, isn't it?'

'Of course it is!' Stock snapped. Then he straightened up, pulling his shoulders back.

'Poor love,' said Stephie. 'He gets so spooked. One thing about Catholicism, it teaches you not to be *too* afraid of what goes bump, right? Look, Mary—'

'Merrily.'

'Right. Sorry. Look, am I . . . suitably dressed for this? I could go up and change.'

'You'll be fine,' Merrily said. 'I was saying to Gerard earlier, I don't like this kind of service to seem sinister, because it's basically about liberation. We're asking God to give you back your home and at the same time free Stewart's spirit from this earth and let him go into the light. In fact, it could be that when we've finished, you'll notice a difference here.'

'What, lighter?'

'Let's just see what happens.'

'Wow,' said Stephie.

She seemed very young to Lol. Although she had to be over thirty, she still had the confidence of inexperience – innocence, even. He couldn't understand, seeing her now, why she'd kept such a low profile locally, why neither Prof nor Simon had ever met her. It couldn't be that Stock had kept her penned up like some exotic pet; she didn't seem the kind of person you could treat that way. And anyway, she was the one who went out to work while *he* stayed at home.

'So, how much time have you got?' Merrily asked her.

'Well, I'm currently temping for this big car-dealer and it's *quite* busy . . . but I guess I've got two hours. Is that enough? I mean, I can phone them . . .'

Let's see how it goes. Erm . . . Stephanie, I've already asked Gerard, but is there anything else *you* think I ought to know?'

'About Uncle Stewart?'

'About anything.'

'Well, not really, I'm just – I'm just glad you're doing this for Gerard. I'm glad someone's taking him seriously.'

'But how do *you* feel about it?'

'How do I *feel?*'

'You don't seem too scared.'

'What's to be scared about? He's my uncle. My charming, camp old Uncle Stew.'

Merrily smiled tentatively. Lol could see her dilemma. Trying to put them at their ease, saying she didn't want it to be sinister. But this girl seemed more at ease than the exorcist.

'OK, then,' Merrily said. 'Let's make a start. I want to organize some things in the kiln area. What I'd like the two of you to do is sit quietly and think about . . . about what this is for. Think about

Stewart. Think about *helping* Stewart. Maybe recall some happy memories of him?'

Stock snorted mildly.

'*I* can think of some,' Stephie said.

'Good.' Merrily beckoned to Lol. 'And, Gerard . . . maybe you can think in terms of reconciliation, like we talked about.'

The airline bag was open at her feet. She brought from it one flask and placed it on the table.

'This was once a hop-crib,' Lol observed. 'See the crosspieces? There'd be like a big canvas hammock thing hanging here.'

'Gosh,' Merrily said, 'you know your way around hops, then.'

'There's a museum down the road. They've got several cribs.' Lol sensed that Merrily was less sure about all this now, after meeting Mrs Stock. He wondered if he should tell her about the Lady of the Bines.

He looked around the circular wall of old bricks, some of them actually blackened by the furnace. It was like being in a big chimney and nearly as dark. Apart from the stove and a tall, juddering fridge everything in here seemed to be still hop-related. Even the shelves on which crockery was piled looked old and stained.

'OK,' Merrily said quietly. She looked around the kitchen, then took down one of the coffee cups, put it in the centre of the table. She bent and took a small canister out of the airline bag, stepped back, closed her eyes.

Lol moved away, looking down at his trainers. He couldn't quite believe he was doing this. He felt privileged to be here, but that didn't make him feel any closer to her. She was The Reverend Watkins.

Merrily said softly, 'We come to bless this place and pray that the presence of God may be known and felt in it. We pray that all which is evil and unclean may be driven from it. As a sign of the pouring forth and cleansing of God's Holy Spirit, which we desire for this place, we use this water. Water has been ordained by Christ for use in the sacrament of Baptism . . .'

She poured water from the flask into the coffee cup, whispered to Lol, 'We're guarding against anything else that might be around.'

He nodded. The fridge rattled.

'Lord God Almighty, the Creator of life, bless this water. As we use it in faith, forgive us our sins, support us in sickness and protect us from the power of evil.'

Merrily made the sign of the cross, opened her eyes and picked up the small canister. She took off the lid: salt. She blessed the salt, sprinkled some on the water. 'Water for purification,' she explained softly to Lol. 'Salt representing the element of earth. A formidable combination. In any religion.'

Merrily stepped back from the table. 'You up for this, Lol?'

Lol nodded.

'Think calm.'

'Sure.'

Merrily put her right hand briefly over his. Her fingers were cooler than Stephie Stock's. The light, at close to noon, glanced off her pectoral cross. Lol thought, unhappily, of vampires.

'I think we can bring them in now,' Merrily said.

TWENTY

# The Metaphysics

It was particularly during a Requiem Eucharist that images of the departed had been known to appear, sometimes standing next to the priest. They would usually look solid and entirely natural, an extra member of a select congregation.

Sometimes, as the rite was concluding, they would smile.

*Gratitude.* The received wisdom was that the hovering essence, presented with an overview and offered assistance, would usually recognize the pointlessness and the tedium of haunting. '*Nine out of ten cases,*' Huw Owen had told his students, '*they're not going to resist you. They'll not fight. Most times you'll get a welcome like an AA van at a breakdown on the M4.*'

And so sometimes they appeared. Smiling.

Actually, this had never happened to Merrily – either that or she wasn't sufficiently sensitive to have noticed. Always nervous enough, anyway, before it began. Who was she to go dancing on the great boundary wall?

'*Never, never, never show nerves,*' Huw Owen would warn his students. '*All the same, don't let them think it's a bloody tea party.*'

A balancing act, then, these dealings with the dead.

Initially, Merrily had prepared for a Requiem for Stewart Ash. The dining table, the converted hop-crib, was to be her altar. On it, she'd set out wine in a small chalice she kept in the airline bag and communion wafers in a Tupperware container.

And then – woman priest's privilege? – she'd changed her mind.

'*Question of sledgehammer and nuts,*' Huw had said more than once. '*You don't even get out the nutcrackers if you can squeeze it open between finger and thumb.*'

So she ended up telling the Stocks she didn't think there were enough people here for a valid requiem – not enough committed Christians (she didn't actually say that). She'd explained to them that she proposed, in this first instance, to offer a prayer commending the soul of Stewart Ash to God, and maybe a prayer of penitence for his killer, followed by a blessing of each room, a sprinkling of holy water.

A Eucharist for Stewart would be the next step if all this proved ineffective.

Gerard Stock had nodded: whatever the priest thought best.

Stewart's book on hop-growing still lay on the table. Merrily was unsure about this. Perhaps it should have been taken away; it represented his work, part of his attachment to the earth which it was now necessary to break. His other known attachment had been to young men; how strong was that now? The pull of earthly obsession: weakened, but not necessarily severed by death.

In the otherwise-silence of the kiln, the growling refrigerator was an unstable presence; its noises varied and fluctuating, as if it were trying to tell her something.

'Our Father . . .'

It remained the most powerful prayer of all, an exorcism in itself. This was how they all should begin.

How you took it from there . . . well, there was always an element of playing it by ear, by sensation, by perception – always remembering that, in the end, it wasn't you doing this; you were only the monkey, you didn't have any powers. You could only respond to signals.

In the kiln-house kitchen, the sun shone through as best it could; the fridge still shivered. The timing seemed about right: nearly noon, the time of no shadows. Nothing sinister.

Merrily offered the prayer conversationally, with only a little extra stress on the crucial line ' . . . and deliver us from evil.'

*Us.*

Four of them in a semicircle in this half-lit brick funnel. Gerard Stock with shoulders back, eyes closed, lips invisible in the beard. But she knew now that those moist, rosebud lips were clamped tight on

Gerard's hidden agenda – oh, there *was* one, something raging inside him, like the fire in a brick furnace. Merrily was sensing anger and frustration made unbearable by fear. Even Fred Potter, the journalist, had picked up on that. But fear of what, exactly?

'For ever and ever. Amen.'

'Amen.' An echo from Gerard Stock and Lol.

'Sorry.' Stephanie giggled. 'Amen.'

Convent girl, huh?

There was – and face it, it could be relevant – almost certainly a problem in Stock's marriage, no concealing that. Stephanie's eyes were wide open, the twist of a smile on her lips – not taking this seriously and not caring who knew. There were perhaps twenty years between her and Gerard. Maybe he'd been slim and successful when they'd met – glamorous parties, cool contacts. Now he was looking florid and finished – career-wise, anyway.

Stephanie was standing between the two men, but closer to Lol than to Stock, their shoulders sometimes even touching, and Stephanie's was bare, her strap slipping, and Merrily felt a stirring of—

Whatever the emotion was, she squashed it. She was the priest here.

All right: the metaphysics.

Had the transition of Stewart Ash simply been too sudden? Merrily caught a cold, shocking image of the spirit flung out, flailing and struggling, as the skull went *crack, crack, crack, crack* on the flags, an implosion of shattered bone and dying brain cells. Huw Owen again: '*Most hauntings are imprints, caused by the atmospheric shock of sudden death. Your imprint is no great problem – a tape loop, a magic-lantern show. It's with the insomniacs and the sleepwalkers you need a bit of one-to-one.*'

Or was there, as Gerard Stock had suggested, a powerful, residual sense of injustice because the nature of the crime had been misunderstood, the wrong people convicted?

Merrily prayed silently to understand, to get a feeling of what was needed, and then intoned aloud: 'O God, forasmuch as without You we are not able to please You, mercifully grant that Your Holy

Spirit may, in all things, direct and rule our hearts, through Jesus Christ our Lord. Amen.'

'*Amen*' – Stock and Lol. Nothing from Stephanie – she looked hazy, suspended in the column of the midday sun. Next to her Stock seemed dense, leaden. Was Stephie already building another life for herself, away from here? And where would Stock be if she left him? This was, after all, her house.

'At this point, we'll have . . . a period of quiet,' Merrily said. 'If that's OK.'

'Sure.' Stephanie's voice was crisp, and Stock glared at her, like a disapproving father, but said nothing. Merrily turned her face away from a collision of light beams emanating from the tiny trinity of windows, and looked down at the flags where Stewart Ash had been taken down, and then closed her eyes.

Greyness.

*Stewart . . .?*

Careful not to reach out for him or call him back. It was about being receptive. She kept her eyes shut, allowing any unfocused thoughts to drift away. There was a metallic shudder from the fridge, then comparative quiet.

In her head: *Stewart . . . don't be afraid to let go. I know it's very confusing for you. You must have been utterly terrified – and outraged. You must have felt, along with the pain, a terrible sense of betrayal. Perhaps you're still feeling that. But there's no progression without forgiveness. Try to release your resentment, the sense of injustice. We're with you. God's with you. Let go. Please.*

She lifted her face towards the central window, now framing the full sun, an orange glow through her eyelids. Appealing now to Jesus Christ to come into this place, because it was always better to welcome in the light than simply drive out the darkness.

'Jesus, we ask that Stewart might be free of all earthly bonds. Free to go into the light and the warmth and the sublime reality of Your eternal love.'

She bent her head.

The commendation came next: a call to the spirit, in the name of its creator, to leave this world. An appeal to God to send His angels to meet Stewart, guide him home. Something told her to omit the prayers of penitence for the killers. Keep the killers out of this, whoever they might be.

Next: the cleansing.

'Father, You have overcome the power of death, strengthen us now with Your spirit and make us worthy to perform correctly the blessing of this home. Let evil spirits be put to flight and may the angel of peace enter in. In the name of Jesus Christ our Lord. Amen.'

Lol thought, *This has to be a scam. But who's using who?*

He watched the priest, his friend, through half-closed eyes – her hands together, the tips of her fingers parallel with the bridge of her nose, the pectoral cross catching the sun through the inverted V of her black-sheathed forearms.

Doing her best for these people: no scam, no sham.

*Merrily. If there was only . . .*

Stephanie Stock's bare arm slid up against his own, again. He tried not to think about it.

Merrily opened her eyes to a light lancing through the central window, was momentarily blinded and felt an intense heat all around her, as though there was still a furnace in here and the doors had been flung open.

She felt sweat on her forehead and a harsh rawness at the back of her throat. She fought the urge to cough.

*Oh God.*

It had caught her off guard. Until then, there'd been nothing: a growing sense of anticlimax, no sense at all of Stewart Ash. Now the kiln seemed claustrophobic, suddenly stifling, and when the fridge grated like a passing container lorry she realized what she'd forgotten to do.

She saw Lol watching her, a flaring of alarm in his eyes. She put a hand to her throat, swallowed. Her throat was burning. She was gasping on a stench of gunpowder and rotten eggs and the smell of cheap fireworks from when she was a kid, fierce and searing as a jet from a blowlamp, hot breath of hell.

# TWENTY-ONE

# The Brimstone Tray

Sulphur?

As she struggled for breath, she was asking herself *Is this real?* and turning to glance at the stove in case it was pumping black smoke.

It wasn't.

Then Lol's voice: 'Merrily . . .?'

His normal voice – no wheezing, no coughing. He wasn't getting it; none of the others were. She began to utter in her head the lines of St Patrick's Breastplate: *Christ be with me, Christ within me . . .*

Hand to her mouth, she crossed the room and pulled open the door leading to the hop-store-turned-living-room. Rushed in and grabbed a wooden dining chair to wedge the door open.

*Christ behind me, Christ before me . . .*

Huw Owen coming through. '*What've you forgotten, Merrily?*' Huw putting them through their paces in a Victorian chapel in the Brecon Beacons. '*DOORS! All of them . . . cat-flaps . . . cupboards . . . open and wedge . . . firmly . . . come on . . . it's not a joke! Do it! Open and wedge! OPEN AND WEDGE!*'

She dragged open the door of the huge old fridge . . . a cold, white bulb blinking on inside. Then the heavy door began to swing back on her and she pulled down two bottles of Chardonnay from a shelf inside to set on the flags and wedge it open. When she turned back into the room, Lol was moving towards her.

She croaked, *'No!'*

One of them must have jogged the hop-crib table, because the chalice instantly tipped over and the red wine began dribbling into the cracks in the wood. Why hadn't she put away the sacrament when her plan for the Eucharist was shelved? Why hadn't she done that?

She snatched the flask of holy water to safety as the spilled wine dripped down and pooled in the outline of Stewart's bloodstain on the flags below.

When she could manage to speak, she said, 'It's all right. Not what I thought.' It came out both hoarse and shrill, no kind of reassurance.

What she meant was: *It's not Stewart Ash.* Something was loose, playing with her senses, but it wasn't Stewart.

'Grant, Lord—' She broke off and took a deep breath, watching droplets of holy water from her flask twinkling in a channel of sunlit dust. 'Grant, Lord, to all who shall work in this room that in serving others they may serve you.'

But in *her* voice, the recommended blessing for a kitchen sounded as potent as watered milk. She'd blown it. She'd been unprepared, had come in here, unforgivably, as a partial sceptic, her mind absorbed by something else, and whatever was here had known it and gone for her and only her.

*What is it? What's here? Who* are *you?*

She cleared her throat, hands trembling around the flask. She could still taste the sulphur. Stephanie Stock was watching her, amused, as if storing up the whole event for a party anecdote – Stephie's famous impression of the loopy woman who thought she was an exorcist.

'The living room?' Merrily asked.

Gerard Stock nodded. He kept glancing at the small pool of wine on the floor, now a stain on the stain.

Coincidence? *Coincidence!*

But Stock was sweating, wet patches the size of dinner plates under each arm. *I've lost it,* Merrily thought in horror, *I've let it through. It's come through me!* She was aware of Lol watching her intently, as if there were only the two of them here. Lol, who rarely judged, almost never condemned – because he was a loser and a wimp, he'd insist.

Stock began to lead the way into the living room. She stopped him, a hand on his arm.

'Gerard, I think I . . . need to go first.'

How ridiculous *that* must sound from the smallest person in the place, and plainly incompetent. She saw Stephanie suppressing a smile, with difficulty. '*And then she goes, "Gerard, I need to go first . . ."*' *Howls of laughter.*

In the living room, the only smell was a faint aroma of mould from the two heavy armchairs and the lumpy sofa. Merrily called on God to unite all who met therein in true friendship and love. It sounded trite and hollow. She saw a wood-burning stove and over it a framed photograph of a younger, slimmer Gerard Stock with two people she didn't recognize and the late Paula Yates.

'Bedroom?'

Of course, she should already have known where it was. She should have been up there already. Should have been all round this place.

'Through that doorway,' Stock said, 'and the stairs are on the left.'

'Thanks.'

The bedroom was instant vertigo.

Lol came last up narrow, wooden stairs that were not much more than a loft-ladder, passing through where a trapdoor must once have been, joining the Stocks and Merrily on the platform where hops had once been strewn to dry. It was floorboarded now, but it didn't feel safe, somehow – probably because you emerged gazing straight up into the apex of the big timber-lined cone, the witch's hat of the hop-kiln, all that dark-stained wood rising to the wind-cowl.

Someone had switched on lights – metal-cased bulkhead lamps bolted to the sloping walls. Just as well; the only windows up here were like the arrow slits in a church belfry. On a stormy night, Lol thought, it would be either wildly exhilarating or terrifying.

'We've got quite a lot to do up here yet, as you can see,' Stephie Stock said, as if they were potential buyers viewing the place.

'Shut up,' Stock rasped.

What a turnaround: bullying, boisterous Stock become all edgy and anxious. Swaggering Stock turned sober and tense. His back to the wall. His back to Stephanie. And to the bed.

The only furniture – apart from a modern sectional wardrobe, its louvred doors now being flung open by Merrily – was a double bed without a headboard, still unmade. Stephie went to sit on the edge, crossing her legs. Lol was aware of a slightly sour amalgam of scents, including – he was fairly sure – hops. Hop-pillows, maybe . . . or the residue of millions of rustling hop-cones?

*Sleep? Fucking hops work like rhino horn. Fact, man. Me and Steph, we're living in an old kiln, walls impregnated with as much essence of hop as . . . as the beer poor old Derek can't pump. My wife . . . leaves scratches a foot long down my back.*

The other Gerard Stock. The one who did not bring his wife to the pub.

From the bed, Stephie gave Lol a conspiratorial smile. Her golden-brown hair was in provocative disarray, her eyes still and knowing; she was now the only one of them who appeared entirely relaxed.

Lol smiled briefly, uncomfortably, turned away to look for Merrily. Something had happened to her down there, maybe just an attack of nerves, and she'd temporarily lost the plot and then recovered. Now she was moving round the sloping wall with her bottle of holy water, and she looked forlorn, vulnerable, like a child.

He felt useless – worse than that, faithless; he didn't believe this exercise was helping anyone, least of all the murder victim. He didn't know why they were here at all, what Stock was after. He felt superfluous and embarrassed, an extra. He felt Merrily was being made a fool of – joke vicar. He felt an irrational and unusual urge to put a stop to this melodrama, demand an explanation – what Prof Levin, with style and finesse, would have done ages ago.

Only two people were taking this seriously now, pressing on.

'Stand up,' Stock said tiredly to his wife. 'Please.' It was clear to Lol now that, whether Stock believed in the power of the Holy Spirit or not, this was something he still very much wanted to happen.

Stephie came languidly to her feet, stood by the bed. Merrily moved into the centre of the room, and they formed a small circle, the boards creaking.

'Lord God, our Heavenly Father,' Merrily began, 'you, who neither slumber nor sleep, bless this bedroom . . .'

Water flying again like a handful of diamonds. The bedroom formally cleansed and blessed, but nothing, for Lol, seemed to have changed. At the end, flask in hand, Merrily stood at the top of the stairs. Her forehead was gleaming. She faced the bed.

'Lord God . . .' Her voice was louder now, Lol sensing defiance. 'Holy, blessed and glorious Trinity.' With her right hand, she made the sign of the cross. 'Bless . . .' Another cross. ' . . . Hallow and . . .' Again. ' . . . Sanctify this home, that in it there may be joy and gladness, peace and love, health and . . .'

The noise came out of her surplice. She drew a wretched breath and closed her eyes, carried on.

' . . . Goodness, and thanksgiving always . . . to You, Father, Son and . . .'

It didn't stop; it shrilled and shrilled, piercing the prayer like a skewer, over and over.

' . . . Holy Spirit,' Merrily's voice shook. 'And let Your blessing rest upon this house and those who . . .'

With a peal of pure joy, Stephanie Stock reeled back on to the bed. A shoulder strap slipped all the way down, half uncovering a breast, with two livid scratches forking up from the nipple.

'I think you'd better answer that, vicar,' Stephie squeaked, convulsed. 'It might be God.'

The minutes after midday. A brutal sun. Global warming: so un-British. *Christ*. Merrily pressed her back against the ouside brick wall. She'd pulled off her surplice, and she buried her face in it for a moment.

'I'm so . . . so sorry.'

'These things happen.' Stock was beside her, sour with sweat.

'I switched it off. I was sure I'd switched it off. I distinctly remember switching it *off*.'

'You don't understand.' He leaned his face into hers, suddenly almost aggressive, his eyes red and squinting in the full sun. 'These . . . things . . . happen *here*. They happen. I thought you *knew* this stuff.'

In a pocket of Merrily's cassock, the mobile phone went again.

'Answer it,' Stock said. 'Go on . . . answer it. There'll be nobody there. I guarantee there'll be nobody there.'

'Don't go,' she said. '*You* don't have to go.'

Skirt hitched up, shoes kicked off, she was squatting at the top end of the bed, her head back against the wooden wall. She raised a hand. A double click, and two of the bulkhead lights went out, leaving only the one over the bed still on. She was very much in shadow now, and there was no doubt at all any more. She was from his dreams.

'Look.' She was reaching down now, to the side of the bed, then underneath. A rustling. 'Remember . . .'

Merrily had left very quickly, making the sign of the cross, then almost stumbling down the stairs, with her phone still screeching; she couldn't seem to switch it off. Stock was right behind her, Lol making to follow, until Stephanie had called him, sultry siren in a slippery tennis dress, slipping off. She glanced down at it, then back at Lol, blinking hard as if trying to wake up. 'He won't come back,' she said rapidly. 'He'll see the vicar off and then he'll go to the pub, drink himself stupid, come crawling home in the early hours. Collapse on the couch, like the sad pig he's become.'

'I'm sorry?'

'What's to be sorry about?' She lifted a forefinger, crooking it at him. Baring her teeth. She said something he didn't understand, which began with a sibilance. '*Usha . . .*' He didn't like it. He started down the wooden steps. It was the sound that made him look back – he had to – and he saw her haloed under the utility lamp, fingered by the slitted sunlight.

Garlanded again.

'. . . *A kam mangela.*'

She was breathing hard, her breath surrounding her, it seemed, like a chilled mist.

'I warn you,' he heard, 'don't say no to me now.'

The voice came rolling warmly out of the phone, so loud Merrily had to pull it away from her ear. Stock heard and *hmmmph*ed and walked away, shoulders hunched, hands in his pockets.

'Merrily! Wasn't sure I'd get you. Knew you couldn't be in church, this time of day. Least, I *thought* you wouldn't.'

'Charlie?'

'You had lunch yet, Merrily?'

'Charlie, listen, I'm with somebody right now.'

'Oh, I *am* sorry,' Charlie Howe said. 'Just that I've got some information for you, my dear. Talking to Brother Morrell last night about this sad business with the Shelbone girl, and a couple of things rather clicked into place, and I thought . . . *I* thought you ought to know about them, that's all. And, of course, I also thought you might like some lunch.'

'Well, thanks, but . . . actually, I don't feel too hungry. I was thinking of— Well, it's been a complicated morning.'

'A coffee, then. I'll be here for an hour or so yet.'

'Where?'

'The Green Dragon in Broad Street? If you don't manage to show up, look, give me a ring tonight – though I'll be out till quite late. But you might find it worth your while, I'll say n'more than that.'

'All right. Thanks. That's very good of— Charlie, how did you get this number?'

He laughed. 'That Sophie Hill's a hard one to crack, but her armour's got its weak points, like everyone else's. My, you do sound a bit subdued, girl. Nothing else going wrong in your life, is there? Can't take on *all* the troubles of the world.'

'No.' She saw Gerard Stock walking back towards her and realized how badly she wanted to get away from here. 'I'll try and get over there. I'll do my best.'

Gerard Stock had made an irritable circuit of the yard and, as he came beefing back, she saw the change at once and got in first.

'Gerard, would you do something for me?' He looked suspicious. 'If I give you some prayers, would you be sure to say them?'

He stared at her.

'I've got some appropriate ones printed out in a case in the car,' she said. 'I'd like you to say them at specific times. Both of you, if possible. If not . . . one of you will do.'

'That going to help, is it, Merrily?'

For the first time, he was challenging her. Was this because she'd quite clearly messed up in there? Or was it because his wife was no longer with them? *So where is she? And where's Lol?*

'It *will* help,' she assured him. 'But I'd also like to come back again. I think this may need more attention. And more preparation than we were able to give it today.'

'You and liddle Lol?'

She sighed. 'Like I said, I've known Lol Robinson for some time, although I didn't know he was living here. He's somebody I can trust, that's all.'

'He's a bloody psychotherapist. That why you brought him? Just tell me the truth.'

'No. Really.' She shook her head. 'And he's not yet officially a therapist, anyway.'

'So what was it that made up your mind?'

'I'm sorry?'

'What I'm asking—' he tilted his head, scrutinizing her sideways '—is what happened, liddle lady, to make you decide I wasn't after all just a scheming townie trying to shaft his neighbours?'

'I'd never decided you were.'

'Because something *did* happen in there, didn't it?'

She took a breath. 'All right, something happened.'

'So tell me. I've got to go on living here.'

'Tell *me* something. What does sulphur mean to you?'

'Why?'

'Is there anything around here that might . . . or might once have . . . released sulphur fumes?'

'Not now. Not any more.'

'Meaning what?'

He shrugged. 'I'll show you.'

She followed him back into the kitchen. The gloom seemed at once oppressive – or was she imagining that? He went straight to the wall where the implements hung, brought down a short pole with what looked like an ashpan from a stove or grate attached. He sniffed at it.

'Can't smell anything now.' He thrust it towards her. 'Can you?'

'What is it?'

'Was known, I'm told, as a brimstone tray. Used for feeding rolls of sulphur into the furnace.'

'Why'd they do that?'

'Some sort of fumigation. It also apparently made the drying hops turn yellow, which the brewers preferred for some reason. Made the beer look even more like piss, I don't know. I don't think they do it any more.'

'Would sulphur have any special interest for Stewart Ash? Can you think of—?'

'You're saying you smelled sulphur.'

'Quite powerfully.'

He tilted his head again. 'Fire and brimstone . . . Merrily?'

'That was what it smelled like. Could be argued it was subjective, I suppose.'

'Oh . . . *subjective*.' Stock held the wooden shaft of the brimstone tray with both hands like a spade. 'There's a good psychologist's word. Why don't we ask *Lol* what he thinks?'

'Like you said, things are inclined to go awry in there. A few minor elements which, when you put them together, suggest a volatile atmosphere. Not necessarily connected with the murder of Stewart Ash.'

'Volatile?'

'I *would* like to come back, Mr Stock.' She saw Lol in the doorway. 'What about tonight?'

'To do what?'

'There are quite a few things—'

Stock hurled the brimstone tray to the stone with cacophonous force.

Merrily flinched but didn't move. '—Things we can still try.'

'You don't really know what the fuck you're doing, do you?' Stock snarled.

Lol walked in.

'No . . . geddout . . . both of you.' Stock picked up the chalice and the Tupperware box of communion wafers, shoved them in the airline bag, tossed the bag to the flags near Merrily's feet. 'You're a waste of time, Merrily. I heard you were a political appointment.'

Merrily bit her lip.

'Been better off with the fucking arse-bandit,' Stock said.

'Well . . .' Lol picked up the bag. 'This is actually quite reassuring. For a while back there, I was almost convinced you'd been possessed by the spirit of a nice man.'

Stock looked at him silently, then back at Merrily. He was waiting for them to go.

Merrily paused at the door. 'I'd like to come back. If not me, then someone else.'

'Geddout,' Stock said.

## TWENTY-TWO

# Barnchurch

'Merrily!' Charlie Howe stood up, tossing his *Telegraph* to one of the tables in the hotel reception area. He was wearing a creased cream suit and a yellow tie with the lipsticked impression of a woman's red lips printed on it, as though it had been kissed. He looked genuinely delighted to see her. Putting an arm around her shoulders, he steered her into the coffee lounge. 'What a job you've got, girl: devils and demons on a wonderful summer's day.'

She'd shed the cassock, was back in the T-shirt. 'How d'you know I wasn't doing a wedding?'

'Contacts.' Charlie tapped his long leathery nose.

'Sophie'll be mortified.'

'When Mrs Hill wouldn't tell me where you were, look, nigh on forty years of being a detective told me a wedding wasn't an option.'

'Smart.'

'Pathetic, more like.' He pointed to a window table. 'Over there?'

'Fine.' She followed him. 'Why pathetic?'

''Cause I miss it, of course.' They sat down. 'Don't let any retired CID man tell you he don't miss it. I'm even jealous of my own daughter.'

'*I*'m jealous of your daughter,' Merrily said ambivalently.

Charlie laughed and patted her wrist. 'Scones,' he said. 'I feel like some scones. You don't diet, do you?'

'My whole job's a diet.'

'Scones, my love,' he called to the waitress before she'd even made it to the table. 'Lashings of jam and heaps of fresh cream. And coffee.'

'Just spring water for me, please, Charlie, I'm afraid I don't have very long. I'm sorry.'

She and Lol were due to meet at the Deliverance office in the gatehouse at five. Lol had said he had things to tell her, but neither of them had wanted to hang around Knight's Frome. It was a blessing, in Merrily's view, that someone like Lol had been there, seen the way it had gone, the two faces of Gerard Stock.

'We better get down to it, then,' Charlie said. 'Brother Shelbone.' He clicked his tongue. 'Not wrong about that one, were you, Merrily? As for the little lass . . .'

'Little lass?'

He looked pained. 'Give me some credit, girl. This suicidal Shelbone child and that kiddie getting messages from her dear dead mother, courtesy of Allan Henry's stepdaughter – one and the same, or what?'

'You never retired at all, did you?'

'I tell you, my sweet,' said Charlie Howe, 'the longer you live in this little county, the more you wonder how anybody manages to keep anything a secret. There are connections a-criss-crossing here that you will not believe.'

'Really?'

'She was very lucky, mind – the child. The version I heard, the mother only found out because she'd got a headache herself, and saw the aspirins were down to about three in the bottom of the jar. Another half-hour and your colleague over in Dilwyn would've had a *very* sad funeral.'

'I didn't know that.'

'No cry for help, this one. Kiddie must've been messed up big-time. You were dead right, and Brother Morrell was dead wrong, out of touch.'

'He didn't know the full circumstances.'

'Nor wanted to, Merrily, nor wanted to. I tell you another thing – nobody who was at the Christmas Fair's likely to forget that girl of Allan Henry's. Jesus Christ, no . . .' He looked suddenly appalled.

'Oh, I *am* sorry. Easy to forget what you do, Reverend, when you're out of uniform.'

'Doesn't offend *me*, Charlie, long as it's not gratuitous. Keeps His name in circulation.'

Charlie Howe raised both eyebrows. The scones arrived. 'Put plenty of jam on,' Charlie said. 'You'll be needing the blood sugar.'

Then on to David Shelbone. 'Got to admire him, really,' Charlie said. 'Sticks his neck out for what he believes. You know anything about listed buildings?'

'I live in one.'

'So you do.'

'Frozen in the year 1576. I pray we never get an inspection, because my daughter's created what she calls The Mondrian Walls in her attic . . . all the squares of nice white plaster and whatever between the beams are now painted different colours.'

'Good example,' Charlie said. 'Most listed-buildings officers would let that one go, because you can always paint them over again in white. Brother Shelbone – forget it. A stickler. Told one of our lady councillors she had to take down a conservatory porch she'd put on her farmhouse. When the good councillor tries to square it with the department under the table, it gets leaked to the press. Red faces all round. That's David Shelbone: staunch Christian, not for sale.'

'And that's bad, is it?'

Charlie grinned. 'Oh, it's not bad. It's good, it's remarkable – and that's the point. In the world of local government, a very religious man who cannot tell a lie or condone dishonesty of any kind *is* remarkable.'

'Meaning a pain in the bum.'

'Correct. It was widely thought that when the councils were all reorganized, he'd get mislaid, as it were, in the changeover. But he survived.'

'*He looks after the old places, makes sure nobody knocks them down or tampers with them.*' Hazel Shelbone in the church. '*They offered him early retirement last year, but he said he wouldn't know what to do with himself.*'

Merrily licked jam from a finger. 'His wife indicated he'd been under some pressure.' Migraines, Hazel had explained. 'Maybe that's not been a happy household for a while.'

She didn't look at Charlie Howe, helped herself to a second scone. Anything said to her by Mrs Shelbone ought to be treated as confidential; on the other hand, Charlie expected give and take. After forty years in the police and now local government, it would be how his mind worked.

'Pressure,' he said. 'Oh, no question about that. Brother Shelbone's under serious pressure. Over Barnchurch alone.'

'The new trading estate, up past Belmont?'

'Source of much weeping and gnashing of teeth,' Charlie confirmed.

'Well, it *looks* awful,' Merrily said. 'There was a time, not too many years ago, when Hereford used to resemble a country town. I mean, do we really need a supermarket every couple of hundred yards? DIY world? Computerland? It's like some kind of commercial purgatory between rural paradise and traffic hell.'

'My, my.' Charlie added cream to his coffee.

'Nothing personal.'

He leaned back, hands clasped behind his head. 'What do you know about the origins of Barnchurch? The history of the site.'

'Fields and woodland, home to little birds and animals.'

'Gethyn Bonner? You know about him?'

'Not a thing.'

'Thought you'd know about Gethyn Bonner. He was a preacher. Came up from the Valleys in the 1890s, sometime like that.'

'Ten a penny,' Merrily said with a small smile.

'Tell a few of my colleagues that. Tell English Heritage.'

'I'm not following.'

'Gethyn Bonner was an itinerant firebrand preacher with a big following, who came out of Merthyr Tydfil and decided Hereford was the land of milk and honey.'

'As you do.'

Charlie drank some coffee. 'Hadn't got a chapel of his own, but a good Christian farmer, name of Leathem Baxter, had a barn to spare. A few local worthies, including a craftsman builder, all gathered round and they put a big Gothic window in the back wall, and in no time at all Leathem Baxter's barn was a bona fide church.'

'Barnchurch.'

'Exactly. Well, in time, Gethyn Bonner falls out of favour, as these fellers are apt to do, and moves on up to Birmingham or back to the Valleys, I wouldn't know which, and Leathem Baxter dies and the church becomes a barn again, and the Gothic window gets bricked up . . . and it's all forgotten until the Third Millennium comes to pass.'

'And, lo, there came property developers . . .' said Merrily.

'Barnchurch Trading Estate Phase One. Should be completed in time for Christmas shopping. Phase Two, however . . . that's the problem. Nothing in its way except a derelict agricultural building, not very old – Victorian brick – and falling to bits.'

'I see.' Merrily poured some spring water.

'Well, even before work started on Phase One, the developers had been assured by the Hereford planners that there'd be no bar at all to flattening this unsightly structure – which, as it happens, also blocks the only practical entrance to the site of Phase Two. Reckoning, of course, without Brother Shelbone.'

'Suddenly, I like him a lot.'

'Who helpfully points out that, although the building itself is of limited architectural merit and not, in fact, very old, its historical curiosity value makes it a monument well meriting preservation.'

'It's fair enough,' Merrily said. 'They should've consulted him before they started.'

Charlie leaned forward. 'Merrily, nobody in their right mind consults David Shelbone, they just pray he's otherwise engaged at the time. Brother Shelbone gets involved, it's gonner cost you: time and money. And the stress factor.'

'So he's put a preservation order on the Barnchurch. Can he do that on his own?'

'What he does is gets it spot-listed. It then goes to the Council, with a report and a recommendation from Shelbone. Well, this is seen as a very significant project, with considerable economic benefits for the city, and the Council, by a small majority, goes against the advice of the Listed Buildings Officer and declares that the Barn-church can be flattened.'

'I don't remember reading about this in the papers.'

Charlie smiled thinly. 'The authority has a certain leeway these days to conduct business not considered to be in the public interest less publicly.'

'Which stinks, of course.'

'But is quite legitimate. Anyway, David Shelbone isn't a man to be put off by petty local tyranny. He goes directly to the body responsible for conservation of historic buildings – English Heritage – and *they* step in. So then—'

'Which way did you vote, Charlie? Just so we know where we are.'

Charlie Howe grinned, whipped cream on his teeth. 'I abstained, of course.'

'Ah.'

'Didn't really think I knew enough about the issue.'

'Why do I find that hard to believe? So, can English Heritage overrule the Hereford Council?'

'Not just like that. It'll have to go to Central Government for a decision. Because what had happened, see, was that the developers had already lodged an appeal contesting the scheduling of an old heap of bricks as a building of historical merit. There'll be a public inquiry before an inspector from the Department of Culture – or the Ministry of Arty-farty Time-wasters, as one of my colleagues likes to call them.'

'Which will take time to organize, I suppose.'

'Months and months – and then more months waiting for a decision. Even if they get the green light at the end of the day, it's going to've cost the developers a vast amount of money, what with all the delays and their contracts with prestigious national chains on the line. In the meantime, some of those firms are bound to go elsewhere. The situation is that Barnchurch Phase Two's already looking like a financial disaster on a serious scale.'

'And all because of one man.'

'You got it.'

'Who are the developers?' Merrily asked.

'Firm called Arrow Valley Commercial Properties.'

Merrily shook her head. 'Not heard of them.'

'Subsidiary of Allan Henry Homes,' said Charlie. 'You with me, now?'

Merrily put down her scone.

Charlie Howe's arms were folded. She studied his face, tanned the colour of lightly polished yew. She knew very little about him, either as a councillor or a former senior policeman, but if she had to guess why he was going out of his way to feed her controversial information, she wouldn't get far beyond the fact that he clearly enjoyed causing trouble – stirring the pot.

'Gosh,' she said.

'You talk for a bit and I'll listen.' Charlie glanced around. 'You're all right: no witnesses.'

'Well . . . phew . . . where do we start? David Shelbone may well have got himself crossed off Allan Henry's corporate Christmas-card list.'

Charlie poured himself more coffee. 'You ever actually come across Allan Henry, Merrily?'

'He doesn't go to *my* church.'

'He's an ambitious man, and a very lucky man. Things've fallen his way. Just a moderately successful small-time housebuilder for quite a few years, then his horizons got rapidly wider. Took over Colin Connelly's little workshop development beyond Holmer when Colin had his accident. And then things started falling into his hands. A few slightly iffy Green Belt schemes, but he got them through. One way or another.'

'Erm . . . would you say he found success in ways that might have interested you in your former occupation?'

Charlie Howe said, very slowly, 'I am saying nothing that might incriminate any of my colleagues on the council.'

'I see,' said Merrily.

Charlie drank the rest of his second cup of coffee.

'So David Shelbone could be getting in quite a few people's hair.'

'I think I said as much earlier.'

'Why are you telling *me* all this?'

He cupped his hands over his eyes and nose, rubbed for a moment before bringing them down in the praying position.

'Got nobody else to tell any more,' he said. 'Last thing Annie wants is the old man on her back. Most of the people I mix with . . . well, you never know quite who you're talking to, do you?'

'What happened to your . . . to Annie's mother?'

'Oh, it was a police marriage. Average life expectancy five years. Better nowadays, actually. Now there are plenty of professional women around, so you can take up with one who understands all about funny shifts and late-night callouts and having to cancel your fortnight in Ibiza because you're giving evidence at Worcester Crown Court. Back then, it was this huge majority of full-time housewives and mothers who didn't understand at all.'

'I'm sorry.'

He grinned. 'Don't be bloody sorry, vicar. I've had a lot more fun in twenty-five unencumbered years than I had with her. Anyway . . . I met you there at the school and I liked your attitude and I thought we were likely to be on the same wavelength on certain matters. And then that little girl taking the overdose – that rather clinched it.'

'Well . . . thanks.'

'I don't much like Brother Henry,' he said. 'I don't like him as a businessman or as . . . as a man.'

'Because?'

'Because . . . well, he's ruthless and he's vindictive, for starters. The rest I'd need to think about.'

'And Layla Riddock's not even his daughter.'

'He brought her up, though,' Charlie said, 'didn't he?'

'I don't know.'

'Me neither, really. I don't know how long he and Shirley Riddock have been together. But it makes you think, don't it just?'

'He must've been very disappointed when certain people failed to persuade David Shelbone to take early retirement.' Merrily broke off a small piece of scone and then put it back on the plate. 'Oh hell, this is getting ridiculous.'

'Nothing's ridiculous,' said Charlie Howe. 'Hello . . .?'

Merrily looked up. A man had come in through reception and was walking directly towards their table.

'Well, well,' Charlie said.

Merrily recognized Andy Mumford, Hereford Division CID. Being promoted to Detective Sergeant in the twilight of his career must have given him new heart, because he'd lost weight. Sadly, it had made him look even more lugubrious.

'Andrew Mumford, as I live and breathe.' Charlie beamed but didn't stand up. 'This your local now then, boy, in keeping with your new-found status?'

'Hello, boss,' Mumford said heavily.

'Dropped in for some career advice, is it? Stick it as long as you can, I'd say. Half these so-called security jobs, you're just a glorified caretaker. Have a seat.'

'I won't, thank you, boss. In fact, it was actually Mrs Watkins I was looking for.'

'Well . . . you can study for the ministry up to the age of sixty,' Merrily told him, 'but at the end of it, caretakers still earn more money.'

Mumford didn't smile. 'Mrs Watkins, Mr Howe's daughter and my, er, governor would like it a lot if you could come to her office for a discussion.'

'Oh.' She sat up, surprised. 'OK. I mean . . . Just give me half an hour. Because I do need to pop over to *my* office first.'

'No, Mrs Watkins,' Mumford said. 'If you could come with me *now* . . .'

'Only somebody's going to be waiting for me, you see.'

'If it's Mr Robinson you mean,' Mumford said, 'we've already collected him at the Gatehouse.'


Mumford's unmarked car was parked in one of the disabled-driver spaces at the top of Broad Street. He drove Merrily across town and entered the police car park, from the Gaol Street side.

It was the pleasantest time of day, layered in shades of summer blue. Mumford didn't have much to say. He'd evidently been warned not to spoil the surprise. But he'd said enough.

Annie Howe had been given a new office. Merrily couldn't remember how they reached it. She didn't notice what colours the walls were. She didn't remember if they'd taken the stairs or the lift.

She felt like she was walking on foam rubber through some bare, grey forest in the wintry hinterland of hell.

Howe's office door was pushed-to, not quite closed; they could hear voices from inside.

Mumford knocked.

No answer.

He pushed it a little. 'Ma'am?'

Inside, the room was dim, the window blinds pulled down. Merrily could see a TV set, switched on. The picture on the screen looked down at a group of people standing about awkwardly, looking at each other as if they didn't know what to do next.

'. . . oom?' a woman said.

One of the others, a man, nodded and walked across the screen and out of shot.

'Better wait here a moment, Mrs Watkins,' Mumford said.

On the TV screen, nobody moved for a second or two, then a woman, much shorter, followed the man.

The sound was not very good, with lots of hiss; you could hear the voice, although you couldn't see who was speaking.

The voice said awkwardly, 'Gerard, I think I . . . need to go first.'

# TWENTY-THREE

# Poppies in the Snow

'Sit down, Merrily.' Annie Howe switched off the TV. She went over to the window and reeled up the blind, revealing a small yard and the back of the old magistrates' court.

It was possibly the first time she'd said 'Merrily', rather than 'Ms Watkins'. Using the first name the way police talked to suspects – patronizing, to make them feel lowly and vulnerable.

Right now, it was entirely superfluous. Merrily sat in an armless chair, one with aluminium legs. She felt sick, wishing she'd said no to the scones. And to Gerard Stock.

The last time she and Annie Howe had been face to face, Howe had said, '*I don't know how you people can pretend to do your job at all. To me, it's a complete fantasy world.*'

Merrily put her hands on her knees. 'Where's Lol?'

'Robinson's being interviewed separately, by Inspector Bliss.'

'Frannie Bliss?'

'If you only knew,' Howe said, 'how badly I'm wishing there was something I could charge you with.'

She was in white blouse, black skirt. Her ash-blonde hair was tied back. She was wearing maybe a little eyeshadow, mauvish. If she'd worn glasses they would doubtless have been rimless, like a Nazi dentist's – Jane's line. Merrily thought, *There is absolutely nothing I can tell this woman that she's going to believe.*

She bit her lower lip. The whole office was painted butcher's-shop white. There were no plants, no photographs. The calendar did not have a picture; it was framed in a metal box, and you expected it to have ten days in a week, ten months in a year. Andy Mumford sat in the corner by the door, presumably in case Merrily should try to do a runner.

'Still,' Annie Howe said, 'I suppose by the time you leave here, you'll at least be in a better position to assess your own degree of responsibility.' She ejected the videotape from the machine. 'At some point you and I will have to watch it all the way through, to verify certain points. Did you know you were being recorded?'

'No. It never even occurred to me.'

'Two cameras.' Howe went to sit behind her desk, which was away from the limited distraction of the window. 'Semi-professional: one digital, one hi-eight. Both of them wedged between timbers in the ceiling. It's a fairly primitive ceiling, with small holes and gaps all over it, so all he had to do was prise up a couple of boards in the bedroom and position the cameras underneath – one wide-angle, one focused on the table. Why do *you* think he wanted it all on tape?'

'I don't know.'

'Of the suggestions so far, the most likely is that he may have been planning to make the material available for some future television documentary. I'm told he's always looking to the main chance. Perhaps – let's not overestimate the man's intelligence – perhaps he thought he might even capture something looking vaguely para-normal.'

'Media-oriented, I suppose. He's a . . . professional PR man.'

'Really? According to people in the village, he's a washed-up drunk.'

'He wasn't drunk when I was with him,' Merrily said.

'No, amazingly, he wasn't. So you didn't even hear the cameras? One was quite old and noisy.'

'There was a big fridge, which made a lot of noise. If I heard anything, I would have assumed it came from that.'

Howe thought for a moment, expressionless. It was hard to credit she was probably only thirty-two years old.

'Doesn't seem to have been a very successful exorcism, does it, Ms Watkins? Or are they always like that?'

'They're all different, in my limited experience. But no, it wasn't as . . . productive as I might have hoped.'

'Depending on how one interprets the word "productive".'

Merrily winced.

'What time did you leave?'

'I'm not sure exactly. It couldn't have been long after midday. I'd suggested we might go back tonight.'

'He didn't seem to take that proposal terribly well.'

'No.' Merrily was looking down into her lap. Her hands were on her knees, but they wouldn't stay still.

'My impression from the tape is that he'd about had enough of you.'

'Yes.'

'He described you as amateurish.'

'I remember exactly what he said.'

'You and Robinson left at the same time?'

'Yes.'

'Where did you go?'

'I drove back to Hereford. I had an appointment to meet someone at the Green Dragon.'

'Who?'

'You know who; your dad.'

'Why?'

'Why don't you ask him?'

'I'm asking you.'

'It was in his capacity as a school governor. He rang me while I was at Knight's Frome to tell me he had some information relating to an attempted suicide by a young girl whose parents thought she was . . . spiritually troubled.'

Howe's top lip lifted in disdain. 'And was this attempted suicide before or after you were called in to assist this child in her alleged religious distress?'

Merrily didn't answer.

'Really not your week, is it? Did you go directly to the Green Dragon?'

'No, I went to the Deliverance office first. I parked on the Bishop's Palace forecourt which, as you know, is only a couple of minutes' walk from the Green Dragon.'

'Was Robinson with you?'

'He followed in his own car. We had a brief discussion, and then I had to go and meet your father. Lol and I agreed to meet up afterwards.' She shook her head. 'Can't get my— I can't believe how quickly this all happened.'

'If it's any help, the videotape shows that it happened precisely eleven minutes and fourteen seconds after you and Robinson made your last appearance on the tape.'

'Useful, that videotape.' Merrily moistened her parched lips.

'From our point of view, it's unique. Like being handed a case gift-wrapped with a pretty bow on top.' Howe stood up, looking down on Merrily. 'We can even say that it was approximately sixteen minutes after the event itself when Gerard Stock telephoned here, asked to be put through to CID and baldly informed DC Little that he'd just slaughtered his wife.'

It was an interview room with a tape machine, for suspects, and that didn't help. DI Francis Bliss was about Lol's age, with red hair, a Merseyside accent and a chatty manner, and that didn't help either.

It all took Lol back to when he was twenty, a baby rock star . . . the accused. '*So hard to tell with young girls these days, isn't it, Laurence? How old did you* think *she was?'* Stitched up by the police and a ruthless bass-player called Karl, and by the parents of a nice girl called Tracy Cooke. Prelude to the great psychiatric symphony.

'Listen, I'm gonna get yer another cup of tea,' DI Bliss said.

'I'm all right, thanks.'

'You're not, you know. You're in shock. Be a shock for anybody.' Bliss perched on a corner of the interview table. 'Sorry about this room, but I'm not based here, so I've not gor an office of me own. Known Merrily long?'

'Just over a year.'

'And you two just met up in the village this morning, after not seeing each other for a few months, and she told you what she was doing and she asked you to go in with her, yeh?'

'I know that sounds . . .'

Bliss put out placatory hands. 'I'm not trying to catch yer out, Lol, I'm just trying to get the basic picture, that's all.'

'I was worried about her doing it,' Lol said.

'Because of what you knew about Mr Stock?'

Lol nodded.

'That's fair enough, I'd've been a teensy bit worried meself after reading that stuff in the papers . . . and the local vicar himself refusing to have anything to do with him.'

'It was the vicar who suggested I should try and talk her out of it.'

'Was it now?'

'He was suspicious of Stock's motives. But Merrily doesn't like to prejudge people.'

'She's a very nice person,' Bliss agreed fervently. 'I was there during that thing, back before Christmas at . . . Oh, what was that little church called? Anyway, she was giving it a spiritual clean-out after this bugger broke in and hacked up a crow all over the altar. She wasn't very well that night, mind.'

'I wasn't there.'

'She was with this priest looked like an old hippy. Hugh some-body. He took it over in the end, 'cause she wasn't well.' Bliss had a gulp from a can of Diet Pepsi. 'See, unlike the Snow Queen in there, I've gorra very open mind about all that stuff. Comes with being raised a Catholic in a big Catholic city. You're a Christian yourself, obviously.'

'I'm not sure what I am,' Lol admitted.

'Just a good friend of Merrily's, then, Lol.' Bliss put down the can. 'Listen, pal, I do know a bit about what happened to you way back, and I accept you may've had a bad time with coppers in the past . . . but I do like Merrily and I fully understand the problem she'd got with this guy. And I know it's her job, and I realize that after that stuff in the papers there was no way she could duck out of it.'

'No.'

'So, you've gorra believe me when I say I'm not trying to stitch her up, I'm not trying to stitch either of yer up – it's just we've got a feller down the cells putting up both hands to the big one and, before we start talking seriously to him, we want as much background as we can get. Make sense to you?'

Lol nodded. He decided that, for Merrily's sake more than his own, maybe he should open up a little to this cop. To a point . . . a point stopping well short of the Lady of the Bines.

'Sorry,' he said. 'I just—'

'You're all right, pal. Take your time.'

'Truth is, I was on edge from the minute we went in there. I mean, I didn't think – not in a million years – that the guy was going to do anything like . . .'

'Goes without saying.'

'But everybody who'd had anything to do with Stock was on about what a conman he was, and a manipulator, and how he'd drop you in it without a second thought. Also, I'd seen him in the village pub a couple of times when he was well pissed. Had a big chip on his shoulder about this bloke Adam Lake – virtually suggesting he was behind Stewart Ash's murder, rather than the two lads who went down for it.'

'Let's not open that can of worms for the time being, eh, Lol?'

'I was just worried he might try and involve Merrily in that.'

'How?'

'I don't know, but she doesn't like to turn away from anyone.'

'So what was he like when you and Merrily went along today?'

'Not himself. I mean, he couldn't've been nicer.'

'Why was that, you reckon?'

'Well, it *might* have been genuine. Maybe he was serious about needing an exorcism, and he didn't want to put her off or make her suspicious. That was what I started to think, but now . . . I suppose that'd be for the tape, wouldn't it? Like, if he was videoing the thing, he'd want to appear on it as a sincere and honest man, genuinely concerned about what was happening in his house.'

'That's a good point, Lol.' Bliss thought about it. 'Mind, he wasn't being very appreciative at the end, was he, when he threw yer out?'

'But he'd got it all in the camera by then, hadn't he? Everything that counted. The Deliverance stuff. He could just have wiped the end of the tape afterwards.'

'True. Why'd he turn nasty, you reckon? Apart from his wife's attitude.'

'I don't think there *was* anything apart from that. Stephanie started taking the piss, so Stock took it out on Merrily.'

Bliss nodded. 'Certainly the times you see him looking at her you can tell he's trying to keep his temper – or something. But then, she was a lot younger than him. And clearly not too worried at being in a haunted house. Or was that bravado?'

'She was a Catholic, like you. Protected. She said earlier – maybe before we went into the kitchen – that she didn't think Uncle Stewart would do her any harm.'

'Oh, we're not scared of ghosts, us Catholics?' Bliss blew out his lips. 'News to me. How did Merrily react to the wife?'

'Tried to ignore it. Just carried on.'

'A true professional.'

'A good person,' Lol said. 'Doing the best she could.'

'You're fond of her, aren't you?' Bliss smiled. 'Who wouldn't be, eh?'

Lol said, 'You haven't told me exactly what he did.'

'How he killed her?'

Lol looked at Bliss: pale skin, freckles, an unusually small nose.

'What happened when you all went upstairs, Lol.'

'Well, just . . .'

Lol had a terrifying thought: the only cameras in the bedroom were the ones under the floorboards, pointing downwards, but suppose their microphones had picked up the voices from above, during Merrily's blessing of the upstairs room? And during what happened afterwards, when Merrily had followed Stock downstairs. If there *was* anything on the tape, the quality would be terrible. But they could work on that. Someone like Prof Levin could clean up the thinnest of recordings.

' . . . Just more or less what happened in the kitchen,' he said. 'With different words.'

He *could* tell Bliss about Stephie's implicit invitation. But it sounded too incredible, unless you knew about the Lady of the Bines incident. Which he'd also kept quiet about. Which he hadn't even told Merrily about.

Lol blanked it out. He was terrible at cover-ups. He would look furtive, he'd sweat.

Bliss said, 'Nothing happened up there you think might throw more light?'

'Not . . . not that I can think of.'

'You wanna see the tape, Lol?'

'Not really.'

'Don't blame yer. But . . . I think you're gonna have to. I think we're gonna have to take the both of you through it. I'm sorry.' Bliss thought for a moment, then sighed. 'Look, all right, I'll be frank wid yer – he's not saying a lot.'

'Stock?'

'In fact, the bugger's not saying a thing. Won't see a solicitor, won't make a formal statement, just sits there like some bloody big Buddha.'

'But he phoned you to confess . . .'

'Oh aye. When we get there, he hands us the videos. Looking relieved, if anything. He won't talk about it, though, won't explain. That's why you and Merrily are so important to us at the moment.'

'I see.'

'Don't tell the Snow Queen I told you that.'


Annie Howe said, 'Have you heard of the case of Michael Taylor?'

'Yes.'

*She's loving this*, Merrily thought. *A case on a plate.*

*Me in the toaster.*

She was desperate for a cigarette, but she wouldn't give Howe the satisfaction. She was also desperate for silence, somewhere to collapse and think and, if necessary, scream. Nothing made any sense. Nothing had made sense for days. She felt a welling hatred for Gerard Stock and a bitterness towards Simon St John who had known enough to shut the door in his face.

'Happened near Barnsley, in Yorkshire.' Howe was back behind her desk. 'In the mid-seventies. I know most of the details because of the pseudo-Satanist person we found in the Wye last year. I called up some background on Satanism and related issues, and this case was the first to come up on the screen.'

Merrily closed her eyes and inhaled on an imaginary cigarette.

This was one of Huw's cautionary favourites, which Howe would just love relating.

'Michael Taylor was thirty-one, a good Christian, a family man – and a member, with his wife, of some local religious group. At some point, for reasons I've never found entirely understandable, he came to believe he'd been taken over by the Devil.'

Howe had a set of files on her desk. She opened one and extracted a cellophane folder.

'Two church ministers agreed that Taylor appeared to be possessed by evil, and they spent all night trying to exorcize him, claiming to have expelled – I think – forty demons – the statistical exactitude here obviously adding important credibility to what most people might consider an inexact science. However, Taylor left the priests early the following morning, went home—'

'I *know*,' Merrily screwed up her eyes in anguish. 'I know what he did, there's no need to—'

'He went home and, with incredible savagery, attacked his wife with his bare hands.'

'Yes . . .'

'He tore at her skin, ripped out her tongue. And her eyes.'

Merrily leaned her head back, stared at the ceiling.

'Eventually, she choked to death on her own blood,' Howe said.

'And Taylor claimed, in his statement to police—' Merrily's voice was starved; she couldn't look at Howe '—that he loved his wife very much but there was an evil inside her that had to be destroyed.'

'Not, I think it's fair to say, the Church's finest hour.'

'Exorcism of a person is a complex and dangerous process,' Merrily said. 'But this . . . this case wasn't anything like that.'

'Wasn't it?'

'It wasn't an exorcism. I made that completely clear to Mr Stock from the start. I even decided to hold off the customary Requiem Eucharist because it might look too much like Christian magic. It was prayer, that's all – prayer as the first stage in dealing with a suspected spiritual presence, there being no reason to suspect any demonic infestation.'

'Let's go back to Taylor,' Howe said. 'Found not guilty by a jury for reasons of insanity. Caused quite a stir, didn't it?'

'What *should* be said about that verdict . . . although Michael Taylor had been, by all accounts, a friendly and popular man with no history of violence, nobody – not the judge, nor the jury, nor the media – seemed prepared even to consider that he might actually have been possessed by a metaphysical evil.'

'He was considered insane.' To Howe the difference between insanity and possession would be indiscernible. 'His mental decline appears to have coincided with his taking up membership of a Christian group. His recourse to almost unimaginable violence immediately followed his so-called exorcism by two Christian ministers, isn't that true?'

Merrily could only nod, knowing now where this was going – a goods train with a toxic cargo inexorably picking up speed, and nothing she could do to stop it.

Howe was still flipping through the file on her desk. 'I'm trying to find what the local bishop said at the time.'

'I can tell you more or less exactly what he said.'

'Here we are . . . "Exorcism is a type of ministry which is increasingly practised in Christian churches. There is no order of service for this; it is administered as the situation demands. Clearly a form of ministry which must be exercised with the greatest possible care and responsibility." '

'But this was *not*—'

'Ms Watkins, the tape clearly shows the sacrament laid out on your impromptu altar, and the sprinkling, by you, of water, which I assume is what you regard as *holy* water.'

'The sacrament wasn't even used, it was—'

Annie Howe wasn't listening; she was back into the report, flipping pages.

'Yes . . . the Taylor case was also commented on by the then Archbishop of Canterbury, Donald Coggan, who said, I quote: "We must get this business out of the mumbo-jumbo of magic. I do not see exorcism as something set off against and in opposition to medicine. Far from it. I think there are many cases where the more rash exorcists have bypassed the work of psychiatrists." ' Howe looked up. 'Partly as a result, I believe, of the Taylor case, there was a re-examination by the Church of the usefulness of exorcism and how such disasters might be avoided in the future. As a result, the guidance now to exorcists is that they should always work with community psychiatric resources. Is that correct, Ms Watkins?'

'Before an exorcism is carried out on an individual, it's recommended that they should be seen by a psychiatrist, to make sure they aren't, for instance, schizophrenic. Yes.'

'And when an exorcism takes place, it's advised that a qualified psychiatrist should be present. Is *that* correct?'

Merrily sighed. 'Yes.'

Howe rearranged the papers in the report, applied a paper clip and slipped them into the folder. She smiled pleasantly at Merrily.

'So, is your idea of deploying community psychiatric resources – in carrying out a ritual that might loosely be described as "mumbo jumbo" at the behest of a notoriously unstable, possibly alcoholic, individual – to take along with you—'

'That's not what—'

'—take along with you, as your expert medical consultant, a former psychiatric patient with a police record?'

'You stay the fuck away from me!' Stock screamed. 'You do not come near me!'

He was backing into shot. His shirt had come out of his trousers. The sweat patches under his arms were the size of hi-hat cymbals, Lol thought.

And it was all so beautifully bright. This was what video did; it compensated for the conditions. Clear and clinical, then, even if the quality was not great; Bliss had said these were quickly-made VHS copies of the two originals. The one they were looking at was wide-angle, evidently shot from a camera position just above the fridge. The constant picture included all of the table and an area of flagged floor about three feet around it.

On the table were Stewart Ash's book on hop-growing, and a wine stain.

Franny Bliss froze the tape.

'I think, boss, that this bit gives the lie to the theory that this whole thing was like some big theatrical production . . . that he even had an idea how it was gonna end. Whatever she's doing now, you can tell he's not expecting it.'

'Not necessarily,' DCI Howe said. 'We can't even see Stephanie at this point. We don't know that she's doing anything. She might not even be there. This could be part of his act.'

'He'd have to be bloody good.' Bliss started up the tape again.

Stock was shaking. He just stood there trembling, almost full-face to the camera. His beard was shiny with sweat and spittle.

The fridge noise was rumbling out of the TV speaker. Lol thought of rocks before an avalanche. He thought of Stock in the seconds before he'd spouted a gutful of sour beer over Adam Lake. He prayed that both Stock and his wife would be out of shot when the killing happened.

'If I didn't know the circumstances, I'd say he was shit-scared,' Bliss said. 'What would he be scared of, Merrily? What could she be doing that would put the fear of God into him?'

'I couldn't give an opinion on that.' Merrily's voice was all dried out.

'We're looking for ideas, that's all,' Bliss said. 'Doesn't have to be a thesis.'

Merrily had been placed near the covered window, DCI Howe standing next to her chair like the angel of death. They'd brought Lol into the room, but only just, seating him near the door, between Frannie Bliss and the other detective, Mumford; he couldn't even exchange glances with Merrily.

'Not saying much, is she, young Stephanie?' Bliss said. 'She still taking the piss? Is she taunting him, you reckon? What's she doing, Lol? What d'you reckon?'

Lol said nothing. Why should Bliss think *he* would know? Had he given something away, with a reaction, an expression? Had Merrily told them that Lol and Stephanie had been alone together, upstairs, not long before the killing?

'Bearing in mind that her body was unclothed,' Bliss said, 'when we found her.'

'I don't . . .' Lol was thinking of Stock that first night in the pub. Derek, the landlord, must certainly have overheard when Stock had said, '*My wife leaves scratches a foot long down my back.*'

'Stock implied that his wife was highly sexed,' Lol said. 'He talked about it in the pub a few nights ago.'

'Boasting?'

'Kind of.'

'He's not looking too turned-on now, is he?'

There was a movement on the screen – Stock reaching up to the wall.

'Recognize that thing, Ms Watkins?'

'Yes. It's a hop-cutter's hook. It was part of Stewart Ash's collection of hop-farmers' implements. Stock said—'

Breaking off because Stock had walked out of shot again. Carrying the hook. Lol had seen enough. Both Howe and Bliss had gone quiet and were watching the screen. There was nothing to see there now but stone flags, a curving brick wall and a table with a book on it. The fridge was going *whump, whump . . . whump* – irregular, as though its metal heart was about to fail.

After about a minute, there arose, from somewhere in the house, perhaps everywhere in the house, this cavernous, animal bellow, mingling with its own echo and the sound of the fridge.

*Rage and terror*, Lol thought, numbed.

Then only the sound of the fridge.

'What were you about to say, Ms Watkins?' Howe asked mildly, as if the TV was merely screening some corny old melodrama they'd all seen many times before. '*What* did Stock say?'

'He told me he'd sharpened it himself.' Merrily's voice was flat. 'He said that, because of what had happened to Uncle Stewart, he'd become afraid of someone breaking in at night, and so he . . . he wanted to be ready.'

On the TV screen: flags, table, book. The only sound was the fridge.

Frannie Bliss said delicately, 'I wouldn't think there's any particular need for Merrily to watch any more, would you, boss?'

Lol heard Merrily saying, 'He said it might seem ridiculous, but he just didn't trust the countryside.'

'Boss . . .' Bliss said plaintively, 'do you *really* think this is . . .?'

Annie Howe didn't reply.

Lol was still hearing '*But he just didn't trust the countryside,*' repeated like a loop in his head, when Gerard Stock walked casually back into the kitchen.

He wasn't carrying the hop-cutter's hook any more. The picture quality was crisp and suddenly very pleasant, the midday sun throwing a bright path from the middle window across the flags, creating a golden alley. Into it, Gerard Stock – the stains on his white shirt as startling as poppies in the snow – put down Stephanie's head.

# Part Three

*If a terrible crime has been committed in the area
— especially if justice has not been properly carried
out — the disturbances will be potentially very
unpleasant. The entity is inflamed by a combination of fear and anger for the injustice it feels
has been committed against it. If a person believes
that they have been especially wrongfully treated,
they may be inspired to curse the individual who
they blame or else the locality in which the wrongful
action has taken place.*

Martin Israel: *Exorcism — The Removal of Evil
Influences*

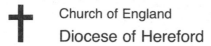

Church of England
Diocese of Hereford

# Ministry of Deliverance

email: deliverance@spiritec.co.uk

Click

Home Page
Hauntings
⌐ Possession
Cults
Psychic Abuse
Contacts
Prayers

## Possession

For a number of reasons, possession is the most misleading and dangerous term in the Deliverance dictionary.

The first thing to remember is that satanic or demonic possession is **extremely rare**, and offers of practical help or exorcism should be treated initially with caution, as misguided treatment could make the situation worse.

If you think that you are in spiritual danger or someone close to you has become the victim of demonic or spiritual interference, it may help to read the following pages before deciding which kind of assistance might have the most immediate benefit.

# TWENTY-FOUR

# Being Lost

Traffic had faded, the shops and the city library were all well closed. Broad Street was cooling into torpid evening and the trees were draping long shadows over the Cathedral green.

Inside the gatehouse, Merrily sipped tea the colour of engine oil, not tasting it. Furrows of concern on Sophie's forehead were dislodging strands of her fine white hair.

'I mean, what was the woman trying to *do* to you?'

'Doesn't matter.' Merrily watched a man aiming a camera up at the gatehouse. Just the one camera, not very big – a tourist, then. It would be the real thing soon enough, the pack unleashed. 'She probably did the right thing in the circumstances. Until we saw the video, I don't think I quite believed it. Thought maybe I was being set up – or that he'd told them he'd killed her, but he hadn't . . . not *really*. She was probably right to show us.'

'I shouldn't have gone in with you,' Lol said. They'd both had to make full statements, which had taken another hour and a half. 'It isn't as if I was any use in there.'

The three of them were hunched close to the window, as if putting on lights might draw the eyes of the world. Siege mentality already.

Sophie looked at Lol. 'Mr Robinson, were you *posing* as a qualified psychotherapist when you went into the kiln with Merrily?'

Merrily smiled wanly. 'He's not good at posing. Even if he *was* qualified, you'd never get him to admit it.'

'Quite,' Sophie said. 'So there's no real argument, is there? A –

neither of you was suggesting that Mr Robinson was there to fulfil the psychiatric or psychological function. *B* – this was a minor exorcism-of-place, for which a psychiatrist would hardly, in normal circumstances, be considered essential anyway.'

'That's not how it's going to read, though, is it?' Lol said.

'The fact remains,' Sophie told him severely, 'that, for reasons of her own – resentment, religious antipathy, whatever else – Detective Chief Inspector Howe is fabricating a spurious scenario.'

'It doesn't *matter*,' Merrily almost howled. 'A man's murdered his wife. Would that still have happened if I hadn't gone there and done what I did? Possibly. But possibly not. And *possibly not* is enough to hang me. But more than that—'

'Just don't hang yourself first,' Lol said. 'You know really that you didn't have a choice.'

'—More than that, I've got to live with the killing of a young woman. And the inference – the increasingly *strong* inference – that it . . . *it* doesn't work. Or when *I* do it, it doesn't work.'

'Don't be stupid,' Sophie snapped.

'So what do *you* think God's telling me?'

'Look—' Sophie raised a finger. 'If – *if* any one person can be said to carry any blame here – and I don't necessarily accept that anyone should – then it has to be The Reverend Simon St John, doesn't it? Whatever St John knew about Stock to convince him to stay out of it, he kept it to himself.'

'You don't understand . . .' Merrily lit a cigarette and, for once, Sophie didn't frown. 'I was approaching this right on top of the Amy Shelbone issue.'

'Oh, Merrily, that—'

'No, look . . .' Merrily glanced apologetically at Lol. 'I'll explain this properly sometime but, in essence, I was being accused of not responding to a situation with sufficient effectiveness. Following which, a young girl tried to take her own life.'

Sophie hissed, exasperated. 'For heaven's sake, Merrily, Dennis Beckett—'

'Look at the facts: here's me driving down to Stock's place this morning with a head full of Amy Shelbone and, like, totally insufficient background about Stock's own problem – in fact, not really believing he *has* a problem. And then, while talking to him and coming to realize there *is* a situation, am I not then subconsciously thinking, *God, I can't underplay this one as well?* Less concerned with finding out what the hell's going on than with covering myself? Was I—'

She stopped, realizing her speech was becoming swollen by sobs, and aware of Sophie getting decisively to her feet.

'Drink your tea, Merrily. Pull yourself together.'

Through a film of tears, she saw Sophie walking over to the door, beckoning Lol to follow her.

Sophie Hill almost dragged him down the stone stairs. Her expression was taut and her eyes were like grey stones in the half-light.

'Mr Robinson, I don't know what your current relationship with Merrily *is*, but I think you'll agree that what we need to do now is get her out of here, before she does or says something from which there'll be no going back.'

Lol nodded, bewildered. 'Anything I can do. Anything.'

Sophie took his arm, led him to the foot of the steps and even then kept her voice low. 'I was very much playing it down in there, as you probably realized.'

Lol nodded. He instinctively liked Sophie, wished she didn't have to keep calling him 'Mr Robinson'.

'This is actually rather grim.' She opened the door leading out to the stone archway. 'We both know that the press and the Church of England are going to hang Merrily out to dry, and if she thinks she's in any way at fault she won't even fight back.'

He remembered Merrily in Howe's office, what he could see of her: cowed, shattered. 'In any situation, she always tends to feel responsible.'

'All right,' Sophie said, 'let's examine the situation. First – I can't see them charging Stock with murder tonight, can you?'

'Not unless he's had a change of heart and given them a full statement.'

'They won't charge him even then, not immediately. And you know what that means.'

'Gives the press free rein to rake over the story. They go back to the original piece in the *People* and they find that quote from Merrily saying she's going to be looking into it carefully, and they'll want to know if she ever did.'

'And whatever answer they get will be the wrong one. If she didn't actually do anything, the Church was being fatally neglectful. And if they find out the truth . . .'

'Merrily's dog food,' Lol said.

Sophie stood in the gatehouse doorway, gazing through the stone arch towards the Bishop's Palace yard. An elegant, white-haired Englishwoman with a cardigan draped over her shoulders. Formidable.

'I don't know how much you know about the Church of England, Mr Robinson, but I can tell you with some authority that, like any large secular organization, it's essentially self-serving and self-protective.'

Lol said nothing. It was hardly a revelation.

'For the Church, it's going to be more than Merrily on trial, it's the credibility of the entire Deliverance Ministry – arguably one of the few dynamic arms we have left. They may not even try to defend her, simply wash their hands of it all. They'll have an inquiry, at the end of which they'll agree that she behaved in an arbitrary fashion, reacted too quickly, disregarded the guidelines, failed to take advice.'

'Can they throw her out of the Church?'

Sophie looked him in the eyes. 'With what you know of Merrily Watkins, would they need to?'

Merrily stood at the window, staring down at the evening light on Broad Street. Stephanie Stock's severed head lay in the middle of the road. She wondered when Stephanie's head would no longer be visible everywhere she looked, with its smile slashed to double-width and one of its eyes fully open – and the other one missing.

In fact, she realized that she and Lol must have been spared the worst. They'd only seen Stock's video. The police's own footage, while it might have less narrative tension, would be far more explicit. She'd heard Frannie Bliss and Andy Mumford talking in the corridor, and so she knew that Stephanie had not died by having her head cleanly cleaved off, like Anne Boleyn, but that Stock had gone at her, at the bottom of the stairs, like some barbaric Dark Age butcher.

This had happened immediately in the wake of what the papers would inevitably describe as an exorcism. A botched exorcism. Howe hadn't exactly been concealing the existence of Stock's video; its contents would inevitably be leaked.

And had this supposed exorcism, it would be asked, brought out something savagely malevolent, long dormant inside Gerard Stock?

It wouldn't matter that, unlike Michael Taylor, Stock had not been personally exorcized – no induced convulsions, no speaking in guttural tongues, no green bile, no *Out, demons, out.* Wouldn't matter that it had been simply a modest entreaty to God for the Stocks' home to become dweller-friendly again.

Merrily's fists tightened. How could that possibly cause a man to go into a murderous rage? *How could it?*

It wouldn't matter.

*Tell her to throw some holy water around and leave by the back door.* She wondered if Bernie Dunmore would even remember saying that.

The phone rang.

She turned slowly. Perhaps this was Bernie himself, fresh from the conference on Transsexuality and the Church, disturbing gossip having reached him while he sat nursing his single malt in the bar of Gloucester's swishest. Casually approached by some journalist, perhaps, as he debated with the Bishop of Durham how best to react to an archdeacon's new breasts.

She started to laugh, and let the phone go on ringing.

A clattering on the stairs. Sophie rushed in. 'Don't *touch* that.'

'Wasn't going to.'

Sophie sat down behind her desk, took two calming breaths and picked up the phone.

'Diocese of Hereford, Bishop's Palace. Sophie Hill speaking.'

Lol came in, looking a little brighter; Sophie could do this. *Don't depress Merrily.*

'No,' Sophie said, 'I'm afraid she's on holiday. Is there anything I can do for you?'

*She?* The only two women working from this office were Sophie and Merrily.

'When?' Sophie said. 'Well, I don't know, precisely. I know she was supposed to have left yesterday, but I believe she delayed her departure for some reason . . . No, I couldn't. I'm afraid that's not the sort of personal information I'm permitted to give out.'

Merrily held her breath and moved away from the window: they could be out there somewhere, on a mobile.

'No, I've no idea, I'm afraid. You'd have to ask Mrs Watkins herself about that sort of thing . . . No, the Bishop's away at a conference. He'll be back on Thursday night . . . Look, I'm sorry, but I'm only a secretary. I'm really not party to that kind of information. I should try our press officer tomorrow. Goodnight.' Sophie hung up. 'The *Daily Telegraph*.'

'Why am I on holiday, Sophie?'

'For the sake of your health.'

'Not good enough.'

'For the health of the Christian Church, then,' Sophie snapped. 'Look, I've just been asked if you conducted an exorcism today at the home of Gerard and the late Mrs Stephanie Stock. What would *you* have said if you'd been asked that question?'

'I'd have explained that it wasn't exactly an exorcism.'

Sophie and Lol exchanged glances.

'Yeah, I know. And they wouldn't have believed a word if it.' Merrily reached for her cigarettes, glared from one to the other of them. 'I'm supposed to run away?'

'Yes,' Sophie said. 'For the moment. At least until such time as the police charge Gerard Stock with murder and the media are formally gagged until after the trial.'

'What about the Bishop?'

'I'll phone Gloucester and advise him to stay in his hotel room and lock the door.'

'And where am I spending my holiday? Learning Welsh in Pembrokeshire with Jane?'

'You can stay at my house tonight.'

Sophie lived with her husband in one of the streets behind the Castle Green.

'Which would implicate you,' Merrily said. 'Thanks, but forget it. Anyway, I have to go home and feed the cat.'

'Don't throw up silly barriers,' Sophie said irritably. 'Phone

Gomer Parry. He has a key to the vicarage, doesn't he?' Sophie knew everything. 'Or Mr Robinson has an alternative suggestion,' she said.

In the fields to either side, cut and turned hay lay like a choppy green sea. The road and the fields and the woods lay in shadow, but the Malverns above them were caught in the sunset, their foothills glowing as if lit from underneath, like a Tiffany lamp.

It was serenely beautiful. And yes, she had to agree, it was the last place anyone would think of looking for her.

Eye of the storm. Merrily lit a cigarette. She felt a little scared, actually. Trepidation – or the electric, arm-bristling fear of another imminent revelation.

Lol had driven her back to Ledwardine Vicarage, and she'd packed a case and phoned Gomer Parry. Gomer had been round in minutes: how about he move in tonight, feed the cat, keep the newshounds off the premises? He'd caretaken once before, when Merrily and Jane had been armlocked into a family wedding in Northumberland. Now widowed and restless, he liked being the guy who looked out for them both . . . which also brought him closer to the action. Good old Gomer.

'A holiday.' Merrily inhaled and leaned her head over the torn back of the Astra's passenger seat and closed her eyes. 'So what's that like, exactly?'

'Boring,' Lol said, 'as I recall.'

'We had a few odd days, when Jane was younger. Not for a while, though.'

'How is she?'

'Raging. Eirion's stepmother seems to think she enjoys being a nanny to her youngest kids.'

'Taking a risk there.'

'And can she even begin to know how much of one?' Merrily closed her eyes. 'Don't really want to get there. I want to drive through the night talking inane crap. Like when we were young.'

'*That*'s a holiday. I remember now. Inane crap with bits of sex in between.'

'You and Alison?'

'Once. Five days in Northern France. You ever see Alison in the village?'

'Well, she's still with James Bull-Davies, if that's what you mean. They say she's really taken him and his decrepit house in hand. But they don't come to church.'

'So who sits in the Bull pew now?'

'Nobody. People are so superstitious, aren't they?'

She felt the car slow and turn, and when she opened her eyes the road had become an alley between rows of short wooden pylons. Entwined around them, luxuriant growth seemed to be surging towards the awakening stars.

It was Lol who was shivering. He pushed his compact body back into the seat to stop it, but she felt the tremor and she knew his hands were tightening on the wheel.

'Time to abandon The Prince of Wales Guide to Making Stupid Conversation, I think.' Merrily caught some ash in the palm of her hand. 'What haven't you told me?'

Lol watched the road winding between the hop-yards, put on his headlights. 'So exactly how long have you *been* a vicar?' he said.

She recognized the church, embedded in shadow, fusing with the bushes above the river bank. There was a light on in the vicarage, just one. It was the kind of light you left on when you went out for the night, to create an illusion of habitation.

The Astra crawled through the village, if you could call it that. There were several cars on the forecourt of the pub. One was a station wagon with its rear hatch flung up, a man pulling out a black tripod.

'Didn't take them long, did it?'

Lol drove slowly past. He even managed to give the man a suspicious glance, like a true local in his battered old car. Subtle. '*There are rooms at Prof's studios,*' he'd said. '*It's not finished yet, but it's quite respectable.*' Who else would be there? '*Only me, in a loft, out in the stables.*'

The road curved out of the village, up a slight incline and down again. The Malvern Hills disappeared and reappeared, undulating with lights like gems mounted on a jeweller's velvet tray.

'Is this going to help?' Merrily said. 'Us coming here?'

'Trust me, I'm a drop-out trainee psychotherapist.'

'Well, *I'm* not any kind of psychotherapist.' She squeezed out her cigarette, turned to look at him, her back resting against the passenger door. 'But I've learned enough about your little ways in the short time we've known each other to know that when you're at your most facetious it usually means you're also kind of scared.'

Lol turned through a gap in the hedge, went very slowly downhill and eventually came to a stop. She could see the humps of buildings but no lights. What had she expected: *The Prof Levin Studios*, in neon?

'You're obviously not scared of the dark, though,' Merrily said.

'No, I like the dark.'

'Yes, you would.'

Lol switched off the engine. 'When . . .' He hesitated. 'When I first came here . . . I went out for a walk in the dark. Well, actually, it wasn't that dark, bit like tonight. I walked down there.' He pointed through the windscreen to a line of poplar silhouettes. 'Over the river bridge, then I picked up a path and wandered into a wood. Then I got a bit lost.'

'Your thing, being lost,' Merrily said softly.

'Is it?'

'But it's produced some lovely songs. Ask Jane.'

'She's just being kind.'

'She'd take that as a serious insult. Go on – you went for a walk. You got lost.'

'And then I came to this abandoned hop-yard. Everything cleared or dead, with the poles and the frames naked.' He paused. 'And a woman – Stephanie Stock. She was naked, too.'

Merrily stiffened. The summer night gathered around the old car, opaque now like November fog.

# TWENTY-FIVE

# Soured

Down past the inn, at the edge of the old harbour, there was a stony footpath, and if you followed it for about half a mile you came to a fairly secret cove. Or at least it *seemed* secret at night; there was probably an oil refinery beyond the headland.

'You *can't*.' Eirion stood with his back to a millpond sea. There were just the two of them on the beach. One of the great things about Pembrokeshire was that you could still find lonely beaches in July.

Jane climbed onto a rock so that she was looking down on him. Post-sunset, the sky was luminous, almost lime green.

'*What?*' Hoping her eyes were glittering with an equally dangerous intensity.

Eirion backed off, the heels of his trainers almost in the water. 'Well, yes, all right, of course you *can*.' He would always start to sound Welsh when he was agitated. 'You can do what you want. You're free, you're sixteen years old, you're—'

'English.'

He moaned to the brilliant sky. 'Don't start that again! Please, *please*, don't hit me with that racism stuff again. They've just been brought up to be proud of their language and their culture.'

'Oh, right,' said Jane. 'Their *culture*.'

This evening they'd been to the movies, to a cinema in Fishguard. Well, not actually a cinema, a cinema *club*. Where they'd seen this thriller, with not-bad car chases and a couple of half-hearted love scenes and a leading actor who Jane recalled from TV and who was moderate totty, in his fresh-faced way.

It had actually helped that it was in Welsh and that snogging had been rendered impractical due to two small girls sitting in between them with their chocolate ripples. It had allowed Jane to contemplate the terrible turn events had taken, and the element of guilt she could no longer reject.

An unexpected wave hit Eirion's ankles and pooled into his trainers. He groaned. 'Jane, please don't do this to me. Stay until the weekend, at least, then we can think of something.'

'I've thought of something. I've thought of a taxi. I've thought of the nearest station. I've thought of . . . lots of things.'

'But there's nothing you can *do* there!' Eirion sat down in the sand and took off his trainers to empty the sea out of them.

'I let her down.'

'Don't be daft.'

'I dumped her in it.'

'That's ridic—'

'Because I didn't have the guts to say to Riddock, "This is naff, this is dangerous, this is *wrong*." '

Jane came down from her rock, and began to ramble up the beach – but slowly, always keeping Eirion in sight. People here still talked about that couple who were murdered years ago on the Pembrokeshire coastal path and nobody was ever caught. English couple, as it happened, on holiday.

'Jane, we're all—' Eirion picked up his trainers and ran barefoot along the sand towards her. 'We're all braver after the event. She's not going to hold it against you. You think she doesn't understand how hard it is? You think she was never in that position herself, of having to keep her street cred at school?'

'Huh?'

'Plus, she's your mother. Plus, she's a – you know – a Christian. And also a very nice woman.'

Jane stared at him in pity. 'Irene, did I even *mention* my mother?'

'You'll have to excuse me,' Eirion said. 'I'm a stranger on your planet.'

'OK.' She stopped. 'This evening, when I went up to change

before we went to see the film, I pinched the cordless from the sitting room – leaving three quid in the dinky little box marked *ffon*, I hasten to add – and I locked myself in the bathroom and found the number from directories, and I tried to ring Amy Shelbone.'

'Ah.' He sighed. 'I did wonder if you might.'

'She'd fitted me up, Irene. She'd lied. She was supposed to either put that right or give me a bloody good reason why not. She wouldn't talk to Mum but she'd have to talk to me. Also, I was gonna tell her what a disgusting old slag Riddock was and how she should tell her to piss off out of her life. Try and put her right, you know?'

'All right.' She felt Eirion's hand close around hers. 'That was a reasonable thing to do, but why'd you have to be so secretive about it?'

'Wasn't anything to do with anybody else.'

'Thanks.' Eirion had trodden on an old bottle in the sand, and let go of her hand to rub his bare foot.

'I didn't mean you. I'm sorry, I'm a bitch, I'm a bitch, I'm a bitch . . . Anyway, she wasn't in. I got her mother, and I said like, when *will* she be in? I didn't say it was me, of course, just a friend from school. But then her mother, she's just like . . . screaming at me: "*Don't you go claiming to be one of her friends, she hasn't got any friends, just enemies.*" And then she goes, "*You're evil, you're all evil! But you won't hurt her again, she's not going back to that school.*" And I'm like . . . *what*? Gobsmacked, obviously. I mean, come on, let's get this thing in proportion, you know? Oh, for Christ's sake, Irene, put your bloody shoes on!'

She walked up a couple of steps, where the beach joined the stony path, and waited for him to pull on his trainers. She could see a light far out in the bay. This was such a romantic place.

'And then it came out,' she said. ' "*As if you didn't know*," she's screaming. "*As if you didn't know, you Godless wretch!*" '

'Know what?' He reached for her hand.

'Amy tried to top herself.' Jane pulled away. 'Overdose of aspirins.'

'Oh, dear God,' said Eirion.

'Yeah.' Jane picked up a big pebble, pulled back her arm as if to hurl it at the sea, then let it drop by her feet. 'Could you live with that?'

Eirion said, 'It doesn't mean—'

'It does, Irene.'

'It'll all come out now, though, won't it? There'll be an investigation.'

'You reckon?'

'Probably.'

'Proving what? Gonna nail Riddock, are they? Not a chance. Her old man – her mother's husband – is one of the fattest fat cats in the entire county. It'll *never* come out, unless . . .'

'Oh, shit,' Eirion said.

Jane glared at him. 'How do we know there aren't other kids being terrorized? I think it was actually you who said the other night that when you're nine, an eleven-year-old could seem like Charles Manston.'

'Manson.'

'Didn't you?'

'Yes,' hissed Eirion through his teeth.

'What kind of holiday do you think I'm gonna have, dangling my toes in the ocean, listening to Sioned trying to teach me the complete works of Taliesyn and all the time thinking about the evil that slag's wreaking?'

'And what could you do if you *were* back home?'

'Loads of things. I could speak out about it for a start. I know this woman, Bella, at Radio Hereford and Worcester. I could go on there live and talk about it and I could just like name names before anyone could stop me.'

'They'd pre-record you,' Eirion said. 'And then they'd edit out the names.'

'I could do *something*. I could get that slag. I *will* get her.'

They both stood looking at the light out at sea, Jane thinking, *What a magic night, what a magic place to make love. What an incredible memory to have for the rest of your life.*

Too late now. It was all soured.

# TWENTY-SIX

# Cats

Lol *would* keep pausing, glancing at her to see if she believed him. As if she might be thinking he'd invented these two bizarre, creepy and sexually provocative encounters with Stephanie Stock, both of them ending with him walking away. But this, in fact, confirmed it: walk away was what Lol would do.

Of course she believed him. But what was it all supposed to convey, apart from that Stephanie had been as mad as Gerard?

As she followed Lol across the yard, a sensor switched on two lamps projecting from the stable wall, revealing the cottage in front of them. She could see it had originally been quite small, a typical Herefordshire farmworker's timber-framed home: two up, two down and a lean-to. There was a brick extension, probably nineteenth-century, longer and taller than the original dwelling.

'Just the four bedrooms at present.' Lol had a long key for the cracked and ill-fitting front door. 'But there's scope for conversion of a few more outbuildings, if Prof can get listed-building consent.'

Merrily thought that with David Shelbone around this could turn out to be more of a problem than Prof might figure.

Unexpectedly, she discovered she was starting to feel less depressed. It was clear that the case of Gerard and Stephanie Stock had several dark and, as yet, unprobed levels, was more complex than either the police or even she had imagined and went deeper than a violent rage inflamed by a botched Deliverance.

If she could be convinced of this, it was a start. She wouldn't be able to live with herself – as an exorcist, a priest or a person – if she thought anything she'd done had led, however indirectly, to the slaughter of Stephanie Stock.

'It's a nice idea, in principle,' Lol was saying. 'Musicians can come and stay, no real time limit, and help out generally around the place when they're not recording. Van Morrison on orbital sander – that's yet to happen, but people will do all kinds of things for Prof.' He pushed open the front door and put a hand inside, feeling around for light switches. 'This is the living room. It's still a bit, er . . .'

Merrily stepped inside, looking around by the harsh light of two naked bulbs. She saw several wooden packing cases, a bubblewrap mountain, an inglenook full of CDs, a TV set on a tea chest, two deck chairs and one padded garden recliner in the middle of an ice floe of polystyrene packing.

'Lol, this is a dump.'

'Yes,' he said. 'That's, er . . . that's one way of—'

'It's the only way, Lol.'

'The bedrooms are tidier,' Lol said.

Which was true. Merrily chose the smallest of them, which contained just a tiny porcelain washbasin, a rag rug and a bed. It was in the old part of the cottage but had recently been done up – fresh plaster between the beams. The three-quarter bed had no headboard, but there was a new duvet lying on it, still in sealed plastic.

It was stuffy in here. 'It was supposed to be my room.' Lol prised open the window – one pane, eighteen inches square. 'But for some reason I keep going back to a camp bed in one of the lofts over the stable.'

*Yes, he would do that; he'd need the feeling of impermanence.*

Merrily sat on the bed. She felt like an asylum seeker in a hostel; tomorrow seemed as impenetrable as Prof Levin's living room.

'Hang on a minute.' Lol went off and came back with a small wooden reading lamp with a parchment shade. He placed it on the deep windowsill and plugged it into a socket underneath. With the ceiling bulb switched off, the lamp turned the room a hazy buttermilk. Monastic cell to cosy boudoir in two clicks.

Lol asked if could bring her up a drink. 'Probably better if you didn't see the kitchen tonight.'

'Bad?'

He shrugged. 'The rats live with it.'

'Is there a kettle, say, and a teapot that we could perhaps bring up?'

'Sure.' He was hovering in the doorway. 'I'll . . . fetch your case in, then?'

'You want some help?'

Lol held up both hands. 'Stay. Luxuriate.'

She spread the duvet on the bed and sat down again, staring at the rough plaster. She and Lol had shared some secrets again. She wondered if he still had the sweatshirt with the Roswell alien motif.

With Lol, it all went back to a teenager called Tracy who had a mate called – Kath, was it? Karl Windling, the aggressive and un-pleasant bass-player in Hazey Jane, had fancied this Kath and set Lol up with Tracy – she was about four years younger than Lol, but you probably wouldn't have known, seeing the two of them together, and *he* certainly wouldn't have suspected. And then Windling had decided he wanted Tracy as well, and it had all turned nasty, and Windling had squirmed out of it, leaving Lol – innocent in everyone's eyes but the law's – with a conviction for having sex with an under-age girl, six months' probation and rejection by his family.

That was the start of it. A long time ago. A long time for anyone to remain an alien. But it would partly explain his reaction, both times, to Stephanie Stock.

'You must have thought she was unreal . . . a ghost.'

'I'd've been happier with a ghost.' Lol put down the tea tray.

Merrily thought back to his involvement with the ethereal Moon, who'd lived on Dinedor Hill. 'It's like cats, isn't it?'

'Cats?'

'Put a cat in a room with someone who's afraid of cats or allergic to cat hair, the cat invariably heads straight for them, jumps onto their laps.'

'I like cats.'

'Well, I know that. And you quite like women, too – I realize this is an inexact analogy. I'm talking about women with problems.

Weird women. They tend to come on to you like cats. And you put out a tentative hand, and then experience tells you to back off.'

'I'm not proud of backing off.'

'I don't like to imagine what might have happened if you hadn't.' Merrily poured the tea. 'Could she have been stoned?'

'Or was she ill?' Lol wondered.

'What? Something long-term? Schizophrenia? Could that have been why Stock kept her apart from the community? Was he drinking to excess to cope with it? The mad woman in the isolated kiln? But you can't really do a Mr Rochester these days, can you? You can't keep this kind of thing secret any more – if she was on medication, for instance . . . and schizophrenics are almost invariably on medication.'

'*And* she apparently went out to work.'

'Yeah, but *did* she?'

'She said she was temping for a car-dealer in Hereford.'

'But was she?' Merrily leaned her head against the side of the bed. 'All this will *have* to come out.' She looked at Lol. 'That night in the hop-yard – was she aware of you?'

'Yes.' Lol drank some tea. 'And no.'

'Good answer. Helpful.'

'It was dark.'

'She was aware of you in the bedroom, though. And she was *certainly* aware of you downstairs before we began.'

'Well . . . coming on to me like I used to be this big rock star – what kind of crap was that? She'd probably never heard of me until Stock mentioned I was staying at Prof's. But she gave absolutely no sign of recognizing me from the hop-yard. Not then, anyway.'

'But you recognized *her*?'

'Wasn't sure at first. Not till we were upstairs together and she was on the bed and you and Stock had gone . . . and then suddenly she *was*.'

'Because of the hop-bine?'

'The Lady of the Bines? Who never existed? Who is an invented ghost?'

'Remind me about that again.'

Merrily lit a cigarette; she'd smoked it by the time he'd finished.

'So the museum woman made it up. You been back to ask her, Lol?'

He shook his head.

'Hops.' Merrily tapped the tea tray with her fingertips. 'Think hops.'

'Hop-pillows? Stock said hop-pillows were supposed to give you a better night's sleep. But not in this case.'

'Hops as a turn-on? The first time you saw her, she was naked and winding a hop-bine around her. And up in the bedroom, she was playing with an old hop-bine again – a hop-bine, which she was again using in a . . . lubricious fashion. How did you feel?'

'Embarrassed. Scared.'

'And maybe just a bit . . .?'

'I'll stick with scared and embarrassed.'

'Basic nymphomania?' Merrily wondered. 'That can be a mental illness, can't it? I mean, people have a good laugh about it. Men in pubs always like to pretend they wish their wives would catch it, but it's a mental illness, isn't it?'

Lol considered. 'I don't even think it's a clinical term. There are no criteria to back it up. It's applied to women who want "too much sex" – but how much is too much? And what do you call a male nymphomaniac? Could be a purely sexist term, because a woman who lives for sex is a slut, while a man who can't get enough is a role model.'

'Wow,' Merrily said, 'you really have been on a course.'

He looked uncomfortable at that. He pulled off his glasses and began to polish them on the hem of his T-shirt. Merrily slid down to the rug and leaned back against the side of the bed, her bare arms around her knees. She was aware of the irony of being alone in a bedroom talking about sex with a man she'd always found attractive, but in circumstances that rendered the whole subject forbidding. Like going into a tobacconist's to discuss emphysema.

'We're going round in circles, Lol.'

He told her about the odd words uttered by Stephie in the bedroom, the foreign language which definitely wasn't French, might have been Welsh. And then '*Don't say no to me . . .*'

'As if someone else *had* been saying no to her? Well, Stock's a lot older than she was and probably close to being an alcoholic, which—'

'—Is no cure for impotence,' Lol said. 'And I think I'm right in saying the number one reason for men killing their wives is being drunk and on the receiving end of taunts about not being able to perform. And Stock's an arrogant guy. Very, very hard for someone like that to admit to sexual inadequacy. And if he doesn't say another word to explain why he did it, that's probably what they'll put it down to.'

'If,' Merrily said heavily, 'there hadn't also been what they will insist on describing as an exorcism.'

They were both silent. It occurred to Merrily that she might have done rather better if Lol *had* accompanied her as a psychologist, part of her putative Deliverance team.

He stood up and leaned against the windowsill next to the lamp. 'How about if I go back to Bliss and tell him about Stephanie?'

She looked up at him. 'You'd hate to have to do that.'

'It might alter the direction of their inquiries. And it's the truth.'

She went and stood next to him. 'They wouldn't believe you.'

'*You* did.'

'Also, Howe would take enormous pleasure in bringing up your . . . past record.'

He smiled. 'Hazey Jane Two?'

They looked at one another; she saw his face soften. It was the kind of confluence of gazes that might normally have progressed rapidly to a meeting of mouths.

But the moment passed, and Merrily went and sat on the bed.

'Call this a vague guess,' she said, 'but it's my feeling that if there's one person who could explain much of this, it's Simon St John.'

Lol used a phone plugged into the wall next to Prof's garden recliner. The call was answered in seconds.

'Who's this?'

'It's . . .' He always found it hard to identify himself. 'It's Lol.'

A sigh. 'Sorry, mate. Thought you were the media. About to tell you to fuck off.'

'You said that to the papers?' He really didn't care, did he? What must it be like not to care? 'Had many calls tonight?'

'Not as many as I expected.' Simon sounded tired, though, like he'd been doing a lot of talking.

'But the police have been round?'

'Briefly.'

Lol said, 'So you know everything.'

'This is the English countryside,' Simon said. 'Everybody within a six-mile radius knew everything by teatime.'

'You don't sound surprised.'

'I'm getting over it.'

'The thing is,' Lol said, 'Merrily Watkins is here.'

'Good for you.'

'It's not looking good for her.'

'I can imagine.'

'We thought you might like to talk. Now . . . or tomorrow morning? There's quite a lot to—'

'No, there isn't,' Simon St John said curtly. 'It's over. Let the police sort it out.'

'Hang on, how can you—?'

'It's *over*, Lol.'

The vicar hung up on him.


The old pine door of Lol's loft opened on to a rickety wooden gallery directly above the mixing board, overlooking the studio floor – moonlight now falling through the skylight on to snaking cables and the Boswell guitar on her stand.

It must have been after three a.m. when he came out and stood there, leaning on the basically unsafe rustic railing. Times like this when you smoked a cigarette. Maybe he should start, if only to get through the nights.

He'd just dreamed of the Lady of the Bines again, weaving and rustling towards him, and this time she *was* a ghost and she came in a shroud of cold, and her eyes were like smoke, and Lol had shuddered awake.

He stood on the gallery – the minstrel's gallery, Prof called it – and thought about Merrily, lying no more than forty feet away, thought about how close he'd come to kissing her. Clearly it just wasn't meant; as she'd pointed out herself, only weird cats jumped into his lap.

And although he thought about her every day, only negative circumstances had ever brought them together, and even then . . . He was aware that tonight they'd attempted to analyse *his* experiences but hadn't even touched on hers: whatever had happened to her in the kiln, whatever it was that had made her appear to choke, sent her dashing around the place flinging open doors.

'*It's over,*' Simon St John had said. Was it?

Was Gerard Stock lying awake in his cell at Hereford Police Station, going back over the day, screening the movie? Lol tried to see that movie – Stock, still angry after showing Merrily the door, walking in on Stephie . . . *Don't say no to me* . . . Predatory Stephie. Gerard Stock imploding, like an old radio blowing all its valves.

It struck Lol that Stock could still virtually walk away from this. Only in exceptional circumstances these days did the perpetrators of hot-blooded domestic murders get life. A domestic killing was a one-off, the killer no danger to the public. In this case, the killer had been under massive stress, heightened by an exorcism that hadn't worked.

It could, in the end, be Merrily who came off worst. A career wrecked. More than a career, a calling.

*It's over.*

In the hour before dawn – the only way to cool the fever of his thoughts – Lol wrote a song and, as the sun came up, sat in the shadows of the booth with the Boswell guitar and played it through, complete.

It even had a title: *The Cure of Souls.*

TWENTY-SEVEN

# Scalding

As she opened her eyes, a shaft of sunlight from the one small window threw her back into the kiln-house. She tasted sulphur, heard the shrill, cold calling: *beep . . . beep . . . beep . . . beep . . .* invoking dead Stephie, racked with laughter. '*I think you'd better answer that, vicar. It might be God!*'

She clawed around the bare boards for the mobile. 'Yes?'

'Merrily?'

'Sophie . . .' She sat up in the bed – no headboard: stone and rough plaster against her back and shoulders, dungeon-like. 'Where are you?'

'I'm in the office, of course. Are you alone?'

'I'm in bed. Yes,' she said, 'I'm alone.'

'I have the morning papers here.'

'Oh. Do I want to know this?'

'Gerard Stock was charged last night with the murder of Stephanie Stock.'

Merrily closed her eyes.

'I think that for you we can take that as a . . .' Sophie hesitated. 'I was about to say reprieve.'

'Think the phrase is "stay of execution".' Merrily fumbled for her cigarettes. 'What do they actually say?'

'It's made page one in the *Mail* and the *Telegraph*. All the reports identify the Stocks as people who complained that their home was haunted, and how it was the site of the murder of Stewart Ash. Nowhere, I'm relieved to say, is there any mention of an exorcism

272

taking place, although the *Telegraph* reminds us you'd voiced an intention of looking into the problem. I would think that they've said all they consider themselves allowed to say until after the trial.'

'Which, since he's confessed, may be not too many months away.'

Sophie said calmly, 'Has he?'

'What?'

'Confessed.'

'He was the one who called the police.' Merrily tried to grip a cigarette between lips that felt slack and rubbery.

'But you don't know if he's made a formal statement, do you?' Sophie said. 'We may not even find out. He'll probably be shipped off to a remand centre, if he hasn't gone already.'

'Well . . . it means I'm back in circulation, at least.' Merrily looked around the tiny monk's cell and felt a small pang of regret. Safe haven. Sanctuary. 'For the present.'

'Ah,' Sophie said. 'About that. I've . . . spoken briefly to the Bishop at his hotel in Gloucester. He feels, as I do, that – since we've already told several people that you're away on holiday – perhaps it would be best if you were to remain away. For a week, at least.'

'What about the parish?'

'That's all been arranged. A locum's been organized for the Sunday services, if you agree. It's the ubiquitous Canon Beckett, I'm afraid. Jeffrey Kimball's back in Dilwyn tomorrow, so the Canon's available again.'

'Oh.'

'I imagine DCI Howe will need to talk to you again, but I wouldn't make the first move there if I were you. I'd keep your head well down.'

'What's Bernie's attitude?'

'Guarded,' Sophie said.

'That's a useful word.'

'And there's something else. Someone else wants to see you. I pass this on now, but I've also told him you're going away.'

'Who?'

'Mr Shelbone. David Shelbone. Perhaps you could talk to him on the phone, if you must.'

'Something's happened?' Merrily swung her feet to the bare boards.

'Well, it seems Mrs Shelbone's done something rather drastic.'

'Oh, Jesus . . .' The unlit cigarette fell from her lips.

'Nothing like *that*,' Sophie said hastily. 'What's happened is that she's apparently left home and taken the child with her. Convinced – *he* claims – that, in the wake of her attempted suicide, social services will try and take Amy away from them and put her into care. Mr Shelbone reckons there's a story going round that he and his wife are religious extremists and the child may be psychologically dam—'

'Does he know where they are?'

'If he does, he isn't saying.'

'Sophie, I need to talk to him.' A couple of days ago this would have seemed like a serious breakthrough, and it was still important. 'Maybe Lol could give me a lift in.'

'If you must do this, I'll pick you up. An hour? Don't wear a dog-collar.'

First time Sophie had ever said that.


Lol had somehow produced scrambled eggs in the microwave. He'd spread a clean tablecloth on a packing case. Merrily looked around, felt quite touched. Either he'd lied about the condition of the kitchen or he'd been up for a long time, scrubbing.

He brought her more toast from the toaster. He was actually wearing his old Roswell alien sweatshirt, faded now to light grey – big slanting eyes on the chest, holes in the elbows. She told him about Sophie's call and that the worst of the heat was off, for a while. She also told him about the Shelbone situation, why it was important for her to go back to Hereford.

'And afterwards?' Lol said lightly.

'I'll get Sophie to bring me back here. If that's OK with you.'

Lol smiled.

'Or maybe I'll just pick up the Volvo. Not as if it's got a Deliverance sticker in the window. Sophie was perhaps being a little overcautious last night.'

'I just don't think she trusted you on your own,' Lol said. 'How do you feel now?'

'Well – I'm eating . . . thank you.' She looked at the remains of her breakfast, then at Lol. 'Can't say I feel a more seasoned human being for having seen a man carrying his wife's head around like a potted plant.'

First shudder of the day. Get it over with. Why had Stock done that – brought in the head, put it down in a beam of light, like a Stone Age priest with a sacrifice commemorating the arrival of the midsummer sun? She carried her plate to the sink, turned on hot water.

'Lol, when – when I said Stock had confessed, Sophie said, "Has he?" Like there was some doubt.'

She watched his reaction. Lol was looking unhappy.

'Am I missing something?'

'Well . . .' He picked up a tea towel. 'Maybe she means, what if he pleads not guilty?'

'But he did call the police, didn't he? He did actually tell them he'd killed his wife?'

'But he's had time to think about it, hasn't he? I didn't like the idea of him refusing to make a statement. He's clever. Suppose he gets a smart barrister and they try to hang the whole thing on exorcism?'

'You mean on *me*, right?'

'I don't know. You studied law for a while, didn't you?'

'But saying what?' The backs of her legs felt weak. 'That Stock had acted out of character due to a sudden infusion of the Holy Spirit? I don't think even that was quite suggested in the Taylor case.'

'But you said that was over a quarter of a century ago. Probably twice as many people going to church as there are now. We've become a secular country very quickly. *You* might talk about the Holy Spirit . . .'

'I imagine some barrister would argue that's become a meaningless term. Mythology.'

'They'd probably bring on a tame shrink,' Lol said. 'There are dozens of the buggers out there – university professors . . . authors of distinguished textbooks, theses. Awesomely eloquent, frighteningly fluent, oozing with . . . certainty. I've been listening to them for months. They're scary. Not necessarily *right*, but convincing.'

He put down the tea towel, and came to lean against the stainless-steel draining board. Merrily let the hot water run over her wrists. This *was* a new Lol, wasn't it?

'So they screen Stock's video in court,' he said. 'The jury see you at work. Then they see Stock at the end, when he's about to throw you out. He's angry, almost irrational – this is the real Stock, of course, but the jury don't know that. The first Stock *they* saw was this quiet, subdued, compliant character who just wants peace restored to his home. They're thinking to themselves, what happened in there? What brought about this change?'

'He was annoyed at Stephanie, the way she was behaving.'

'But on the video he isn't going for Stephanie, he's going for you. And me – he's questioning what *I'm* doing there. Am I there as a psychotherapist in case he's bonkers? So what's this other guy *about*? the jury asks itself . . .'

'Is *directed* to ask itself,' Merrily said, 'by the smart brief.'

'Meanwhile, back on the video, Stock's trying to find out what's been achieved there, and he's not satisfied with the answers. He loses it completely, hurls the brimstone tray to the floor. And what do *we* do? We just walk out, leaving this unstable and clearly violent man—'

'With the offer of a few prayers to tide him over,' Merrily said bitterly.

'And then they . . . I suppose they put *you* in the witness box.'

'And screen the – what they'll keep on calling an exorcism. They take me through it, prayer by prayer, line by line, demanding explanations, justifications. They ask: What happened to you when you looked like you were choking? Why did you suddenly start rushing around opening doors?'

'Why *did* you do that?'

'Well, that was . . . that was just something I should've done before we started. You're supposed to open all the doors.'

'So the evil spirits have nowhere to hide?'

'I . . .' She stared down into the sink. 'Something like that.'

'You actually had an awareness of evil?'

'Maybe.' The water was very hot on her hands and wrists, but she didn't remove them.

Lol took a step back. '*Did* you?'

'Yeah, I know – how do I *qualify* that? How do I *define* evil?'

'No,' Lol said. 'This is me, not the barrister. *I* want to know. *Did* you feel an evil?'

'I . . . I smelt sulphur. I tasted sulphur. It went to the back of my throat in this raw, searing way that sulphur does. I can't explain that, but it did feel like I was choking. For a couple of seconds I felt like I was going to—'

The water began scalding the backs of her hands and she pulled them back with a small scream. Lol wrenched a hand towel from a hook on the wall.

'—Die.' She pushed her hands gratefully into the towel. 'Now that sounds *really* stupid, doesn't it? Imagine having to say that in court. But yeah . . . I mean, obviously, what happened afterwards took the edge off it in a big way, but for one terrifying split second I really thought I was about to choke to death, or at least pass out, lose consciousness. So I started to say in my head something called St Patrick's Breastplate, which is a complete spiritual self-defence thing, surrounding yourself with the power of Christ, and I went around opening doors, and it . . . it went away. And I got my act together and carried on. How would your psychologist and your agnostic barrister react to that?'

Lol didn't reply. He was holding her hands, still wrapped in the towel.

'Go on.' She felt her voice shrink. 'Finish the scenario.'

Crunch of tyres on the track outside. Sophie?

Lol took his hands away. He stood there in that same old alien sweatshirt, those same sad, whipped-puppy eyes behind his brass-rimmed specs. But this was Lol back from psychotherapy school – six months exposed to concerned humanism, sympathetic psychobabble. He was right: he did know these people now.

'They'd take me apart, right?' Merrily said. 'They have full access to science and psychology and scepticism and cynicism. I'm—'

'Look,' he said, 'I'm sorry. We shouldn't've started this. It could be that none of it will happen.' He followed her to the door. 'I was just playing devil's advocate.'

She turned and stared at him, and he realized what he'd said and smiled ruefully, eyebrows rising above his glasses.

'Jesus,' he murmured.

'Two thousand years of exorcism on trial,' Merrily said.

It seemed so ridiculous when you put it like that.

So why was she sweating?

TWENTY-EIGHT

# A Religious Man

Lol followed Merrily out to the grey Saab, its engine running. She was wearing a short, orange-coloured skirt and a crumpled white jacket and carrying a canvas shoulder bag under an arm. The exorcist.

He thought: *They'll do it. They'll sacrifice her.*

At the car, as though she'd simultaneously reached the same conclusion, Merrily turned to him, tried for a smile but failed. She shrugged instead.

Her image misted. Behind her, in the meadow sloping down to the Frome, the hay had been cut and turned and lay heavy, like acres of gold leaf, a heat haze hanging over it.

From behind the wheel of the Saab, the stately Sophie raised a hand in formal greeting, like the Queen or somebody. She wore a dark blue business suit and no smile. She revved the Saab like a getaway driver. Sophie would do her best for Merrily. Probably even the Bishop would do what he could. But in the end they'd both have to walk away.

Lol watched the Saab turn, crunching baked red earth, vanishing around the curve of the track. A cold electricity was branching through him as he walked rapidly away, down the footpath, across the hay meadow, to the river that seeped below the brambles, under the hedge and the fat, purple-spotted banks of willowherb.

The River Frome, flowing invisibly. Like the truth.

Just when it seemed entirely unimportant, the substance of the final verse of his river song seeped unbidden into his head.

What you did, Lol realized, was join another river.

Walking through Knight's Frome, he saw nobody: no police, no press. He crossed the bridge, to the small, sunken church. The churchyard was wilderness, so overgrown around the perimeter that you couldn't tell where the countryside began, several gravestones even poking out of bushes.

Lol stood in the porch and listened: no voices, no clatter. He went in, letting the iron latch fall behind him.

Sometimes they still oppressed him, churches, with their rigidity and weight, the ungivingness of them, their atmospheres dense with the residue of humourless old hymns. This one was almost frugally plain, the air inside ochre with sunlight and dust. Lol went and sat in a back pew, over in a corner. He couldn't quite see the altar; that was OK.

He sat for a while in silence. The prayer-book shelf was thick with dust; in it, someone had finger-drawn two sets of initials and a heart.

Lol took off his glasses, wondering how often Merrily did this, how many times a day – how long it took to break the ice. His feeling was that it could be like meditation, that you'd have to connect with your deepest inner self, the part that flowed into some collective unconscious, rippling under the light of whatever it was you called God.

Rivers again.

'Listen,' he whispered, when the level seemed beyond his reach. 'I mean, we don't really know each other – at least, I don't know you. But we've got one mutual interest, and I hope you're not going to let her down.'

His eyes had half closed and all he could see was a dark yellow haze, with blobs of white where the windows were.

'Because she's not going to help herself, you know that. She'll just keep on telling the truth as she sees it, and that might be the wrong kind of truth for certain people. And I realize we only learn by suffering, by screwing up, and maybe she did screw up . . . but her heart was in it, and what else can you ask? And if she goes, she won't come back, and I don't think that's going to help anybody. I mean, how do you want to play this? You want a church run by politicians or by people who actually give a shit?'

He glanced over his shoulder towards the vestry, which Merrily had entered as a woman and emerged from as a priest. He leaned back and thought for a few minutes.

'So, like . . . don't you think some things need to start coming out? I mean, don't know how far this goes back, but I think it probably pre-dates Stewart Ash. I think something bad happened there, apart from Stewart's murder. And I think that Stewart, as a lingering presence . . . was an irrelevance, and I think Stock knew that. So what did Stock really want? Why did he want an exorcism? Why did he approach Simon and then go after Merrily?'

Talking to himself, now. He'd tried to puzzle it out last night and early this morning as he'd mopped and scrubbed the kitchen. But puzzling had produced nothing. He just didn't know enough.

'Sorry,' he said. 'This is bollocks, isn't it?'

He stood up. Nothing resolved. No revelation. No inspirational feedback from his inner self.

When he put on his glasses, the white blobs hardened into pearly Gothic windows. He slid wearily out of the pew and across to the church door.

Daylight filled the crack around the door. When he put a hand up to the latch, he found it was already up. Which was odd, because he was sure he'd closed the door and heard the latch fall into place.

It was probably warped. He opened it and went out, and there she was in the porch, blocking his path with her wheelchair.

'A religious man after all, then, is it, Lol?'


There were no unfamiliar cars in the palace yard; no-one was waiting under the arch or at the top of the stairs.

Sophie unlocked the office door. 'If he doesn't show up now, I think I shall be very annoyed indeed.'

Inside, the phone was ringing. They heard the machine pick it up. *'This is for Mrs Watkins. We've met before. Tania Beauman, formerly of the* Livenight *programme, now researching for the* Witness *series on Channel Four. I'd appreciate a call back. Thank you.'*

Merrily drew a surprised breath. 'She's got a nerve after last winter's fiasco.'

'Don't worry about it,' Sophie said. 'I can handle this. I didn't tell you, but we've had a similar approach from *Panorama* at the BBC. They're all thinking ahead to the court case. They make a background programme in advance, to be screened immediately the case is over and the shackles are off. The *spiel* is that they're going to make the programme anyway, and if you don't agree to appear, your views may not be fully represented.'

'What did you tell them?'

'I said we'd discuss it when you returned from your holiday, adding – God forgive me – that I was sure we could trust the British Broadcasting Corporation to produce a balanced and accurate account, with or without your help.'

There were two other messages on the machine, one from the Bishop, nervously demanding an update, the other from Fred Potter, of the Three Counties News Agency.

*'Look, nobody can print anything now, so I won't be on your back for a good while. I just wanted to say thanks for your help, and if there's anything I can do to help you at all . . . because, you know, I've heard one or two things which don't sound that promising from your point of view . . . so, if you think there's anything I can maybe tell you . . . you know where I am, OK. Thanks. I'll give you the number again, just in case . . .'*

'Little shark.' Sophie lifted a finger to delete the message.

'No, I'm going to ring him.'

'You're *not!*'

'What have I got to lose? Besides, he was—'

'Everything,' Sophie snapped. 'For a start, you're supposed to be on holiday.'

But Merrily was already tapping in the Worcester number. The young woman who answered said Fred was on the phone, asked who was speaking.

'It's Mrs . . . Sharkey, from Hereford. I'll hold.'

When Fred Potter came on the line, Merrily said quickly, 'Just don't say my name aloud, or I'll have to hang up.'

'Mrs *Sharkey?*'

'Never mind.'

'Well, thanks for calling back, Mrs Sharkey. Hold on a moment. Ah, Sinead, you don't fancy getting me a tuna on rye from the sarny bar? Plus whatever rabbity morsels you allow yourself. Excellent, thank you. This enough? Cheers.' Pause. 'Right, Mrs Sharkey, we're on our own. Bloody hell, that was a bit of a turn-up, wasn't it?'

'A turn-up. Yes, it was.'

'You know about the video?'

'Video?'

'All right, I'll be honest. I knew Stock had the place bugged and wired up for sound and pictures. He told me himself.'

'*Did* he?'

'He had one camera wedged into a shelf at the time, and of course it fell over while I was there, and it was dangling by the strap. He asked me if I'd mind keeping quiet about it. Said he was convinced he was going to get something mind-blowing on tape that would prove he wasn't making it up. That's why I said I believed he was on the level – I couldn't tell you, I'd agreed to say nothing.'

'That's OK.' *Thanks a bunch.*

'Besides, I was thinking, if he *does* get something mind-boggling . . .'

'Seems like he has,' Merrily said.

'You reckon he thought something might appear during the exorcism?'

'You're just trying to find out whether I did one or not.'

He laughed. 'All right, forget it. Anything I can tell you, stuff you might not know? No notes, no recording, swear to God.'

'What did you think of *Mrs* Stock, Fred?'

'Good question. Er . . . well, the first thing I thought was, he's landed on his feet there, hasn't he just, jammy bugger?'

'Meaning what's a clapped-out old drunk doing with a charming young thing like that?'

'I wouldn't say say charming. Sexy. Not beautiful, but she'd got a certain . . . It's funny, he was going on about what it had done to them, living in that place, making them withdrawn, nervous, all this . . . and she kept very quiet while I was there. But after it came out about the murder, when we'd got all we could in the village, I drove into Hereford and hung around outside the secretarial agency where Stephanie worked, back of Aubrey Street, and I had a word with a few of the girls when they came out. And I got just a *completely* different story.'

There was a tapping on the door. Merrily glanced up as Sophie let in a man who had to stoop in the doorway. She saw grey and white tufted hair, a face like a tired horse. David Shelbone?

'In these situations,' Fred Potter said, 'you're just after kind of, "We're all absolutely shattered, she was a lovely person who remembered everybody's birthday" – predictable stuff, because this is the victim and it usually helps if the victim's a nice person. You normally find the workmates or the neighbours've already had the cops round and the initial excitement's worn off a bit. But on this occasion, as it happened, I was in there first. These women didn't *know* about it.'

Sophie offered the visitor a seat. Merrily put a hand over the phone, whispered, 'Sorry, I'll be one minute.'

'So what I was getting was genuine, off-the-cuff reaction,' Fred said. 'The women looking at each other, shocked, naturally, gasps of horror, as you'd expect, then grilling *me* for information. But the quotes I was getting from them were not what I was looking for. In the end I put the notebook away because I was getting a load of stuff I couldn't have used – asking more questions than it answered. And we weren't going to *get* any answers, not now, with her dead and him—'

'Questions?'

'What I was getting was not a lot of genuine sorrow, to be honest. She'd worked for that agency four or five months. When she first arrived, she seemed very, *very* quiet. Very proper, very polite, butter wouldn't melt. The kind, if she met a bloke on the stairs, she'd shrink into the wall to avoid him brushing against her.'

'Stephanie Stock?'

'And when she talked about her husband, it was like he was some sort of guru – her mentor, her guardian. Gerard this, Gerard that. "Oh, I don't know, I'd better ask Gerard." "No, I don't think Gerard would approve." This was when she talked at all.'

'So what happened?'

'She changed.'

'Damn right she changed,' Merrily said.

'Not overnight; it was a continuing process. If I'd been writing it up for the tabs, I'd've had the girls saying something like, "Stephanie was very quiet at first and hard to get to know, but the job really brought her out of herself, and in her last few days she'd been full of life and getting on with everybody."'

'Meaning?'

'You're clergy, Mrs Watkins. I can't . . .'

'Oh, sod *off*—' Merrily looked up, uncomfortably, with a strained smile for Mr Shelbone.

'All right,' Fred Potter said. 'There was a bloke upstairs, an accountant. Divorced. Sports car. There's always one, isn't there? The one *no* woman likes to meet on the stairs on a dark morning. The one where *they* always prefer to hold open the door for *him*, yes?'

'I know.'

'Again, this is one of those bits where the girls're exchanging knowing glances, and frankly I don't think any of them knows exactly what happened between Stephanie and this randy accountant. But someone saw her coming down from his office one lunchtime, and after that the man was *very* subdued.'

'More than he bargained for?'

'No, he was actually *scared* – that was the consensus. I don't know if this was an exaggeration, but they said he was working from home the rest of the week. Like he was frightened.'

'You serious?'

'Yeah,' Fred said. 'Yeah, I am actually.'

'These women – they didn't like her.'

'I think it's fair to say they did *not* like poor Stephie. One of them started whispering that she was probably a bit mental, and who knows what her husband had to put up with, and then another one's shouting, "Hey, this isn't going to be in the papers, is it?" and of course that was it for me – everybody clams up. Well, no *way* was it going in the papers, even if he didn't get charged last night – this is the victim; if you make a victim sound too much like a slag, the level of interest goes right down.'

'Meaning the amount of space you get, the amount of money . . .'

'Well . . . yeah.'

'What about the haunting? Did she ever talk about that at work? I mean, she must have, after that spread in the *People*.'

'Somebody apparently said something like, "How can you go on living there?" but she just laughed, and then the boss sent her off to this garage, Tanner's, temping, so they never saw her again.'

'What's the name of the agency?'

'The Joanna Stokes Bureau.'

Merrily made a note. 'Thanks, Fred.'

'Thank *you*,' he said. 'I've been wanting to tell somebody. It's like I've been carrying her around.' A little laugh, part cynical, part embarrassed . . . part something else.

'It's different, isn't it,' Merrily said, 'when a murder victim is somebody you knew, however slightly. Somebody you'd seen not long before it happened.'

'Yes,' Fred Potter said, 'it's different. Look, is it OK if I ring you again, if I . . . if you . . .?'

'Of course.'

She gave him her mobile number. She didn't usually do that. It was that phrase '*carrying her around*'.

# TWENTY-NINE

# The Plagues of Frome

Even from a few feet away, it looked as though the wheelchair was gliding through the undergrowth, cutting brambles like Boudicca's legendary chariot with the knives in the wheels.

In fact, Isabel knew where the overgrown path went burrowing through the tangled churchyard to the bank of the Frome. Where the wheelchair stopped you could see the river down below, like smoked glass.

'Look at that,' she said contemptuously. 'No rocks, no rapids. Seemed such a nice boring place, it did, after Wales. No historical baggage, see – no ruins, no megalithic sites. No history at all that wasn't to do with hops.'

She wore a short-sleeved tropical top, with big golden flowers, and cord jeans. Her hair had amber highlights. There was a thin, grey shawl folded on her lap.

'Perfect, it was,' she said. 'Perfect for us. And now – blood every-where.'

'Everywhere?'

'Not yet.'

'Huh?'

Isabel shook her head. Apparently, she'd sent the vicar off on a pastoral visit to the farthest of his four parishes, up towards Ledbury. Missionary work.

'Starting to mope, see. Becomes dangerous when he mopes.' She looked up coyly at Lol. ' *"You want a church run by politicians or by people who actually give a shit?"* I like that. That's telling Him.'

Of course, she'd overheard it all, every whispered word.

'And now you're throwing it all back at Simon. Can't blame you for that. Fair play, though, he did say bring her along to see him first, if she had plans to go into that place.'

'We tried,' Lol said tonelessly. 'You weren't at home. You were in Hereford, shopping.'

'My fault. He was moping, and I got the feeling he was getting ready to . . . go in there himself.'

'To exorcize the kiln?'

'Or whatever was needed.'

'He'd made it pretty clear he didn't think anything was needed!'

'Ah, well,' said Isabel, 'what he says and what he *thinks* . . .'

'You're saying—' Lol looked up in despair at the flawless sky '—he *did* think something was needed.'

'I'm not saying *what* he thought. You can blame me, like I said. I didn't want him in there. I didn't mind him warning your lady friend, that was only right. But I didn't want him *in* there. So you see . . . It's me to blame.'

Lol didn't say anything. Isabel wheeled herself back from the river bank, along the path, to the base of an arthritic-looking apple tree.

'*Funny*, though, isn't it, this whole religion business? God working in mysterious ways. How do people *expect* Him to work – bolts of lightning all the time? And there I am, sitting at the door, and you pleading for enlightenment: "*Isn't it time it all came out?*" Me thinking, I must be *it* – the mysterious way. What a bloody honour.'

Lol shook his head, mystified.

Hands folded on the shawl on her lap, Isabel fixed him with a gaze blazing now with what looked like a fearsome candour, and her voice acquired a flint edge.

'Time for us to talk, isn't it, boy?'

She got him to push her back to the vicarage gates and then down towards the main road. The haze had been burned out of the sky and the tarmac was beginning to sweat. There were hops on either side of them now, high on their frames, the fruit tight and green on the bines.

'Preserve the beer, they do,' Isabel said. 'And the memories, I bet. And all the old hate.'

Lol sensed a stage being set out and climbed up onto it. 'So who do *you* think killed Stewart Ash?'

'Does it matter?' Isabel gazed downhill towards the just-visible roof of the hop museum. 'Wasn't Adam Lake himself, was it?'

'No?'

'Hasn't got the balls. Big man, macho image, but no balls. I reckon, see, that what Stock was trying to suggest the other night was that Lake got somebody else to do it. No balls, plenty of money – that's what Stock was saying.'

'But like Lake said, would he really kill somebody just get back another little bit of his old man's estate?'

'Ah, well,' Isabel said, 'you've got to look at the whole picture, isn't it? Son of his father, when all's said and done.'

Lol recalled what Gerard Stock had said in the Hop Devil about Conrad Lake. 'You mean some kind of Nazi?'

'Wasn't far out. They still don't say too much out loud, round yere, about all that, because old Perry-Jones isn't dead yet, and Perry-Jones and Conrad Lake were part of the same disease.'

'Armbands, Stock said.'

'Nothing so obvious. Right-wing politics, racist stuff – you don't get so much of that in the country. You get *Tories*, of course. They're all bloody Tories, the old kind, stuck into their Little England feudal ways. No tub-thumping, though, no rabble-rousing. It's the cities where the real extremism starts, isn't it, the cities where all the immigrants go? How many black faces you ever see behind the wheel of a tractor? Life just trundled on in places like this: the same families, the same faces, the same hairstyles . . .' Isabel reached out and fingered a bine. 'Except in September, of course.'

'The hop harvest.'

'September, see, that was when the people of the Frome Valley had a taste of what life was like in the cities – drunkenness, debauchery, robbery, violence. All those thousands of common working-class folk from the Black Country and the Valleys. People like me. In fact my mam and my auntie used to come round yere hop-picking when they were young. Great times, she always says. Hard work, but a lot of laughs.'

'Debauchery?'

'Oh, no more than you'd expect with all those thousands of people and not much to do at night but drink and flirt. Got out of hand sometimes. And there was jealousy and rivalry . . . bar brawls, beatings, the odd stabbing. The Hop Devil – that was a no-go area for local people until about halfway through October. Bit like the Wild West. Then, one night, a farmer's boy . . . they found his body in the Frome.'

'What, murdered?'

'Never proved. This was the early fifties, they didn't have fancy forensics back then. But it was enough for Perry-Jones. He was off . . . *"These barbarians . . ."* '

'The Welsh?'

'Thank you, Lol. No, the Welsh, mostly they just sang. This was the gypsies.'

'Ah.'

'The Welsh looked like everybody else, but the gypsies looked like foreigners, another race. The gypsies weren't sociable. Clannish. Set up their own camps and only mixed with their own kind. Not that they weren't loyal to their employers, because they were – more than any of the others, in some ways. But they were a race apart, and they knew it. What are they, originally? From India or somewhere?'

'I think so.'

'And heathens. Oh, Perry-Jones made the most of all that. Ambitious, he was, see – only a young man, then, in his twenties, and a firebrand. Didn't care what he said. Well, nobody did back then. No such word as racism. You call the gypsies a bunch of no-good, lying, evil, murderous bastards, nobody's going to jump on you for not being politically correct. *"Get them out!"* he's screaming. *"Clean this filth from our farms!"* '

'He said that? With the war not long over? What about the Holocaust? All the gypsies who went into the death camps? Was that not fresh in people's memories?'

'If you listen to my mam, Lol, all that was fresh in people's memories back then was the war itself and what a relief it was all over. Besides, I think it was years later before they even knew the extent of the Holocaust. Anyway, Perry-Jones, he was up for the County Council and looking for a future in Parliament, and he got a fair bit of support, blaming the gypsies for every bit of trouble. A lot of people, they have a natural fear of anything they don't know about. And nobody knows about the Romany folk, do they, except other Romanies? Not to this day.'

Lol recalled that Al Boswell had been among the Romany pickers at Knight's Frome, back then, and wondered how he'd managed to drink in the same bar as Oliver Perry-Jones. *Non-confrontational is all we are*, Al had said. He'd have to be.

Isabel explained how Perry-Jones was forever on at Old Man Lake – this was Conrad's father – to ban the gypsies from Knight's Frome for good. In the nineteen-forties and fifties, the Lakes owned the two biggest farms in the village.

'But Old Man Lake, he said the gypsies were good workers and that's all that concerned him – wasn't one of *his* boys that wound up dead in the river.'

'But if there was no proof—'

'No proof whatsoever. But then the old man, he died, and Conrad took over, and Conrad was very ambitious, too, went at it like an industrialist, buying up every bit of ground going, until he owned what amounted to the whole of Knight's Frome. And he was around the same age as Perry-Jones, and a close friend of his, and Perry-Jones was on the council by then and oiling wheels for Conrad. So . . . well, the first thing Conrad does is cut the gypsy pickers' pay, hoping this will drive them away. Didn't work – they still came back. Resentful, sullen, but they came back. No loyalty to him now, mind, and a good deal more poaching and theft, including his wife, it was said.'

Lol stopped pushing. They were at the crest of a rise, and the land before them sloped panoramically away, low hills and woodland, towards Hereford.

'His wife?'

Isabel peered over her shoulder at him. 'Nobody's told you that?' He shook his head. Isabel smiled.

'His first wife, this was, not Adam's mother. Caroline, her name, and quite a prize – high-born beauty, god-daughter of the Earl of so-and-so. And, well, she just disappeared one day, isn't it? Gone. Vanished. And it was *never* explained. Well . . . the police certainly weren't called in, so it's clear that Conrad must've known where she was and was too proud to let it out. But this was the height of the picking season, and the rumour was she'd been bewitched by the gypsies – seduced, kidnapped, spirited away. That's what they do, isn't it, gypsies? Conrad never mentioned it, never a word, but that was it for the Romanies . . . and the tinkers and what-have-you. Conrad's manager told them to take their money, clear out and never come back.'

Lol pushed the chair into a passing place near the bottom of the lane and sat on the grass verge in front of Isabel. 'When was this?'

'Oh . . . early sixties? You don't hear the full truth about it, ever, because this was the time when machines were taking over from the hop-pickers, generally, so most of them were going to be out of a job soon anyway – the gypsies, the Dudleys and the Welsh, all of them together. And some people still say Conrad kept quiet because his wife had run off with one of his own friends, and he just took it out on the gypsies because they were there and because Perry-Jones was his best mate. Today you'd have questions asked, but in the early sixties people knew their place – though *that* was about to change, mind – and Conrad Lake was the boss, and he owned the whole bloody village, so . . .'

'This was when he was living at the house that was originally behind Stock's kiln?'

Isabel's eyes shone. 'Correct. It was after Caroline left, he started building his new place. Turned his back on the old farmhouse, knocked it down, just left the kiln. As if the house itself was responsible for the failure of his marriage.'

'And the gypsies all went?'

'Oh, they *went*. In their own time and their own way. The hop-picking, see, that was part of their seasonal cycle – Hereford, for the hops and apples, then down to Evesham for the plums, what have you? They *went* . . . but not before buildings were set on fire, fences cut, stock loosed into the hop-yards. And that was when the police arrived in force.'

292

'Not very non-confrontational.'

'The police?'

'The gypsies. Al Boswell says the Romanies are essentially non-confrontational.'

'Aye, well, what had happened, they accused Lake, or one of his managers, of taking one of their own women. An enormous outcry, there was. Police out searching for her. In the end, I think the cops decided the gypsies had made it up, to get back at Lake. The gypsies of course, were saying – *still* say – that the coppers never really tried to find her because she was only a gypsy, see, and not worth shit. Maybe something in that. At least some things have changed for the better since the sixties.'

'What do you really think?'

'Well, *I* don't know, Lol. But Stewart Ash thought he did. Gone into it all, he had. And of course it was all going to be in his book, in detail.'

Lol blinked. 'Which book?'

'The book he was working on when he died. The book the Smith boys were supposed to be helping him research. He was going into the whole business: the reasons the Romanies were banished from Knight's Frome, never to return – if you don't include Al – and what *really* happened to the girl. Rebekah, she was called, with a k and an h. Rebekah Smith.'

'Smith?'

'Oh, it's a big tribe, Lol, the Smiths. None bigger. Doesn't mean she was related to the boys who killed Stewart.'

'It does give them a reason for *not* killing Stewart, though, doesn't it?'

'I suppose you could say that.'

'And did Stewart claim to know what happened to this Rebekah Smith?'

'I don't know. The thing is, Lol, you can't libel the dead, and if Stewart wanted to suggest that Conrad Lake was in some way connected with the so-called disappearance of Rebekah Smith, there was nothing much to get in his way . . .'

'Except Adam Lake, maybe. How much does Stock know?'

Isabel spread her hands. 'Who can say? Especially now.'

'Is there a manuscript?'

'I've no idea. I don't even know if he'd started writing it before he was murdered. But, yes, you're right, of course, it wouldn't make young Adam feel any more at home to have some book on sale for ever and ever in Bromyard and Ledbury and Hereford, linking his late father with some nasty old scandal. Especially—' Isabel smiled gently '—as the local people have always said – and Sally Boswell will confirm this for you – that the terrible collapse of the Lake family hop-empire is down to what you might call a very traditional Romany curse.'

'Of course.' *The aphids, the red spiders, the white mould . . . and the Verticillium Wilt.* The four plagues of the Frome Valley.

And the Lady of the Bines – where did she fit in?

Lol stood up. 'So that was where Stock was coming from.'

'Bit clearer now, is it?'

'That's a joke, right?' Lol said.

'You asked God,' said Isabel, 'and God, in His mysterious way, asked me to fill you in on a few basics. Can we go back now? I need a wee, I do, and I can't just nip behind a bush any more. Not till I've been to Lourdes.'

Lol pushed the wheelchair back into the lane. He wondered when God might think it appropriate to ask her exactly why she'd been so afraid of Simon going into Stock's kiln?

THIRTY

# Element of Surprise

Eirion took the big roundabout at Carmarthen on two wheels, it felt like, throwing Jane into the passenger door. 'There's a station here, right?' she demanded, but he didn't react. He drove on, until, quite soon, there was only open countryside in front of them.

'I did not ask for this,' Jane said. 'I did not want this.'

Eirion was heading north towards Llandeilo. He was, like, serious. He was even wearing his baseball cap the right way round.

'I'd really hoped,' Jane said, 'that you were not going to turn out to be one of those guys who think women can't transport themselves from A to B on their own.'

He still didn't respond. *Well, stuff it,* Jane was thinking now, *why should I complain if he wants to drive me to Hereford and then turn the car around and drive all the way back to the bosom of his incredible family? Except . . .*

'This is Gwennan's car, isn't it?'

'She lets me use it,' Eirion said through his teeth, eyes fixed on the road. 'And anyway, they've still got Dad's car.'

'As I understand it, she only lets you use it because you've got some heavy dirt on her. Like that she's really English or something?'

'If you're just trying to make me dump you at the roadside,' Eirion said, 'it won't work.'

'I was merely trying to envisage the scenario when little Sioned and little Lowri returned from *y siop*, maybe half an hour ago, to find out that we'd pissed off without them, and their mummy discovered she was obliged to take care of them for the *entire* day. I would have gone on to make the point that whatever dirt you have on her – and I would be the last one *ever* to ask – would then count for like . . . not a great deal. I just make the point.'

Eirion slowed the BMW. She saw that, despite the air-conditioning, he was sweating.

'I just don't want you to get disinherited in favour of those spooky kids, is all,' Jane said. 'It would like distress me if you were to be taken away from the Cathedral School and forced to work as a rent boy in Abergavenny.'

'What makes you think I don't already?'

'You're not pretty enough.'

'Why don't you call your mum?' Eirion said.

'It's not your problem.'

'Then why did you tell me about it?'

'We've been through this. I just didn't want you to think it was a racial thing when I went over the wall.'

Eirion pulled into the side of the road. Though it was a main road, it was still fairly quiet. The hills were low and green and there were broadleaf woods. Apart from the colour of the soil, it didn't look dramatically different from Herefordshire.

Eirion turned to face her and took off his baseball cap. His eyes were solemn, his famously amazing smile now in cold storage.

'I'll be straight with you, Jane, I'm going to be in deep shit over this. Gwennan and Dad have a big lunch today in Tenby with some Arts Council people and National Assembly delegates and a cultural delegation of Irish-speakers from Ireland. It's informal, but there could be a significant PR contract in it for Gwennan, in connection with this pan-Celtic cultural festival.'

'Turn the car round *now*,' Jane said with this, like, dark menace.

'No. They'll deal with it. They'll find someone to look after the kids. Things will be a little tense for a while. I may have minor transportation problems – nothing I can't handle.'

'Why are you telling me this?'

'Brownie points, that's all,' Eirion said. 'I mean I'd really hate you to think I was in love with you or anything like *that*.'

He turned on the engine and pulled back into the traffic without looking at her.

Jane sank back into the leather. 'Holy shit,' she whispered, almost to herself.

They stopped for lunch at a roadside diner, where they were served chips only slightly broader than matches, then made it through Llandovery and Brecon without once being stopped by the Welsh National Assembly Cultural Police looking for a stolen BMW, and reached the outskirts of Hereford by early afternoon.

It was like Eirion had crossed over some barrier, and nothing emotive was touched on again. His mood was lighter, but Jane also sensed an underlying determination, and by the time he pulled into a side road off Kings Acre it was clear it had *never* been his intention to drop her off at the bus station.

'Where exactly do we find this suicide kid?'

'It wasn't my intention even to try,' Jane said. 'It would mean getting past her old lady. That could take time. She sounded like a very difficult woman.'

'Then let's be sensible about this and go and see *your* mother.'

'You're missing the point. My mother is in an invidious position. And if she gets involved with Riddock it will like rise off the scale of invidiousness.'

'So you want to go and face up this Riddock?'

'Christ, no. She'd chew us up. Especially you.'

'Thanks.'

'You're a guy. Guys she eats for an aperitif.'

'An aperitif is a drink, Jane. Try hors d'oeuvre.'

'I thought children of your ethnic persuasion had to do Welsh instead of French.'

'I didn't *need* to do Welsh, Jane. It was my first language – well, almost.'

'Sometimes you scare me, you're so alien.'

'Bollocks,' Eirion said. 'Neither, somehow, do I believe this Riddock scares you.'

'Doesn't *scare* me, exactly. I just don't want to go near her until I've got the means to, like, bend her to my will. No, listen . . .' Jane hammered both fists on her knees. 'Listen, listen, *listen*, I can work this out. You were right, of course. There was no way I could go to the media with half a story. We have to know first what the complete score *is* with this slag. Like, are we talking extortion? Because when I first sat down at that table in Steve's shed, the first thing Kirsty Ryan asked me was had I got the ten quid. I mean, was that a joke? Or have they actually been taking money off little kids for letting them talk to their dear departeds?'

'Little kids tend not to have dear departeds,' Eirion said. 'Death doesn't mean that much to them.'

'Jesus,' Jane said, 'when did you have *your* mid-life crisis?'

'Besides which, I thought you said she had this rich stepfather who bought her a yellow Porsche.'

'Mazda. Look, we don't know enough, OK? Therefore, we need to talk to someone who does. Turn the nice German wheels around, and I shall endeavour to direct you. And . . .'

'Yes?'

'I'm very grateful to you for sacrificing your cultural heritage on the altar of, um . . .'

'Don't embarrass us both,' Eirion said. 'We have all the time in the world for that crap.'

'Wasn't that in an ancient James Bond film?'

'Sorry?'

'Bond's like, "We have all the time in the world." Then his woman gets shot.'

'You have to turn everything into wide-screen, don't you, Jane?'

'It's a cultural thing,' Jane said. 'It's about seeing the big picture – being outward-looking, rather than . . . all right, forget it.'

She had a vague idea where the farm was because Kirsty and her sister had thrown this barn-rave for Kirsty's sixteenth, about a year ago, and these little maps had been given out. Despite her old friend Dr Samedi doing the music, Jane hadn't gone along in the end because . . . well, because of a nobody-to-go-with kind of short-term situation, if you wanted the truth. But she remembered the name of the farm.

'The Bluff?' Eirion said. 'Is this an omen?'

He was taking it very slowly because this was, after all, Gwennan's car, and they were into rough tracks now. He'd left a terse but nervous message on his dad's answering machine, explaining about the car. All Jane knew was that it was terse and nervous, because it was also in Welsh.

'I could've sworn this was right.' She was sitting up, peering from side to side: fields full of hay like big rolls of butter, a distant church steeple that could be Weobley. The Bluff implied high ground, but this was all fairly flat.

It was getting very hot; she wished she'd worn shorts.

'You didn't say you'd never actually been here,' Eirion said crossly, the BMW lurching on a baked rut. 'And you don't know she's going to be there when we find it. In fact, you haven't really thought this out, have you?'

'I'm an emotional, volatile, *charged* kind of person, Irene. When I see what has to be done, I just go for it. I thought that was one of the things you—'

'Don't push it,' Eirion growled.

'All right,' Jane said. 'I'd have rung her, if I'd thought about it. But anyway, I always think the element of surprise works best, don't you?' She looked over the back of the seat, through the rear window. 'You know this . . . this has got to be right, Eirion. If Weobley's over there and Sarnesfield's back there—' She pointed across the field. 'OK, look, there's a guy on a tractor. Why don't we just ask him? Just like drive across, you're OK.'

'I can't just drive across his field!'

''Course you can, he's already done this bit.'

Eirion changed down; the BMW chugged across the spiky surface of the mown meadow. When they got to within about ten yards of the tractor, the big machine stopped and the driver was jumping down, walking slowly towards them. The driver wore a red shirt and jeans and a dark blue baseball cap with *Ford* across the front.

The car couldn't go any further; they were into this rolling sea of cut hay. There was another guy messing about with whatever you called the piece of machinery the tractor was pulling. He looked up. Both of them looked sweaty and knackered. Eirion wound down the window and hot, urban music came in, along with the industrial juddering of the tractor.

'Sorry to bother you—'

The driver whipped off the cap, uncovering short red spiky hair and unshadowing a face that was, despite its deepening tan, not a happy face.

'Right, mate – deal. You show me the sign that says "picnic site" and I won't ram you into the bloody ditch.'

'Oh.' Jane leaned across Eirion to the open window.

The tractor driver peered past Eirion at Jane.

'Er . . . hi,' Jane said. 'Hi, Kirsty. You got a couple of minutes?'

Kirsty Ryan wiped the sweat from her nose with the back of a hand, and a clinking of the outsize nose-rings not allowed in school. She looked butch and she looked sullen. She also looked like she knew exactly what this was going to be about.

'Piss off, Watkins,' Kirsty said. 'We got nothing to say to each other.'

'Element of surprise,' Eirion murmured. 'Yes, that always works best.'

# THIRTY-ONE

# Little Taps

David Shelbone didn't look well. There was something static about one side of his long face, as though he'd had a stroke.

'No, I'm all right, quite all right,' he'd kept saying to Sophie, as she offered him more tea, a paracetamol. 'I've always suffered from migraines; this is nothing.'

Merrily didn't like to stare, but she wondered if perhaps he had only one eye. He was not what she'd imagined. Charlie Howe had led her to expect some stern prophet type, wielding the banner of Christ and the Law of Listed Buildings. But David Shelbone had a diffident, faraway look, like some ageing poet weary of words.

Sophie had read something in his manner. Announcing that she had some papers to collect from the Bishop's Palace, she left them alone. Merrily led Mr Shelbone into the little Deliverance office. A few weeks ago, she'd turned the desk around, so she now had her back to the Palace yard and was facing the door – a *feng shui* arrangement, recommended by Jane. She had to admit it did feel better-oriented; she felt more in control. Even this morning.

'I owe you an apology.' David Shelbone didn't have a local accent like his wife; there was something vaguely northern about it, and his voice was flat but thin, like card. 'When Amy came home from hospital, we had a talk. She told us your daughter was not one of the organizers of this spiritualist circle, that she in fact only attended once and was virtually dragged into it.'

Merrily nodded. 'That's my understanding, too.'

'Amy said it had been on her conscience. She felt pressured – not so much by you as . . . Anyway, I'm very sorry. There was, I'm afraid, some overreaction.'

'That was understandable.'

'We were going to write to you, to apologize.'

'No need. How is she? It must've been—'

'It could have been a lot worse. We thought there'd have to be a stomach pump, but fortunately she was very sick in the ambulance. Anyway, I rang Canon Beckett last night, and he said I should talk to you, although he wasn't sure whether or not you'd gone on holiday yet. Failing that, he thought I should go to the police. But we'd rather keep the authorities out of this. She's our only child, you see, the only child we'll ever have now.'

*Police*? 'Erm . . . Sophie said your wife and Amy had gone away somewhere, because you were afraid social services might— I mean, can they do that? *Can* they take her away, if she's been formally adopted?'

'It's complicated, I'm afraid, Mrs Watkins, but broadly, yes, they can take away any child they might consider to be in danger.'

Merrily thought of all the battered wives, abused children in unstable homes. She didn't understand.

Mr Shelbone coughed nervously. 'Also, you see, I'm . . . This is going to sound ridiculous.' There was a patch of white stubble on his neck, a grease spot on the collar of his faded grey shirt.

'Which is what most people say when they come here,' Merrily told him.

'Normally, I abhor talk of victimization . . . vendettas.'

She said carefully, 'We *are* talking about Amy here? We're talking about school?'

'Er . . . not entirely.' He cleared his throat. 'Or at least, we . . . we're probably also talking about me.'

'I see. I think I see.'

'Do you?'

'Possibly. I happened to be talking to one of the councillors.'

His eyes flickered: a hunted look. 'Which one?'

'Well, I don't think I'd better . . .'

'No,' he said. 'Of course not.' His breathing had quickened.

'But someone who I think you could say is neutral on the issue of the Barnchurch development,' Merrily said.

He blinked hard then looked almost relieved, closed his eyes for a moment. The wall clock clicked on 11.55, and Merrily remembered, with an inner shudder, precisely where she'd been standing this time yesterday.

'I have to be careful what I say here, Mrs Watkins,' Mr Shelbone said. 'As you may have heard, I'm not a very popular person in some quarters. Though I try to do what is right and Christian.'

Merrily nodded. *Tell me about it.*

'The problem with councils,' he said, 'is that, although different departments – let's say planning and social services – have very different functions, and officials rarely encounter one another in the course of their work, they're all closely linked, through the elected members.'

'In that a councillor who serves on – shall we say, planning . . .'

'May also serve on social services.' He nodded. 'You're being very perceptive, I think.'

'No, I'm just putting two and two together from what I've been told. You've a history of getting in the way of certain people's plans. They'd like you out. Your wife indicated you'd been offered some sort of early-retirement deal, but you wanted to go on.'

'We all feel we're here for a purpose, and protecting the past is mine,' he said simply. 'How could I relax at home, knowing wrong decisions were being made and important buildings were in danger of disappearing for ever?'

'Especially religious buildings?'

He bowed his long head, like a shire-horse over a gate.

'So someone who might be adversely affected by a planning decision influenced by a ruling from you,' Merrily said slowly, spelling it out, 'might seek to use any influence they might have in social services to damage you in other ways.'

'Knowing that if I became ill or . . . disgraced in some way, it would be difficult to continue. You don't believe people would behave like that?'

'To get rid of someone seriously damaging their potential incomes? Of course I believe it. But, just so we know where we are,

are you suggesting a bunch of councillors are on the take from Allan Henry?'

'I doubt it's as simple or as provable as that. It might involve a new garage or an extension to someone's house. All peanuts to Henry, of course. But I'm not naming names.' He looked directly at her, eyes full of pain and fatigue. 'All I want to convey to you is that if anyone took Amy away, it would destroy Hazel. There'd be nothing left for either of us. Ever.'

'These fears are very much in the wake of Amy's overdose?'

'Gossip travels fast in Herefordshire. In no time at all, people were linking Amy's sudden hospitalization . . . to the incident in the church.'

'They *were* linked, weren't they?'

He looked defiant. 'It was a horribly stupid and dangerous thing to do, and she knew it. I said to Hazel, if Amy wanted to draw attention to herself, she's certainly done it now.'

'Is it your feeling she was just trying to get attention? Rather than . . .' *Wanting to be with her mother?*

'And it's all horribly exaggerated, I'm sure.' Avoiding her question. 'Because serious churchgoing is so unfashionable these days, people have accused us of being fanatics, forcing Amy to go to church all the time, operating a strict religious regime at home. I . . .' He passed a hand across his eyes. 'There've been all kinds of stupid stories. People are so needlessly cruel and vindictive. And social workers have big ears.'

'You don't need big ears when somebody's whispering into them,' Merrily said. 'Have there been any formal inquiries? Any contact at all from Social Services?'

'I have *some* friends left in the office. I've been discreetly warned, put it like that.'

'As a result of which, Hazel's actually taken her away?'

'I – no. No, she hasn't, of course. That was untrue.' When he half turned, she thought it was to hide tears, but he was putting a hand into an inside pocket.

He slid a folded paper across the desk to her.

Merrily unfolded it carefully. Though the message was word-processed, it didn't looked official – probably something to do with the fact that the paper was pink and had a kitten in the top right hand corner.

*Oh God.*

Dearest Mum and Daddy,
I am so very sorry. I have behaved abbominably and feel I am ruining both your lives. I pray that you will understand what I am doing and support me in this and not worry for my safety because I have definately learned my lesson and you need have no fears on that score any more.

I know it is not your fault and that you were only trying to protect me by not telling me the truth about Justine, but I know now, beyond all doubt, that my real mother is very unhappy and cannot rest in spirit and I know I cannot live a normal life until I have done all I can to help her.

By the time you read this I will have been to a cash machine and drawn out the money that you said was mine from your account. I am sorry I borrowed your card and will post it back to you.

Please try to understand how important this is to me and do not try to find me or tell the Police. I am quite safe, but if I find out that they are looking for me I will be very upset and might do something stupid, so please trust me and I shall return home in a few days, when Justine is at peace.

 Yours sincerely,
 Your loving daughter,
  Amy

Merrily folded the letter. *Oh God, oh God, oh God.*

'Erm . . . I'm with Dennis,' she said as calmly as she could. 'I think you should take this to the police.'

David Shelbone reached for the letter and quickly pocketed it.

'No,' he said very quietly.

'David, just a couple of days ago she tried to kill herself.'

'Tell me, do you trust *your* daughter when she tells you something?'

'I . . .' It was the things Jane *didn't* tell you about . . . 'Yeah. I suppose I do.' She thought quickly. He wouldn't want to go to the police for two principal reasons: *one*, that Amy might indeed do something stupid if she thought there was a search on for her, and *two*, it would confirm any social worker's suspicions.

But this development might be more serious than David Shelbone could imagine. For instance, how much did he know about Layla Riddock? Anything at all?

'She's never lied to us, you see,' he said. 'Not from being a small child. Not about anything. It's the way she was brought up, certainly, but also the way she is.'

Merrily sighed. 'She lied – I'm sorry, but she lied about Jane, didn't she?'

'No!' he insisted. 'She didn't. She said your daughter was there. The rest was implied. She didn't lie.'

'So when you told Sophie that your wife—'

'*I* lied. Hazel's gone to try and find her.'

'She knows where to look?'

'She has a good idea, yes.'

'Where?'

'Up near Birmingham. It's where Amy was born. And where her mother died.'

'And Amy knows this?'

'We assume she does.'

'From . . .'

'Initially, from the so-called messages she received.'

'The spirit messages?'

'Whatever they were, they were horribly accurate. And so, in the end, we had to tell her where she came from. And what happened to her mother.'

Merrily said, 'Do you think you could tell *me*?'

She'd been born Amy Jukes at Tipton in the Black Country. Her parents were even married before the happy event. Just about.

Justine was seventeen when Amy arrived and not yet a heroin user. She came from a respectable family, was doing A levels, hoping to become a doctor. This was what the court was told.

The father, Wayne Jukes, was twenty-two, an 'assistant manager' at a night club. What this actually meant was that Wayne had been responsible for selling various stimulants to the punters. He also did a little pill-peddling around the schools and colleges, for a bit of extra cash, and that was how he met Justine. Wayne wore nice suits and a tie and was smooth and plausible. He had a Toyota sports car, so it didn't take long.

Justine's parents were disappointed, naturally, but they thought Wayne was a presentable enough boy, with an apparently promising managerial position. They helped Wayne and Justine get a house, a little semi on a not-bad estate, ready for the baby.

David Shelbone knew all these details from the Social Services people in the Black Country and in Hereford. He'd also gone out of his way to obtain the inquest and court reports in the local papers – destroying them, of course, before Amy learned to read. He'd even traced Justine's parents. David was very thorough: anything that might help understand Amy better, he and Hazel wanted to know.

Justine had been very young, had never really wanted this baby, found it awfully hard work, especially with Wayne out most nights, pursuing his junior managerial role. Justine, at home with the infant Amy, had very rapidly become depressed, and it became clear that Wayne Jukes had taken to slipping her a little something to make life seem easier. Sometimes he'd even keep her company.

They thought they were cool, rising above it. They thought because he was in the business somehow that meant they could control it. And they were young, too young for life to appear seriously bad. When you were young, you bounced.

It was a long time before Justine's parents realized what was happening. By then, Wayne was himself using more than he was selling – too far gone to realize he was being eased out of the club operation because he was becoming untrustworthy, careless, a risk.

And the mortgage wasn't getting paid, and the baby cried too much and Justine complained sometimes – to the extent that Wayne had found it expedient to give her a little tap from time to time.

David Shelbone was telling the story in his colourless, hesitant way, but Merrily was seeing it in harsh documentary flashes, hearing the voices, the accents, the head-spinning, squashy, bloody, sobbing reality of those little taps.

There was a serious falling-out with her family, and Wayne and Justine sold the house and got a small flat in a run-down area, at the end of one of those streets that went on for ever, a greasy ribbon of tatty garages and betting shops, chip shops, half-dead pubs.

At the very end was a church, which had been a big parish church back in the days when this had been a village street but now had a congregation of about seven pensioners. Some days Justine would retreat into the church, taking the baby, when Wayne was in one of his moods.

Which was most days, because Wayne was drinking heavily now as well. He'd made friends in one of the half-dead pubs and Justine had found it best not to be around – or to be there but completely out of it – when Wayne got home.

It was worse at night, obviously. A neighbour, who cleaned the church for the vicar – who had four other collapsing congregations to try and shore up – became concerned for Justine and gave her a key to the side door next to the vestry, and some nights that was where Justine would go, carrying the baby and a carving knife in case there was anyone already in there.

And one night there was.

Wayne had been wondering for a long time where Justine went, the times she wasn't there when he came home in need of some kind of action. So one night he left the pub twenty minutes earlier than usual and waited in a derelict doorway across the street and followed her when she came out with the kid. Next day, he found the church key in the back pocket of Justine's jeans and had a copy cut for himself.

And that same summer night, when Justine came into the church with Amy, Wayne was waiting for them behind the dusty, moth-eaten drapes in front of the vestry door.

It might have ended differently if Justine hadn't done some business of her own that afternoon with a bloke she and Wayne used to know when Wayne was at the club – a bloke who gave her a little something for her trouble. If Justine hadn't shot the little something into her arm before she came out, if she hadn't been up there and ready for anybody, Wayne included, it might have ended with just a few more little taps.

'And Amy saw all this?' Merrily said. 'How old was she?'

'Nearly three.'

'Dear God, that's old enough to absorb everything. Even if she had no conscious memory, it would all be there.'

'The Social Services were very careful about where she was taken,' David Shelbone said. 'The grandparents didn't want her – they'd recently taken in an elderly relative, and, well . . .'

'Mmm.'

'It was an emergency, obviously. They wanted to get the child well out of the area, and we were experienced, reliable foster-parents, unencumbered at the time. We were approached, told the background. We were fully prepared.' He fell silent.

'And?'

'Nothing to cause alarm. Not ever. No particular problems at all – and, believe me, Hazel and I have coped with some very taxing children in our time. But Amy settled down remarkably quickly. No nightmares beyond the norm. Nothing to suggest suppressed memories of violence. She was always a very well-balanced, if rather serious child. Our daughter. We both decided very quickly that, if at all possible, she should stay with us and become our daughter.'

'There were no indications at all that she might have remembered something?'

'Not until . . . I mean, yes, I *have* sometimes wondered if her serious and rather . . . orthodox approach to life didn't reflect a sub-conscious need to impose an order that would in some way cancel out the chaos of her early years. But it's not something that's greatly worried me, and Hazel was always most emphatic that Amy should never be exposed to any kind of psychological assessment. We were naturally glad when she – without any coercion from us – began to embrace Christianity from quite an early age . . . perhaps four or five. Hazel always believed that if she ever required solace she would find it there, rather than in counselling or therapy.'

Merrily recalled Hazel Shelbone's reaction to the suggestion that some kind of psychiatric assessment would be needed as a preliminary to exorcism.

'What did you tell her when she asked you about her real parents?'

'We told her we understood there'd been an accident – and she never questioned that. We always accepted that there may come a time when we'd have to tell her the real truth, but not until she was old enough to deal with it.'

'So when, after years of going happily to church, she suddenly knocked the chalice out of Canon Beckett's hands and—'

'It all ended at the altar, you see,' David Shelbone said. 'That's the point. That was what frightened us the most.'

No one knew exactly *how* it had ended. Wayne Jukes had presumably either decided or been told that it would help his defence if he was unable to remember anything after emerging from behind the curtain to find the baby sitting on the font and his wife crouched, snarling – the Kitchen Devil glinting in the feeble light, swishing the air.

Less than half an hour later, police – summoned by neighbours who had been afraid even to go in – found the threadbare chancel carpet already slippery with blood, Wayne standing in the aisle, with his face opened up from eye to chin, Justine vomiting blood over the altar rail.

Amy sitting on the altar itself, laughing.

'Justine had stab wounds to the lungs, throat and stomach,' David Shelbone said. 'She died in the ambulance.'

The trail of blood apparently suggested that Justine had first slashed Wayne and then picked up the child and run to the chancel, the trail of blood along the aisle showing how Wayne had blundered after her.

'She'd put Amy on the altar and then either she'd put down the knife in horror at what she'd done, and he picked it up and attacked her with it . . . or he overpowered her, and in the struggle—'

'What happened to Wayne?'

'I gather he's out of prison now,' David Shelbone said without emotion. 'Doing youth work in Bristol.'

Merrily felt faintly sick, thinking not about Justine Jukes but Stephanie Stock and Gerard with the wild poppies on his shirt. Domestics: the most common kind of murder.

'Why didn't Hazel tell me about this at the very beginnning?'

'We'd never told anyone – *anyone*. Besides, Hazel and I both fervently believed that the way out of this was through Christ. Her mother died in church, so Amy had some sort of flashback – again in church.'

'So Hazel never really believed that Amy was possessed by Justine?'

'It didn't *matter*,' David Shelbone insisted. 'She was possessed by the past. If the memories could be reawakened by these foul experiments then they could be exorcised by Christ. We have old-fashioned values, Mrs Watkins. Today we'd probably never be accepted as foster-parents.'

'When did she go missing?'

'She wasn't there when we got up this morning. That was a terrible shock. Her bed hadn't been slept in. Her mobile phone was gone. We've tried ringing it, but it's always switched off.'

'And you think she's somehow made her way to the Black Country. Does the church still exist?'

'Oh yes. And also . . . we searched her room. Something we've never done before. We found an old road atlas of mine under the bed. The area was ringed. Hazel set off for there about three hours ago.'

'How much money has Amy got?'

'There was five hundred pounds of her money in the account. She can draw two hundred a day from a machine.'

'And what do you think Amy might do there?'

'I don't know. I haven't a clue what they'd do.'

'They?'

'I doubt she's on her own. That's one reason I wanted to talk to you. Your daughter would know who the other girls were, wouldn't she?'

'Didn't you ask Amy herself?'

'She wouldn't tell us . . . except for naming your daughter. This was when Mr Beckett— We asked her again, later, as I was ready to go to see the headmaster, but she insisted it was all over.'

'She told you that?'

'I honestly believe she thought it *was* over. And it was clear that if we tried to take it further she'd throw a tantrum. She once said if we attempted to find out, she'd— Mrs Watkins, you have to understand this is not the way she normally behaves. It's clear, looking back, that she's under someone else's influence. And I rather doubt we're talking about her dead mother.'

So he actually didn't know yet about Layla Riddock? He didn't have the information to make this other, very meaningful connection with Allan Henry?

And how, in his present state, would he react if she told him about it? Merrily wasn't prepared to put it to the test.

'Erm . . . my daughter's on holiday with her boyfriend's family. I'll try and get hold of her, OK? I don't know how long it'll take, but if I find out anything I'll . . . I'll get back to you at your office. And if Hazel finds her—'

'I'll get straight back to you, of course,' he said. 'Thank you, Mrs Watkins. Thank you.' He stood up. 'There is one more thing. If Hazel finds Amy and brings her back, I don't think it'll be safe for her to come home. I wondered if the Church had any place of – of sanctuary, I suppose, somewhere you could recommend as safe for both of them. I mean Hazel as well. I'm sorry to put this on you.'

Merrily stood up too. 'If you think it's necessary, we'll find some-where. Until all this is sorted out. Even if it's in my vicarage.'

She smiled.

This was all she needed right now.

'I'll help you *all* I can,' she said. 'But if Hazel doesn't find her by tonight, I really think you should go to the police.'

When Sophie returned, Merrily laid the whole story on her, including the information she'd had from Charlie Howe at the Green Dragon, before Andy Mumford's arrival had rearranged everyone's priorities.

Sophie's eyebrows rose several times.

'What was I supposed to do?' Merrily asked her. 'Do *you* think I should've warned him about Layla Riddock?'

Sophie thought about it, hands clasped on the desk.

'That would be giving him a target,' she said at last. 'Not good. Especially if the target's Allan Henry.'

'What do you know about him, Sophie?'

'I know that he isn't what one might call a Friend of the Earth, particularly the Herefordshire earth. He began by buying small der-elict properties in villages and hamlets – a petrol station that went out of business, that sort of thing – demolishing them and developing the sites. And then somehow those sites would start to expand into adjacent fields. His own thoroughly tasteless dwelling began that way. He gets away with things. Luck of the Devil, as it were.'

'Charlie Howe said that.'

'And there's a man who'd recognize it,' Sophie said darkly. 'However, you have no proof whatsoever of any connection between this girl's evident persecution of Amy Shelbone and her stepfather's grudge against David Shelbone. No, I think you did absolutely the right thing in not telling him – at this stage, at least. I think you have enough to worry about, without having an already distressed individual behaving in a probably irrational fashion because—'

'Because of something I did.' Merrily sighed.

Sophie glared at her. '*I* certainly intended no parallel with the Stock business.'

'But what if Amy Shelbone *is* out there with Layla Riddock? This is a girl even Jane is scared of.'

Sophie thought for a moment, then reached for the Hereford phone book. After a couple of minutes tracking along columns of names, she slammed it shut.

'Ex-directory.'

'Only to be expected,' Merrily said. 'I imagine there's quite a lot of people would like to ring Allan Henry late at night. Well, at least we know where he lives. A little bit of Dallas in Canon Pyon.'

'Oh no,' Sophie said. 'You stay away from there. What would be the point?'

'We could at least find out if Layla's there. If she is, she can't have gone off with Amy – and then it all falls down, doesn't it?'

Sophie scowled. 'Why doesn't that man just tell the police?'

'But he hasn't. He's told *me*.'

'Almost as if he knew you,' Sophie said with bitterness.

'And, whatever he says, Amy *did* lie. She claimed Jane had approached her initially, to lure her into the circle – Jane, not Layla. She also tried to stitch me up when I went to the bungalow when her parents were out. So we know that Amy *does* tell lies.'

'But the attempted suicide . . . why did she do that?'

'Well, there was a vague mention of "pressure",' Merrily said.

'But it was clear he didn't want to talk about it. I don't think – and this is possibly the most worrying thing of all – I honestly don't think he knows *why* she did it.'

# THIRTY-TWO

# The Big Lie

'I mean you're not gonner scare *me*, Watkins,' Kirsty said. 'I don't give a toss who you've talked to. The school year's over. The slate's wiped clean. They can't touch any of us now and like, by the time we go back, those time-serving gits en't gonner want to remember. Also, I may not even *go* back. I'm undecided. I may've had enough of education.'

She sat down with her back to a tractor wheel, stretched out her legs, fanned herself with her baseball cap. Jane thought she looked disgustingly smug.

'Came to me, couple of months ago: OK, you get your A levels, you go to university, you get some pissy little job in some nasty, overcrowded city, so that in twenty years' time you can afford to take your kids to live in the country. It's insane, ennit?'

'You've got a point,' Eirion agreed. 'But—'

'But meanwhile – yeah, yeah – Amy bloody Shelbone.' Kirsty closed her eyes in a kind of weary contempt. 'Why don't you just let it go, Watkins? The kid's neurotic. She tried to kill herself, so-called, but she didn't make it. After an hour or so on the end of a stomach pump, or throwing up, whatever, she en't gonner do that again in a hurry, is she, stupid little cow?'

Jane stared at the chunky girl sprawled in the hay. The other guy had gone, just slipped away. Kirsty didn't need back-up, she was wholly self-sufficient; this was her place. But for the tractor and the blast of Massive Attack from its cab, she could have been part of a scene from centuries ago.

'Questions are being asked all over the place,' Jane said. 'And it isn't you in the frame, or Layla, either. It's me, right? I'm the only one she named – like to the doctors and the police and people like that.'

Jane didn't know if Amy had named her to anyone except her parents, but she needed to bring it down to a personal level that Kirsty Ryan just might relate to.

'Tough,' Kirsty said. 'Go tell Morrell about it.'

'Like you said, why should Morrell care? School's out. But I am *so* not gonna sit here and take the shit for you and Riddock. I'm going public on it. You ever heard of Bella Ford from Radio Hereford and Worcester?'

'Nope.'

'Well, she's a mate of mine, anyway, and I'm going over there to see her tonight, and I'm putting you and Riddock in the frame for bullying and terrorizing this younger kid into trying to top herself.'

Kirsty's eyelids flicked up.

'Believe it,' Jane said grimly.

'I only listen to Radio One,' Kirsty said. 'Therefore, I don't give a monkey's.'

'OK.' Jane shrugged. 'So you won't hear it.'

'So why you telling me?'

''Cause I'm kind of a straight person. I don't go behind people's backs. I just wanted to tell you why I was doing it, is all.'

'And to warn you they'll probably be ringing you up for a comment,' Eirion put in swiftly. With his news-reporting ambitions and his dad having fingers in BBC Wales, HTV and the Welsh-language outfit, S4C, Eirion knew quite a lot about radio and TV. 'They're obliged to do that, to give you a chance to get over your side of the story.'

'Well, they can piss off, can't they?'

'Sure. Sometimes it's easier for them if you do refuse to comment. They only need to give you the opportunity.'

Jane said, 'It's just, you know, that I'd started to feel a bit bad about you. Thinking maybe you weren't as majorly responsible as Layla, and I wanted to tell you what I'd done. And now I've done that, so, like . . . we'll go now.'

She turned away. It was beginning to get uncomfortably hot in this field, anyway, like the hay was extracting all the juice out of the sun.

Eirion pulled the car keys out of his jeans.

Kirsty sat up. 'You're an *evil* little cow for a vicar's daughter, aren't you?'

Less than ten minutes out of the centre of Hereford, you could be into deep countryside. There weren't many cities like this any more and, the way things were going, Merrily thought – as she thought almost every time she drove out of the city – it wouldn't be long before Hereford had become like the rest. Rampant megalomania, disguised as essential economic growth.

Ego-tripping councillors and unscrupulous developers.

Allan Henry.

Sophie stopped the Saab with two wheels on the grass verge, near the top of a low hill a mile out of the straggling village of Canon Pyon.

They were in a quiet lane, looking down on sloping woodland. On its lower fringe, the sun was reflected darkly from the huge picture windows on the side of a long, brick villa that had been built on so many levels it seemed to cascade down the hill.

Where they were now parked was probably the only place you could get a good view of Allan Henry's home. The surrounding trees failed to conceal a wall with railings enclosing about two acres of garden, suggesting Allan Henry must also own the land between the wall and the lane. In fact, Merrily supposed he owned the whole hill.

'What do we do now?' She was in need of a cigarette, but Sophie had a yellow and black *no smoking* sign on the dash, and she meant it.

'I suppose that depends on to what extent you think Henry might be implicated,' Sophie said. 'Personally, I wouldn't even get out of the car.'

'Think about it. If we assume David Shelbone is costing him hundreds of thousands of pounds, maybe millions – because, if the Hereford bypass goes through there, the Barnchurch estate would be gold dust – then anybody might feel frustrated to the point of . . . I mean, people have killed for less, haven't they? Much less.'

Sophie nodded. 'It's frightening when you think about it. Which is why, if I were you, I wouldn't get out of the car.'

'So . . . accepting that killing people can seriously damage your future, Allan Henry's looking for ways of neutralizing a sober, clean-living, God-fearing man who can't be bought. What are the most important things in Shelbone's life?'

'His family,' Sophie said reluctantly. 'Wife, daughter . . . and his religion.'

'*Adopted* daughter. Originally a foster-child taken in by the Shelbones under very difficult circumstances. Now, David Shelbone might think Amy's origins are a secret, but quite a few people in and around social services will be aware of the history – including councillors, present or past.'

'In some quarters it would be quite an open secret,' Sophie agreed. 'It wouldn't take much for the information to get back, via certain councillors, to Allan Henry.'

'Whose stepdaughter goes to the same school as Amy.'

'This is very much the tricky part, Merrily.'

'But if you work from the premise that Allan Henry initially asks his stepdaughter what she knows about Amy Shelbone, and Layla tells him that Amy's this prissy, stuck-up little swot . . . And from then on, Layla starts to take a particular interest in Amy. Now, why – as a teenager – would she particularly want to help her stepfather?'

'No,' Sophie said. 'They don't, as a rule, do they? Not without an incentive, usually monetary. Has her stepfather told her the full background, do you think? That this girl's father is a serious thorn in his side who could affect their future standard of living? Does he perhaps exaggerate that situation?'

Merrily thought of Robert Morrell on the phone the other night: '*like a lot of wealthy men with potentially problematical stepchildren, he's been throwing money at her for years.*'

'Mmm. Maybe he tells Layla that if the Barnchurch project goes down, his business will be in ruins and her lovely new sports car will have to go?' She caught a glimpse of shimmering turquoise behind Henry's villa. 'Or even the swimming pool? I mean, maybe he isn't exaggerating at all – we don't know the size of his stake in Barnchurch.'

'I don't normally like to encourage flights of fancy,' Sophie said. 'But I suppose there is a certain tainted logic to all this.'

'At some point Allan Henry tells Layla what he's learned about Amy Shelbone's history – the background even Amy herself doesn't yet know. So *then* what happens? Most girls would simply confide it to a best friend, and within a couple of days it'd be all round the school. And Amy would probably become a more popular figure as a result – attracting a lot more interest, even some sympathy, for a change. But Henry realizes that Layla, being Layla, is going to come up with something *far* more elaborate.'

Merrily thought of Gypsy Layla: black hat, dark veil, predictions of death and destruction. Had Layla also been aware that it was the father of Amy Shelbone who'd complained about her at the Christmas Fair and ended her show – the very same David Shelbone who was now trying to shut down Allan Henry's show?

'So Gypsy Layla becomes Madame Layla, confidante of the dead, in session every lunchtime in the caretaker's hut. She has at least one friend in on the secret and, between them, they work the glass. She has a lovely name to play with – *Justine*. She takes it very slowly, feeding out bits at a time to Amy . . . there are probably usually other girls involved as well so it won't look suspicious – like Jane, in fact. And slowly and exquisitely, little Amy is hooked.'

The barb really taking hold when Amy went home and asked Hazel Shelbone certain questions – saw the instant dramatic effect on Hazel. Immediately, Amy would feel herself to be at the centre of this awful conspiracy – her beloved adoptive parents had been lying to her for all these years. The only person who wasn't lying to her was her real mother, reaching out from beyond the grave. Layla, with her sense of drama, could create whatever kind of Justine she needed for the purpose: lonely, sad, unloved, imploring.

And horribly seductive to an adolescent who perhaps *did* sometimes feel like an alien – without previously having known why. *Had* something previously hidden been unblocked, horrific memories awoken?

'So gradually Layla was feeding it out to Amy: blood in the church, blood on the altar. Then here's Dennis Beckett in his vestments, with his chalice: "*The blood which he shed for you . . . The blood of Christ keep you in eternal life.*" And Amy Shelbone, kneeling in the chancel, is getting a whole different slant on this.'

*All smelly and musty and horrible, and it's full of dead people . . .* There must have been some ghastly images in her head by then – Wayne Jukes, maddened with pain and shock, half his face hanging off, plunging the kitchen knife into Justine. And 'eternal life' was some church-bound, tortured spirit.

'The big lie, the great cover-up.' Merrily was rocking in the passenger seat, everything suddenly making blinding sense. *He watches us suffer and die and he doesn't help us, ever, ever, ever . . . Nobody's going to ever save you. It's all a horrible sick lie!* 'Amy only knows one church, one altar. She's imagining her mother dead . . . *in Dilwyn Church.*'

She stopped, hearing what else Amy had screamed from her room: *And I don't . . . I don't want to die in . . .* Had 'Justine' predicted that Amy too was going to be killed or at least die in church? Had she given some kind of terrible warning that made suicide seem like a soft option?

'The essence of all this,' Sophie said, 'is that the child has been virtually programmed to turn against everything the Shelbones cling on to. If that's true, then, in its insidious way, it's actually extremely sophisticated. Almost Satanic in its . . . Do you know what I mean?'

'In the way the poison's been introduced.'

'However, I don't even see that any laws have been broken. And I *still* don't think you should get out of this car.'

'You bastards.' Kirsty Ryan lay flat in the churned hay, staring up at the deepening blue. 'I don't know whether you're lying to me, or what. It don't matter either way to me, though, look, 'cause I en't catching no armful of shit for that bitch, I can tell you that much.'

'Why don't you just tell us everything?' Eirion suggested.

Kirsty rolled her spiky head back into the hay. 'Who *is* this guy thinks he's Geoffrey Paxman?'

'Just a friend,' Jane explained.

'Thanks, Jane,' Eirion said.

'Well, all right, a really good friend,' Jane conceded.

Kirsty grinned. 'Then why'n't you both just go and have a roll behind that hedge and leave me alone, eh?'

'Please, Kirsty.' Jane leaned over her. 'This is really important.'

Kirsty sat up. 'All right. Siddown. Got any blow? Naw, forget it. Only kidding. Wouldn't do at the vicarage, would it? Listen, I'll go so far and no further, so don't go asking me more stuff when I say *no*. And you keep me out of this, right? Else I'll come after you with the four-ten.'

'OK.' Jane sat down in the mown grass. Kirsty with a shotgun – that was entirely believable. 'We never even spoke to you.'

'This thing, it got out of hand, right? I went so far with it then I was out. Finished. I even tried to bust it all up, but that didn't work. So that was it, I was outer there. Plus, I mean, in school you need diversions, right? You gotter have things to get you through it. Though I don't need that now, do I? I look like I got time to mess with the mind of some stupid little cow?'

'No,' Jane said.

'All right, well, it's simple enough. Layla knew some things about Shelbone, look – about her parents, her *real* parents.'

'How did she—?' Eirion began , but Jane put a warning hand on his knee and he shut up.

'Like, for instance, that her dad knifed her ma to death in this church,' Kirsty said.

Jane clutched at the hay.

'Both of them bloody junkies. Both parents junkies and her dad's a murderer – and Shelbone's this holier-than-thou, pain-in-the-arse, stuck-up little cow who'd grass you up to the teachers soon as— Unbelievable, ennit?'

'Where did this happen?' Eirion asked.

'Somewhere up the Midlands. Not round yere.'

'In a church?' Jane felt numb.

'Now Layla, she had a very good reason to bring down that family. On account it was Shelbone's ole man, her *adopted* ole man that messed it up when Layla done that gypsy thing at the Christmas Fair.'

'I wasn't there. I was sick.'

'Well, I'll tell you, Jane, that was real scary, that stuff she was coming out with. When she gets in that gypsy gear, it's like she's another person. Wouldn't have *my* fortune told by her, *no* way. But that's beside the point. The point is ole man Shelbone protests that it's unChristian and he gets it stopped. So in Layla's view they all got it coming to them now, big-time. Gypsies don't forget, right? And she done me a few favours, mostly money, you know? So I couldn't say no.'

'To helping her stage the ouija?'

'But, after a while, I could tell this was fucking the kid up, serious.'

Merrily gazed over the glass waterfall that was Allan Henry's home. She thought about getting out, going for a meditative walk around, with a cigarette. Perhaps there was something obvious she was missing.

'Where's her mother stand in all this?' she asked suddenly.

'Sandra Henry,' Sophie said. 'Sandra Riddock?'

'You *know* her?'

'Not personally, but she worked for an estate agency where my sister was manager for a while. It was how she met Henry. They were the agents for one of his first shoddy housing estates – twelve, fifteen years ago? She was quite a beauty, apparently. I remember my sister saying that no one knew she even had a child, then.'

'The father was a gypsy, Jane says.'

'I wouldn't know. But you're right – I do wonder if Sandra Henry knows what her daughter's been up to.'

'I wonder if she's in. I wonder if she's down there now – on her own. I wonder if Layla's away, supposedly staying with friends or something equally suspicious.'

Sophie stiffened. 'On what basis would we be calling on her?'

'We? Well, me, I'd have to play it straight. I'm a minister of the Church. I've just found out my daughter's been involved in experiments to contact the dead, along with Mrs Henry's daughter and a girl who attempted suicide. As a priest I'm naturally very worried about that. What's she going to do, laugh it off, turn me away?'

'You'd be using Jane.'

322

'I'm not *using* Jane. Jane didn't even tell me about it. Dennis did.'

'All right.' Sophie started the car. 'Let's try and find the entrance to the drive. I'm told it isn't obvious. I won't say "On your head be it." It's both our heads.'

'You're a mate, Soph.'

'Oh, shut up.' Sophie pulled into the lane, drove very slowly down the hill. It was very quiet; there were no other houses or farms in the vicinity. No cows or sheep grazed the hill. As far as Merrily could recall, no other vehicle had passed them since they'd stopped.

'Likes his privacy.'

'Evidently.' Sophie stopped opposite a tarmacked opening on the right. 'You think this is it?'

'Try it.'

Sophie drove into the entrance – the deep shade of big forest trees immediately closing over the car. After about fifty yards they came to the perimeter wall with its railings on top, a couple of brick gateposts, eight or so feet high, with metal gates, open. A black sign on the left-hand post decreed, in yellow lettering, NO UNAUTHO-RIZED ENTRY.

'Probably be security cameras, somewhere,' Sophie guessed. They passed a small bungalow with a van outside. 'Staff there, I expect. We supposed to check in, I wonder?'

'Nobody about, anyway. Carry on.'

On the left was a clearing in the trees. Sophie braked.

'Good heavens. Either it's a reproduction or a museum piece.'

'Or Layla's dad's dropped in.'

The *vardo* stood alone. It was crimson and gold, like an outsize barrel organ. It had ornate, gilt-ribbed panels, a porch with side-brackets like golden wheels, and brass carriage lamps. The windows had intricately patterned shutters. The *vardo* looked immaculate, out of a children's picture book.

Really *has* thrown money at her, Merrily thought. For a couple of seconds she even wondered if Amy Shelbone was in there with Gypsy Layla.

'Too easy,' Sophie murmured, and drove on.

After a few yards, the full sky reappeared as the drive widened into a forecourt with three vehicles in it: a Range Rover, a black Porsche Carerra and a small sleek yellow sports car. There was a flight of about five stone steps up to a front door that was about the size and thickness of the one accessing Ledwardine Church.

A man came down the steps. Merrily got out of the car.

'I'm looking for Mrs Henry.'

'*Are* you, indeed?' He wore jeans and an old cheesecloth shirt, open to the waist. Gardener? Handyman? Security?

'This is the right house, isn't it?' Merrily said.

'And you are?'

'My name's Merrily Watkins.'

He nodded slowly, waiting.

'I just wanted to talk to Mrs Henry on a private matter. I would've rung first, but it's ex-directory.'

'So it is,' he said. 'Well, she's not here.' He looked her up and down like she might have a set of burglar's tools under her jacket. 'Maybe I can help.' He put out a slow hand. 'Allan Henry.'

Kirsty Ryan said she'd first started to get cold feet when she realized that Amy Shelbone had actually *not* known about her real dad killing her mother until they pulled the spirit scam on her in Steve's shed.

'Even Layla was surprised how easy she went for it. We'd give her a bit of a spirit message from her ma, and she'd write it all down, like it was tablets of stone, and next day, half-twelve on the dot she'd come scampering across the field, desperate to contact her ole lady again – I'm saying ole lady, she was just a kid herself when the bastard carved her up. I was getting pissed off with it. I mean, a joke's a joke, but you don't let it take over your life.'

'Whose life?' Eirion asked.

'*She* needed it as much as the kid by then.'

'Layla?'

'Don't get the idea she's playing at this, mate.' Kirsty pushed a hand through her foxy hair. 'She's into the gypsy thing in a *big* way. Whole shelves of books, wardrobes full of exotic clobber – the veils and the hats and the flouncy skirts. She got crystals and a dozen packs of Tarot cards. She got her own gypsy caravan. She mixes herbs and things. She'll do you a love token to get the bloke you want –

involving locks of your hair and his hair and ribbons and stuff. Calls herself a *shuvani*, a gypsy sorcerer. Like – OK – once, there was this bloke I fancied and I wanted to know if I was wasting my time, right? Layla's like, OK, wait for the right time of the month, gimme a Tampax—'

Jane recoiled. 'Gross!'

'We make this necklace of beads out of clay and menstrual blood. I was supposed to hang it on the guy's locker and then if the beads had like dissolved by morning it meant he wasn't gonner be interested. In the end, I bottled out, threw it away, said somebody must've nicked it. I mean – what?'

'She really believes this stuff?' Eirion said.

'It's her *life*, mate.'

'So she didn't think it was entirely a scam – the spiritualism?'

'It started *out* that way, like I said. But when it began to *work*, when the kid's really gone for it, she's like, "Oh this is how it happens, this is how it happens." You know?'

'Not really.'

'It was like she believed the kid's ma really was in touch. Now, she believes she's got the power. All the things she told people at the Christmas Fair, ever since, she's been like, "Oh, Mrs So-and-So just died, you hear that? I told her she was gonner die!" Going on like that.'

Jane shivered.

'They're really cooking, you know, her and the kid. I don't know how she found out about the murder, I really don't. But then she reckons a load of other stuff's coming through that she *didn't* know. Layla is very excited, not that you'd know that, if you en't known her as long as me. Come the holidays, no way does she wanner let go of little Shelbone. That afternoon, after the heavy mob crash into Stevie's shed and bust us up, I'm like, right, that's it, you can count *me* out, sister, I got better things to do. But she's already making other arrangements.'

'So you haven't been in contact with Layla since school broke up?' Jane said.

'She rang me a couple of times. I said I was too busy. Next thing, I hear about the kid chucking up in church – well, nobody knew what that was about except me. I thought, this has gone too far. This is well over the bloody top. *Next* thing I hear, she's tried to do away with herself. That's spooky, ennit?' Kirsty stood up. 'There it is. You got the lot now.'

Eirion said, 'You've known Layla a long time then?'

'All my life, give or take. We were at the same little school at Eardisley. 'Course, they weren't rich then, her and her ma. When Allan Henry come on the scene, he wanted to take her away from Moorfield to some private school, but she wouldn't go.'

'You never met her father?'

'*She* never met her father. She used to have like fantasies about him, this mysterious gypsy. He was probably some travelling scrap-metal dealer, but she had him roaming Europe in his romantic caravan, seducing women with love potions and doing the business.'

'The business?'

'The magic. Doing the magic for his friends and cursing his enemies. She got all the books, and whenever there was gypsies in the area she'd spend hours with them. She even went off with the buggers once for two nights, her ma went bloody spare. And then . . . Oh yeah – she cursed a teacher once. We had this gym teacher at Moorfield, Mrs Etchinson. Gave us a hard time. Gave everybody a hard time – team spirit, all this shit. Layla was never a team player.'

'Cursed her how?' Jane asked. 'This was probably before my time.'

'It must've been before your time, because everybody knew about it. I dunno what she did. The evil eye, the bad words . . . grave-dirt in an envelope.'

'What happened?'

'Put it this way – within a few months it was confirmed she'd got multiple sclerosis. Not good for a gym teacher.'

'That takes years to come on,' Eirion pointed out. 'She must have had it already.'

'That was what we said,' Kirsty said. 'But it does makes you think, don't it?'

It didn't give Jane a good feeling. She stood up, too. 'What did she do for Steve, to get him to lend her his shed?'

'More what she didn't do, if you ask me,' Kirsty said enigmatically. 'Like being considerate enough not to shrivel his genitals.'

'But she's still seeing Amy?'

'Look, all I know is, when she rang me she said Amy was coming out to meet her at night. Like *really* at night – when her parents were in bed. She'd ring Amy on the little phone that Amy kept under the pillow, and Layla would say the word and Amy would be up and dressed and out the front door and Layla would pick her up at the bottom of the lane.'

'Where would they go? I mean she'd need somewhere with a table, to lay all the letters out and—'

'No way,' Kirsty said scornfully. 'That is *history.*'

'What?'

'That's primitive stuff, now. They got *well* beyond the glass and the little bloody letters.'

'What's that mean?'

'You don't wanner know, Jane.' Kirsty started to walk away. She looked back over her beefy shoulder. 'Or, more to the point, *I* don't wanner know.'

## THIRTY-THREE

# Item

Allan Henry's sitting room had one wall that was all plate glass, perhaps forty feet long. It had wide green views across to one of the conical, wooded humps known as Robin Hood's Butts. Appropriately, according to legend, the Butts had been dumped there by the Devil, making him Hereford's first sporadic developer.

'And this is your . . .' Allan Henry studied Sophie, evidently trying to decide whether she was mother or sister.

'Secretary,' Sophie said quickly and firmly. She and Merrily were at either end of a white leather four-seater sofa, one of two in the vast snowy room. Under their feet was a pale grey rug with an unusual design – a tree growing through the centre of a wheel.

Merrily didn't recall ever seeing Sophie looking more agitated. Sophie wanted out of here. Sophie was Old Hereford to the core; to her this man *was* the Devil.

'Vicars have secretaries now?' Allan Henry said.

'Sophie works for the Cathedral,' Merrily told him.

'And what do *you* do, Mrs Watkins? Specifically.'

'Erm . . . official title: Deliverance Consultant. I'm afraid I don't have a card or—'

'Or a dog-collar. So what *is* a—?'

'It's somebody who deals with problems of a paranormal nature,' Merrily said, for once without embarrassment. 'Used to be Diocesan Exorcist.'

His eyes widened. 'They still *do* that?'

'It's never gone away, Mr Henry.'

'Well . . .' He leaned against the towering brick inglenook, long mirrors either side of it reflecting the greenery. 'I'm now trying to think if I have a problem of a paranormal nature. Let's see . . . when things go bump in the night, I can *usually* explain it. And although I often have people leeching off me, I wouldn't call them vampires. Can I offer you both a glass of wine?' He laughed. 'That is, can I offer you *each* a glass of wine.'

'Thank you, but I'm driving,' Sophie said quickly.

'And I'll be driving in a short while,' Merrily said.

'Not even one glass?'

'Not even one between us. Honestly, we don't have very long. We've got a number of parents to see.'

'Oh, parents, is it?'

His local accent had been planed down to a light burr. He was probably in his late forties. He had strong, lank hair, deep lines tracking down his tanned face from eyes to jaw. A modest beer-belly overhung his jeans, but you had the feeling it was being gradually ironed out.

'So why did you want to see my wife rather than me?'

'We didn't think you'd be here,' Merrily said. 'We thought you'd probably be out somewhere building something.'

'With my bare hands.'

'We all have our fantasies,' she said, and then realized there were two ways he could take that. Sophie frowned at her. Sophie was sending out the message: *Get out now, make some excuse, this is a mistake.*

Allan Henry laughed. He laughed, Merrily was noticing, with a confidence that was almost self-conscious. Maybe he'd had a lot of costly work done on his teeth, was determined to get his money's worth. Otherwise, she sensed around him a kind of conserved energy. She could imagine him in board meetings, relaxed and expressionless and then jumping on someone without preamble, like a jungle cat. Laughing, maybe.

'Rare afternoon off,' he said. 'You were lucky to catch me. And my wife's away, as it happens. The only parent here is me. A parent from my first marriage, that is. The youngsters live in France now, so I don't see them very often.'

'Perhaps we'll come back when your wife's at home.' Sophie half rose. 'It's nothing terribly pressing.'

'Unless it's about Layla, of course,' he said.

'She's with her mother?' Merrily asked him.

'I hardly think so. Her mother's on a cruise around the Azores, with her sister, who was recently widowed, poor woman. Thing is, I don't think of Layla as a child any more. And she's my wife's daughter, not mine. This *is* about Layla, yes?'

As he leaned forward, a medallion on a black leather thong swung out from his bare chest. It was clearly made of gold. Engraved on it was the symbol of a wheel.

'Yes,' Merrily said. 'It's about Layla.'

Sophie sank back in her seat, with a leathery creak that sounded like a cry of pain.


Jane said, 'I remember Mrs Etchinson now. It was at one of the prize-givings. She was in a wheelchair. A guest of honour. Everybody was making a fuss over her and she was smiling so much that you thought it must be hurting her, all that smiling. And somebody said she used to be a teacher and she had MS, and I remember thinking, *God, she's so young.*'

She flopped back into the soft leather and felt for Eirion's hand and squeezed hard, as if to make sure she still could.

They were parked on the grass outside a farm shop overlooking the Ledwardine valley, the sunlit steeple of her mother's church poking out of the surrounding orchards like a terracotta rocket.

'Listen, Jane . . . that's how they get these reputations,' Eirion said. 'They utter a curse and then something like that happens, and everybody conveniently forgets how many curses have been laid on people who go on to have completely trouble-free—'

'It's the fact that she could even *do* it!' Jane could feel tears of anger coming on. 'Wish illness and misfortune on someone.'

'You never done that, in a fit of pique? Wish that someone would have a bad time?'

'Yeah, but I don't ever believe it's gonna have any effect whatso-ever, and then I take it back anyway in a couple of minutes. Or a couple of hours. Or before I go to sleep. Whereas Riddock, she believes, like, totally that she can do it . . . and then she does it. It doesn't matter whether she gave Mrs Etchinson this awful degenerative disease with the grave-dirt in the envelope or whatever. The fact that she wanted to, that's just as bad, isn't it?'

'It comes back on you, though, doesn't it?' Eirion said. 'Karma.'

'Allegedly. But not necessarily in this life.'

'Sounds to me,' he said thoughtfully, 'like she needs this kid, Amy, as much as the kid needs her. You know what I mean? She lays a curse and somebody falls ill or dies or something, well . . . She isn't *really* sure, is she? She might like to fantasize, but she knows that's all it is. But when she sets up this spiritualism scam, then suddenly she's getting what seem to be *real* messages from the Other Side.'

'How?'

'Trance? Automatic writing? Whatever it is, it's proof to her that she's got the power. She's a medium, now, she's a shaman. And maybe that's never happened before, except with this young kid.'

'Who's so precious she drove her to attempt suicide?' Jane said.

'What do you want to do, then? It's getting a bit late, if I'm going to get the car back before nightfall . . .'

'You've got hours yet. But sure, by all means, drop me somewhere.'

'To do what?'

'I'll think of something.'

'There's only one thing you *can* do. You can go home and lay the whole lot on your mum and leave it to her.' Eirion nodded down at the valley. 'Stop putting it off.'

'She'll probably be a bit gobsmacked to see us.'

'Why do I doubt that?' Eirion said.

What they told Allan Henry was that a teenage girl had tried to take her own life after being drawn into ouija-board experiments at school. The Deliverance service was trying to establish how widespread the craze was and whether other children were at risk or in distress. Merrily said finally that a number of kids had mentioned Layla Riddock as the girl presiding over psychic sittings at Moorfield High School.

Close as it was to the truth, the story sounded worryingly thin to Merrily, and foreboding arose just a second or so before Allan Henry got to work on it.

'Well.' He sat in a steel-framed swivel armchair, his left ankle resting on his right knee. 'I didn't know about this.'

'It came out through the hospital where the child was taken.' Sophie had evidently assumed responsibility for any necessary lying. 'When a schoolchild takes a potentially lethal overdose, quite a lot of people start wanting to know why. In this case, as the parents are churchgoers—'

'No, that's not what I meant. What I didn't know, Mrs Hill, was that the Anglican church had its own investigative branch.'

'It's not *quite* like that,' Merrily said.

'Because, you see, I find that very disturbing. Are the *lay* police also involved?'

'Not yet,' Sophie said.

'*Not yet.* I see.'

He was silent for a short while, during which Merrily became aware of a gilt-framed painting on the wall, high in the alcove to the right of the great fireplace. In glowing colours, style of Gauguin, it showed an unsmiling black woman, robed and veiled, with either a crown or an ornate halo over the headdress.

'OK, let me get this entirely correct,' Allan Henry said slowly. Neither the tone nor the pitch of his voice had altered, only the sense of laughter had gone. 'On behalf of the Church of England, you are accusing my stepdaughter of psychologically abusing young children.'

The absolute accuracy of this left Merrily's mind momentarily blank. She couldn't meet his eyes and went on staring at the picture of the Black Virgin.

'We don't *accuse* people, Mr Henry,' Sophie was saying. 'We try to help them where we can.'

'Mrs Hill . . . is it the *Reverend* Mrs Hill?'

'Certainly not.'

'You have to excuse me for feeling threatened, Mrs Hill. You two women arrive at my door like Jehovah's Witnesses, with some assumed authority—'

'Look,' Merrily said, 'it's not about the individuals involved, it's about the practice itself. And what it can release . . . psychologically, if you like. It might seem harmless, a game, though I don't think it is. But this is certainly not a witch-hunt.'

As soon as the word was out she wanted to snatch it back, but it was too late. Allan Henry caught it in the air, like a fist closing over a fly.

'*Witch-hunt?* Now that's a *very* interesting term. The Church has a long history of persecuting minorities.'

'I'm sorry . . . persecuting kids?'

'Minorities, I said, not minors. If we look at the Romany culture, for instance, they've been subjected to *the* most appalling discrimination and persecution over the years, the world over, because of their customs, their lifestyle and, of course, their—'

'Well, yes, but—'

'No, no, let me *tell* you about Layla. She's a very serious young woman, very mature for her age, with a brilliant academic career ahead of her. And she has Romany blood. Which gives her a striking presence that some people find intimidating. And also certain abilities that some people can't accept. Ignorance breeds prejudice. 'Twas ever thus, Mrs Watkins. Ever thus.'

Merrily was aghast. 'You're implying there's something racial behind this?'

'Again, *your* term.'

'Mr Henry, all I'm concerned about—' she wished she was the other side of the plate glass; she would run and run, all the way to Robin Hood's Butts '—is kids dabbling with the dead. That kind of worries me. I can't stop them. All I can do is advise them that they could be messing with something that can't easily be controlled.'

'In your culture. Can't be controlled in *your* culture.'

'Let's say not easily.'

'I think,' he said, 'that you need to consider your position very carefully before you come here and accuse someone you don't know of pressuring a child into suicide, like one of those mad Californian cult-leaders.'

'Oh, you know that's not—'

'We should go, Merrily.' Sophie stood up.

Allan Henry didn't move. '*I'm* not pushing you out. I'm just warning you to be very, very sure of your ground. These are terribly serious allegations. Which could have repercussions.'

Merrily felt mauled. He hadn't even raised his voice or moved his ankle from his knee. *Persecution?* she wanted to cry out. *What about David Shelbone?* But she knew the most that would get her would be a writ or an injunction by morning. He hadn't got this far without being able to push people over with one finger, like dominoes.

She suspected there would indeed be repercussions from this. Everything she'd touched lately, there were repercussions.

'OK. I'm sorry if . . .'

She stood up. Her face felt hot. As she rose, she became aware of a group of objects laid out on a ledge in a small cavity inside the fireplace: acorns, two dice, a magnet, something that might have been a rabbit's foot.

'Allan . . .?'

A woman had entered the room through a narrow archway at the furthest end. She had on a full-length black kimono, open over a tiny white bikini. She wore sunglasses. She carried a champagne glass, half-filled.

'Allan,' she said, 'I didn't leave my mobile—?'

Allan Henry stood up. 'Layla,' he said warmly, 'we were just talking about you.'

Merrily could almost feel Sophie's stomach contract.

Ethel met them on the driveway and Jane picked her up and carried her round to the back, where they found Gomer Parry, placidly weeding the path.

'Welshies throw you out, is it?' Gomer said.

'They found my arms cache, and there was this car chase, but we made it over the border. Hullo, Gomer. Where's Mum?'

'Ah, well.' Gomer laid his trowel on the gravel, straightened up, blinking a few times behind his bottle glasses. 'The vicar en't yere, see, Janey. Her's been called away.'

'How long's she been gone?'

'Oh . . . day and a half, mabbe.'

'*Huh?*' Jane clutched the cat to her chest. Mum spending a night

away, without a word? This did not happen. This just did not—
'Something's wrong, isn't it? *Gomer?*'

'Nothin' exaccly *wrong.*'

'So like . . . where is she?'

'Out east,' Gomer said. 'How are you, Eirion boy?'

'Not too bad, Gomer. You're looking—'

'*East?* What's that mean? Norwich? *Bangkok?*'

'Bromyard way, I believe,' Gomer said.

'Jesus, Gomer.' Jane slumped in relief. 'So it's a job, right?'

'Som'ing of that order. Her spent the night over there and mabbe
a few more to come. I does the days yere, feeding the cat, doing
what's gotter be done. Give her a ring, I should. Her'll likely explain.'

'A few more? A few more *nights?* I don't understand. Where's
she staying? Who's she with?'

'You can get her on the mobile. Her's, er . . .' Gomer scratched
an ear. 'Her's staying with young Lol Robinson, ennit?'

'Oh.' Jane bent to put Ethel down and to conceal her expression.
Bloody *hell.* 'I . . . didn't know Lol was living in Bromyard.'

'Not livin', exaccly. Just mindin' a place. Like me.' Gomer gestured at the back door. 'You stoppin' a bit, Janey? Only I gotter be
off in a coupler minutes. Gotter help young Nev sink a new cesspit
up by Pembridge.'

'We'll probably just get something to eat,' Jane said.

Well, bloody hell. All those hints she'd been dropping, like for
months. *Heard anything from* Lol *lately? Lol still doing that stupid
course, is he? Why's he wasting his time on that crap when he's so cool
and talented? Somebody should take him on one side, somebody he really
trusts and believes in and . . . Why don't you invite* Lol *over sometime?
You know he's never going to invite himself. You ever think about the
future, Mum – what it's going to be like when I've gone?*

Actually, Jane felt kind of resentful, if you wanted the truth. Mum
going behind her back, giving it a little try at Lol's love nest in
Bromyard, to see if things worked out, and if they didn't that would
be it, and Jane would be none the wiser – if she called her on the
mobile, she could pretend to be at home, anywhere. Bloody sneaky,
really. Just when you thought you knew how certain people would
react to a given situation, they did something to surprise you – shock

you, even. In a way, it made Jane feel a lot better about not immediately telling Mum what had gone on in Steve's shed.

'She's still fairly young,' Eirion said when Gomer had gone and they were in the kitchen.

'Yeah,' Jane said airily. 'Sure.'

'It's always hard to imagine your parents still feeling—'

'Oh, come *on*, I know that. Don't be patronizing, Irene.'

'He's a good bloke,' Eirion said.

'I know that, too. And interesting – an artist. And vulnerable. Women like guys who are vulnerable and a little . . . askew.'

'Askew?'

'You know.'

Eirion was sitting at the kitchen table with his chin in his hands. He eyed her sheepishly, eyebrows disappearing into his hair. 'What would a guy have to do to appear . . . a little askew?'

'Hmmm.' Jane came to a decision. Little bloody Sioned and Lowri weren't here. Gomer had gone to sink a cesspit. Mum was Out East finding out if everything still worked after all these years. Even Ethel was a cat of the world.

'Irene,' Jane said. 'Did I ever tell you about the Mondrian Walls?'

Eirion lifted his chin out of his hands. 'This would be in your . . . apartment? On the—'

'Top floor. Formerly attics.'

'Where you painted the plaster squares between the timbers in different primary colours in the style of the great Dutch abstract painter?'

'Correct.'

'It sounded very . . . experimental.'

Jane nodded. 'I thought maybe you could give me your expert critical assessment.'

'Well . . .' Eirion stood up. 'I'm not an expert.'

'Good,' Jane said.

Jane wasn't wrong. There was something forbidding about Layla Riddock.

A big girl with a mature, not to say ripe figure, a mass of dark brown curly hair still slick from the pool. She had smoky brown eyes under heavy brows. She was seventeen going on thirty-eight, and darkly radiant. And she was here.

She was *here*.

*As in, not in the Black Country with Amy Shelbone.*

'Layla, love,' Allan Henry said. 'Excuse me, but these ladies would like to know if you have much regular contact with the dead.'

Layla Riddock backed away, mock-startled, wrapping her kimono and her arms around her.

'We talking about necrophilia?' She cocked her head. 'Necrophilia's useless for women, isn't it? I mean, rigor mortis doesn't last, right?'

Allan Henry laughed again, for the first time in several minutes, as if a little light had come back into his life.

'No, actually, Layla,' he said, 'this could be very serious. For somebody. This is Mrs Hill and Mrs Watkins. Mrs Watkins is a minister of the Church of England, and it seems one of her parishioners, a young girl from your school, has attempted to take her own life.'

Layla nodded casually. 'Amy Shelbone.'

'Oh . . .' he said. 'You know about this, do you?'

Merrily was watching him closely now. She saw nothing. No obvious reaction from Henry to the name Shelbone. And there really should have been, shouldn't there?

'Sad,' Layla said. 'But horribly predictable, I'm afraid. That's one disturbed little girl.'

'Really.' Allan Henry looked at Merrily and Sophie in turn, triumph in his eyes, then back at his stepdaughter. 'Layla, would you tell us about this?'

'About what?'

'About any previous dealings you might have had with this young child. Please?'

Layla shrugged. 'Not much to tell. I've never made any secret about my bloodline, and so I'm always getting approached by kids who want their palms read, or their cards, or something. Anyway, one day – a few weeks ago, I suppose – up comes this rather solemn little girl, says would I help her contact her mother, for heaven's sake. Her mother is, you know . . . dead.'

'She approached *you*, did she, this little girl?'

'Oh yeah. Very politely. I told her not to be silly. I told her that whatever she may have heard about the Rom, we have great respect for the dead but we *don't* get involved with them on a personal level. I said – you know – like, run along.'

'And that was the last you heard?'

Layla sighed, wrapped her kimono tighter in frustration. 'Wish I could say it was. Next thing I hear that some other students – principally a girl called Kirsty Ryan – have taken Amy under their wing and they're holding these kind of seance things, what d'you call them – where you lay out letters in a circle and have a glass upside down?'

Merrily said nothing.

'Anyway, I thought I'd better check it out. There's a lot of this stuff about the school lately – little witchcrafty groups popping up. Awfully childish. I don't like to see kids playing at it. If you have psychic skills, it's your responsibility to develop them sensibly. If you haven't got it . . . don't mess with it. So, yeah, I found them in this shed on one of the fields and I . . .' Layla paused and smiled. 'I'm afraid I arranged a little surprise.'

Layla glanced around. Holding court, now. *A dominant kind of girl*, Robert Morrell had said. Perhaps the kind of girl where all the teaching staff, both sexes, would be relieved when she left school.

It was hard to believe this woman was only about a year older than Jane.

It was also hard to believe she'd want to waste time on a little girl like Amy Shelbone.

'What did you do, Layla?' Allan Henry was taking a back seat, playing the feed, the straight man – and proud to do it, Merrily thought.

Which was interesting in itself.

'I grassed them up,' Layla said smugly. 'I discreetly tipped off one of the staff. And there was a raid.'

'Caught them at it?' Allan Henry said.

Layla put up both her hands. 'Absolutely nothing to do with me!' She wore five rings, all gold.

Everyone was quiet. It was not so difficult to believe that Layla

Riddock would consider her natural peers to be found among the staff rather than the pupils.

Allan Henry glanced at Merrily and Sophie in turn again. He was smiling gently.

*Very mature for her age.*

'Good for you,' Merrily said hoarsely to Layla, and the schoolgirl smiled at her, too, the tip of her tongue childishly touching a corner of her mouth. But her eyes were cold with malice. Merrily felt sure it was malice.

*You can't touch us*, the smile said. *You can't get near us.*

Neither of them said a word until they were in the lane, heading back towards Canon Pyon. Merrily was expecting a hard time. *Stay away*, Sophie had advised back in the office. *What would be the point?* And then, in the car, *If I were you, I wouldn't get out.*

When had Sophie ever not been right?

She was looking at her most severe, sitting stiffly, eyes on the road, both hands positioned precisely on the wheel, like she was taking her driving test. Merrily sat with her bag on her knees, a hand inside playing with the cigarettes. She couldn't keep the hand still.

'I'm sorry, Sophie.'

Sophie said nothing, but you could almost hear her thoughts ricocheting like pellets from the upholstery and the windscreen and the dash.

'It was a very bad idea,' Merrily said. 'I should not have dragged you into it.' She'd crushed a cigarette, strands of tobacco teased between fingers and thumb. 'I don't know how he'll get back at us, but he will. I was useless in there. I let him walk all over us. A corrupt developer, a crook, and I let him . . . let them *both* walk all over us.'

Sophie turned right, towards Hereford, and the car speeded up. A mile or so along the road, she said mildly, 'They're an item, aren't they, those two?'

The sky was flawless, the blue deepening. Across the edge of the city, you could see all the way to the hooked nose of The Skirrid, the holy mountain above Abergavenny.

Merrily closed her bag on the tobacco mess. 'I'm glad you said it first.'

'Is Sandra really away on a cruise, I wonder?'

'Maybe she's buried in the garden. He can do anything, can't he? He's got everybody in his pocket, and now he's sleeping with his stepdaughter!' Merrily was momentarily horrified at how high her voice had risen.

'He might sail close to the wind,' Sophie said, 'but he's not stupid. I expect Sandra *is* on a cruise. Quite a long cruise.'

'So you think she knows?'

'Wouldn't you?'

'I wonder how long it's been going on.'

'A more interesting question is, which of them initiated it?' Sophie said.

*A very lucky man*, Charlie Howe had observed. *Things've fallen his way.*

And people have fallen out of his way.

Sophie said, 'The girl was lying rather cleverly, wasn't she?'

'Beautifully. Forget about the trinkets, that's probably the best evidence of genuine Romany ancestry.'

'I'm sorry?'

'They're supposed to consider it an art form.'

'Lying?'

'Mmm.'

'And what else do you know about them?'

'Not enough. Not yet, anyway.'

'Well, forget about it for tonight,' Sophie said. 'Get a good night's sleep. If Inspector Howe or anyone else rings wanting to speak to you, I'll put them off.'

'No, put them through.'

'You're getting personally involved. That's not helpful to anyone.'

'I *am* personally involved. And now there's a child missing.'

Only two, three years between Amy Shelbone and Layla Riddock, but one was a child and one was a woman. Merrily folded her hands in her lap, couldn't keep them still. A teenage girl had done this to her. She closed her eyes, breathed in.

'Sophie,' she said. 'Could I possibly have a cigarette?'

# THIRTY-FOUR

# The Cure of Souls

'Ha,' he said. 'The *drukerimaskri*.'

He seemed to be dancing in the last of the dusk, will-o'-the-wispish. The late evening was rich and close, the atmosphere laden with herbal scents. There was going to be a full moon.

Merrily said, '*Drukeri*—?'

'—*Maskri*. It's a Romany term.' Al Boswell's white hair flurried as he did a little bow. She suspected he was mocking her.

A lantern hung from the bowed roof of the *vardo*, a thick candle inside it. On the grass in front of the waggon, a heavy wooden table was set up, with bentwood chairs. A shaggy donkey browsed nearby. In the distance, beyond the building housing the hop museum, glittered the tiered lights of Malvern.

Al Boswell presented himself in front of Lol, hands behind his back. 'Where's your guitar? Why didn't you bring your guitar? We could have played for the moon.'

Lol told him Prof had insisted the guitar was a short-term loan. 'Besides, it didn't seem—'

'Appropriate?' Al Boswell arched his back like a thin, white cat. 'Relevant? Seemly?'

'All those,' Lol said. 'Plus—'

'You can't surely be afraid to play alongside an old man whose arthriticky fingers slur drunkenly over the frets?'

'Tonight, I can manage without total humiliation,' Lol admitted.

'Certainly not in the presence of the lovely *drukerimaskri*.'

*I am* not *going to ask what it means*, Merrily thought.

'Or are you afraid the *drukerimaskri* would think it was wrong to play for the moon? And besides, look at her: she's in a hurry, there's no time, she's on hot bricks, she needs the information. Therefore, she might find you . . . trivial.' Al Boswell walked right up to Lol, peered into his eyes. 'And that would *never* do.'

'Al, for God's sake!' The beautiful, frail silvery woman in the long skirt came down the steps of the waggon, carrying a tray with glasses on it. 'He's such a terrible walking cliché sometimes,' she said to Merrily. 'Except, of course, in the presence of other Romanies, on which rare occasions he's almost withdrawn.'

'She's such a bitch tonight!' Al Boswell howled. He took Lol on one side. 'So, have you heard from Levin?'

The donkey had ambled up to Merrily and she ran her fingers through his heavy fur and gazed into his billiard-ball eyes. There was an unreality about the night or perhaps a hyper-reality – a sensual intensity she hadn't been prepared for. Lol had brought her here, and suddenly she wanted Lol to take her away again; she wanted to be alone with him. Things needed to be said, worked out, if that were possible.

'You're terribly tense, aren't you?' Mrs Boswell was standing next to her. 'And exhausted? I'm going to fetch you something that might help.'

'No, honestly, it's . . .' Merrily let the donkey nibble at the sleeve of her jacket. 'What's his name?'

'Stanley.'

'Does that mean something in Romany?'

'I do hope not.'

Merrily smiled. A wave of tiredness washed over her, and the lights of Malvern blurred.

'About Stock.' Mrs Boswell looked insubstantial in the dusk – like steam, like a ghost. But for the glasses on a chain, you felt you could have put a hand through her. 'There's nothing you could have done. It shouldn't have been allowed to happen, but there's nothing *you* could have done. You weren't to know.'

'Know what?'

Mrs Boswell didn't reply. Merrily let it go: a false trail, probably.

This woman didn't look at all like a gypsy but she'd been married to one for many years.

'What's a *drukerimaskri*?' Merrily said.

'Al called you that? Originally, I think, it meant soothsayer. Then it became applied to Christian priests who could lay spirits to rest. *Drukerimaskro* is the more familiar form, in the masculine: an exorcist, a healer of souls.'

Merrily held on to the donkey and looked for Lol.

*Healer of souls.*

The song had been happening when she got back to Knight's Frome just after seven p.m.

She'd insisted on driving back in the Volvo – which had meant first returning to the office and submitting to two cups of sweet tea, a biscuit, a paracetamol and a dissertation on the parameters of responsibility.

'The Bishop's back tomorrow,' Sophie had reminded her, finally seeing her to the car. 'I'm going to advise him to put off the inevitable formal meeting with you until next week.'

'I'd rather get it over with.'

'And admit to things for which you were not to blame?' Sophie held open the door of the Volvo. 'I don't think so.'

'If I lose the job, I lose the job. There *were* things I got wrong. I'm not just going to keep denying everything to preserve my . . . dubious status.'

'Merrily,' Sophie said very clearly, 'I have to tell you I'd be more than pleased – for your sake, at least – if you were to leave Deliverance behind for ever.' Merrily stared at her in dismay. 'But certainly not under the present circumstances. I'd never forgive myself if you went down for either Gerard Stock or Allan Henry and Layla Riddock. Now go back and get an early night. I'll talk to you in the morning.'

Sophie pushed the car door closed – except it didn't; this was an old car and you had to slam the door. Merrily opened it again to do that, overheard what Sophie was muttering to herself as she walked away.

She'd sat there with the door hanging open – maybe her mouth as well – until Sophie was out of sight. Then, to avoid having to think, she'd snatched the mobile and called David Shelbone at home, intending this time to insist he get the police in.

No answer. In the silence of the Bishop's Palace yard, she'd prayed for the Shelbones and then started the car and put on the stereo very loud, something sparking with ideas but not too profound: Gomez – *Abandoned Shopping Trolley Hotline*.

At 7.03 p.m., she'd driven out of the lane from Knight's Frome and on to the now-familiar track, parking the Volvo between the stables and the cottage. Lol's Astra sat there, years older than the trees Prof Levin had planted to screen off his studio. In Prof's absence, nature was running things again – green hazelnuts in the uncut boundary hedge and a gold-dust haze on the seeded long grass of what was supposed to be a lawn.

The stable door was open, and Merrily went into the kitchen area, putting down her bag on the breakfast-bar packing case, walking down the short passage to the studio door. It was ajar. She peered through the gap.

Some of the stable remained as it had been, three of the stalls turned into recording booths. Lol was sitting in one, his back to the door, a guitar on his knee. On the smaller of the two tape machines to her left, she could see spools revolving. He'd be laying down a demo for Prof Levin. She knew he'd had his orders.

There was a pair of headphones hanging from a metal bracket beside the tape machine. She could hear the tinnitus buzz of music and she slipped off her shoes and padded across. The air was still and warm. Feeling like whatever was the aural equivalent of a voyeur, she slipped on the cans.

The music stopped. '*Shit*,' Lol murmured wearily into her head. There was silence, then a string was retuned. The crisp acoustic was frighteningly intimate: she could hear his breathing, the movements of his fingers on the machine-heads.

Lol said, 'Take six.'

The guitar, in minor chord, was awesomely deep and full – this kind of weighted fingerstyle sounding like a piano. She felt like she was inside the soundbox and somehow also inside the heart of the guitarist, and tears came into her eyes as Lol's voice came in, low and nasal and smoky, and the first shockingly resonant line fell like a stone into a deep, deep well.

'*As you kneel before your altar—*'

Merrily froze. Lol stopped. He cleared his throat. He sighed.

'Seven,' he said.

Merrily had been holding on to the sides of the tape deck, as if she was part of the machine, recording it, too, every softly explosive, questioning phrase. She recalled Lol waiting for her in the dappled quiet of the church at Knight's Frome, re-experienced his expression of loss as she emerged from the vestry as a priest.

He began again.

> '*As you kneel before your altar,*
> *Can you see the wider plan?*
> *Can you hear the one you're talking to?*
> *Can you love him like a man?*
> *Did you suffocate your feelings*
> *As you redefined your goals*
> *And vowed to undertake the Cure of Souls . . .?*'

Merrily had hung up the cans and walked rapidly out of the stable with her shoes under her arm, the stones and baked mud brutal on the soles of her feet.

'The Black Virgin,' Al Boswell said. 'Sara *la Kali*.'

Candles in bottles dramatized his goblin profile. He'd calmed down now, after a couple of glasses of wine, and the four of them were sitting around the wooden table outside the *vardo*.

'Medieval French saint,' Merrily recalled. 'Linked to Mary Magdalene. A servant?' Was this the woman in the unlikely picture on Allan Henry's sitting room wall?

'Gypsies in France became strongly identified with the Catholic pilgrimage of Saintes-Marie-de-la-Mere in the Camargue,' Sally Boswell said. 'This is where the three Marys – Mary Salomé, Mary Jacobé and Mary Magdalene were said to have landed and where their relics are presumed to have been found under the church . . . and later, in a bronze chest, the remains of their black servant, Sara.'

'Why did the gypsies adopt this Sara?' Lol leaned away from the candlelight, his elbows on the table hiding the holes in the famous alien sweatshirt.

'They're a great paradox, the Rom,' said Sally Boswell. 'Flamboyant, volatile, and yet subtle and secretive. They were pagans originally – some still are, but most adopted the dominant religion of whichever country they travelled. They may have chosen Sara because she was the humblest of the saints, the most unassuming . . . the least obtrusive.'

Lol nodded. He would understand that. Given the options, she'd have been his patron saint as well, Merrily thought, tears pricking again. She was overtired, that was the problem.

'Or,' Sally went on, 'they may have seen her as a Christian incarnation of the Hindu goddess, Kali. There was talk of blood sacrifice, but I think that's an exaggeration or a corruption of the truth.'

'Hmm,' Merrily said.

After leaving the studio, she'd walked through the fields for a while before going up to her cell in the cottage. She'd washed and changed, come down, and then she and Lol had raided Prof's fridge for scraps of salad, while she told him about Layla Riddock and Allan Henry and the objects in the big white room, the picture on the wall, the conclusion she and Sophie had come to. And then Lol had suggested Al and Sally Boswell might throw some more light on this, and he'd phoned them.

'Can I ask you about some symbols?' she said to Al. 'The wheel, for instance.'

'On its own?'

'Like a cartwheel. With spokes.'

Al glanced at his wife.

'Money,' she said. 'Wealth.'

'So a gold talisman with a wheel engraved on it, worn around the neck . . .?'

'Would obviously be designed to promote wealth.'

'*I* wouldn't wear one.' Al poured himself more wine.

'OK.' Merrily moved on. 'A group of objects: acorns, dice, a rabbit's foot – oh, and a magnet.'

Al drank, then put down his glass. 'To which you might want to

346

add a few gold coins – and a magnifying glass. Because this person, whoever it is, wants – or needs – *considerable* wealth.'

'Why wouldn't you wear the talisman?' Merrily asked.

'*You* would want unearned wealth, little *drukerimaskri?*'

'But *you*'re not a priest.'

His eyes flashed. 'How do you know that?'

'Sorry. I don't know that.'

He sniffed sharply. 'My father was a *chovihano*. Well-known guy – a shaman, a healer. A healer of souls and bodies and the living and the dead. Not many left in the world now.'

'It's hereditary?'

He looked glum. 'Sometimes. But you need to work at it. It's a calling, a commitment. You'd understand that. Me . . . I was a disappointment to my family.' He offered the bottle round, got no takers, poured more wine for himself. 'No, you're quite right, I'm not a priest.'

'You're not rich, either,' Lol said. 'You don't make enough guitars. You could have had a Boswell guitar factory turning out thousands, like – I dunno – the Martin family?'

'Mother of God!' Al half rose, the wine spilled and the candle flame wavered.

'Not that I was actually *advocating* that,' Lol said. 'Just making the point.'

'Valid. Quite valid.' Al shook his head sadly, sat down and topped up his glass again. 'I'm no businessman, Lol, and no *chovihano* – I've lived too long in *gaujo*land. But I try to honour the old code . . . which is about living lightly on the earth, taking what you need, taking selectively, taking secretly sometimes. Taking in a way so that nobody notices that what you've taken has gone. It's not quite stealing . . . if nobody notices it's not there any more.'

This was questionable morality, but Merrily was too tired to ask the questions. She sipped some of the sweet soft drink that Sally had brought her. It apparently contained hops and nettles.

'You want to know the truth of it, I'm still paying back.' Al drained his wineglass in one. 'I'm paying back for the one time when I took . . . and it *was* noticed. How could it fail to be bloody well noticed? And that's how I brought a curse upon my own family, why

I live among the *gaujos* and keep my head down. It's why we have a museum devoted to hops, and most of the Romany memorabilia's in the back room, behind a locked door.'

Sally Boswell said in a low voice, 'You *could* have paid.'

'You get off my back,' Al growled.

There was an uncomfortable silence. A bat flittered in an arc over the table. Merrily had one more question.

'What about a wheel with a tree through it?'

Al looked up. 'Where did you see that?'

'It was a design on a rug. In the house of the man with the wealth talisman.'

'Nothing particularly to do with wealth.' He poured the last of the wine, a dribble, and pulled over another bottle. 'The wheel would be the medicine wheel. The tree is the Tree of Life. Comes in three sections. The branches are in the Upper World of vision and inspiration. The middle, where the wheel goes through, is about our life and dealing with it. The roots are in the lower world of the ancestors . . . and the dead.'

'The gypsy dead aren't in the Upper World?'

Al smiled ruefully.

Sally said, 'Not all gypsies believe in a heaven. And anyway, the dead are gone, and must stay gone. The dead are unhealthy. Death pollutes a place meant for living, so when someone was dying it used to be that they were taken out of their home and put in a tent or a bender. The person is always washed and dressed in fresh clothes *before* death.' It was coming out pat now, Merrily thought – the museum curator's voice. 'Also, in Romany society, the names of recently dead people must never be mentioned lest this might call them back. At one time, when a gypsy died, his *vardo* would be set alight with all his possessions, so there would be nothing in this world to *draw* him back.'

'Of course, these days,' Al said, 'the *vardo* is worth a lot of money, but it's still usual for something to be ritually burned. Something closely associated with the dead person.'

There was an important question here; Merrily couldn't untangle it.

Lol did. 'So gypsies don't try to communicate with the dead?'

'Not recommended,' Sally said.

'But isn't that what a shaman does – talks to the spirits?'

Merrily nodded gratefully – this was it.

'Their ancestors, mainly,' Sally said, 'which is different. Also spirits of nature. Spirits of living things. Everything has a spirit . . . this table, those trees, the River Frome.'

'A guitar?' Lol said.

Al turned slowly. 'Smart boy.'

Merrily saw that Lol's face was alight with understanding. 'All the wood for each guitar, you take sparingly,' he said, 'so that it isn't missed. So maybe even the tree doesn't have to die?'

'Aha.' Al leaned back, a knuckle depressing his cheek, two fingers making a V around an ear.

'So that the living spirit of the tree – or trees, all those different species – goes into the guitar,' Lol said. 'And maybe you consult the tree spirit first to make sure it's OK to take the wood?'

Al pointed a long forefinger. 'And I'll tell you something else, Lol, boy – if you ever bring that instrument back, you'll be *insulting* those spirits . . . have you thought of *that*?' He flung back his head and laughed. Directly above the table, Merrily was aware of the full moon, the colour of custard cream. It seemed warmer than the day had been, as if the moon was putting out its own heat.

She said carefully, 'So a gypsy who was attempting to arouse the dead, for whatever reason—'

Sally said, 'You know of a gypsy doing this?'

'I know of *somebody* trying to do it. Somebody claiming to have a gypsy father.'

'A *posh rat*?' Al Boswell asked.

'Sounds vaguely appropriate.'

'Half-breed. Is this the same person seeking wealth?'

'Seeking even more wealth would be more accurate. And ensuring his wealth involves damaging another person. A family, in fact.'

'Have nothing to do with this person,' Al said.

'Erm . . . it's my job, Mr Boswell.'

His face was blank in the milky moon and candlelight. 'What, at the end of it all, is so important about a bloody job?'

'It's a *gaujo* thing,' Lol said.

'Black magic,' Al said flatly. 'Raising the dead to damage another person or acquire wealth – that's the black arts. And also, let me tell you, it's far too stupid a thing for a traditional Romany ever to go near.'

'There are no evil Romanies?' Lol said.

'You don't understand, boy. Romanies respect, sometimes consult the ancestors. But they let the dead lie. Most of us don't even like to touch a body after death. This is about *fear.*' He leaned towards Merrily and into the candlelight, as if he was concerned that she should see how agitated he was. 'Listen to me, *drukerimaskri*, I want to tell you – and this also concerns the other thing, the thing in the kiln – I want to say to you, don't ever trust the dead.'

In Merrily's bag – she jumped – her phone began to shrill, just like it had in the Stocks' bedroom when she could have sworn it was switched off. She didn't touch the bag. 'Go on,' she said to Al.

The phone went on bleeping – Al glancing nervously at the bag, as if this might be a spirit coming through.

'I'll get it if you like,' Lol said. Merrily nodded gratefully, dug in the bag and pulled out the phone, handed it to him. Lol took it over to the boundary fence.

'We have a word,' Al said, and he whispered it. '*Mulo.* This is the Romany word for a ghost. The same word . . . this word is also used for a vampire: the living dead.'

Sally Boswell was silently observing her husband's melodramatics with a faintly sardonic expression, but her skin looked whiter than the moon.

'The point being, I think, that we don't see that much of a difference,' Al said.

Merrily didn't know how to react to this. Was she supposed to say something inane about not all ghosts sucking your blood? The moon picked out a circle of pink, as perfect as a tonsure, on the crown of Al's white head.

'This is our dead I'm talking about. We don't worry about *your* dead – we'll settle down to sleep in your cemeteries any night of the week. We believe that the Romany dead . . . we believe they don't come back for no reason. And they'll leech off you. They'll steal your life-energy. They'll keep on taking it until you're a cored and cancerous husk. We are very afraid, *drukerimaskri*, of the vengeful power of our dead.'

She didn't really know what he meant. She didn't understand what he was saying to her.

Lol came and sat down again, but said nothing. Nervously, Merrily drank some more of the nettles and hops. The night was suddenly swollen with tension.

'Whatever it is,' Sally said to Lol, 'you'd better tell her. We'll go away and leave you.'

'No, it's OK. It's no big secret.' Lol handed the phone across the table to Merrily. 'It was Sophie. The police are trying to get hold of you.'

Merrily drew a fearful breath. She was thinking of Amy Shelbone . . . David Shelbone not answering his phone.

'There's been an incident at the remand centre in Shrewsbury where Gerard Stock was taken. He, um—' Lol cleared his throat. 'Stock's hanged himself.'

THIRTY-FIVE

# Left to Hang

The turned hay was a rich confection, baking under the moon. Merrily stood on the hard mud track that bisected the meadow below Prof's place, the mobile damp against her ear, a cigarette in her other hand.

The air was so very still and DCI Annie Howe's voice so crisp and distinct and authoritative, it was like the news was being broadcast to the whole valley.

'Easier for them to do it in remand centre,' she explained, as if she was talking about laundry or something. 'Fewer personal restrictions there. As they haven't been convicted of anything, they're not forced to wear prison clothing.'

*The full moon*, Merrily was thinking, outraged. She and Lol had walked all the way back from the Boswell hop museum before she'd felt able to make the call to Hereford police. *Why the hell don't they watch them more carefully under a full moon?*

'Unfortunately, it's not too infrequent an occurrence,' Annie Howe said. 'There's more of an element of loneliness and despair among remand prisoners. But a man of Stock's apparent intellect and resilience – I have to say I wouldn't have expected it from him, and I do wonder what pushed him over the edge. Did he suddenly realize he enormity of what he'd done? Was it remorse? Or had something . . . perhaps altered his state of mind?' Meaningful pause. 'What do *you* think, Ms Watkins?'

Merrily thought about the court scenario Lol and she had built

352

from what they knew of the mind of Gerard Stock. She didn't like Howe's innuendo, but she let it go.

'How did he do it?'

'With his shirt,' Annie Howe said. 'The shirt was torn and soaked – he'd urinated on it and rolled it up tight.'

'Not a cry for help, then,' Merrily said dully.

His white shirt. White for innocence. White for the side of the angels. Out in the endless darkness, Gerard Stock's heavy body was revolving slowly, his feet inches from the floor. '*Don't really know what the fuck you're doing, do you? You're a waste of time. Geddout.*' Stock revolving slowly for ever: an obscene enigma.

'I do feel obliged to warn you,' Howe said, 'that all legal barriers must now be considered down. No impending court case any more, only inquests. No one's freedom's at stake, so the gates are wide open. The media can go in now, with all its fangs bared. You under-stand what I'm saying?'

Merrily said nothing. She imagined Howe in her half-lit office, relishing the moment.

'It means they can exploit the exorcism angle to the full,' Howe said. 'They can print whatever they like. *I* can't stop them.'

*Even if you wanted to.*

'And it means, of course, that they'll come after you, Ms Watkins. If they aren't after you already.'

'I expect you'll give them a full description,' Merrily said, 'so they don't miss me.'

Everything under the full moon was bright and sharply defined: the crisp ridges of hay, a line of graceful poplars, Lol – still and compact, standing looking down at his trainers.

'I should get some sleep,' Howe said. 'It's been a fairly stressful couple of days for you, I imagine.'

She didn't say, *But nothing compared with the stress to come.*

Eirion sat up in horror, staring around the moon-washed attic. 'Oh my God. Oh my *God.*' He bounced out of bed, ran to the window. 'Look at it!'

'What?'

'It's bloody *dark*. It's got to be after *ten*.'

Jane put on the light. 'Five past. No sweat.' She looked at him, head to bare toes. She smiled. 'Doesn't take the little guy long to shrink, does it?'

'Jane, I'm dead.'

'I wouldn't go that far.' On the Mondrian walls, the moon spotlit the yellow rectangle and the blue square, and Jane sighed in some kind of weird rapture. 'Irene, isn't life sometimes so . . . really quite good, in spite of everything?'

'It—' Eirion came back and sat on the bed and tenderly stroked her hair. 'Well, yes. Yes, it is. But there's always a vague downside – like we fell asleep. We weren't supposed to fall asleep afterwards, were we, Jane?'

'It happens.' Jane shrugged knowledgeably. 'Release of sexual tension.'

'Even if I leave now, I'm not going to get back until the early hours.'

'So don't leave.'

'They'll have locked me out.'

'You've got a key.'

'They'll have barred the doors, out of entirely justified spite.'

'Just say the car broke down.'

'Jane, it's a two-year-old BMW. It's still under warranty. Plus, we didn't even say we were going anywhere.'

'You know what?' Jane said.

'What?'

'I don't actually care a lot.' She linked her hands behind her head. She felt, like, *all woman*. 'The car, your family . . . all this is *so* not a problem.'

Eirion looked into her eyes.

'And Amy Shelbone?' he said.

'Ah.' Jane went quiet. *That* was a problem. Yes. Oh God.

'I think we were going to *see* Amy, weren't we?' Eirion said. 'Either before or after or instead of ringing your mum. If you recall, we looked up the address in the phone book. Some hours ago.'

'Irene, what are we going to do?' She was confused: part of her wildly happy, the rest horribly anxious, the combination bringing her to the brink of tears. 'I mean what are we going to do about Amy *now*?'

'Yes.' He stood up again. 'I guess we do have to do something.'

'Because that would like destroy everything, wouldn't it, if it—?'

'Don't go imagining things, Jane.'

'Irene, that stuff... you *couldn't* even imagine it.' Everything came back to her, in the tough, no-shit tones of Kirsty Ryan: '*They're really cooking, you know, her and the kid.*' She covered herself with the duvet, as if some astral Layla Riddock might be watching her from the shadows. 'You couldn't dream it up, could you?'

'No.' Eirion walked around, discovering into which corners he'd thrown his clothes. 'How long would it take us to get over there?'

'Dilwyn? Ten, fifteen minutes. But suppose she's already in bed.'

'Then she can get up, can't she? At least if she's in bed she's not going to run away. Go on, get dressed. I won't watch.'

'You don't want to watch?'

'Yes, I'd love to watch. That's—' Eirion gathered up his jeans '—why I'm getting dressed in the bathroom.'

'Irene?' Jane slipped on her bra. Eirion paused at the door. 'You will come in with me, won't you? At the Shelbones'. You're more likely to convince the parents than I am.'

'Sure. We're ... an item, aren't we? Official.'

'I ...' Jane smiled a little stiffly, wondering how she felt about that, like, *post-coitally. Hey!*

She reached down to the little pile of her clothes lying beside the bed.


'Maybe he left a suicide note,' Lol said.

They were on the wooden footbridge. The river was down there somewhere, but even the full moon couldn't find it. Lol was standing over the Frome which went nowhere in particular, maybe aching to join another river before it was too late.

'If he refused to make a statement,' Merrily said, 'I don't see him leaving a note, do you?'

Lol didn't have an answer to that. He couldn't imagine why a man like that would ever have hanged himself – taking Gerard Stock out of the picture, robbing the world of a sensational trial at which he might easily have put up a strong defence, with Merrily Watkins left to hang.

'Sophie mention the media?' he asked.

'Yes.'

'So, do you want to risk staying here?'

'Risk?' She was wearing a blue cotton skirt, a top the colour of the moon, a small gold cross on a chain. She looked very small. 'What are they going to do to me? The press are only people.'

'In the pack, they tend to lose their humanity.'

'We'll see what happens. Look, I . . .' She brought out her phone. 'I'd better call David Shelbone again.' She switched on the phone and the screen came up green. Merrily put in a number and listened. 'Engaged.'

'What was it Al told you?' Lol said. 'When I was taking the call. What was Al so keen to tell you?'

'Oh, he'd . . . had a little too much wine.'

'Something about not trusting the dead.'

'He was talking about the gypsy dead. Romany ghosts. What he called the *mulo*. He said gypsies were terrified of their own ghosts, though they didn't give a toss about ours. It didn't seem entirely logical to me. But what do *I* know?'

'He say anything about there being a presence in the kiln?'

'Only in passing.' She stepped onto the footpath on the other side of the bridge. 'But it doesn't matter now, does it? Nothing to explain to the Crown court. Just an inquest.'

Lol followed her. 'And yourself. If you can't somehow explain it to yourself, you'll never trust Deliverance again, will you?'

'Well, sure, I'd rather have got myself shredded in the witness box, have the whole exorcism thing held up as some kind of tawdry medieval spoof, than lose another life.' She waited for him by the first of the poplars, the moonlight on her face, shadows under her eyes. 'Or maybe I'm fooling myself? Maybe I'm secretly glad he's dead, because he'd already set me up and he was probably going to do it again.'

'You don't have it in you to be glad anyone's dead,' he said.

'As a vicar.'

'Not even – let's be honest here – as a person.'

356

'Oh, well, you – you kind of stop being a person when you join the Church,' Merrily said. 'You have to learn to suffocate your feelings.'

It went so quiet you could even hear the Frome moving below.

'Ah,' Lol said.

'Redefine your goals. That kind of thing.'

'Damn,' Lol said.

'Nice tune,' Merrily said.


They both stood with their backs to the door, so there was no way out, short of physical violence. And although they were both seriously into middle age, they were big people. She was kind of pudgy-armed and hefty and he was tall and thin and, although he didn't look too well, he did look desperate enough to damage somebody.

Like, for instance, somebody who might know where his daughter was but was refusing to tell him.

'Honest to God,' Jane said, scared, 'we didn't even know she was missing. We came here to *see* her.'

Invoking God because it looked like this might well cut some ice here. The room was too bright from a big white ceiling bowl loaded with high-wattage bulbs. There was a wooden crucifix on the mantelpiece over the Calor gas fire and round the walls these really awful religious paintings by one of those pedantic Pre-Raphaelite guys who thought it was important to paint every blade of grass individually.

'I wouldn't lie,' Jane insisted. 'My mum's a vicar. I wasn't brought up to lie, OK?'

'Your mother knows you're here, then?' said Mr Shelbone. He had a weak voice that sounded kind of laminated, and Jane felt slightly sorry for him; it was clear his wife called the shots.

'Of course she doesn't,' Mrs Shelbone snapped. 'Her mother seems to know very little of what goes on.'

Jane let the slur go past. 'No, she doesn't. But only because I feel responsible for dropping her in it when I didn't tell her at the time because I didn't think there was anything particular to worry about, but now I know I was wrong, and I want to put it right.' She drew a long breath.

'Why should we believe you?' Mrs Shelbone demanded. 'How do we know you're not just sensation-seeking?'

'This is silly. Jane's only trying to help.' Eirion's Welsh accent coming through. 'That's all she wants – and to find out what's going on.'

'And what,' said Mr Shelbone, '*is* going on, in your opinion?'

Jane swallowed. It was one thing telling Amy what kind of psychotic slag Layla Riddock was; it was something else laying it on her parents in her absence. Serious as this whole thing could turn out to be, it broke some kind of code of honour. You didn't grass until you reached the stage where it was impossible to deal with it yourself.

This didn't seem to worry Eirion, however. Maybe he'd just had it with the whole thing. Or maybe he thought this *was* the stage.

'It comes down to bullying, Mr Shelbone. Your daughter's been picked on by an older girl, who evidently thinks she's . . . something special.'

'Picked on?'

'Ensnared. You must know what I'm talking about. Especially as it's been suggested to us today that she – this girl – might have wanted to use Amy to get at— well, to get at you.'

Mr Shelbone was silent. Once Eirion mentioned the Christmas Fair, Layla Riddock would be in the frame. Best to leave it here, Jane decided. They should say as little as possible, get out and go and grovel to Mum, let her decide what to do.

'Sit down.' Mr Shelbone indicated a sofa in a pine frame, like the bottom half of a bunk.

Jane said, 'We have to be . . .'

Eirion just shrugged and went over to the sofa and sat down.

'Now then, son,' said Mr Shelbone. 'Let's start at the beginning.'

'Well, her name's Layla Riddock,' Eirion said.

## THIRTY-SIX

# Confluence

Lol tensed. There was the tower across the fields, just as he'd seen it the first time, the tip of its witch's hat askew, as if a low-flying aircraft had clipped it. He remembered how he'd thought it looked like a fairy castle, with that glow in the window.

Where a glow was now.

'What?' Merrily demanded.

'There's—' He sagged, his back to a tree trunk, the breath forced out of him as if he'd been punched. 'Sorry, it's just the moon. It's just a reflection of the moon.' It seemed to be everywhere tonight.

'What did you think it was?'

'How about we go back?' He searched for the path, then spotted where he'd gone wrong the last time: there was a stile he could have climbed over to follow a circular route back to the bridge, and another path that led into the tangled wood. 'Merrily?'

'Erm . . . Lol, how do I get to the old hop-yard? Where you saw Stephanie that night?'

'*Oh* no.' Lol stood in the middle of the path, 'I really don't think so.'

'Lol . . .'

'Merrily – *tell me*. That's why we're here?'

'Look,' she said, 'I haven't got the gear, I haven't got the holy water, I haven't got the sacrament. But I can pray. I can do the words.'

'Words?'

'Words to get them out of here.'

'Who?'

'Stock, Stephanie . . . Call it precautionary. Call it—'

'To stop them becoming earthbound, right? To fix it so nobody in the future goes for an innocent walk in that field and—' Lol actually shivered '—sees something.'

'All right, to *try* and fix it. You've got to try, haven't you? It's what I do. Like I keep telling people. I'm actually trying very hard to believe it's what I've been put here to do.'

'Cure of souls,' Lol said. He sensed how close she was to tears.

'Yes.'

'Souls of the living or the souls of the dead?'

'Don't you *know*?'

'Merrily, it's just a phrase I heard with the right balance, the right metre. If it sounds right, use it. What *does* it mean?'

'It's—' she shook her head at him '—just an old description of what we do – what we're supposed to do. Implies we have curative powers, which I suppose we don't, most of us. We just know how to ask nicely. And all I want to do now is say, Please God, will you accept the souls of these two people, help them break the bonds of obsession, anger, lust, hatred – help them leave it all behind. Is that so bad?'

'You've known you were going to do this ever since we left the Boswells, haven't you?'

*Something to prove*, he thought. Stock's death must have made her wonder if she wasn't so much a force for good as a force for chaos.

'It kind of grew,' Merrily said. 'It's a responsibility. Least I can do. You don't have to join in or anything. Just point me in the right direction. If you think it's crap, that's OK.'

Lol nodded. 'Joining another river,' he murmured.

'Sorry?'

'Just another song.'

The trees were closing overhead, the moon shining through a grille of high branches like the wires around a hurricane lamp. He wasn't even sure of the way, but he was in no doubt that they'd get there.

He wondered if Merrily was secretly hoping that if she prayed in the haunted hop-yard God would mystically grant her knowledge, an explanation of the deaths of both Stephanie and Gerard Stock.

Because it seemed unlikely that anyone else could.

'You know what I'm beginning to think?' she said, with alarming synchronicity. 'I'm thinking Stock – because of his professional history, because of his attitude – was sorely misjudged. I'm tempted to think he approached Simon St John out of pure need, having come to the conclusion – very gradually and very reluctantly, no doubt – that Stephanie was possessed by something evil. I think it was *her* he wanted exorcized, not the kiln.'

'But wasn't the type of guy who could ever come out and say that.' Lol held up a branch for her to duck underneath. 'So he laid it on Stewart. The obvious ghost.'

'The e-mail he sent to the office was very straightforward and very sincere,' she said. 'He appealed to me as a Christian. He said he and his wife were being driven to the edge of sanity. I also spoke to a journalist today, called Fred Potter, who spent some time talking to Stephanie's colleagues at the agency where she worked. She seems to have gone through a radical personality change, from mouse to . . . someone altogether more predatory.'

'Are you actually talking about possession?'

'I don't know. I'm the only person who ever has to consider that possibility. So I try not to.'

'I think it was Conan Doyle who had Sherlock Holmes say— *Oh.*'

Just as he'd done the first time, Lol almost walked into it: the first of the abandoned hop-poles. They walked out of the wood and into full moonlight, into the first alley of hop-frames, the moon overhanging the hop-yard, making the lines of naked frames gleam whitely like prehistoric bones.

'God,' Merrily whispered, 'you were right. It isn't nice at all, is it?'

She took his hand and led him to the centre of the hop-yard – the field of crucifixion. They stood together beneath a broken frame, the crosspiece hanging down, a frizzle of bine dangling from it. Lol had an image of Stephanie, with the bine in the bedroom. He blinked hard and shut it out.

'Has to be done tonight, you see,' she said, 'because this place will probably be crawling with people tomorrow.' She looked around. 'I'd like us to get protection first against anything else that might be here. So we'll do St Patrick's Breastplate – *Christ be with us, Christ within us* . . . you know? And perhaps we could visualize a ring of light around the hop-yard and the kiln, spreading out to Knight's Frome.'

'Sure. I mean I'll try.'

The truth was, he felt an unexpected, slightly shameful excitement. This was nothing like the cleansing of the kiln. Just the two of them this time. And the big full moon.

She said, 'To be honest, I'm not sure I could do this alone, tonight.'

'Well, I'll do whatever—'

'Just *be* here. And think no harm of them. Wish them . . . love. Maybe repeat a few things after me.'

'Merrily, I . . .'

'Mmm?'

'I believe you can do this. I believe in you.'

'I know.'

They were quiet for a few moments, looking across at the kiln-house, soot-black now against the creamy sky.

'Erm . . . it's about guiding the undying essence to God,' Merrily said. The moon was full on her face and she didn't look like a saint or a goddess. She looked like a woman. 'That's Deliverance.'

He said on impulse. 'Merrily, how can you love Him? How can you commit your—?'

'Can I love Him like a man?'

'Words to that effect.'

'You want this straight?' He nodded. 'When I pray, I don't see a man. Or a woman. I just experience – it started out as imagination, but now it truly exists – a warmth and a light and a great core of . . . what you'd describe, I suppose, as endless, selfless love. Which asks for nothing in return but an acceptance of it . . . which is faith. It sometimes comes in a kind of blue and gold – but that's subjective.

It's just some incredible benevolence, so beautiful and so close, so intimate that . . . No,' she said, 'this is not a man. It's completely different.'

Lol was glad, for a moment. 'You feeling any of it here? The benevolence?'

'No. That's what worries me. Somehow I can't get going until I feel there's something – some small light – something to . . . connect with.'

'So what exactly are you feeling?'

'Scared?'

The moon hung in the black wires, several feet above them. The moon was not Christian; it was not about selfless, undying love; the moon was cold rock and had no light of its own.

They stood together between the poles, looking down a whole avenue of poles towards the wood, and then Lol was aware of them turning and facing one another, and he didn't actually perceive Merrily coming into his arms, she was just there, a small, warm, slippery animal, not a saint, and her mouth was soft and moist, not like the marble mouth of some sacred statue, and the air around them was full of the caramel essence of tumbled hay.

'Oh God,' Lol murmured, drawing back in final, fractional hesitation and then lowering his head again as he felt her lips part and her breath meeting his breath, a confluence, her breasts pushing against him. He felt the two of them were pure energy, blown down the alley, the poles to either side blurring in the warm, racing night. He felt this was the moment his soul had been rushing towards, through days and months and years and lives and . . .

. . . And yet it was wrong.

It was sickeningly, shatteringly wrong.

It grew cold. The air around them grew as cold as the moonlight. Lol heard wooden poles creaking, as if one had cracked. They were old poles, some had fallen, many were probably rotting inside their creosote shells. Held inert by a damp dread, he heard a crumbly rustling that his mind translated into images of brittle hop-cones on mummified bines. He heard the humming in the wires and looked up at stringy clouds in the luminous green-grey northern sky, through the hop-frame, a black gallows.

'*No!*' he heard behind the studio silence, the crisp eggbox acoustic. '*Come out!*'

Merrily's back felt cold against his hand, the cold of an effigy on a tomb. Their faces were apart, a chill miasma around them, as if they'd dropped into a vault, and Lol felt sick with the wrongness of it and sick at heart with what this implied.

# THIRTY-SEVEN

# Rebekah

Close to midnight. Sweet, black tea. A cardigan around her shoulders. A warm summer's night, and she was still cold under a moon that now looked pocked and diseased.

The iron table was wobbling between clumps of couch grass on the cracked flagged yard in front of Prof Levin's studio, the four of them seated around it, Merrily between Al and Sally Boswell, with her back to the hay meadow and the moon.

'I called you,' Sally was telling her. 'Didn't you hear me? I stood in the clearing and I shouted to you to come out of there. My voice—' she looked at her husband in sorrow and some irritation '—doesn't have the carrying power any more.'

'She means I should have gone in for you, but she thinks I was afraid.' Al was sitting with his back to the stable wall. 'I wouldn't go further than the little wood.' He put a hand over Merrily's. 'Well, maybe. But the real truth is, I'd only've made it worse. My father was the *chovihano*. I just make guitars.'

Sally said, 'After you'd gone, we talked about it and then we came after you. With Stock dead, there seemed to be no reason at all any more why we shouldn't tell you . . . everything, I suppose.'

Opposite Merrily, with his chair pulled a little further back from the table than the others, Lol was looking down at his hands on his lap. Merrily felt his confusion. Also the distress, coming off him in waves.

Al was talking to her. ' . . . Like we were saying earlier about the

Romany custom of burning the *vardo*? Was this your Christian way of ensuring that the Stocks did not—?'

'Maybe.' It seemed such a long time ago. Had she actually done that? Had she completed her impromptu apology for a Deliverance? Had she even started it?

Couldn't remember.

Couldn't *remember*.

'Brave girl,' Al was saying, 'but maybe not so wise. That yard – the yard in the shadow of the last kiln – they tried to turn it into pasture once, and the cattle kept aborting.'

Why couldn't she remember? Was it the potion Sally had given her? She said, 'Can someone tell me what happened? Did something happen in there?'

Lol looked up, bewilderment in his eyes.

'We couldn't see what was happening' Sally said quickly. 'Too many poles.'

'Laurence brought you out,' Al said. 'I respect him for that.'

She didn't understand.

Lol said to Sally, 'Why don't you tell us about the Lady of the Bines? That's what this all comes back to, isn't it? Rebekah Smith.'

Sally shot him a glance. 'The Lady of the Bines . . . there's been more than one, of course.'

Lol nodded.

'But the original, I suppose,' Sally said, 'was Conrad's first wife. Caroline.'

It was the local secretary of the National Farmers' Union who had got into conversation with Sally. This was in the mid-seventies, when Verticillium Wilt first hit Herefordshire in a big way. They wanted to discourage young trespassers who might carry the disease from yard to yard, and Sally had said, in fun almost, why not put a ghost story round?

And she'd thought then about the Emperor of Frome and how much more resonance the story would have if it carried echoes of the truth.

According to the 'legend', the Knight of Knight's Frome had banished his wife because she could not give him a son. It wasn't quite like that with Caroline, but the basis was there. It was true that she couldn't have children, threatening Conrad's dynastic dreams – Conrad, collector of farms, with his lust for land, each new field turned into a sea of stakes, a medieval battleground. Eight centuries earlier, Sally said, Conrad would have impaled the heads of his competitors on hop-poles as a warning to other potential rivals.

And yet, he could be charming. Especially away from his domain, on one of his wild weekends in London or at someone else's house party. He'd charmed Caroline, still in her teens, a city child with dreams of vast green acres and dawn walks through wildflower meadows.

Caroline had actually loved the hops – the exuberance of them, their mellow smell, much nicer than sour old beer. Caroline had loved, especially, the month of September when the Welsh came, and the Dudleys and the gypsies. She loved to talk to them – especially the Romanies who did not *want* to talk, who reeked of mystery.

Conrad had said she should not mix with them, the lower orders – lower species, he'd implied. Conrad would drive among the hop-yards in his Land Rovers, a royal visitor. He looked on his pickers, it was said, much as the American cotton kings had regarded their slaves.

The fifties, this was, and the early sixties: feudal times still in the Empire of Frome.

'It was said the gypsies took Caroline away,' Lol said, explaining quickly that Isabel St John had told him a little of this – some of the dirt on Conrad Lake, which would have been published in Stewart Ash's book.

'And I suppose they did, in a way,' Sally said.

Caroline became particularly close to one family after helping them get medical assistance for a child who turned out to have meningitis. Caroline called out her own doctor in the middle of the night and the condition was diagnosed in time to save the child. This was something the Romanies would not forget and, from then on, the doors were open to the young Empress, the mysteries revealed. Under the tutelage of an old lady – the *puri dai*, the wise woman –

and some others, she became aware of an entirely new way of looking at the countryside, the world.

She learned about living lightly on the land. Taking what you needed and no more and then moving on. Fires from the hedgerows, water from the springs. The secret of *not owning*.

'Ecology . . . green politics . . . all this was far in the future.' Sally's face shone in the light from the stable walls, and her hair was like steam. 'To Conrad it was simply communism, of course. Conrad lived *very* heavily on the land. For a while, she thought she could change him – women do, as you know, and sometimes they succeed. But Conrad was already middle-aged and heavy with greed, and Caroline, still in her twenties, was learning fast . . . too fast.'

'They gave her a present,' Al said. 'The Romanies, this was. The mother of the baby she helped save made her a dress, a beautiful white dress, exquisitely embroidered. She wore this wonderful garment, with pride, to a party at the end of the hop season. This was the first and the last time she was to wear it.'

'The Emperor went into her wardrobe and took out the dress,' Sally said. 'Took it into the kiln – yes, yes, *that* kiln. Gave it to the furnace-man to put into the furnace. The furnace-man couldn't bear to do it and took it home to *his* wife, who wore it to a dance. The word got back, and the furnace-man was sacked, of course. After this, the dress was considered bad luck, but no one wanted to destroy it. It was passed from hand to hand and . . . well, we have it at the hop museum now. One day, I like to think, it will go on display. When it's safe. When the full story's told.'

'What *did* happen to Caroline?' Merrily asked. 'She left him, presumably.'

'Yes, after . . . I – I believe that Conrad began to abuse her in a more direct sense.'

'Physically?'

'Conrad was an *owner*. Body and soul. Caroline had to leave him, of course she did. She had a little money of her own, and the gypsies had awoken in her a need for *more* . . . within less. There was – we assume – a discreet divorce. She joined a community set up to develop human potential – at Coombe Springs with J.G. Bennett, who had been a pupil of the Armenian guru, Gurdjieff, at Fontainebleau. And she embraced Schumacher. But Caroline is not so important to our story from then on. If she ever came back, I imagine it *was* to haunt Conrad's hop-yards.'

'She's dead?'

'She's not important,' Sally said. 'Rebekah Smith's the important one now.'

The Rom were always very protective of their women. The term 'communal existence' didn't come close; it was a vibrantly crowded life among siblings and parents, grandparents, great-grandparents – eating together, sleeping together, part of the same chattering organism, Al explained.

The point being that young gypsy women did *not* go for solitary walks. Outside the camp, even outside the *vardo*, they were always within sight of the brothers and the uncles. Part of the traditional defence mechanism.

So how could Rebekah disappear?

'I'll show you some photos of her sometime,' Al promised. 'You'll see the long, coppery hair, the wide, white gash of her mouth as if she'd like to seize the whole world in her teeth. It gives you a small idea of what went wrong.'

No one could explain how Rebekah came to be quite as she was. *Poshrat, didekai?* No way. Her lineage was impeccable. This was a good family, and Rebekah was deeply grounded in the traditions. Also, she had the sight, had been *dukkering* from early childhood. Rebekah could read your palm and your very eyes. Rebekah could look at you and *know*. They used to say a true *chovihani* was the result of some dark union between a Romany woman and an elemental spirit. Well, everyone knew who Rebekah's mother's husband was. But her father?

'If you look carefully at the pictures, you'll see the courage and the arrogance. She was not afraid to be out there,' Al said. 'She was twenty-three years old, and they all said she ought to have been married.'

When she wanted to go off, for a night or longer, she'd always outwit the brothers and the uncles, who would suffer the consequential tirades from the wizened lips of the *puri dai* every time they lost her. But lose her they would, whenever Rebekah decided it was time to make one of her forays into the *gaujo* world.

It was as if something would be awakened in her during the hop-picking season in Knight's Frome, when the gypsies were as close as they ever came to being part of a larger community. After she went missing, the police discovered she was already well known – or at least very much noticed – in some pubs in Bromyard and Ledbury, also further afield, Hereford, Worcester. A woman of the world, it seemed: two worlds, in fact. Rebekah Smith, once away from the camp, wore fashionable clothes, was never even identified as a gypsy. Where did she get those clothes? Who bought them for her?

It was clear she wanted out, the police said. She wanted the bigger scene. She'd be in Birmingham now, or Cheltenham or London. Or even in America. Wherever she was, she'd have landed on her feet. She was twenty-three years old, said the travellers. She should have been married.

She was dead, said their *puri dai*.

But no body was ever found.

And the Emperor of Frome, still raging in private over the corruption and defection of his wife? Oh, he was never even questioned in any depth.

Al looked like he wanted to spit.


Sally Boswell said, 'We look at the nineteen-sixties and we tend to think that was not so very long ago. The young musicians now are all influenced by sixties music – the Beatles and the Rolling Stones and the Grateful Dead and people freaking out on hallucinogens, the voice of youth.'

She leaned forward under the wall-light, as if to make herself more real, her museum curator's voice taking over. She must have been breathtakingly beautiful back then, Merrily thought.

'But the sixties were a *long* time ago,' Sally said.

Particularly the early sixties, when there was still an almost mystical aura around the Royal Family . . . when, in the countryside, this was still feudal England . . . when the Lakes were the squirearchy, clear descendants of the Norman marcher lords. And when their actions were not subject to examination.

Conrad Lake's friends included MPs and would-be MPs like Oliver Perry-Jones. The Emperor dined and drank with senior councillors, magistrates, chief constables . . . and this was the time when the senior police would tend to be ex-army officers with medals from the Second World War, men for whom stability meant the preservation of a hierarchy – and the structure – at all costs. When the police knew their place.

'Conrad was himself a magistrate for a time,' Sally said. 'He was also Worshipful Master of the local Masonic lodge. And the gypsies were vagrants, and their so-called culture was primitive. And they lied, of course. And they also had a grudge against Conrad. So when the police were told that Rebekah Smith had been seen getting into Conrad's car . . .'

'And they *were* told,' Al said. 'There was more than one witness.'

'Uncles or brothers?' Lol asked.

Al smiled. 'You see the problem.'

Merrily saw how intense Lol had become, as though he'd channelled his confusion and distress into an urgent need to know.

'Isabel told me the police finally concluded the gypsies had simply made it up to get back at Lake for banning them from his hop-yards,' he said.

Sally nodded. 'That was one suggestion, yes.'

'But she also thought Stewart Ash had evidence linking Lake to the disappearance. Does that mean he just spoke to the gypsy witnesses who the police chose to disregard?'

'Oh, more than that,' said Al. 'It would have to be more than that.'

'Like what?'

'Like photographs. She took a very good picture, did Rebekah.'

Merrily stayed quiet. Lol hadn't told her any of this – not that there'd been time.

'Especially naked.' Al's eyes glinted metallically. 'Gypsies aren't the most inhibited of folk, and Rebekah – well, she was not the most inhibited of gypsies. I imagine there would have been times when she had Conrad crawling to her feet.'

'Conrad took many photographs,' Sally said quickly. 'He liked to

371

have photos of his land and the things he owned – or wanted to own. He'd bought all the most expensive equipment.'

'You sound as if you *know* that Stewart had pictures,' Lol said.

'Well, of course.' Al extended long hands that bore no signs of arthritis. 'We know Stewart found some of them when he was carrying out his rudimentary renovation of the kiln. Stored behind the furnace, like a private porn collection. For a long time, Stewart preserved the old furnace. I guess it would be – when?' He looked at his wife. 'Early last year? When he decided it was going to have to come out to make more kitchen space.'

'It was certainly well into the spring when he showed you one of the photographs and asked you if you recognized the woman.' Sally turned to Lol. 'When the furnace came out, the builder had found a space at the rear, well away from the heat, where the bricks could be removed. And that was where an old briefcase had been stowed. It contained, apparently, about two dozen photographs. Of the same naked woman.'

'Though not necessarily the same hop-bine,' Al said.

Merrily saw Lol flinch slightly. She drew the cardigan around her. She didn't like where this was going.

'And those pictures of Rebekah,' Lol said. 'They were going in Stewart's book, right? So where are they now?'

Al laughed. 'You tell me. He showed me just the one. He said he had the others. We became excited, naturally, that an old mystery might be solved, an old injustice exposed. But I warned him to keep quiet. Obviously, it must not get back to Adam Lake.'

'And did it?' Merrily asked. She wasn't convinced this would have exposed an injustice. What was there to link these pictures to Lake?

'Well, if it did, it wasn't us who told him,' Al protested.

'If it did get back to Adam,' Sally said, 'it was probably through Stewart himself. Consider: Stewart bought the kiln at a knock-down price, after the receivers moved in – Conrad's death being almost contemporaneous with all this.'

'The Emperor became old quickly and died quickly,' Al said, with evident approval. 'When his second wife left him, taking the child, Adam, they said his mind was already going. They said he drove her away. Eventually, the old bastard had a timely coronary while out patrolling his shrinking domain. He was found by a walker, dying in the hop-yard below the kiln. Yes . . . *that* hop-yard. I like to wonder if, knowing the kiln was being sold, the Emperor was on his way to retrieve his photos when he was struck down . . . and died knowing his final crime was there to be discovered.'

'Why would he keep them there?' Merrily asked.

'We can't know, can we?' Sally said. 'Perhaps it was his old hiding place, going back to when the kiln was part of his farmhouse. He knocked down the house in the bitter wake of his first marriage, built the new house for his second.'

'That's another thing – why did he knock down the house and leave the kiln standing?'

'We don't know,' Sally said, too quickly.

'Why would he have kept those pictures at all?'

'Obsession, Mrs Watkins.'

Merrily didn't ask her to expand, didn't think it would get her anywhere, not yet. 'You were about to tell me why Stewart might have told Adam Lake about the pictures.'

'To get him off his back, of course,' Al said. 'Obsession again. Adam's obsession was to recover what he could of the old empire – especially *that* bit. Maybe he even knew there was something in that kiln, maybe that was another reason why he was so anxious to get it back that he was prepared to make Stewart's life a misery. Maybe Stewart told him about the pictures and tried to blackmail him. Who knows?'

'Al,' Lol said softly. 'Who really killed Stewart?'

Al's head tilted. 'You're asking *me*?'

'You couldn't let Stewart turn those pictures over to Adam Lake, could you? Not at any price. If Stewart had let Lake have the pictures, they'd have been destroyed. So the truth would never have come out.'

Al looked down at his long, guitarist's fingers. 'Yes,' he said calmly. 'Quite right, Lol.'

'And he would have, wouldn't he?' Lol said. 'He'd have given them away in exchange for money or just the removal of the big blue barn – just to be left in peace and a decent amount of light to get on with his books. I mean, I never knew Stewart, obviously, but I don't see him as any kind of investigative writer. The idea of publishing those photos – that would've scared him to death, probably. I mean, how often do you find soft porn in a local-history picture book? The story of Conrad Lake's war with the gypsies, maybe culminating in an undiscovered murder – it wasn't exactly an *obvious* sequel to *The Hop Grower's Year*, was it?'

Merrily stared at Lol with, for the first time, a kind of awe. She wondered how long he'd been brooding about all this? And what had happened in that cold, sterile hop-yard to sharpen his focus.

There was momentary quiet around the table. Then Sally Boswell pushed away her mug of cooling tea.

'You're right, of course. Stewart Ash was a gentle soul. I feared very much for him, with the appalling Adam Lake pursuing the kiln. He was so happy there – compiling his little books, talking to the locals about the old days. Taking his careful photos with equipment so old that Conrad Lake would have discarded it without a thought. You're right – poor Stewart just wanted to be left alone in his beloved kiln-house.'

Sally said she'd once asked Stewart to whom he planned to leave the place. It would have to be his favourite niece, he said – despite her dreadful husband. And so it was Sally who had suggested, half humorously, that he make a will leaving it to the most obnoxious of his relatives, with a clause pre-empting resale . . . and then tell Lake what he'd done. On the other matter, the book, Sally had asked Stewart if he'd consider turning the photographs over to her, saying she was prepared to write the book and publish it, too, and sell it in the museum if no one else dared take it.

'He could keep the profits, for all I cared,' Sally said.

'And what did Stewart say?' Lol asked.

'He was thinking about it,' Sally said. 'He was still thinking about it when he was killed.'

'By who?'

Al exploded. 'Mother of God, there's no big mystery here, boy. Stewart was gay. He was doing a book on the hop-pickers of yore, and his bits of research did indeed bring him into contact with some very nice gypsy boys. Most gypsies have very few hang-ups about sex.

Twenty quid for a three-minute hand job would sound very reasonable indeed.'

'And these are nice boys,' Sally said cynically. 'Very friendly. He can trust them. So perhaps we weren't the first ones to see those photographs.'

'Let's just imagine,' Al went on, 'that Stewart – no doubt more interested in the hop-bine than the naked girl – gives one of the photos to the Smith boys and asks if any of them can tell him who the girl is. They say they'll take it back to their family and ask around. They return the picture a day or so later, heads shaking: "Terrible sorry, guv'nor – nobody d' recognize this one at all." '

Al flashed his goblin's grin around the table.

'But in fact someone in the family whose opinion you do not, under any circumstances, discount, has said to the Smith boys, "*It is your duty to the family to go back and get the rest of these photos and if you know what's good for you for the rest of your dishonourable lives, you will not return without them . . .*" '

'So the Smith boys *did* do it,' Merrily said.

'Never any doubt in my mind. It was probably much as it was told to the court – an attempted burglary. They went for the pictures – all of them. And the book, too, whatever stage it was at, to find out how much Stewart knew, find out what really happened to Rebekah Smith. Oh, a mission of *great* importance. And had it been anything else – anything but his precious book – Stewart would've said, "Go ahead, take it, take it all." ' Al sat back. 'Anything but his bloody book.'

A large moth, with black rings on its wings, landed in the centre of the table, moved around it for a few moments and then fluttered away.

'There goes Stewart now,' Al said whimsically.

Lol kept asking about the pictures. Where were they now? Did the Smith boys take them, or did they panic and leave empty-handed, as had been implied in court? If the Smiths *had* taken them, would they have had time to pass them on before they were brought in by the police?

Merrily thought Lol seemed obsessed, as if he was determined to spread out all the mysteries of Knight's Frome, like the cut and turned hay under the full moon.

'If the family have the pictures,' Al said, 'they'll keep bloody quiet about it now, at least until after the appeal. No stronger evidence of the boys' guilt. And it's all spoiled now, anyway. Who could ever justify the murder of an innocent man to prove the guilt of another who's already dead?'

'Besides which,' Merrily said, 'it's just a photograph of a naked girl – no proof of who took it and no suggestion of what happened to the girl.'

Lol looked at Al and then at Sally. 'And what did happen to the girl?'

'No one knows,' Sally admitted. 'We don't know how the relationship between Rebekah and Lake came about, which of them seduced the other, who exploited whom. But everything I know of Conrad suggests that it was probably going on before Caroline left him. He would have taken a perverse delight, knowing of her friendship with the Romanies, in forming one of his own. However, Conrad's idea of a relationship was not . . . a two-sided thing.'

'But he picked the wrong woman.' Al pushed long white hair behind his ears. 'He picked the woman with the mouth which would eat the world. It's likely that the departure of Caroline would have fed some ambition into her head. So what does he do? Does Conrad Lake, good friend and supporter of Oliver Perry-Jones, marry a gypsy? Out of the question. Can he pay her off, perhaps? Ha! Does even the Emperor of Frome have enough money to pay off Rebekah Smith? I think not.'

Sally said, 'I don't know how he killed her. Probably strangulation. But I think I can guess how he disposed of her remains.'

Merrily stared at Sally, and the night quivered around her.

Vision, when it came, could knock you sideways.

*The burning stench of gunpowder and rotten eggs, the smell of cheap fireworks from when you were a kid, fierce and searing as a jet from a blowlamp, the hot breath of hell; brimstone.*

Just because the pictures of Rebekah were found in the kiln, didn't mean—?

Merrily put a hand to her throat. She saw the sudden concern in Lol's eyes, recalling his anxiety in the kiln, during the Deliverance – the utterly needless deliverance of the soul of the inoffensive Stewart Ash to God. It wasn't Stewart, it had never been Stewart. Stewart wasn't the *type* . . .

Al Boswell put his head on one side. '*Drukerimaskri?*'

'Is it possible,' Merrily said, 'that Rebekah Smith might have died in the kiln? Was this the conjecture at the time?'

Sally Boswell raised up her glasses on their chain, put them on, gazed through them into Merrily's eyes. Her face was severe and, for once, she looked her age.

'Oh yes,' she said.

'And could she have choked?'

'Sulphur,' Sally said. 'Do you know what sulphur does?'

'Yes. I've a strong idea.'

Sally spoke in her museum curator's voice, without emotion. 'What happens in a hop-kiln is that when the sulphur is to be burned, everyone gets out very rapidly. Sulphur, in small quantities or as an element in spa water, can be beneficial to health. Sulphur burning in a confined space can be horribly poisonous. It causes extreme reactions very quickly. It attacks, the eyes, the throat, the lungs, the skin. It turns hops yellow. I think that anyone exposed to sulphur fumes, in a confined space and unable to get out, would be . . . grateful to suffocate.'

Al said, 'Lake always took his women to that kiln. Common knowledge.'

'Women? How many women did he have?'

'How many sheep in a flock?' Sally said. 'And after the cursory search for Rebekah was over, he became less cautious. He'd pick up prostitutes in Hereford and Worcester and bring them back – right up to his death. He had a mattress in the loft.'

Al regarded Merrily gravely. 'How do *you* come to know of this?'

Merrily's phone began to shrill.

Al suddenly smashed a fist down on the iron table. 'He locked her in, didn't he? He locked Rebekah in the fucking kiln with the sulphur rolls burning blue in the brimstone tray?'

'I *don't* know that,' Merrily said. 'I just—'

'He turned her *yellow!* And then he came back and did whatever else was necessary, and then he fed her to the furnace. The reliable old oil-fired cast-iron furnace, burning at two million BTUs . . . cremation guaranteed!'

Merrily stood up and found she was shaking. She took the phone to the edge of the weed-choked terrace.

'M–Merrily Watkins.'

Behind her, Sally was saying, 'We'd always suspected he must have spread her ashes on the hop-yard, then had them dug in.'

'*Mum* . . .'

'Jane?'

'Mum, I swear to God we thought we were doing it for the best but it, like . . . it's all gone wrong.'

'Where are you?'

'We're in the car. We're on our way to Canon Pyon.'

Merrily said tightly, 'I didn't know there was a Canon Pyon in Pembrokeshire.'

'Oh, Jesus Christ, Mum, we went to tell Amy Shelbone to stay the hell away from Layla Riddock, but she's piss— she's run away . . .'

Behind her, Lol was saying, 'What do you mean, "in the real sense"?'

'Jane,' Merrily said, 'what have you done?'

'So we were in this like really difficult situation, and we ended up telling Mr and Mrs Shelbone about Layla Riddock, but it was only when—'

'You did what?'

'It was only when I said, just, like, in passing, that Layla's stepfather was – was Allan Henry . . .'

'Dear God,' Merrily said drably.

When she came back to the table, Al Boswell was saying intensely to Lol, ' . . . Drains him, you know? Exhausts him sexually, but it's like a drug, until he doesn't know what day it is. You know what I'm telling you, boy?'

THIRTY-EIGHT

# Physical Dependency

If the Shelbones knew they were being followed, it didn't seem to bother them. Their Renault was puttering steadily along like this was some little jaunt to the all-night supermarket. Even in his seriously unstable condition, Mr Shelbone was driving with impeccable care, slowing for every bend.

'And she said what, exactly?' Eirion was keeping a steady distance between them, all the same.

'She said kind of, you know, be careful,' Jane said.

'These were her actual words?'

'Close.'

'She said "Go home", didn't she?' Eirion didn't take his eyes from the tail lights ahead.

'Well, yes, she did. She said that, too.'

'But the phone signal wasn't great at that point, I would guess.'

'Maybe the full moon affects them.'

The road at this stage was absolutely dead straight, probably an old Roman road, and there was no other traffic, so Eirion let the Shelbones increase the space between the two cars. 'What did we have to lose, after all?' he said morosely. 'There was only one parent left to alienate.'

'The point is, Irene, she doesn't know what we know, and she wouldn't let me explain.'

'Jane, you really think *we* know everything? You see the looks those Shelbones were exchanging as soon as they heard Layla Riddock's name? What was that about?'

'It was the Christmas Fair thing, of course. And anyway that was your fault for telling them. The Shelbones are immensely strange people. All those awful, sombre pictures? You can tell why Amy's turned out the way she is. If they've got a shotgun in the car with them, Allan Henry's blood will be on your hands.'

'But she *is* coming out here?'

'What?'

'Your mum.'

'Oh, yeah. And Lol, I expect. And OK, she did say to keep out of it, but what she really meant—'

'What she *really* meant was, keep right on top of it so you don't miss any of the action.'

'I would not forgive myself if something happened I could've prevented. Riddock's psychotic, and Allan Henry's some kind of semi-criminal with pockets full of councillors and police – bit like your dad.'

Eirion let this go; there were some issues beyond argument. They drove through Canon Pyon, which was strung out like a Welsh village.

'What is it with you, Jane?'

'Maladjusted?'

'Angry,' Eirion said.

They drove in silence, eventually leaving the village lights behind. Then Jane said, 'Actually, that day in the shed, when Riddock – when she kind of dominated me – it was like she was a woman and I was just a little girl. I was feeling screwed up and insecure. Whereas now . . .'

Eirion braked slowly as the Renault in front indicated right. The moon shone down on woodland.

'Don't say it,' Eirion said. 'Do not even—'

'Whereas *now* . . .' Jane smiled grimly. 'Now, I reckon I should be able to take the slag, no problem.'

Lol drove. His old Astra wasn't as fast the Volvo, but when you lived in the country you knew that speed didn't help, because cars didn't own country roads. He headed straight for Hereford, the most direct route to Canon Pyon; at least there'd be no hold-ups, past midnight. He concentrated on his driving; there were issues he didn't want to think about until there was something meaningful he could do – if there ever could be.

At the Burley Gate crossroads, Merrily said, 'Lol . . .' He heard her groping in her bag for cigarettes. 'Lol, I have to—' All kinds of stuff rattling in the bag, getting thrown about. 'Look, what happened back there . . . in the hop-yard—'

*Oh God.*

'Nothing happened,' Lol said.

*Nothing at all.*

'That's not entirely true, is it?' Flick of the lighter. 'What I remember feeling was . . . what you might describe as a – at that moment, an unseemly need. I mean, don't get me wrong, there've been times, and – and quite recently, when it would not have struck me as unseemly. Not at all.' He heard her sink back against the vinyl. 'God, the older you get, the harder it is to talk about these things. Or is that just me?'

'Could I have a cigarette?'

'You don't smoke.'

'Yes, I do.'

'Since when?'

'Since after you hand me one. No, all right, forget it.' He sighed. 'If you're asking, was it normal, healthy, adult passion, well, I would love to have thought it was. But in the end . . .'

'Thanks,' Merrily said.

There was a long silence.

'Where does that leave things?' Lol said.

'I don't know.'

Lol swallowed.

After a while, Merrily said, 'What did Al say to you when I was on the phone?'

'You know – gypsy stuff.'

He heard her blowing out a lot of smoke. 'Al is saying that the presence in the kiln is this Rebekah Smith, isn't he?'

'That's what he seems to be saying.'

'And even though he knew Rebekah – had known her since she was a child – he's very much afraid of her now, isn't he?'

'He . . .' Lol could see clusters of lights in the distance, maybe the city itself. 'The difference apparently is that *gaujos* – *we*'re ambivalent about our ghosts. We have bad ghosts, we also have vaguely tolerable ghosts. But the Romanies – I may be wrong, but I think *mulo* is the only word they have for a ghost.'

'And it can also mean vampire,' Merrily said, 'in the real sense.'

'They don't have to take your blood, Al says. They'll just take your energy.'

'That's . . .' He sensed her strained smile. 'I was going to say "normal". It's usually suggested by those who accept these things that spirits need to absorb energy in order to manifest. Hence cold spots in haunted houses. Hence, in extreme cases, possession.'

'In the case of the *mulo* or *muli*,' Lol said, 'it seems to be . . . sexual energy. It's sexually voracious. Sometimes it comes back to its old partner. In the old gypsy stories, it would come out of its grave and appear in its lover's waggon and spend the night. The next day, the lover would be physically drained. And this would go on. And eventually the lover would die. Exhausted. A husk. Maybe become another *mulo*. Something like that. I don't know. Al was losing it by then, and you were just coming off the phone.'

'This is not going to be pleasant,' Merrily murmured. 'It's going to be much worse than I could have imagined.'

'When you asked Sally why Conrad Lake would have knocked down the house but kept the kiln – I mean, why would he? Especially if that was the place where he'd left Rebekah to die, where he'd burned her body. You'd think it would be the very first place he'd choose to demolish, wouldn't you? Unless the kiln was the place where they used to meet . . .'

'And would perhaps go on meeting?' Merrily said.

'Yes.'

'And if he had to keep going back there. I mean *had* to. He said—' Merrily coughed. 'Boswell said Lake became old quickly and died quickly. He said he virtually drove his second wife and the child away – as if he wanted to be alone there. People were saying his mind was going.'

Lol heard Al talking. '*Exhausts him sexually, but it's like a drug, until he doesn't know what day it is. You know what I'm telling you, boy?*

'As if he had to be alone with her,' Merrily said tonelessly, 'and with what he'd done. Killed a gypsy, but he couldn't kill the need. Kept her pictures in the kiln. A memorial. A shrine. And she was still there. In his head. A physical dependency.'

Lol glanced at her. She was holding the cigarette between finger and thumb, eyes focused on its smouldering tip.

'But he wasn't always alone there,' he said. 'According to Al, he'd pick up prostitutes in Hereford and Worcester and pay them to come back with him. I believe that. You can't take women regularly in and out of the kiln without somebody noticing. But people would keep quiet – at least until such time as Conrad no longer had any money left to pay them.'

'Still found money for the women, though?'

'Because *she* needed them.'

'Rebekah.'

'Yes.' Lol drove faster as he saw the lights of Hereford gathering ahead and then surrounding them. He wanted them to get there soon, wherever they were going. He didn't want to talk about this any more. He didn't want the theory expanding to take in Stephanie Stock and the scratches she'd made down her husband's back – maybe Stephie and Rebekah between them. Stephie and Rebekah on the bed with the bine.

Stephie and Rebekah in the hop-yard, rustling and crackling with the cold electricity of the dead, and the keening in the wires.

Had Stewart Ash known this would happen when he left them the house? But why would he do that to his favourite niece? The answer, Lol supposed, was simple: Stewart was unaware of it. He was gay, so Rebekah's *muli* could never have reached him. It had taken predatory males to destroy Stewart.

Lol drove into half-lit Hereford with its shutters up, its pubs long shut, a cruising police car waiting at the traffic lights.

He thought of Merrily finally in his arms, breath on breath, the warm confluence, then the passion turning cold as they became a foursome: Lol and Merrily and Stephanie and Rebekah.

The lights changed. He felt her hand on his arm.

# THIRTY-NINE

# Rich Girl With a Hobby

Big, black, metal gates. Not decorative gates, but gates with bars more than an inch thick, and with spear-prongs on top. Gates designed to keep you out. White security lights pooling the turning circle in front of them.

The Renault was stopped outside them with its engine running and its headlights on full, and its horn was blasting, an unbelievable noise down here in the woods.

What was more unbelievable was that this was adults, in the old-fashioned sense: staid middle-aged people. It was kind of shocking. And, sooner or later, it was going to have to get a reaction.

It was cooler now, in the hours before dawn. Jane, in her old fleece jacket, was hunched down by some rhododendrons about ten yards behind the Renault. She'd got Eirion to drop her at the end of the drive and she'd walked down through the trees while he'd gone to find a place to park the BMW – so it would be ready for a fast getaway, he said; also so it wouldn't be damaged in the event of—

—Whatever happened.

Jane couldn't blame Eirion for being cautious; he was in enough trouble, domestically. And anyway she wasn't in any mood to blame him for anything tonight. Right now, stocky, solid Eirion was very OK; Jane still carried that warm glow, warmer than the fleece, and her body felt different, felt stronger; felt like a complete unit – though maybe the unit now was her and Eirion: *an item, official*. Yeah, OK, cool. It felt like the start of a journey. Scott Eagles and Sigourney Jones? Had it come to this?

*'STOP THAT NOW!'*

This guy was inside the gates, on the edge of the area floodlit by the headlamps – big guy in a leather jacket and jeans.

The horn stopped, though Jane could still hear it in her head, so the silence was kind of shattering. Mr Shelbone got out and stood next to the Renault, staying behind the headlights, a long silhouette.

'I want to speak to Allan Henry.' His voice sounded harsh and fractured, the way cardboardy voices did when they were raised.

'We've got an office,' the guy in the leather jacket said. 'You can phone in the morning and ask for an appointment like anyone else. Now go away.'

'You tell Allan Henry I want to see him *now*. Tell him it's Shelbone.'

'Do you *know* what time it is?'

'Tell him if he doesn't come out, I shall stay here all night, blowing my horn.'

'You won't, you know. Because if you aren't away from here in two minutes, I'm calling the police.'

'And you are?'

'The gardener. Don't you even know it's illegal to sound a car horn after dusk? Now get back in your car and get out of here, before I get annoyed.'

Oh yeah, he really looked like a gardener. The kind of gardener who planted people.

Mr Shelbone got back into his car, like he'd been told – and just leaned on the horn again. It filled the night like a wild siren. Jane felt a little scared. If this was a bunch of kids, like drunk or stoned, it wouldn't mean a lot, but these were quiet, suburban, middle-aged, extremely Christian people, and they believed this man and his stepdaughter had somehow taken away their precious child.

And Jane was now inclined to believe this, too, though it didn't make any proper sense. It was one thing for Layla Riddock to be very turned-on by the idea of real communication with the spirit of Amy's murdered mother, something else entirely to kidnap the kid. And bring her here, thus connecting Allan Henry to it?

An arm around her waist. She screamed.

'Sssh.'

'Irene!'

'Not so loud, *cariad*.' He pulled her down into the rhododendrons.

'*Cariad?*'

'Welsh term of endearment. What's happening?'

'I know that. They're demanding to talk to Allan Henry. That
guy claims to be the gardener, would you believe? Where've you left
the car?'

'There's a little clearing about thirty yards back. I turned it round
and tucked it under some trees.' She had the feeling that now he was
sure Gwennan's car was safely off the road he was almost enjoying
this. 'He's breaking the law, making that noise. He drove here like
he was on his driving test, and now—'

'He knows. The gardener guy's threatened to call the police.
Shelbone's just ignored him.'

'Maybe he *wants* them to call the police. Maybe he realizes that
if he went to the police himself and asked them to start questioning
this Allan Henry's daughter about the disappearance of his kid, it
would be quite a long time before they even took him seriously.'

'Yeah,' Jane said. 'That's good thinking, Welshman.'

'But if Henry does know where that kid is, getting the police up
here's going to be the last thing he'll want.'

The gardener guy was no longer visible. Maybe he was taking
instructions on the phone. Shelbone was still blasting away on his
horn.

'He's even beginning to annoy *me*,' Eirion said.

Jane became aware of a small gate, set into one of the big gates
– became aware of it because it opened, and the guy in the leather
jacket came through and walked around to the driver's door of the
Renault.

'Open the window!'

No reaction. The horn went on blaring. You could just make out
the Shelbones – heads and shoulders front-facing, neither of them
moving. You felt they ought to have placards in the windscreen: *Save
our Child*. They were a little crazy.

'*Open it!*'

No movement inside the car. The guy in the leather jacket swung an arm and stepped back. There was a faintly sickening snapping sound.

'Jesus,' Jane whispered.

'He's smashed the wing mirror.' Eirion's arm tightened round her waist. 'I can't believe he did that.'

'Open the window,' the guy said, almost conversationally, like he was into his stride now.

Shelbone revved the engine a little but stayed on the horn. The guy's arm went back again; there was a glint of moonlit metal.

'Bloody hell, Jane, he's got some kind of big wrench.'

The arm came down fast and there was this massive crunch.

'Oh my God, Irene, he can't—!'

The gardener had begun smashing in the driver's door and the side panels, his arm pumping with a deliberate, workmanlike savagery, which reminded Jane of those disgusting clips of the bastards beating baby seals to death. The whole car was rocking with each blow, the horn intermittent now, fractured *beeps*, Mrs Shelbone screaming, the woods echoing to a scrapyard symphony of violence.

Eirion let go of Jane. 'We can't just stand and watch this.' He pulled out his phone, thrust it at her. 'Call the cops.' He stepped out of the bushes.

'No!' Jane grabbed his arm. She'd seen lights coming on, some way behind the gates. 'Wait.'

The guy in the leather jacket backed away from the car as both metal gates started to swing back.

Then this man in a check shirt and jeans strolled coolly out, making these casual but authoritative side-to-side wiping movements with his hands until the gardener guy and his wrecking tool went back into the shadows.

And the man just stood there, waiting – until the horn stopped, and Mr Shelbone's door began to open with this really horrible rending noise. The man didn't move, didn't wince. Mr Shelbone got out, unsteadily – kind of top-heavy like a wallflower that had come unstaked.

'It's David Shelbone, isn't it?' The man was talking like this was a cocktail party. 'From the Planning Department.'

Mrs Shelbone shouted, 'David, don't go near—' But the rest was

387

muffled by Mr Shelbone slamming the car door and taking a step towards the casual guy, who just stood between the headlight beams, his arms by his sides.

'Well,' he said, 'I was going to say I'd be surprised if this were an official visit, Mr Shelbone, at one in the morning. But then, on reflection, I suppose I wouldn't be surprised at anything you did.'

Shelbone was breathing hard, 'Where is she, Henry?'

'What? Who? What are you talking about? This your idea of a night out, is it, Shelbone? Taking a tour of historic buildings in the moonlight to make sure nobody's replaced any slates with the wrong colour—'

'Tell me where she is.'

Allan Henry stood with his legs apart. He wasn't the puffy, bloated tycoon-figure Jane had imagined. He looked quite young from here. He looked fit – a lot fitter than Mr Shelbone.

'So what've you got against me, David? It's just your name keeps cropping up time and time again. Everything I do to bring new business into this town, improve the local economy, create jobs – you're there trying to sabotage it. I don't understand – it's just *you*, every time. A reactionary little man, a deluded loner with a grudge. Nobody at the council can figure you out. What's the problem? What's the matter with you?'

'You and your thugs!' Mrs Shelbone was out of the car, now, a big, bulky woman, arms flailing. 'You can have your thugs destroy our car, but you won't intimidate us, with the . . . with the Lord Jesus Christ on our side!'

'Destroy your car?' Allan Henry looked for a moment like he was going to laugh but in fact, Jane thought, his expression had turned suddenly menacing. 'Thugs? You arrive at my private residence at one in the morning in a car that's either been in an accident or been . . . quite deliberately damaged by you and your husband and you wake everyone up – to accuse me and my gardener—'

'You—' Mr Shelbone stabbed a quivering finger at him. 'You're *filth*. God will punish you!'

'Ah, you're a sad and a sick old man, David Shelbone,' Allan Henry said, almost lazily. 'You should be having treatment. You should be on medication.'

'It's *you* that's made my husband ill!' Mrs Shelbone shrieked. 'And you've turned our daughter . . . You and that . . . *witch.*'

'Ah, *yes.*' Allan Henry turned on Mrs Shelbone. 'That's something else, isn't it? I had a silly little woman vicar here allegedly investigating some ludicrous allegations against my stepdaughter. I might have known where all *that* came from.'

Jane began to quiver. Eirion put a hand over her mouth. 'Save it,' he whispered. 'Just remember everything that's said. You're a witness.'

She thought she caught a movement behind Allan Henry, a figure flitting like a moth. Eirion took his hand away.

'You . . .' David Shelbone's rigidly pointing arm began to shake suddenly. *God,* Jane thought, *what if he has a heart attack?* 'You tell me . . . where you've got—' his voice rose to a howl of helpless anguish '—GOT MY DAUGHTER!'

And suddenly Allan Henry was losing it. 'Shelbone!' Advancing through the gate in the illumination from the headlights. 'What would *I* want with your fucking daughter? Truth is, you and this mad old bat should never have been allowed to adopt that child, and if she's run away, then you've driven her away. We—'

He half turned as headlights appeared behind him. There was the mean, throaty snarl of a powerful engine, and then the lights were full in Jane's eyes.

'It's coming out!' Eirion yelled. He started to drag her back into the rhododendrons.

Jane heard Mrs Shelbone scream, saw the woman throwing herself in panic across the bonnet of the Renault as the yellow car came through the gates. There was a vicious scraping of metal on metal, a small splintering crunch as it tore a tail light from the Renault and spun off into the bushes, no more than a foot from Jane's legs, to get past and back onto the drive. She heard tyres spinning and then the wheels hit the tarmac, skidding, and the car took off into the night, and Jane yelled,

'Layla!'

Eirion was frantic. 'You OK? Jane? *Jane!*' Feverishly pushing foliage aside, like he might find both her legs severed at the thighs.

'That was Layla Riddock!' Jane cried. 'Where's the car? Get *after* her!' Her legs worked. She began to run back up the drive. 'Come on!'

'What?'

'Please, Irene, go, go, go – *go!*'

Nice idea. Quick thinking in the circs. Except that when the BMW reached the lane, there was no sign of the yellow car. She could have gone either way, either left towards Dilwyn or right to Hereford. Jane was sobbing in frustration, scanning the horizon for tail lights, but the horizon was no more than five yards away, here: high hedges either side of the twisty road.

'Right! Irene, go *right!*'

'Why?'

'I don't *know*, but we've got to try something. It just seems more likely. Just do it.'

'Call the police.' Eirion was poised at the junction, holding the car on the clutch. 'The phone's on the dash. Dial 999.'

'And tell them what?'

'Tell them there's a disturbance at Allan Henry's. Tell them you're a neighbour and you heard crashing and screams.'

'There aren't any neighbours. Please, Irene, go – *go!*'

'Call the police! And if you really want to help the Shelbones, give the cops our names as witnesses.'

'Oh, all right!' Jane stabbed at the phone, and Eirion sent Gwen-nan's car racing towards Hereford, Jane half hoping that after a couple of hundred yards they'd find the yellow sports car upended in some ditch.

'*Emergency – which service?*'

'Police.'

Eirion made pained noises as Jane described the sounds of what could have been a massacre coming from the Henry spread, and then conveniently got cut off.

'Why the hell did you—?'

'Just keep going, Irene.'

'Why? What's the point?'

'Haven't you figured this out yet?'

'Forgive me, I'm Welsh.'

'She's got the kid in the car,' Jane said. 'She's got Amy.'

Merrily was breathing again. In the confining darkness of Lol's car, they'd approached the absurd, cornered the chimera . . . been able to talk about something that otherwise might have remained undiscussed, possibly for ever, putting a permanent distance between them – a gap that might never have been crossed.

Now, she was feeling closer to Lol than she had to anyone except for Jane, Sophie sometimes and – curiously – Gomer Parry, since first coming to Ledwardine and taking on this impossible job and discovering that the people she could trust to try and understand her were all too few.

Ironically, Lol remained unconvinced about the threat posed by Layla Riddock – maybe because, without her, they wouldn't be here, wouldn't have reached this level of communication.

'She's seventeen,' he said as they neared Canon Pyon. 'She's just a rich girl with a hobby.'

'However,' she reminded him, '*she* clearly believes that being half-gypsy gives her access, a power base.'

'*Imaginary* power base.'

'And she's now got remarkable influence over one of the richest developers in the county.'

'It happens.'

'Taking over his house, his bed? From her own mother?'

'She's a young girl, he's a rich middle-aged man,' Lol said sadly. 'The gypsy magic could be entirely superfluous.'

'And the fact that she's also assuming responsibility for conserving and regenerating his finances? And somehow being *allowed* to?'

'It's *not* a fact, though, is it?' Lol said. 'It's only what she thinks. He scatters her mystical charms and talismans around, it keeps her sweet. He doesn't believe any of it, and they both know it won't last.'

'Maybe.' She watched Lol driving, the slit-eyed alien on his sweatshirt lit green by the dashlights. The mature woman's dream: a nice-looking man who, targeted by a young girl, *any* young girl, could be firmly relied on to run like hell. 'So, what about the persecution of the Shelbones? It starts as a game, becomes a serious fixation for the persecutor as well as for the principal victim. And it's working.'

'*Why* is it working?'

'It just does,' Merrily said.

'Black magic just works?'

'In the short term, it works. People who go down that road find they can get what they want very quickly. Then it starts to mess them up and they can't get out. I'm not being metaphysical here. Pure, calculated evil works, short-term, because it nearly always takes us by surprise. We're not conditioned to turn the corner and meet the man with the knife.'

'And what happens when we *are* conditioned?'

'Then maybe we also start to carry knives,' Merrily said miserably. 'Then it gets ugly. Hang on, Lol, I think we've just passed the turning.'

She'd spotted a man standing by the roadside, smoking a cigarette.

Lol pulled in and reversed. The man threw down his cigarette and stamped on it. The Astra drew level with him. Merrily wound down her window.

'Good morning, Reverend Watkins,' Allan Henry said wearily.

On the edge of the Holmer industrial estate, at the top of Hereford, there were temporary traffic lights. They took for ever to change. There was already a great wide Dutch container lorry waiting at the lights.

'Mum was right after all,' Jane said. 'There *is* a God.'

Behind the container lorry, its headlights full on, was a chrome-yellow Mazda sports car. Its driver kept revving impatiently. It was clear that if it hadn't been for the Dutch lorry, this particular driver would have shot the lights.

'Just as I was convinced we'd got it wrong and Layla had just kindly taken her home to Dilwyn,' Jane said.

'*We*'d got it wrong?'

'Just don't lose the slag.'

Eirion said nothing. This was not such a happy development for him, evidently.

Over the old city, the moon was very bright. You could see right across to the hills and Wales beyond. Jane didn't think she'd ever felt so wide awake.

# FORTY

# Bleed Dry

They followed the yellow car down to the silent city, past Hereford United's ground and the livestock market, losing the Dutch lorry at the big traffic island.

Just the BMW and the Mazda now and, on Greyfriars Bridge, Eirion let Layla widen the gap.

'You'll lose her!' Jane wailed.

'Not now. I know where I am now. I know all the escape routes.'

'What if the lights turn against us at the bottom, and she's away? You *want* to lose her, don't you?'

'That would be nice,' Eirion admitted, 'but unfortunately I'm an honourable sort of person.'

'Sorry.' Jane glanced back across the River Wye where the Cathedral sat placidly beyond the old bridge, above a nest of modern buildings turned greyly medieval under the moon.

They watched the Mazda go around the bottom island and up towards Belmont and the Abergavenny road, Jane leaning forward, peering through the windscreen to see if there were two heads in there. But the sports car was too low; Amy could be sunk down in the seat. The clock in the BMW said five past two.

'Look – how do we know she's got the kid?' Eirion said.

'It's obvious, isn't it? Layla was there all the time – behind Allan Henry at the gates. I'm sure I even saw her once. She'd have heard everything. She knew the Shelbones were raising hell and the police were likely to be involved. She had to get Amy out.'

'Out of *where*? She was staying with the Henrys? Does that sound likely to you?'

'Irene, the whole thing's sick. I don't know what the arrangement was. For instance, Layla's supposed to have a gypsy caravan somewhere in that wood. Maybe the kid was in there, maybe that's where they were doing their seances, I don't *know*.'

'All this presupposing she's so much under Layla's thumb that she'd let her nearly run her mother down on the way out, without protesting, leaping up, shouting out. Admit it, none of this is making a lot of sense'.

'Just stay behind her.'

They tailed the Mazda through the Belmont District, past the all-night Tesco, another roundabout, a half-mile or so of main road, and then Layla took a left, and Eirion slowed but didn't turn.

'This looks like a *minor* minor road. If we so much as turn down here she'll know we're following her.'

'Who cares?'

'Let's not blow it now, Jane, for the sake of a bit of caution.' There was woodland both sides of the entrance, but it wasn't too thick; anyone the other side would see their headlights. Eirion switched them off. 'I don't think there are many places you can get to from here, anyway, I think it just goes into plant roads.'

'Huh?'

'Industrial development.'

'So like maybe she killed Amy and she's going to have her body set into some concrete foundations?'

'Let's try and retain just a modicum of proportion here.'

'Oh yeah, let's be *sensible*.'

'OK, let's not, then.' Eirion turned left, put his headlights back on. They were into a newly made road through woodland that you could tell was being cleared: another ecological disaster zone. About half a mile in, they came to a fully cleared area washed by sterile, high-level security lamps. Eirion suddenly slammed on the brakes, cut his lights.

Because there was the Mazda, parked outside some utility wire-meshed metal gates. A sign behind and above them said:

**DANGER. KEEP OUT.**
**ALL TRESPASSERS WILL BE PROSECUTED.**

At the side of it, another sign:

*Arrow Valley Commercial Properties*
**BARNCHURCH TRADING ESTATE**
**Phase 2**

'I don't get it,' Jane said.

'Stay here,' Eirion warned.

Jane snorted. What was the point of that? She zipped up her fleece and got out of the car. She walked out into the middle of the clearing, the big lights shining down like this was a prison yard. A lone tree, a Scots pine, towered over the site, its steep trunk filigreed with moonlight.

There was nobody in the Mazda. It was dead quiet, surreal.

After a couple of seconds, Eirion stepped out, too, and Jane turned to wait for him. It was now that a shadow peeled off the base of the pine.

Jane squeaked.

The shadow spoke.

'Little Jane Watkins. The vicar's child. We *are* honoured.'

Allan Henry leaned down to the Astra's wound-down window. 'My solicitor's on his way. Not his usual office hours, but with all the money I pay the fat bastard, he'd've been reaching for his pinstripes even as we spoke.'

He grinned, all those nice white crowns shining in the moonlight: teeth like stars. Basically unworried, Merrily concluded, up against it yet perversely energized; a stroll around the grounds with a cigarette and he was ready for anything. Been here before, and he'd be here again.

'Where are the Shelbones now?' she asked him.

'Finally gone to the police, I imagine. I told them the bloody kid wasn't here, never had been here. They weren't convinced. My own fault: I'd antagonized them – maybe a mistake. Can't believe they

396

got you out again. Those people are frighteningly unbalanced. Look, how about you come down to the house and have that drink, Mrs Watkins. Is that your friend in there, the very proper Mrs Hill?'

'It's my other friend, the very self-effacing Mr Robinson.'

'Boyfriend, eh? What a shame. When you'd gone yesterday, I had a little fantasy about you in your cassock.'

'Thirty-nine buttons to undo, one by one,' Merrily said. 'That's an old one. You haven't seen a couple of teenagers around, boy and a girl?'

'I told you: nobody here but me.'

'But you're a notorious liar, Allan.'

'I swear on my Swiss bank account.'

'OK.' Merrily got out, Lol too, leaving the sidelights on, locking the car.

'What's *he* do, then?' Allan Henry asked. 'Archdeacon?'

'He makes music. He writes songs.'

'I think I feel one coming on now,' Lol said.

'Be careful, my friend,' Allan Henry said, as if by instinct. 'I don't just threaten, I sue. I *always* sue. Go for everything. Bleed dry – it's the only way.'

Layla unlocked the metal gate with a steel key. She was wearing tight jeans and a black cotton top that finished three inches above her gold-ringed navel. Her tumbled hair was dyed black, with a long, streak of gold that seemed to have been spun from the moon. Jane could tell Eirion was unexpectedly impressed; he'd gone very quiet.

'You don't know about the Barnchurch, Jane?' Layla's voice was throaty, almost gravelly.

It stood no more than twenty yards behind the gates. All the ground around it had been cleared, and a small mountain of sand had been dumped a few yards away. It was a regular red-brick building with a slate roof. There were brick steps up the outside, tough grass sprouting between them.

It looked like, well, just a barn, and not a very old one – except that, where the gable end was half-lit by the security lamps, you could make out where a Gothic window had been bricked up, just the ridge now, like an old operation scar.

'This Welsh miracle-worker used to preach here, way back,' Layla said. 'Sinners reborn, the sick taking up their beds and walking out, angelic visitations. Powerful stuff. In fact, the farmer here was so impressed he gave him this barn, and all the local people helped turn it into a church, and the miracles went on for a while and then . . . I dunno, the buzz died, or the preacher fucked off back to Wales, or the miracles stopped happening or something, and it became just a barn again and got forgotten about. But, hey, once a holy place – you know what I'm saying?'

'Yeah,' Jane said, though it really wasn't much more than a breath.

'Imagine all that energy shut up with chickens and cows, sacks of feed, tractor parts. Throbbing away on its own for about a century. And then Allan buys the site and it wakes up again – so much energy focused on the old Barnchurch, so much money banked up, so many greasy palms, so much *desire* . . . that it's become really *charged* again.' Layla's face was radiant. 'You go in there, *pow!* Heavy shit, Jane. This place really makes it, where so many real churches are just old dust.'

Eirion said, 'Where is Amy?'

Layla turned to appraise him. 'Boyfriend?' She walked right up to Eirion, gazed arrogantly into his eyes from about three inches away, her breasts almost touching his chest. Eirion blinked. Jane tensed.

'Hey, this boy's had nooky tonight!' Layla spun away from him. 'Was that with you, Jane?'

Jane said nothing.

'Where's Amy?' Eirion said stolidly.

'You want to keep this boy, Jane? You'd like to stay together? I can actually fix that, if you like. I can show you *kitan-epen*. I fixed it for Eagles and Sigourney, did you know?'

'Ms Riddock,' Eirion said, 'is Amy Shelbone with you?'

'She's probably in there.'

'In the barn?'

'She's got a key. She's very trustworthy. She's got a key to the main gate and a key to the Barnchurch itself. She comes on the bus. Isn't that sweet?'

Jane stared. 'She's been *here*? All the time?'

'Just for a couple of nights, approaching the full moon. Making things ready for Justine. You remember Justine, Jane?'

'Her . . . mother. Murdered.'

'Oh, you know all that. Who've you been talking to? Kirsty?'

Jane said nothing.

'There was a full moon the night Amy's daddy slaughtered Amy's mummy, did you know that? The moon's great for that stuff. It moves the tides, and we're nearly all water – but you'd know all that.'

'Sure.'

'You want to go in and see? Talk to little Amy?'

Jane looked back at the wire-mesh fence and the BMW. Actually, she didn't. She wanted to go home.

'After you,' Eirion said to Layla.

'Tell me something.' Layla put the flat of a hand on Eirion's chest and spread her big, fleshy fingers. 'Do you get asthma at all?'

She didn't wait for an answer, let her hand fall and walked away towards the brick steps, big hips swaying, the sliver of gold breaking up and reforming as she tossed back her hair.

Eirion swallowed. Jane looked at him questioningly.

'Haven't had an attack in years,' Eirion said uncomfortably 'Jane . . .'

'What?'

'I don't think it would be a good thing to annoy her, do you?'

They didn't make it to the house, only as far as the *vardo* in its little clearing, to one side of the drive.

Allan Henry noticed Merrily looking at it.

'She's not in there, vicar. Believe me.'

'Can I see, anyway? Would you mind?'

'The holy of holies?'

'Please.' What she needed was to get him talking about Layla. Now, while he was hyped-up, aggressive, his back to the wall. Outside the gates, he'd picked up what looked like the plastic cover of a car's tail lamp and thrown it far into the bushes, without comment.

Allan Henry tutted. 'Can't believe how amenable I'm being to everyone tonight.' There were two wooden steps up to the *vardo*. The door was locked, but he had a key. 'She doesn't know I had this cut. Thing is, I don't like there to be places I can't go. 'Specially not on my own property.'

He went in first. There was electricity: a flicked switch turned on a couple of erstwhile Victorian brass oil-lamps, one on a dresser, one on a wall bracket.

'Gosh,' Merrily said. 'It's a complete little world.'

It was beautifully kept but not like a museum. Although everything – from the decorated and lacquered panels on the dresser to the vaulted ribs in the bowed ceiling – was polished or at least shiny, there was a *used* feel about the place: a pan on the cast-iron stove, a mortar and pestle on the dresser with powder scattered around it, a silk scarf spread on a small camping table, with a pack of Marseilles tarot cards at its centre.

And books: over a hundred on shelves, floor to ceiling, either side of a red-and-black-curtained window. Merrily checked out a few of the titles: a couple of dozen on gypsy lore but mainly general occultism. One was laid horizontally on top of a row: *A Manual of Sexual Magic*.

'How old is she?'

'Coming up to eighteen,' Allan Henry said. 'That means she's been a grown woman for five, six years.'

'Erm – in what context are we talking here?'

'Gypsy girls mature earlier. By Layla's age, most of them are married, with two kids. By my age, there'd be a bunch of grand-children. Like you say, a different world.'

'Which sounds like as good an excuse as any.' Merrily looked at Lol, who was still standing out on the steps. Lol's eyes narrowed.

'However, this is not really any of your business.' Allan Henry picked up the tarot pack and then dropped it quickly, as if it was hot. 'No blood relationship between me and Layla. Don't even have the same surname. I've never been a father to her. She never wanted a father. But, like I say, not your business, Reverend.'

'No, it's between you and Layla and . . . Mrs Henry.'

'Mrs Henry's well taken care of.'

'I bet.'

He grinned. She saw he was still wearing the wheel medallion, representing wealth.

'Where's Layla now?'

'I wouldn't know. She's a free spirit.'

'Just I had a feeling you always liked to know where everything was. Where you could put your finger on it.'

Allan Henry turned and glanced at Lol. 'Before we go any further – some things I don't talk about in front of a third party. Legal safeguard.' The lines either side of his nose were parallel, like a ladder without rungs.

Lol looked at Merrily. 'Go for a walk, shall I?' Merrily nodded.

'Don't go anywhere you shouldn't, my friend,' Henry said over his shoulder. 'The boy in the bungalow's nervy tonight.'

There was a Victorian sofa opposite the cast-iron stove. Merrily sat at one end of it, with her hands on her lap. Henry was at the other, an arm flung over the backrest.

'Costly, this little vehicle?' she said.

'You wouldn't believe.'

'Beats a Wendy house. But she's worth it, is she? Layla?'

'You're not wired, I suppose?'

'I'm certainly not going to invite you to check.'

'Sometimes she's solid gold,' he said. 'Sometimes she's plutonium. We had a big bust-up after you left. She drove out of here during— when my back was turned, but I don't want to talk about that.'

'She gives you Romany talismans to wear, and decorates your house accordingly.'

'Where's the harm?'

'Does it have any effect?'

'On a personal level.' He smiled. 'You bet.'

Merrily glanced up the bookshelf. *A Manual of Sexual Magic.*

'How long have you and she been . . .?'

'Longer than I'm ever going to admit to the likes of you, my dear. Like I say, they mature early, and not only physically. I have no guilt about this. She made the running, in the early stages. She knew what she was doing. And I'm a businessman, not a teacher, not a politician. I'm not obliged to set an example to anyone.'

'But she's still at school.'

'And will be until she gets her four A levels. It's a changing world, Reverend. That's all right by me. You only have one life, live it on the outside track.' He jabbed a finger at the window. 'He famous, that guy?'

'Not especially.'

'Too old to make it now. Nobody in that business sees first-time action the wrong side of thirty. What would you want with a loser?'

'He's not a loser. He just doesn't make much money. Maybe you're the loser.'

'How do you figure that?'

'Just my warped Christian way of looking at things.'

He shook his head irritably. 'What do you want, anyway? Not to help the Shelbones. *Nobody* wants to help the Shelbones.'

'And that would make me your enemy, wouldn't it?'

A fist clenched. 'Where do you *get* that from? The man's got a chip on his shoulder the size of a fucking breeze-block. His colleagues don't like him, the council doesn't like him. He wants to turn Hereford into a museum – how many jobs are there in a museum? Do you have any idea how much money's riding on Barnchurch, how many people go down if it crashes?'

'It's not going to crash because of one barn. It'll just have to be modified.'

'Modified?' His face quite visibly darkened. 'A full-conceptualized multi-million-pound project that *everybody* wants has to be *modified* because of one man's whim? Let me tell you, an out-of-town location, it's got to be big to work – we need the whole fucking space, we don't need a prime plot right on the entrance clogged up with a useless pile of old bricks we aren't even allowed to *adapt*. If this works – *when* this works – it opens up the whole Hereford Bypass corridor . . . and that's *mega*. Let me tell you—'

'—That it makes sense, in anybody's language, to destroy one awkward cranky little family rather than spend a lot more money?'

*Go for everything. Bleed dry. It's the only way.*

'That's a naive oversimplification,' he said.

'And that's an admission,' Merrily said.

*Total darkness at first.

'Amy?' Layla called out. 'Are you there, love?'

Then, gradually, a lozenge of light appeared high up in the furthest wall – the old ventilation slit.

They'd come in from the door at the top of the steps, into the loft where there must once have been pews, Jane figured.

'Amy!'

There was a big echo. It was a cathedral of a place, but it didn't smell like a cathedral. Instead, there was a crude blend of old hay and manure and engine oil and something sourish.

'Evidently not here,' Layla said. 'Come on, we'll go down. You'd better follow me. No electricity, I'm afraid.'

Eirion held Jane's hand. He squeezed it encouragingly. But this was all going so totally, totally wrong. Layla Riddock was supposed to be furious and devastated at being exposed as some kind of spiritual abuser – not playing the affable tourist guide.

Jane remembered, with a wince, her own excruciating cockiness earlier on. *Now I can take the slag, no problem.* The truth was, she was feeling exactly the way she'd felt that day in Steve's shed, when she was just a mixed-up little virgin and Layla was a mature woman, seventeen going on thirty-eight – someone who didn't guess or fantasize, someone who *knew.*

Rites of passage? What a load of bollocks. It didn't make any bloody difference at all, did it? Jane didn't even have as much going for her as little bloody Sioned and little bloody Lowri – at least they had a *culture* around them. Like Layla, in fact – a Romany gypsy, with all the powers *that* seemed to confer. One hand on Eirion's chest and she'd identified him as an asthmatic, something even Jane, his girlfriend, his *lover*, didn't know. Where did *that* skill come from? Jane remembered reading somewhere that gypsies didn't tell each other's fortunes, because that was something they could *all* do – no big deal.

*No big deal.* Wow. If you weren't part of an ethnic minority you were like nowhere these days.

'The steps are quite steep,' Layla called, 'so you'll need to go down one by one. There used to be stairs when this was a church, but they rotted away years ago.'

'I'll go first, wait at the bottom for you,' Eirion said.

Jane could hardly see her way to the steps, which were wooden, with gaps in between, not much more than a wide ladder. At the bottom, there were stone flags.

She could see Layla's dark form moving on confidently down what maybe was once an aisle.

'You say your dad – Allan – owns this place?'

'Yeah. He's going to flatten it in a couple of months. We're just getting some use out of it first. We *needed* a church. We needed to match that energy, you follow?'

'Not really.'

'Where were we supposed to go, Steve's shed?'

'I don't understand, Layla.'

Layla was squatting by a wall. Far above her was the ventilation slit, the only light source. It was a cold light, and Layla's silhouette was blue-grey.

'They go through an identity crisis, Jane, adopted kids – especially when they've got adoptive parents like hers. Weird old fucks. But you saw them at our place, obviously.'

'Er . . . yeah.'

A match was struck, yellow-white light flared, like the light in Steve's shed: a fat candle.

'I'm helping her to find herself, Jane. Very rewarding, for both of us.'

Another match, another fat candle. Two fat candles – on an altar.

'Here she was, little angel in a house full of religious prints, Bible at the bedside, church twice on Sunday. Is that *normal?*'

Jane thought about Mum: no, not normal.

She could make out the altar now. It was obviously not the original one; it was supported on two rough pillars of old bricks, but the top was quite a big, thick piece of wood, varnished and shiny. As well as the candles, it had a chalice on it, a real churchy kind of chalice, perhaps even silver. Layla was loaded, Layla could get hold of these things, no problem.

'And it wasn't Amy, was it?' Layla said. 'Not the *real* Amy, whose parents got pissed and shot up. What this is all about is letting the real Amy come through. This is what her mother wants – I mean her *real* mother.'

As Layla stood up, Jane screamed and clutched at Eirion. A grey-white figure was standing behind the altar.

# FORTY-ONE

# Another Round to the Devil

Lol had walked twice up and down the drive, once exchanging a wave with the nervous gardener through the front window of his bungalow, when a police car nosed in, no siren, no fuss.

He waited for it near the gates. This was slightly awkward, but walking away wouldn't look good.

Both coppers got out. 'Mr Henry? Mr Allan Henry?'

Lol stood blinking in the headlight beams, aware of another vehicle pulling in behind the police car: the solicitor, maybe, arriving with Henry's legal bulletproof vest.

'Er, no,' Lol said. 'Mr Henry's back there. In a gypsy caravan.'

Exchange of glances, then they came slowly towards him, one either side. He leaned back against the gates, arms loose: no threat, not part of this. Where was the gardener – he should be handling it.

'Then who are you, sir?'

'Me? I'm just—'

'Mr Laurence Robinson, as I live and breathe!'

*Not* the solicitor, then. This was a recently familiar figure with red hair and an expression of pleasant anticipation.

'Remember me, Mr Robinson? DI Bliss?'

Like there were several Scouse accents in Hereford Division.

'Remind me,' Lol said.

Bliss laughed. 'What a night that was, eh?' He walked over, car keys in his hand. He looked like he'd come out in a hurry; he was wearing a dark suit jacket over a white T-shirt and sweatpants. 'And what a night this is turning out to be – what's left of it. What you doing here, pal? That your car, is it, on the road?'

Lol nodded. He saw one of the uniformed men had a flashlight levelled at the ground, tracking around.

'Looks like there's been something approximating to an RTA in this vicinity, boss.'

'Does there, really?' Bliss nodded absently. 'Tell you what, Terry, why don't you boys go and see if you can find Mr Henry and make sure he's in one piece. I'll have a chat with Mr Robinson here.'

They leaned either side of the bonnet of Bliss's modest Nissan. Lol was explaining as best he could, covering up very little.

'Two nights?' Bliss whistled thinly. 'A fourteen-year-old girl missing for *two nights*, and no bastard tells us?'

'Hang on,' Lol said, puzzled. 'You knew this, surely. You've talked to the parents.'

Bliss looked genuinely blank. 'I know nothing about any parents, pal. We're just responding to a 999 from a young girl. Sounded like everybody who ever bought an Allan Henry home was arriving to complain *en masse*. I was in bed, I had a call, the magic name was whispered in me ear and . . . as I'd always wanted to visit Southfork, I came. I'll be making the most of that in a minute.'

'Young girl?' Lol said.

'I doubt it was this actual missing girl, if that's what you were thinking. Let me get this right, are you saying Henry's stepdaughter knows where she is?'

'Well, that's what the kid's parents thought.'

'I'll give Hereford a bell in a minute, see if these parents have shown up. Hereford can handle it from their side. Me, I feel much better knowing Mrs Watkins is on the case.'

Lol met his eyes: sarcasm or a feed-line?

'I *like* that little lady,' Bliss said. 'She tries so hard.'

'She does.'

'Allan Henry, mind, that feller's something else again. Not harmed then?'

'Not that I could see.'

'Doesn't sound like it was worth getting out of me pit, does it?'

Bliss stood with his hands flat on the car bonnet. 'So . . . anyone tell you about Gerard Stock, then, Laurence?'

Lol nodded.

'Surprise you?'

'Kind of.'

'C'mon, Lol, I'm not taking a bloody statement here.' Bliss straightened up. 'You're one up on me – you knew the bugger before he was a murderer. What I've learned in the past day or so tells me a bloke like that doesn't clam up then top himself. Now he's gone, there's not much left for us to clean up. But I'd still like to know what it was about. Really. So – what *was* it about?'

'You're asking *me*?'

'I am. I'm asking you 'cause you've got no professional angle on this. And also, well, our governor, Annie Howe . . . very busy little snow queen tonight. She's probably still up in her office right now. Don't get me wrong – good copper, Annie, good thief-taker. But limited vision. And I'll tell you now, Annie's out to stick this on Merrily. Big-time.'

'Why?'

Bliss blinked. 'That's a good question. I never gave it much thought, to be honest. *Why?* Well . . . she's no believer. It offends her a bit, working in a cathedral city, seeing what it all costs, being told by the Chief that she's gorra stay on good terms with the Church hierarchy. And women priests – not that she likes men priests either, but I reckon she actually thinks women should be *above* that kind of superstitious rubbish. Women becoming priests is a sell-out. That's what I reckon, anyway. Women like Merrily are traitors to the cause.'

'That's a new one,' Lol said.

'Yeh, and I never told yer. So, go on. Why did Gerard Stock kill his wife and chop her head off?'

'I don't know.'

'I know you don't bloody *know*, Lol. What do you *think*? What does Merrily think?'

'Well, nothing you could put in a police report.'

'Bloody Nora!' Bliss gazed at the moon. 'I'll decide what can be made to fit into a report – and it might not even need to be a report, as such. Might be a whisper in the right ear at headquarters.

I'm trying to help here, pal. I was raised a Catholic in Liverpool, me.'

'You said.'

'It was a long time before I even started to question whether the stuff in the jug at Mass might possibly *not* have turned into the actual blood of Christ. Still keeps me awake sometimes. So, what I'm saying . . . I'm not gonna laugh, you know?'

'Well . . . Stock gave the impression he thought his place was haunted by the ghost of Stewart Ash. But if you believe it *was* haunted, maybe you're not looking at Ash whose murderers were caught. Maybe you're looking at something that happened there a long time ago but that was never solved at all.'

Bliss blinked. 'Something *else* happened there? Should I know that?'

'Maybe something was left that affected Stephanie more than Stock, because she was a woman. Something that changed her personality.'

'You're suggesting Mrs Stock was possessed, right?'

'I don't know if that's the right word.'

'Tell me,' Bliss said.

So Lol actually told Bliss about The Lady of the Bines. About Rebekah and Conrad Lake. Out here, under a full moon, it didn't sound entirely crazy. While he was talking, a Mercedes drew up and a plump man with a pilot's case walked past them to the gates without a sideways glance.

'Doesn't waste any time, does he?' Bliss commented. 'Right then. You're saying that, whatever the truth of the matter, Gerard Stock, notorious piss-artist of this parish, had every excuse for thinking his wife had been . . . shall we say, infected by the spirit of a woman whose murder had gone undetected.'

'Not only undetected, but undiscovered,' Lol said.

'This is not uninteresting, Laurence. You think if I went back through the annals of the old Herefordshire force, I might find a reference to this missing gypsy? Not that I'm doubting your word, but it might help to have that bit official.'

'I wish you would.'

'I will, son, no skin off my nose. There, that wasn't too hard, was it? I get very upset about how nobody wants to talk to us any more in case it gets taken down and used in evidence.' Bliss patted Lol on the shoulder. 'See, from Merrily's point of view, what would need to be shown was that Stock wasn't just a dangerous mental case who only needed his blue touchpaper lighting – by, say, an unwise exorcism carried out without due forethought, et cetera, et cetera – but in fact an intelligent man forced by circumstances to grapple with possibilities to which he'd not normally have given houseroom.'

Lol noticed Merrily on the other side of the gate. She was talking to one of the uniformed coppers. She had her shoulder bag and her jacket draped over an arm.

'Looks like this is the bit where I'm called on to fence for a while with Henry's foxy brief,' Frannie Bliss said.

'Um, there's something else.'

'Quick as you can, Lol.'

'It's likely Stewart Ash had an unfinished manuscript suggesting Conrad Lake as Rebekah Smith's killer. Also some pictures – photographs – that Lake took of Rebekah, naked, with a hop-bine wound around her . . . the two most important elements in his life, maybe.'

'Or a sadomasochistic symbol of Mr Lake's dominance, if she was tied up in the bine, Lol.'

'That too. Anyway, we know Stewart had them in his possession, and that they've disappeared. Be interesting to know if the Smith boys *did* nick them, and if they got a chance to pass them over to someone before they were arrested. I mean, how long after the killing were the boys brought in? Could they have hidden the papers and photos somewhere? Could that stuff still be found?'

Bliss nodded. 'All right. I'll check it out. Might take a day or two, and I might not be able to tell yer even if I do come up wid something, but you'll know the info's in good hands. Thanks, son. Anything else you think of, you know where to get me. Leominster or Bromyard, usually.'

He moved towards the gates. Lol followed him.

'So what exactly . . . has Howe got planned?'

'Well, it won't come from her, will it? It'll come from the Chief

Constable.' Bliss stopped. 'Not a word, OK? You can tell Merrily, and that's it.'

'OK.'

'I mean it, Laurence. I fuck'n hate this politicking, but I'm not gonna lose me job over it.'

'Sure.'

'Right, this is it. Annie's suggesting the Chief puts out a press statement on the lines of, if the Church can't be relied on to police *itself* on matters of irresponsible exorcism, without psychiatric back-up and the like, then it should be made far more open to legal redress. Words to that effect.'

'You're kidding.'

'I only wish it were so, pal.'

'What's the bottom line?'

'The bottom line, Lol, is that the Chief Constable of West Mercia puts his name behind the suggestion that a priest who performs an exorcism that has unfortunate consequences should subsequently be held legally responsible for those consequences. In this case, for instance, we could even be looking at manslaughter.'

Merrily came through the gate. She looked worried. She was digging in her bag for a cigarette.

Lol said, 'They'd want . . . that she could actually go to prison?'

'That's extreme, but—' Bliss shrugged '—this could serve as an important precedent. Chances are nothing'll come of it – I mean, they repealed the Witchcraft Act, didn't they? But it'll certainly make everybody very nervous for a good while.'

'The Church has no balls,' Lol said. 'No bishop in this country would ever sanction an exorcism again.'

He watched Merrily coming towards them, the ruby glow of the cigarette between her fingers. It wasn't the wider issue that worried him so much as what it would do to her. Prison – OK, unthinkable. But being identified as 'the precedent' would, for Merrily, be im-measurably worse.

The pariah. Goodbye to the clergy, obviously. And then what? He'd never fully come to terms with the awesome concept of her as a curer of souls. But ex-Rev Watkins, the disgraced former priest – the consequences of that didn't bear thinking about.

He couldn't tell her. He had to do something.

'As Father Flaganan used to say to us when we missed mass—' Frannie Bliss winked, without humour, acquired an Irish accent '—*ding-ding*, and there's *another* round to the Devil.'

## FORTY-TWO

# Witch Trials

There was a screen behind the altar in the Barnchurch. Not a rood screen but the sort of concertina thing women used to toss their robes over in Victorian bathrooms.

The grey-white figure was hanging from this screen like a giant moth.

Jane stayed back. The face was chipped and grotesque: the face of a black, dress-shop dummy, greasy white rings smeared around the eyes.

'People touch her clothes, usually,' Layla Riddock said, weaving in the candlelight, 'for healing.'

Jane recalled Kirsty: *Gypsies got their own virgin – like a patron saint or a goddess – the Black Virgin.*

'Sara,' Layla Riddock said carelessly. 'Yes, she helps. Amy's had so much starchy religion pumped into her that we have to bring her down slowly. Sara's the Black Virgin, and you can view that two ways, can't you? A saint or an inversion – or a semi-Christian mother goddess. All ways, she helps. Amy's finding her true mother. And, through that, her true self.'

'Where *is* Amy?' Eirion said.

'Haven't you taught him any other words yet, Jane?' Layla tossed her hair. Jane was realizing for the first time how scarily intelligent she was. 'Watch my lips. I – don't – know. Perhaps she went home. Perhaps she's walking the streets. Perhaps she let a rapist in.'

'*Don't*,' Jane shouted, 'talk like that.'

. . . *alk like at* . . . The walls sent back the echo. This was a big, empty place, bigger than the average parish church. Layla seemed very much at home here.

'Your mother came to see Allan,' she said. 'And me.'

'What?'

'Yesterday. She was with another woman, from the Cathedral, looking for Amy. Didn't you know?'

'No.'

'That's funny, because it sounded like someone had told her all about the Steve's Shed Experience.'

'So?' Jane had backed up against something low and hard, an old manger.

'Well, that wasn't a very nice thing to do, grass up your mates, was it? *And* it caused a nasty little row between me and Allan, making it difficult to get away tonight. I arranged to meet Amy here, but I'm late, and now she's pissed off. Anything could've happened to her. All because you had to blab.'

'What do you expect me to do? My mum was in a hassle with the Bishop, because Amy had laid it all on *me*. Because she was scared to put you in the frame. What was I supposed to *do*?'

Layla shook her head in disgust. The ring in her navel shone like the edge of a coin. Jane was bewildered and furious with herself. How could she have let all this get turned around?

'Anyway,' she found herself saying petulantly, 'it was you who set her up.'

'This is Kirsty again, yeah?'

'It's the truth, though, isn't it? You hated that family ever since her old man got your fortune-telling act pulled at the Christmas Fair.'

Layla smiled. 'Oh, Jane, one forgets, you're so *young* . . .'

Jane gritted her teeth. 'Caution, *cariad*,' Eirion whispered.

'I'd go to all this trouble for *that*?' Layla exploded. 'For fuck's sake, what am I?'

'You predicted all kinds of bad stuff. You sent old women home thinking they were going to die—'

'Oh, for God's sake, I was pissed! I'd spent a couple of hours in the pub with some guys, then I go back to the school, put on the clobber, and I just couldn't *bear* to do all that you-will-come-into-money-and-go-over-the-water shit. So I just let it come through.'

Jane stared at Layla in her black top and her black jeans standing next to the Black Virgin in her white robes and white headdress.

'I can *do* this stuff. The *dukkering*. It's a mixture of insight and scam. You do the patter, and sometimes the real stuff comes through. But you're also observing, judging what kind of a punter you've got and tailoring your predictions accordingly. But I was pissed, like I say. I mean, you wouldn't believe some of the people you get in there. There was this old woman, well dressed, dripping with jewellery, all she wanted to know was whether her friend, who was in the hospice, was going to leave all her money to her. You think, *that* age and all she cares about is more money? I said, yeah, you'll get the money but you'd better spend it quick 'cause you ain't got long yourself, dearie.'

Silence. Jane looked at Eirion. There was a little smile twitching at his mouth.

Layla chuckled in her throaty way. 'The one I was a *little* sorry about afterwards – but, yeah, I said it, sure I said it – was Libby Walker who used to do school dinners part-time. You know Libby? She's about thirty and she's got about five kids, all by different dads, and everybody knows she just does it for a council house and the family allowance, that's how thick and irresponsible she is. And as soon as she came in the booth I could see she'd got another one in the oven, and I just lost patience and told her in this sinister voice that I could see "a withering" in her womb. 'Course, the stupid bitch went bloody spare.'

Eirion made a little noise horribly suggestive of amusement, which made Jane blurt out, 'You cursed Mrs Etchinson!'

'Yeah.' Layla sighed and fingered the hem of the robe of the Black Virgin.

'Yeah, I did that. I cursed Mrs Etchinson, and Mrs Etchinson had got MS and we didn't know it, and that was why she was so bloody ratty all the time. I'm sorry. What is this, the Salem witch trials?'

'Layla,' Eirion said, the Welsh coming out in his voice, 'can we come back to the Shelbone issue? Whatever you think about Mr and Mrs Shelbone, their dear little daughter has vanished and they're worried sick. And they've been treated pretty abominably at your stepfather's house – we saw this. First they had their car smashed in by a man with an aggression problem who calls himself a gardener, then your stepfather blatantly lied about it—'

'Oh, Allan's just a little boy,' Layla said. 'Turns peevish if he doesn't get his own way. Forget all that. He'll get Douglas Hutton, his lawyer, to fix it – money will change hands, faces will be saved. Allan's not a bad guy, he's just a crook, which everybody knows anyway. He needs a gardener on account of so many people want to punch his lights out.'

'Hmm,' Eirion said.

Jane wondered if Dafydd Sion Lewis had a gardener, too.

'Look,' Layla said. 'Shelbone's bonkers, and he's the bane of Allan's life. He's this kind of loose cannon. Puts the blocks on lucrative development.'

'That's necessarily bonkers?' Jane said.

'From Allan's point of view, yes,' Layla said patiently. 'The situation was that Allan had been after some dirt on Shelbone for years. Unfortunately, although he's out to lunch, he's cleaner than the Pope. But some councillor knew about Amy's origins, and Allan told me, and I admit I got so utterly tired of his constant ravings and his threats to have Shelbone's brakes seen to, that I thought maybe if Shelbone was already cracking up, like everybody said – maybe we could destabilize his life enough to push him into early retirement or something. No real harm done.'

'So you admit it,' Jane said.

'Yeah, yeah, yeah, I admit it, big deal. I am a bad, bad person. But, then, my old man was a gypsy who conned his way into my ma's pants and pinched her car and stuff, so it's in my genes. It's a hard and ugly world, Jane. Also, Amy was such a pompous little sod that for quite a while it was very much a pleasure, I have to admit. And I had Kirsty, who's this delightfully amoral creature with no sense of moderation – it was all too funny. But then . . .'

Layla went to sit on the altar between the candles. She looked cool and exotic. She didn't look at all worried, about Amy or anything else. Jane supposed that growing up in Allan Henry's household kind of emulsioned over your conscience.

But the really disturbing thing about all this was that the Layla with the cut-off jumper and the navel-ring didn't really seem such a vicious, evil person. And this weird, echoey half-church, with the grotesque Black Virgin overseeing the proceedings wasn't the best environment for working out whether this was simply because she could be witchily enchanting and insidiously plausible, or—

'The word is, you're quite interested in matters of the spirit yourself, Jane. And I don't mean Church.'

'Er, yeah – kind of . . .'

'Which, of course, was why I let you into Stevie's shed. Thinking you could be relied on. Thinking the last person you were going to tell was your old lady.'

'I couldn't know, could I, that she was going to get called in by the Shelbones, thinking their little girl's possessed or something?'

'Yeah.' Layla tucked her legs under the altar. 'That's what they would think. Me, I just thought she was a pain. I don't think any of us could've known.'

'Known what?' Eirion asked.

Layla glanced at him. 'He OK with this stuff, Jane?'

'He's been around me for months.'

Layla smiled. 'What none of us could've known was that Amy Shelbone is the most— it blew me away.'

'What did?'

'She's a natural. That kid is the most amazing natural psychic I ever encountered.'

'Huh?'

'When we did the ouija – and I know how to do this, right? I know how to move the glass and you would never know I'm doing it. Which was what I did. I started it off – and it was like the bloody Internet. I punch in Justine and *boom* – like a search-engine: "We have forty-six listings for *Justine*." You know what I'm saying? All this stuff comes pouring through, and I didn't have to do a thing, the glass is moving like a bloody piston. Kirsty couldn't write fast enough. She tell you this?'

'Not the way you're telling it,' Jane admitted.

'Ah, she's in denial, is Kirsty. It was just a scam to Kirsty. Beyond that she wasn't interested. All the time, she wanted to think it was me swinging the glass. *I* wanted to think it was me. For a couple of weeks, I *did* think it was me – me as a psychic. I got a little cocky. Then I did it with somebody else.'

'The ouija?'

'Got squat.' Layla looked down at her feet. 'Sod-all. Embarrassing. This was at the end of term. Next day, I called Amy, picked her up when the Shelbones were out, and we came here.' She looked up. 'Jane, what a *blast!* We get into Justine, I ask a question, the glass doesn't move. *Won't* move. I couldn't push it. I ask the question again . . . Amy starts speaking. Only it's not her. It's not the little squeaky *I'll tell my mummy* voice; this is grown-up, it's kind of raunchy – and it's got this *Brummy accent.*'

'Oh, wow.' Jane felt Eirion squeezing her hand. A warning. He was telling her not to take all this as gospel. He was reminding her that Layla Riddock was a notorious manipulator.

But, like, *wow.*

'What I'm listening to is a detailed description of a killing. Little Amy Shelbone sitting there in her prim little summer frock, and her mouth's twisting, spittle on her lips, and this like slurred, bitter voice, going, *"I'm gonna cut him this time, I swear, I'm gonna put him away for ever . . ."* '

'—*way for ever,*' the walls sang. Jane dragged her hand away from Eirion's, shoved it down into a pocket of her fleece.

'So she . . . like, she really *was* possessed, then. Mum got it completely wrong.'

'No.' Layla shook her head briskly. 'No way. She's a *medium.* It's a different thing altogether. The medium has control. The medium can let the spirit come through and shut it off whenever. Jane, *I* am psychic. I get insights. A lot of people are, *you* know that. It's either in the blood or it isn't. But it's nothing I can control. I've spent years trying to master it – since I was about twelve. Read hundreds of books, tried all kinds of stuff. And I'm not a medium. I'm just one of a million people who get insights. She made me very jealous, did little Amy.'

Layla stood up, lifted up the chalice, sniffed the contents and put it back. Whatever Eirion thought, Jane's feeling was that this was the absolute unvarnished truth, as Layla saw it.

'So what did you do?'

'I just marvelled, Jane. I just wanted to understand. The complete *injustice* of it. I wanted to understand how come this obnoxious little— I'm going, "How long's this been happening to you? You had experiences like this before? You *must* have!" She's like "What d'you mean?"'

'Did that mean she hadn't? Or she just didn't understand what you were talking about?'

'I still don't know for sure. What I felt – *feel* – is that she hadn't, or wasn't aware of having had any serious psychic experience. Quite often it's something that doesn't happen until puberty. But also she'd been brought up in this strict religious household, with the fear of the Devil and all this stuff hanging over her, and the Bible on the bedside table. She was surrounded by this big, white wall of sterile, puritanical— You know what I mean?'

'Yeah,' Jane said, excited now. 'You kind of dislodged that. You knew about her past, you did the ouija thing, you pushed out the block. It all came flooding out, and not only these awful suppressed memories, but the whole—'

'The whole wall collapsed.' Layla nodded. 'The wall her parents – the Shelbones – had thrown up around her, maybe thinking they were protecting her, I don't know, but I think more likely they were just making sure she was *theirs*. I've read about this loads of times – often people's psychic side gets awoken by some trauma. Like it could be physical, a bump on the head – or, in this case, something deeply emotional.'

'Like you suddenly find out what your dad did to your mum.'

'No, Jane, you *remember* what your dad did to your mum, 'cause you were there and you saw it all.'

'This is *incredible* stuff,' Jane said.

'Let's not . . .' Eirion walked off into what she could now see was an aisle between, not rows of pews, but stalls and mangers. 'Let's not get carried away, ladies.'

'Doesn't this move you at all, Irene?'

'It makes me a little scared, if you want the truth. But then I come from a stiff, puritanical, religious—'

'But not so much any more.'

'No,' he said, as if this was a cause for regret. 'Not so much any more.'

'So where do things stand now?' Jane said to Layla.

'You tell *me*. It's all out now. The Shelbones are on the rampage. I suppose the police'll be out looking for the kid. I mean, I was excited, sure, but I also felt responsible for her – still do, obviously. A person I don't even like. But it was me that broke her through, trying to help Allan. Does that matter now? Seems so trivial: money, again. He'll go on piling it up, and then he'll die.'

'And you were going to meet her tonight,' Eirion said. 'Here?'

'I've already said. We were both excited. Hyped up for the full moon. Look, it's started to run away with itself. Bit like me when I first found out about my dad. Changed my whole world. She's been rejecting the Shelbones' Church for a while – which is OK. Except she needs something to replace it and what's been replacing it is *her*.'

'Justine,' Jane said. Her own voice sounded hollow.

'Justine was real, God wasn't. I think she thought that tonight she was actually going to see— It nearly happened before . . . I would swear, it nearly happened.'

'What?' But Jane was not sure she wanted to know.

'It was just a haze, a mist – a fine, grey mist. But it was coming.'

'Justine.' Jane was shivering inside the fleece.

'I think.' It was as if the cold was even getting to Layla now, she was hugging herself. 'You want the truth, I'm not sure how much I like Justine.' She looked up, towards the ventilation slit. 'Why doesn't the bloody kid come *back*? She can't think I've deserted her, just because I was late. Sometimes you could almost believe the stupid Shelbones *were* her parents.'

'I think we should call the police,' Eirion said. 'If she's wandering the streets of Hereford . . . Well, it's not the genteel country town it might once have been, is it?'

'Christ, no,' Layla said. 'Junkies out there, muggers, violent people – like Amy's dad. Yeah, give it a few minutes, then call the police. Maybe it's working out for the best, after all. Maybe it's better if she does go back into care. Maybe I let a bloody monster loose.'

'Justine?' That name had a disturbing symmetrical sound for Jane now. She had to keep saying it.

Layla looked up at the Black Virgin. 'I lied about this lady. She's *my* protection – nothing to do with Amy. I always felt this affinity with Sara. The patron saint of gypsies. But more than that, like I said: as long as she's up there, watching over me, I feel protected – against whatever Justine turns out to be.'

'More than *I* do,' Jane confessed. Not that it was hard confessing anything to Layla Riddock any more. It was as if, in these past few minutes, she'd shed some age, was far closer in years to Jane. 'Look, I'm sorry, you know? I got this badly wrong.'

Layla patted Jane's arm. 'We've all got this wrong at some stage.'

Eirion watched them from a few yards away. 'Now *that*,' he said, 'is something I find moving. I'll go out to the car and ring the police. Where . . .?'

'Follow the aisle and you'll find a wooden door at the end. It's barred on this side. Hang on, take a candle with you.'

Layla walked back to the flickering altar, where the grotesque but evidently benevolent Black Virgin hung above it in her white robe.

As she reached the altar, the Black Virgin fell, with a slithering sound, down from the screen, in front of the candles. 'Oh God.' Jane rushed back down the aisle. 'She'll catch light.'

The Black Virgin rose up to meet her, its white arms flapping, which was kind of spooky, but Jane laughed and brushed the cotton robe aside, and then Layla fell into her arms.

'*Oh Jesus!*' Eirion cried out.

Layla was coughing. Jane was aware of movement to her left, but she was too intent on staying upright because Layla was pretty heavy, a big girl. Jane staggered back into the aisle under her weight, her arms wrapped around Layla, who just kept coughing. Jane's chin and neck were hot and wet now with what Layla was coughing up – vomit or bile. Oh, *gross*.

It was when she became aware of the salty, coppery tang that Jane's arms sprang apart in true horror.

One of the candles *did* set light to the robe of Sara, the patron saint of the Romanies. Jane saw the flames suddenly leap. And then, in their light, she saw the girl with straight, blonde hair in a white dress – it looked like a confirmation dress – standing on the altar with the carving knife held high and dripping.

Then Amy Shelbone leaped down from the altar and ran jerkily up the aisle and, as Jane stood there, with Layla's lifeblood on her throat and chest, Amy also stabbed Eirion.

# Part Four

'The healer's role will lie not only in rescuing a lost soul but also in experiencing *that soul's misery and pain, thereby 'capturing' the curse or spell responsible for keeping the dead person out of the grave.*'

Patrick Jasper Lee: We Borrow The Earth

*The spirit of the deceased person is addressed in terms of love and consolation in which the eternal forgiveness of God is emphasized.*

Martin Israel: Exorcism

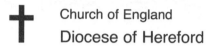 Church of England
Diocese of Hereford

# Ministry of Deliverance

email: deliverance@spiritec.co.uk

Click
Home Page
Hauntings
Possession
Cults
Psychic Abuse
⌐ Contacts
Prayers

## Contacts

If you are in trouble, any Christian priest will be very willing to help you.

However, in all denominations, attitudes towards the treatment of spirtual problems will always differ and, as with any other form of healing service on offer, you should never be afraid to ask for a second opinion.

# FORTY-THREE

# Retribution

When they finally made it home, the dawn was bleeding freely over Ledwardine. Less than half an hour after going to her own bed, Jane appeared in Merrily's bedroom doorway.

It was 6.08 a.m. The sun was well up now. It was already, somehow, humid and airless.

'Cold,' Jane said and slipped into bed beside Merrily.

Eventually, Merrily slept for almost an hour, though it felt like four minutes. All the time, the phone was ringing downstairs. Or so it seemed.

At just after seven a.m., she rose quietly. Jane was still sleeping.

Merrily prayed, in a desultory way, had a quick, lukewarm shower. All the stored hot water had fallen on Jane not so very long ago. Jane hadn't wanted to come out of the shower. Ever.

In towelling robe and slippers, Merrily went down to the kitchen and put the kettle on. The phone was ringing again. She didn't react to it.

She put out both wet and dry food for Ethel the cat. She made herself some tea. Outside, it was as sunny as it had been yesterday morning and the morning before. This would be the last day of the mini-heatwave, someone had said. More little yellow-green apples had fallen to the ochre lawn.

Merrily felt like the world was in colour and she was in black and white and grey.

She felt like a ghost.

\*

In the scullery/office, she sat down in the usual sunbeam with her tea. The phone was still ringing. There were twenty-five messages on the answering machine, which meant that the tape was full.

Merrily unplugged the phone and forced herself to play every one.

There were calls from papers and radio stations she'd never even heard of.

There was a call from a woman, who even gave her name. Mrs Fry said Merrily was a smug, ambitious little bitch who deserved everything she had coming to her. Merrily didn't recognize the voice.

There was a call from someone, a man, who just sniggered and hung up. It was a vaguely familiar snigger, quite possibly a church organist who had once exposed himself to her over a tombstone. Stock's death had been anounced too late for most of the papers; the sniggerer, like Mrs Fry, whoever she was, had probably been inspired by something on the radio or breakfast TV. What did it matter now?

A call from Dafydd Sion Lewis, in Pembrokeshire, began without preamble. 'Mrs Watkins, I consider myself a liberal parent and what my son does in his own time is, for the most part, his own business. However—'

Merrily had already spoken to Dafydd Sion Lewis, awakening him at 3.30 a.m., because she didn't want the police to call him first.

The only useful message was from DS Andy Mumford at Hereford. 'Mrs Watkins, thought you'd want to know we found Amy Shelbone wandering near Clehonger, couple of miles from the Barnchurch estate. We'll be talking to her properly today. And if we could see Jane again, that would be useful. Oh . . . we still haven't found the knife, but we're searching.'

There were several calls she had to make. She plugged in the phone and picked it up.

A man's voice said, 'Hello . . .'

Damn. How could that happen?

'Is that Merrily Watkins?'

Yes, she said. The word didn't come out. 'Yes.'

She decided, at that moment, that whichever paper this was she would answer whatever questions were put to her and she would tell the entire truth. This would save a lot of time and in no way alter the final verdict.

'This is Simon St John at Knight's Frome.'

'Oh.'

'Yeah, I'm very sorry to bother you so early. I was going to leave a message on your machine, actually. I understand from Lol that you've had a stressful night, so you may not want to be involved in this. It's just that I've been talking to the Boswells.'

'Oh.'

'And we . . . decided that something needed to be done.'

'In relation to?'

'In relation to a particular area of ground and the building on its perimeter.'

'Pardon me,' Merrily said, 'but weren't you invited to attend to this particular problem a while ago? Approximately two deaths ago, in fact.'

She waited for him to hang up, the way he'd done with Lol.

'I can understand your bitterness,' he said at last.

'Wouldn't call it that, exactly. I really admire your ability to tell people with problems exactly where they can shove them. I think it's an enviable quality in a clergyman.'

'Well,' he said, 'if you do feel inclined to help, we'll be meeting at the Hop Museum between ten and ten-thirty.'

'Tonight?'

'This morning. It has to be done at noon.'

'What does?

'Al and I agreed this seems to require a more . . . customized procedure. There's a traditional Romany form of exorcism. I believe they have a word or phrase meaning soul-retrieval, but I'm buggered if I can remember it.'

A shadow fell across the desk. She turned in her chair. Eirion stood there. 'Oh.' He backed away. 'I didn't . . . sorry.'

She waved to Eirion that it was OK. 'It's all a bit of a rush, isn't it?' she said to Simon St John.

'Well, it . . .' She picked up either crackle on the line or some agitation. 'Al's in a state. A bad way. And I suppose I'm—'

'What time did you say?'

'Midday.'

'Why?'

'Because it has to be. Al will explain. We were planning to meet as soon after ten as possible.'

'I don't know if I can make that.'

'It's OK,' he said. 'I just . . . thank you for your—'

And now he did hang up.

Lol grabbed the ringing phone, hoping it was Merrily. He'd given up trying to call her at the vicarage. Last night/this morning, he'd forgotten to ask for her mobile number. He hadn't been to bed. He was rediscovering, on the far shores of fatigue, a state of heightened consciousness produced by a cocktail of body chemicals that he suspected was only rarely mixed. It happened sometimes after a whole night in the studio. Afterwards, the hangover would be awesome, but right now he was floating on a luminous pool of awareness.

'Good morning, Laurence,' Frannie Bliss said briskly. 'You're up then. Gorra pen?'

'Not on me.'

'Good. Don't get one.' There was the unmuffled sound of main-road traffic; Bliss was clearly outside, on a mobile. 'Some night, then, in the end, eh? Quite a few added complications to this Shelbone business, sounds like. What's Merrily's take on it?'

'Haven't spoken to her for a few hours.'

'Never mind, not my case anyway. Let's leave that alone; time's short. I got in early this morning, couldn't sleep – bloody full moon. And I was thinking about what you were saying, about Mrs Stock. So I had another look in Stock's computer – we brought his computer in; fascinating, all the things a computer'll tell you about its owner. I got into his Internet files – you click on "history" and the computer very kindly tells yer all the websites Stock and his missus have been into the last months or so. Now, what was the general subject that *most* interested one or the other or both of them over the past few weeks?'

'Gypsies?'

'You're on the ball this morning, son. Aye, there's about ten files on the general subject of gypsies. Which I already knew about, of course – and no big mystery there because that was Mr Ash's main interest, too. But I did begin to detect another element coming through. Either Stock or Mrs Stock was going back to the same sites, following up particular angles. *Gypsies and Death* was a popular one, gypsy death rituals and gypsy ghosts and evil spirits.'

'The *mulo?*'

'Exactly. The living dead. You wouldn't want one, would you? The female version might be all right at first, but she'd start to wear yer out after a while. Couldn't keep up, could you. Go bloody mad.'

'Especially if you were already having problems down there.'

'Precisely. Now – what would you do to get rid of it? Several suggestions came up on this one particular website – you could drive steel or iron needles into the heart of the corpse, or a hawthorn stake through one of its legs. Or you could simply . . . chop its head off. Isn't that interesting?'

'It is, isn't it?' Lol said soberly.

'Course, this is corpses, and I think we can assume Mrs Stock was not one of the walking dead. But then if, as you suggest, the normally rational Gerard had come to believe his wife had been taken over by one of these things, and *if* she was making demands on him he was failing to satisfy – and *if* he'd got in an exorcist to sort her out . . .'

'And if, the minute the exorcist had left the premises, Stephanie appeared to be unaffected or even . . .'

'Go on.'

*Perhaps even perversely stimulated by it,* Lol thought.

'Maybe prayers focused on helping Stewart Ash didn't quite hit the spot,' he said. 'But how was Merrily to know that?'

'How indeed? Because Stock wasn't telling the truth, was he?'

'Why break the habit of a lifetime? You going to tell Howe about this?'

'Not yet. Anyway, it might not have the desired effect coming from me. She's the governor, she decides what line we take. She could tell me to leave the gypsy stuff alone, and that's me silenced.'

'Would she?'

'She might. But let's talk about the disappearance of this gypsy girl in the autumn of '63 and the recent murder of Stewart Ash. What's the connecting factor between these two events?'

'There is one?'

'There is, my son, long as we agree you never heard it from me.'

'Sorry,' Lol said. 'Who are you, again?'

'Good boy. Listen, this is something I can't help you with beyond what I'm about to say. Might be something or nothing. Either way, you'll have to follow it up for yourself. Cherished reputations at stake. I didn't go through official channels, because you leave tracks that way, but I did put in a call, first thing, to a former copper, who I won't name, who used to be based at Bromyard and, as it happened, was one of the PCs involved in what you could describe as the less-than-intensive search for Rebekah Smith. And who, as a local man, was well aware of all the rumours about the womanizing activities of the late Mr Conrad Lake. You with me?'

'All the way.' Lol said.

Merrily brought some tea over to Eirion at the kitchen table.

'How is it?'

'Oh, you know, bit sore . . . stiff.'

'Couldn't sleep?'

'Not really.'

'Is there anything I can do?'

'Well, I'm supposed to go back and have the dressing changed this afternoon.'

'That's not quite what I meant.'

'No,' he said. 'Can we talk?'

'We can try.' Merrily sat down.

The dressing was on his upper arm, just below the shoulder. The woman doctor in Accident and Emergency, stitching up the gash, had said the point of the blade didn't seem to have quite penetrated to the bone. Dafydd Lewis had started saying he'd come over at once, take the boy back to Withybush Hospital at Haverfordwest, but Eirion had insisted he wanted to stay here and see this through. Besides, he assumed the police would want to talk to him again.

'Anyway, I don't deserve any sleep,' he said to Merrily. 'If we'd stayed out of it, this would never have happened.'

'You should never say that. Perhaps something even worse might've happened.'

'Personally,' Eirion said, 'I really can't conceive of anything worse than what did happen. How's Jane?'

'Sleeping.' She'd put Eirion in one of the bedrooms on the first floor.

'Jane's in a bad way about this,' he said.

'I know. She thinks she was guilty of rather demonizing Layla.'

It was the first thing Jane had said when Merrily and Lol had arrived at the Barnchurch: '*Mum, I got her deeply, deeply wrong. We started talking, and gradually she was like really normal – like a friend, a mate . . . oh God!*' Jane was looking like the time when, as a very small girl, she'd found a pot of raspberry jam and got it all over her face and down her front; only it wasn't jam this time and it was even in her hair, so much of it that Merrily'd panicked and thought she must have been stabbed, too, and hadn't bothered to tell the paramedics. '*Layla died. Mum, I watched her dying. I watched her heaving and shivering and struggling for breath . . . Oh, Jesus, Jesus, Jesus . . .*'

In fact, Layla had passed away in the ambulance: multiple stab wounds, at least one believed to have penetrated a lung. It was Eirion who'd had to watch her die on the way to Casualty – the ambulance leaving as the fire engines came in.

The Barnchurch had burned to a shell. The flames had already been into the rafters when Jane and the wounded Eirion had brought Layla out.

'The kid must have been behind that screen the whole time,' he said now. 'Clutching her knife. What was she doing with a *knife*?'

'Well, I – I believe her mother, Justine, used to take a kitchen knife with her as protection when she went to a local church to hide from Amy's father. This was the knife he ended up using on her.'

'I couldn't believe the . . . strength in her. She was like a wildcat, a puma or something. The flames behind her. That white party dress. It was terrifying – sort of elemental. I was just shaking all over, afterwards. I'm sure I'm going to see her in nightmares for the rest of my life.'

'It'll fade, Eirion, I promise. Erm . . . I know the police have asked you this, but what do you think brought it on?'

Eirion drank some tea, trying not to move his injured arm. 'I've thought about it a lot more, obviously, since I talked to the police. I suppose, if you were looking for an ordinary, rational explanation, you'd have to say it was because of what Layla had been telling us. She wasn't being particularly polite about Amy. One of the last things she said before it happened, she called Amy a monster and said perhaps it wouldn't be a bad thing if she was put into care.'

Merrily nodded. 'Mmm. And if we *weren't* looking for an ordinary, rational explanation . . .?'

'Well, earlier, Layla told us how the spiritualism thing had started with her stepfather, Allan, finding out about Amy's history when he was looking for some dirt on Mr Shelbone because—'

'It's OK, I know about that.'

'And then Layla got excited because she assumed *she* was doing it, that it was coming through *her*. But then, the further they went with it, the more they realized that it was actually Amy—'

'*Amy?*'

'Layla said Amy was this incredible natural medium. It was Amy who had . . . raised her mother, if you like.' Eirion drank more tea. 'I think Layla had the idea that if she stuck with Amy, kind of supervising her progress, then she'd see some, you know, amazing things. She said – this is all a bit creepy for me, Mrs Watkins, but she said that it seemed like Justine had been about to kind of, you know, *manifest*. Which was why they were here on the night of the full moon, because there'd been one the night Justine died.'

'And Layla was convinced Amy was the real medium?'

'She said she'd been trying to develop her own psychic side for years, and suddenly here was this awful, repressed little girl who was a natural. She said she was quite jealous. That's more or less what she said. Does this mean Amy could be in some way possessed?'

'I don't know.' Merrily was thinking back to the intense, truncated night in her own church when an eighteenth-century penny had supposedly given her God's spin on the problem: no demonic possession in this case, no possession by an unquiet spirit. 'I suppose,' she said, clutching another of those slender straws frequently offered to you by faith, 'that mediumship and spiritual possession are separated by a degree of control. The medium consents to open herself to the spirit, knowing she can always close the door.'

'That's more or less what Layla said.'

'Except we're not talking about Betty Shine here, we're talking about a fourteen-year-old schoolgirl, and a fairly archaic example of the species at that – impressionable, naive—'

'Will she be charged with murder?'

'I don't see how they can avoid it.'

She was momentarily haunted again by thoughts she'd kept pushing away, about the similarities between this killing and Stock's murder of his wife. In fact, when you examined them individually, the similarities were not so great, since the Romany element was peripheral to the Shelbone issue. To an outsider, the strongest link between the two cases would be herself: Deliverance – failed.

'It's tragic,' Eirion said. 'When you think about it, it's tragic for everyone. Layla Riddock – she was about the same age as me, and she was . . .' There were tears in his eyes. 'She was obviously incredibly intelligent. And there she was, one minute coolly analysing the situation, the next coughing up all that blood, and then in the ambulance . . . What a terrible *waste*, Mrs Watkins. I've heard people say that so many times, but when you actually—'

'Eirion,' Merrily said, 'you really are a nice guy. You risk alienating your family to pursue Jane's whim, you—'

'No, I'm not.' He stared at her, blinking in agony. 'I slept with your daughter!'

His features slumped into comical dejection, like a boxer puppy's.

'I see,' Merrily said softly.

'Last night – well, evening. It was the first time. It was why we were so late getting to the Shelbones. We fell asleep. You see, that's another thing – retribution. If we hadn't . . . been to bed, we'd have got there earlier – and Layla might still be alive. It's retribution.'

'I really don't think so.' Suddenly she wanted to laugh. She'd often thought about what she'd say in this situation, and now she didn't know what she wanted to say. Except . . . 'Well . . . thanks for telling me.'

'I'm sorry,' Eirion said.

'Well, you know, it's not—'

'I do love Jane, you see.'

'Yeah. That's, er, that's the impression I already had.'

'I mean, it wasn't . . . casual sex. I'm a not a very casual sort of bloke.'

'No?'

'In fact this was the . . . you know, the first time.'

'You said.'

'No, I mean for me. For me, too.'

'I see. Does Jane know that?'

'Well,' he said, 'that's probably not the impression I've given her, no.'

'I won't tell her, then.'

'That's very good of you.'

'But just . . . just take good care of her. You know what I'm saying?'

'I think so.'

'I was only about three years older than you when I was pregnant, so I've tended not to come on heavy with Jane, so as to avoid any mention of pots, kettles and the colour black.'

He smiled tentatively. On the shelf beside the Aga, Merrily's mobile began to bleep.

'Excuse me a sec.'

Sophie sounded as if she had a cold.

This was the Sophie who never seemed to get colds, not even in winter.

'I'm afraid the Bishop's back,' she said.

'Good.' Merrily lied, carrying the mobile to the window.

'A short time ago, we took a call from the Church of England Press Office, which has learned of inquiries from West Mercia Police – and also, I understand, from the Crown Prosecution Service – about the Church's guidelines on exorcism. Do you know anything about this, Merrily?'

'Not a thing.' Merrily stood looking out over the vicarage garden. This was only their second summer here; it seemed like half a lifetime.

'The Press Office also understands there may be a statement from West Mercia very soon, expressing dismay at the way the Church of

England reacted to the Stock case. The upshot is likely to be a call for the Church to be held more directly answerable for the effects of what's been described as "irresponsible ministry".'

'But doesn't this pre-empt the result of the inquest? Isn't it usually the coroner who makes comments like that?'

'I think it's more of a reaction from the police to an impending onslaught by the media. It could be weeks or months before the inquest's over. Anyway, the Diocese needs to prepare a counter state-ment, so an emergency meeting's been called at the Bishop's Palace for this morning. The Bishop needs to hear your explanations, in considerable detail, to decide if any of it's—'

'Rational enough to repeat. Hang on, you just said the Crown Prosecution Service. But Stock's dead, so there's no prosecution, only the inquest. Why should the CPS—? Oh.'

'Quite,' Sophie said.

'Oh my God.' Merrily went cold.

'It doesn't *necessarily* mean anyone's contemplating prosecuting either the Church or . . . or . . .'

'Or me.'

'I'm very sorry to have to drop this on you, Merrily.'

'Hardly *your* fault.' *How could it have come to this?*

'The meeting's at eleven a.m.,' Sophie said, 'on the dot. If I were you, I'd—'

'Sophie, perhaps . . . you could make my apologies.'

Pause. She counted six, seven, eight, nine little green cider apples on the lawn.

Sophie said, 'I'm sorry?'

'I've got another appointment, that's all.'

'Merrily, let's be perfectly clear about this: you do realize what your non-appearance would be taken to imply don't you?'

'Things have happened. Don't suppose the news has reached the Cathedral close yet.'

'News?'

'Allan Henry's stepdaughter, Layla – you remember Layla? Black kimono, champagne glass? Layla was stabbed to death early this morning by Amy Shelbone. Who also injured Eirion.'

'What?' Sophie's voice was faint and fractured, like the crinkling of tissue paper.

'That's actually not the reason I won't be able to make it to the meeting,' Merrily said. 'But I thought you should know.'

Lol picked up his keys, locked the stables and drove the Astra up the lane. Despite the window being wound all the way down, the day was already too hot for him. Already, he felt oppressed.

On his way through Knight's Frome, he spotted Simon St John standing on the humpback bridge. Simon started flagging him down.

'I'm sorry, Lol.' He was wearing a black shirt and a dog-collar and very old jeans. He was sweating, and his hair looked like the leaves of a long-abandoned house plant. 'Whatever I said to you the other night, I'm sorry.'

'Don't you remember?'

'Whatever it was, it was probably offensive and I'm sorry.' Simon squinted, the sun directly in his eyes, but he made no effort to avoid it. 'Have you spoken to Mrs Watkins today?'

'Not since first light.'

'Lol, I need her.'

Lol stared at him, said nothing.

'I'm in a lot of trouble.' Simon's eyes were glassy with sunlight and anxiety. 'I phoned her and asked her to come over, but I'm not sure she's going to.'

'Tell me,' Lol said. He didn't have that much time but if this involved Merrily he wanted to know about it.

'It's a priest thing.' Simon started to laugh. 'Oh, fucking hell . . .'

'Why do you swear so much, Simon?'

'Denial. I'm a sick, polluted priest in denial. Pity me, Lol, we're not exactly twin souls, you and I, but I guess we've been to some of the same places. In my case complicated from time to time, as you may have heard, by a certain sexual ambivalence – but, then, in the seventies and eighties an entirely heterosexual rock musician was considered a serious pervert.'

'That's not the pollution, though, is it?' Lol said from his vantage point on the hill of no sleep. What was the point of all this confessional stuff? It was as though Simon was desperate to convey sincerity, openness.

'Oh no,' the vicar said, 'physical pressures I can control. He turned his head and stared at the bridge, the church, the roofs of the village. 'This *bloody* place!'

Lol suddenly thought of Isabel in the churchyard. '*Seemed such a nice boring place, it did, after Wales. No historical baggage. No history at all that wasn't to do with hops. Perfect, it was. And now – blood everywhere.*'

'I'm horribly, horribly sensitive, Lol,' Simon said. 'That's my problem. Like people with a skin condition who can't go out in the sun. Will you tell her that?'

Eirion saw she had other preoccupations and said perhaps he'd take a walk around the village. When he'd gone, Merrily phoned Huw Owen over in the Brecon Beacons.

'Aye,' he said. 'Wondered if you'd be calling one of these days. We do get the papers up here – not necessarily the same day, mind. Anyroad, say nowt, that's my advice. When the trial date's set, we'll happen have a chat about it.'

'There won't be a trial. He hanged himself last night.'

'Who?'

'Stock. In his cell at the remand centre.'

'Simplifies things,' Huw said.

'No, it doesn't.'

'You can get yourself through an inquest. You can tell the coroner why any comparisons with the Taylor case are inappropriate.'

'No. I mean, yes, all that's very much on the cards, and I'm really trying not to think about it yet. But to complicate things, informed sources at Knight's Frome are suggesting there's a remaining problem.'

'At this kiln place?'

'That the killing happened not because Stock was in any way possessed, but because his wife was.'

'By what?'

'A gypsy girl went missing, back in the sixties. There's reason to think she was imprisoned in the kiln and either strangled or choked to death on sulphur, and then her body was burned in the furnace. All I wanted to ask is, have you had any dealings with, or do you know anything about, Romany beliefs?'

'Specifically?'

'Specifically, the *mulo*.'

He didn't say he had, he didn't say he hadn't. 'How long you got to play with?'

She told him, expecting him to laugh.

He didn't. 'Walk away, lass,' he said. 'Just take a holiday. There's no shame in that.'

# FORTY-FOUR

# Avoiding the Second Death

Her hair fell not much more than shoulder-length but was bushed out, maybe a little frizzy; her nose was hooked, her mouth small but full-lipped. The sleeveless white blouse she wore was knotted under her breasts. She had her hands clasped behind her head, her face upturned. Smiling at the sun – eating the world.

Rebekah.

The black-and-white photograph was pinned to the wall above a small inglenook in the back room. Eating the world, and then she choked. It broke your heart.

'That's not one of Lake's?' Merrily asked Al.

'Mother of God, no, it's a blow-up of a picture she sent to *Tit Bits* or *Reveille* – you remember those old glamour magazines? Looking for a career as a pin-up or a model. It was found after she disappeared. The family had copies made to show around, to see if anyone had seen her. They had to conduct their own search, in the end.'

'That's ridiculous.'

'Ah, in those days, as Sally may have said to you, people from ethnic minorities were not considered proper people.' His eyes were quiet this morning. 'Even the beautiful ones.'

The back room of the Hop Museum was not open to the public because it also served as a workshop. It ran the length of the main building, and the two shorter walls were lined with racks of hand tools, probably antiques in themselves. There were a pair of elderly wood-lathes and a bench with a Bunsen burner attached to a liquid-gas bottle. Guitar parts – necks, pine tops, bridges – hung from walls and beams. There was a rich composite aroma of glue and resin and wood.

And hops, of course. The scent of hops was unavoidable in this place.

In a white waistcoat and a spotted silk scarf which, Merrily recalled from childhood, was called a *diklo*, Al had welcomed her with a small bow and a kiss on the hand. Now he was moving around the work-shop, picking up guitar fragments and gently putting them down. A sign down by the road had said: *MUSEUM CLOSED ALL DAY*.

They were still waiting for Simon St John.

'What do you want me to do?' Merrily asked Al. 'I'm afraid I don't really have as much time as I'd have liked.' She'd told him as much as she needed to of what had happened after she and Lol had left Knight's Frome last night. 'And I'll need to be there, obviously, when the police come to talk to Jane.' Al was nodding, but she could tell he was somewhere else.

'*Jane might sleep for hours yet*,' Eirion had kept insisting. '*You go. I can tell this is important. And when she comes down we've got a lot to talk about, haven't we?*'

At least it wasn't far; she could be back in just over half an hour, if necessary. If they could hold off the police until this afternoon, that would help. She'd already called Mumford, asked if this was possible. Mumford had said, '*We've found a knife, by the way.*'

Al was still nodding his goblin chin. 'By one o'clock, it should be over. By one, we'll have done all we can do.'

'But are we trying for the same thing?'

'To bring her into the light,' Al said.

'But is it the *same* light?'

'Light is light, *drukerimaskri*. You know that.'

'I suppose.' She didn't even know if he was a Christian. 'Where's Sally?'

'Gone for a walk. Coming to terms.'

'How happy is she – about what you're proposing?'

'Ah . . .' He picked up an unstained guitar neck, only half fretted, held it up to one eye and looked along it. 'Well, she thinks we should have acted on this when we first suspected something was arising. I tried. I talked to Stock, way back. Told him to sell the place to Lake, take his wife away from here.'

'Did you?'

'Ah, but Stock's patting me on the shoulder, patronizing, like I'm this colourful old rural character. Perhaps I should've had more patience with Stock, told him I was Boswell the guitar-maker, but I didn't want him to know. Consequently, perhaps, I don't suppose he believed a word I was telling him.'

'He must have believed something in the end. He went to Simon St John. And then he came to me.'

'Poor Simon, he doesn't want to do this, even now. He's afraid for himself, and for his wife. He's afraid of what he might bring down on his wife.'

Merrily didn't quite understand, but it was clear that nobody seemed to be entirely happy about this, perhaps not even Al himself.

'Then why today?' she asked him. 'Why the hurry?'

'It's not a hurry for me, *drukerimaskri*.' He put down the guitar neck. 'I've had years to prepare.'

'Why you?'

'Because I'm the only Romany left. And because it's always been my responsibility.'

'Why?'

Al peered around the workshop, as if to record every detail in his mind. As if to hold a memory of it.

'I think Simon's here,' he said.

The address Frannie Bliss had given him proved to be a three-storey Victorian terrace on the main road out of Leominster. Lol parked the Astra half on the pavement, from where he could see the numbers on the front doors.

The man he was looking for lived in the ground-floor flat at the far end of the terrace, but he owned the whole building, Bliss had emphasized, as if this explained something.

Lol sat there for ten minutes, the car slowly turning into a roasting tin around him. He thought about Simon St John, who had once said, '*This is the country, Lol. In the country, in certain situations, everybody lies.*' Had Simon himself really been telling the truth this

443

time? Had he genuinely been too scared to attempt to exorcize Stock's kiln? In which case, why hadn't he referred it directly to Merrily instead of trying to claim Stock was making it up? Lol concluded that in an irrational situation people acted irrationally. How would Merrily react? Would she help Simon now, despite everything?

Stupid question.

No time for stupid questions.

As Lol got out of the car, the front door at the end of the terrace opened and a man in a light blue suit came out.

Lol stayed close to the Astra. The man didn't look behind him, or towards Lol, as he walked out of the entrance. Could this actually be the right guy – wide shoulders, stiff white hair? Stop him now? Accost him before he got into his car?

But the man didn't go to a car. He walked briskly along the pavement. When a woman passed him, he said warmly, 'How are *you*, my dear?' Glanced up into the sky. 'Make the most of it, it's due to break today, I hear.' Rich, rolling local accent.

Lol followed him to where the road widened and you could see a junction with fields beyond. But before that there was a big Safeway supermarket, a commercial palace with a tower, set well back behind its car park. The man almost skipped down the steps towards the supermarket. Lol waited until he'd reached the bottom and was strolling across the car park towards the entrance, before following.

He watched the white-haired man go through the automatic door. Hesitated. Was he supposed to challenge this guy across the fruit counter, maybe block his trolley in one of the aisles?

Lol went through the door, through the porch, past Postman Pat and his black-and-white cat in their van, and on into the store. He looked from side to side: a dozen or so customers, none of them a man in a blue suit – maybe he'd gone to the gents. Lol moved further into the store, uncertain. He felt conspicuous, so he picked up a shopping basket from a stack. He felt hollow. He *was* hollow. He couldn't do this.

The voice was very close to his left ear.

'Looking for me, brother?'

*

A clock made out of a breadboard with a six-pointed star on it put the time at 10.15 a.m.

'Why noon?' Merrily asked bluntly.

Simon St John exchanged a glance with Al.

Al was sitting straight-backed on his stool, determinedly defiant, with his hands in the side pockets of his waistcoat. Simon St John, however, looked as wrecked as his jeans.

'When we travelled,' Al said, 'we camped at night, but we always stopped the waggons at noon: the time of no shadows. Do you understand? Noon is the *dead* moment in time. When the day belongs to the dead – all the energy of the day sucked in. Sometimes, for a fraction of an instant, you can almost see it, like a photograph turned negative. Everything is still, everything – the road, the fields, the sky – belonging to the dead.'

'He means that noon is the time of the *mulo*,' Simon said. 'The only time you'll see one by daylight.'

'No.' Al tossed a guitar bridge from one hand to the other. 'In most cases, you won't see it at all.'

Merrily shrank from the melodrama. *The time of no shadows.* And yet . . .

'You do know, don't you, that we did the Deliverance in the kiln around midday? Stock wanted me to do it at night. I said, let's do it now, in the full light of a summer morning. Let's not make it *sinister.* You did know that?'

'And was this when the sulphur came to you?'

'At midday, yes. Or very close.'

Al glanced at the photograph. 'She could have had you. You were lucky.'

'Or protected.'

'And were you protected in the hop-yard last night?'

Merrily felt herself blush. 'It happened too quickly.'

'Lucky,' Al said.

'What is she?' Merrily asked. 'I need to know. You use these terms – *muli*. Very sinister. But what are we really talking about?'

Simon St John came over to sit down. He had a glass of water. All three of them were drinking water. No alcohol, no caffeine, not today.

'Not quite a ghost,' Simon said. 'Not possession either, in the classic sense. You could say it's a question of borrowing the aura.'

'Very much a Romany thing,' Al pointed out. 'Live lightly and borrow.'

'But the *mulo* doesn't necessarily give back,' Simon said. He kept rubbing his black-shirted arms as though they were cold.

'This is true,' Al accepted.

Simon said, 'When Shakespeare talked about shuffling off the mortal coil, he was probably close to it. Death appears to be a staggered process – when the body dies, the spirit exists for a while in the aura, the astral body, the corporeal energy field. Its normal procedure, at this stage, is to look for the exit sign and get the hell out.'

'But if the cycle's incomplete,' Al said, 'if there's a need for justice, for balance, for *satisfaction* . . .'

Merrily thought about it. 'This is about what's sometimes called the Second Death isn't it?'

'This is about *avoiding* the Second Death.' Simon leaned forward. 'I don't think it's common, not in our society. I don't imagine it's a common occurrence in the Romany culture either. I think it's something they've tended to blow up out of proportion over the centuries – I bloody *hope* it is.'

'It's an unpleasant state to be in,' Al said, 'because the *mulo* is said to require life-energy to maintain its existence. Hence the term "living dead." There *are* tales of a *mulo* or *muli* sucking the blood of the living, but—' he waved a long hand dismissively '—it's all energy. Sexual, mostly. The victim may be the former life-partner – you get tales of people having sex with their dead husbands or wives – or the person held responsible for the sudden death of the subject before their time.'

'In the stories, they talk of a solid physical presence,' Simon said. 'But *we* prefer dreams, or sexual fantasies.'

'You're selling it as psychology?' Merrily asked, doubtful.

'It's *all* psychology,' Simon said. 'That doesn't make it any less real. It doesn't make it any less frightening.' His face was gaunt; it was one of those soft, pale faces which could alternate in seconds between looking youthful and prematurely aged. 'The thought of

Rebekah – or what she may have become – leaves me cold with—
I'm sorry.'

Al stood up and walked over to the photograph. 'It seems to me
that *our* task is to separate the spirit of Rebekah from what's formed
around it. The evil that grows like fungus around hatred and rage.
You follow, *drukerimaskri?*'

'And lead it to God. To the light.'

'And the evil,' Simon said sourly. 'Where does that go?'

'*My* responsibility.' Al walked to the door. 'You two probably
have Christian things to work out. I'm going to the place. I'm going
to talk to my father. Come when you're ready, you won't disturb
me.'

'Al . . .?' Merrily touched his sleeve.

'It'll work out, *drukerimaskri.*' He looked again at the picture of
the young woman amateurishly pouting at the sun. 'She's ripe. She's
swollen. We can't delay.'

He walked out without looking back.


Councillor Howe said, 'Small piece of advice, brother Robinson, in
case you're ever called upon to tail anybody again. Nobody comes
shopping at a supermarket and parks half a mile away. Just a small
point.'

'Thanks.' Lol took the two cups of tea off the tray, along with
Charlie Howe's doughnut. This time in the morning, fewer than a
quarter of the tables in the supermarket coffee shop were taken. They
were sitting at a window table, just up from the creche.

'I take it this en't council business, then.' Charlie Howe's brown,
leathery face was not remotely wary. He bit into his doughnut. Dark,
liquid jam spurted. Charlie licked his fingers. 'And you're not a
newspaperman after my memoirs?'

'Newspaper, no,' Lol said. 'Memoirs, probably.'

'Cost you, boy.'

'Bought you a doughnut.'

Charlie smiled. 'That gets you as far as 1960. Nothing much
happened that year, I was still a beat copper.'

'How about '63?'

'Young DC, then. Still hadn't done my first murder. What did you say you did for a living?'

'Write songs.'

His eyes were deep-sunk in his craggy forehead, like rock-pools. 'So this'd be *The Ballad of Charlie Howe*, then?'

Lol fought the urge to look away, out of the window. 'How about *The Ballad of Rebekah Smith?*'

Charlie raised an eyebrow. 'Don't reckon that's a song would mean an awful lot to me.'

'Maybe you'd only be in the last verse,' Lol said.


Merrily lit a cigarette.

Simon St John eased his stool a few inches further along the bench. 'You always smoke before an exorcism?'

'Sounds like that old joke,' Merrily said. ' "Do you always smoke after sex? No, only when . . ." What did he mean, talk to his father?'

'His father, the *chovihano*, dead these twenty years. Didn't speak to Al for the previous twenty because Al came off the road, married a *gaujo*. Cardinal sin, punishable by lifelong curse. Sally once told me he and Al have been communicating better in the past three years than the previous forty.'

'Candidly,' Merrily said, 'do you *believe* that stuff?'

'Why not? They talk to the ancestors like we try to talk to God. Their own ancestors, not anyone else's.'

'What about you?'

'I have a fairly strict rule. I talk to living people, and I try to listen to God. Anything else I see or hear nowadays, I turn off the fucking set, *rapido*.'

'You're saying you've seen and heard more than most of us.'

He laughed.

'And you've had a bad experience, with that?'

'I've had a whole sequence of bad experiences, Mrs Watkins. I've had the living shit scared out me. I've been afraid for myself, for my friends and – worst of all – for my very dear wife, my soulmate.'

Merrily said cautiously, 'Israel believes all exorcists should be psychic to a degree. Which I suppose means you could be a lot better at this than me.'

'He doesn't, however, say all psychics should be exorcists. Spare a cig?'

'Sorry, I assumed—'

'Periodic vices. All my vices have been periodic – the worst kind. Look, my view on suffering is simple: you ask the question, "Is anyone benefiting from this?" If not, don't fucking suffer.'

'What about Stock?'

'We couldn't help Stock. His only recourse was to get out, and I told him that. Al told him that. But Stock was Stock.'

'So why this, now?'

'It's for Sally.' Simon lit up, holding the cigarette between finger and thumb, like you'd hold a joint. 'Sally didn't want Al doing this on his own.'

'Why does he have to do it at all?'

'Ancestral ties. Who else is gonna do it? Al was trained for years in the Romany mysteries and then backed off. Bit like me, really, but I only backed off to a place that looked safe. Nowhere's really safe, is it? You ready, now?'

'What are we going to do?'

'Deal with this stupid bitch, I suppose.' He went up to the picture of Rebekah Smith.

'I meant, what are we going to do? Those Christian things.'

Simon turned back to Merrily. 'You ever sleep with Lol?'

'No.'

'Poor sod puts you on a pedestal. He thinks you're a much better person than he is, purer, holier. You're going to have to make *all* the running, I fear.'

'People tend to underestimate Lol,' Merrily said. 'Where is he, anyway? I'd somehow expected him to be here.'

'Nah, this is a priest thing. He drove off somewhere.'

She stiffened. 'Where?'

He shook his head. 'Don't worry about it.' He had another deep drag on his cigarette. 'Anyway, I'm very grateful to you for coming.'

'I'm sure you are, Simon.'

'Meaning what?'

'It's a set-up, isn't it? For instance, why can't you and Al do this on your own?'

'Maybe we could.'

'No, you bloody couldn't,' Merrily said, 'because you need a woman. Because of the nature of it, there has to be a woman, doesn't there? It's a female entity, so it needs a woman's energy, a woman's aura. Poor Stephanie underlined that. And who else? Who else before Stephie?'

Simon's eyes didn't move. 'OK, I suspect there was some similar impact on the second Mrs Conrad Lake, Adam's mother. But she was wise enough to get out before too long.'

'And the Hereford hookers?'

'Sure, and the working girls of Worcester. "Come back to my kiln, my dear. Help me recapture some old memories." '

'Each one of them acquiring, however briefly, the essence – the destructive essence – of Rebekah Smith. I just hope none of them ever got into his car a second time. I pray the psychological damage wasn't permanent.'

He grimaced. 'Depends what fucking Conrad did to them. Not much, by the end, I'd imagine. I suppose the times he couldn't get himself fixed up, he'd potter along to the kiln and get auto-erotic over his photographs. And she'd be there for him.'

'Like a drug.'

'A craving, yeah. Until he died. How far you want to take this? I don't know if it's an infection, like the wilt, or a sporadic phenomenon. I don't know whether it's a wilful spirit or an imprint. Should I be poetic here? Should I say it came out of the kiln on the smoke of Rebekah's cremation? Was it scattered with her ashes? How the hell can we know?'

'Until you present her with a woman's aura to enter, you probably won't.' She met his eyes and saw the fear behind the aggression.

'You done this sort of thing before, Merrily?'

'That a serious question?'

'What I meant was, there's nothing in the book on this one, is there? When she comes, *if* she comes, you'll have to be fully aware of her and at the same time have a strong enough sense of your spiritual self to keep her out. At that point, you'll be very much on your own.'

'I do hope not,' Merrily said.

Simon St John smiled tiredly. '*He* might see it as a little test for you. Just . . . don't count on the parachute opening.'

Merrily looked into Simon's light blue eyes for flecks of bullshit. Saw only the faded sorrow of experience.

FORTY-FIVE

# Drukerimaskri

Charlie sat back, with his hands on his knees and his tea going as cold as anything could in this weather. His smile was constant and condescending. Although he wasn't looking directly at Lol most of the time, Lol felt under intense study.

'If this is poker,' Charlie said at last, 'you better show me some cards, boy.'

'Ron Welfare?' Hesitantly, Lol brought out the only name he'd been given by Frannie Bliss. 'PC Ronald Welfare. He'd have been one of your old colleagues?'

'Dead,' Charlie said, with contempt.

'Ron Welfare talked to a bloke who saw a woman closely resembling Rebekah Smith going over to the kiln and the door opening and a man closely resembling Conrad Lake standing there in the light, before the woman was admitted.'

Charlie made no comment.

'There were probably other witnesses, but most of them would have had some family members still employed by Lake. This was a chap from outside the area who'd gone to visit his mother nearby.'

'How're you, Terry?' Charlie called out to a man leaving the coffee shop. 'Don't forget to get that application in before September, now.'

Lol pressed on. He realized no ordinary former copper would even be talking to him by now, but Charlie Howe was a prominent local councillor, a friend to the people, an open book. And maybe his ward was a marginal. And also they were in a public place. And you couldn't tell whether Charlie was worried now, or just curious.

'Ron Welfare was so convinced he was on to something that he even worked on it in his spare time,' Lol said. 'But no police were going to risk grilling Lake, because he was the Emperor of Frome and he owned half the valley, and Rebekah Smith was considered the lowest of the low.'

'Could be you're a journalist,' Charlie said thoughtfully. 'But I don't think so. You don't talk like a journalist.'

'When Ron eventually reported it to his superiors, a detective was assigned to check it out. By this time, Ron had put some more stuff together – reports of the kiln furnace being fired for two days or more, even though the hop season was well over.'

'Not unusual,' Charlie said. 'Furnaces can be used for more than drying hops. You don't talk like somebody works for some gypsy-loving civil-liberties charity, either.'

'Did you never have the furnace checked out for—' Lol struggled to keep the ignorance out of his eyes. '—I don't know – fragments of bone or whatever? Were there *any* forensic tests?'

'No need, boy. Waste of resources, would've been. Seeing as the hunt was called off that very night. Now, I wonder if you're simply someone with a grudge against the Lake family.'

'The witness didn't stand by his story, in the end. Suddenly he said he couldn't be sure. Or maybe somebody made it worth his while to drop it?'

'Or perhaps it's me you're after. Perhaps you or some mate of yours is trying for the council. But that don't make a whole lot of sense. You wouldn't come and face me up with some half-arsed story – less you got a little cassette recorder on you. But you en't even wearing a jacket. No.' Charlie leaned back. 'It's a puzzle. But, for the record, that girl probably left home, like a lot of young gypos did, sick of a life of squalor and ducking and diving. And the gypos, never ones to miss an opportunity, made out she was missing, presumed dead, to get back at Brother Lake for kicking them off his land. Whole bunch of 'em should've been charged with wasting police time. Rebekah Smith, she's probably a suburban granny now, keeping very quiet about her origins.'

'But Ron Welfare never forgot. And he never did make CID. His career kind of . . . stopped right there. For some reason.'

'Ron Welfare left the force years back. Ron Welfare was a second-rate copper and a sick and bitter man.'

'However,' Lol said, 'the DC who went with him to question Lake – he did really *well*. He was a sergeant by the end of the year and he never looked back at all, did he?'

The condescending smile was history. 'Well, now.' Charlie leaned forward, his face close up to Lol's, eyes like knuckle-bones. 'You wouldn't, by any chance, be suggesting this detective was corrupt, would you, brother?'

Point of no return. Lol wondered briefly if he hadn't been set up by Bliss, no fan of Annie Howe, to stir an old pot. He made himself meet Charlie Howe's bruising gaze.

'Lake was a very powerful figure locally. Influential.'

'So Conrad was buying off witnesses and bribing policemen to look the other way?'

'Isn't that how it was in those days? A strong squirearchy, and senior policemen *expected* to be in the Masons?'

'I'll ask you once again, boy, are you suggesting this particular detective was bent?'

'I don't know.'

'Because another alternative about you that occurs to me would be attempted blackmail. Of course, only a very stupid person would attempt to blackmail an ex-policeman. But then small-time black-mailers often *are* very stupid people.'

Lol shook his head.

'And shy,' Charlie Howe said. 'They're often a bit shy. And hesitant – bit timid. See, a real criminal, he'd go and hold up a bloody garage, but your small-time blackmailer, he en't got the bottle. He's quite often someone on the small side of average, maybe unsuccessful in his career – a misfit, a social inadequate with a personality defect. Would that be you, brother Robinson?' Charlie sneered. 'Aye, that could *very well* be you.'

Two elderly ladies brought their trays to the next table, and Charlie broke off to smile pleasantly at them, raise a hand. 'So piss off, boy,' he muttered out of the side of his mouth. 'Take your forty-year-old, cobbled-together nonsense somewhere else, and don't try and play with the pros.'

Lol's hands were gripping the sides of his chair and for about half a second he seemed to be looking down on himself and the white-haired man with the leathery face, that condescending smile returning to it.

'Right, you've done it now, brother Howe.' Surprised at how calm he sounded. 'I'm going to tell you exactly why I'm here . . . just so you'll know that it's nothing to do with money – absolutely the reverse, in fact – and there's nothing you can ever do to scare me off.'

Charlie Howe blinked, just once. It was the first time Lol had noticed him do that.

'And also why,' he went on, 'if I ever find out you *did* take money or favours or even benefit from a word from the Emperor of Frome in the right chief superintendent's ear – or that your old mate Andy Mumford slipped you some pictures and a manuscript he took off the Smith brothers when he nicked them for murder – if I find out any of that I'm going to hang you up to dry so high that, from where you are, I really will look very, very small.'

The old ladies were looking across. Charlie Howe smiled and it was not, Lol noticed, with immense relief, an entirely comfortable smile.

'My place next, I think, Mr Robinson,' he said.

At 10.45 precisely, Merrily and Simon St John drove over to Prof Levin's studio, left the Volvo on the back forecourt and walked down the track through the meadow. The hay lay like stilled waves either side of a causeway. There were still traces of heat haze over the Malverns. Merrily saw the Frome Valley as an airless, spectral nether-land where the real and the unreal wrestled in an amorphous tangle of threshing limbs.

She was afraid.

Not yet eleven on a wonderful summer morning, the kind of morning that dissolved fatigue, the kind of morning from which the uncanny was banished, but she was afraid. Her stomach felt weak; her throat was dry and sore. *Walk away,* Huw had said. *No shame.*

This would probably be her last Deliverance job. Bit of an occasion? In the museum, she'd put on her light grey cotton alb and a large pectoral cross, for the aura.

'A holy cross *is* supposed to condition it, isn't it? The aura?'

'So I believe,' Simon said. 'Just as ordination does. And regular prayer, the celebration of the Eucharist – all protective.'

Simon smiled in a half-hearted way, felt in a hip pocket of his jeans and brought out a heavy gold cross on a chain, slipped it over his head.

'What about Al?' Merrily said.

'I doubt it.'

'I'm sorry?'

'Al won't be looking for protection.'

'Why not?'

'Because gypsies believe in destiny, and Al believes this is his.'

'I don't understand.'

'Oh, I think you do, Merrily.'

They'd arrived at the bridge over the Frome. She stopped and stared down into the dark water of Lol's river. She supposed she'd known since last night.

'It's the unspoken, isn't it? The first Mrs Lake.'

'There you are, then.'

'Does *everyone* know?'

'Not quite everyone. But the Frome Valley people are rather like the Frome itself. Secretive. Protective.'

'Sally?'

'Is her actual first name. Sarah Caroline Lake. She was very young when she married him, of course. It wasn't exactly an arranged marriage but fairly close. Her father was a wealthy enough guy, but nothing compared with the Great Lakes. When she went off with Al, it's hard to know which family was more appalled.' Simon unsnagged a hanging twig from the chain of his cross. 'At the divorce, she took only a small settlement – far smaller than someone in her position would expect today – and distributed it among a number of charities, considering this the only way of laundering, in the old-fashioned sense, Conrad's tainted money.'

'And when Conrad died . . .'

'She and Al were able to return.'

'She's the Lady of the Bines.' The thought made Merrily absurdly happy. 'She wrote her own story and gave it to a ghost.'

'Rather lovely, I always thought,' Simon said.

'It crossed my mind, of course it did. Al virtually told us.'

'And now you can forget it, just like the rest of us have.'

'Well . . . sure.' They followed the path towards the line of poplars, and her flare of happiness faded. 'But going back to Al's destiny . . .'

'Think about it,' Simon said.

'I have. The gypsies genuinely believed Lake took Rebekah because his own wife had gone off with a Romany.'

'Some of them still believe it,' Simon said sombrely. 'And, after all, it may be true. It's certainly why Al's father never spoke to him again – while alive. Why Al became an outcast. A pariah. Cursed.'

Al's profile in the glow of candles in bottles. *You want to know the truth of it, I'm still paying back.*

'He seriously believes he's cursed?'

'Don't underestimate the weight of that tradition, Merrily. He seriously *knows* he's cursed.'

Charlie Howe's high-ceilinged, white-walled sitting room was more than half office: a roll-top desk, a crowded flat-top desk, a wooden filing cabinet, a bookcase full of box files and a computer. There was also a TV set, with satellite box, and a black-leather recliner placed in front of the screen.

Right now, Charlie didn't seem in the mood for reclining. He sat on the deep windowsill.

'The Reverend Merrily Watkins,' he said. 'My latest weak spot. You bastard, brother Robinson. Are you two—?'

Lol shook his head.

'But you live in hope, I imagine. Were you there last night, by any chance, when this Shelbone child . . .?'

Lol nodded.

'Can't beat that for bitter irony, can you? Allan Henry gets his biggest wish in all the world: the bloody Barnchurch burns down –

at a cost. And *what* a cost. What's he gonner do now? Will he build on the very spot where his stepdaughter died?'

'My guess,' Lol said, 'would be a Layla Riddock memorial plaque on a side wall of Debenhams.'

Charlie Howe laughed and pointed at him, one eye closed. 'Dead right, brother! By God, you must be *very* fond of Mrs Watkins. Last time anybody threatened me like that in public, he – but then, I must watch my tongue in front of you, mustn't I? You really *were* going to try and blackmail me, weren't you?'

'Persuade you.'

'Good word. Often used it myself. Persuade me to do what?'

'Just to get your daughter off Merrily's back. She's trying really hard to make sense out of an impossible job, and your daughter's going to turn her into a demon or a martyr. And the Church of England doesn't like either, so we all know what that means.'

'This is the kiln murder, yes? And that's what put you on to Lake.' He scratched his head. 'Fact is, I hadn't even realized this was the same bloody kiln.'

'Well, I'm going to be dead honest with you—'

'Must you, Robinson? Half a lifetime in the police force and a good few years mixing day-to-day with councillors, I en't *comfortable* with honesty.'

'Well—' Lol shrugged '—the truth is I haven't a hope in hell of proving the police had good reason to suspect Lake of killing Rebekah Smith and then pulled back because Lake was who he was. I've got even less chance of proving that somebody in the police confiscated whatever the Smith boys nicked the night of Stewart's murder. All I know is that Mumford made the arrest, and Mumford and you were always close, despite the disparity in rank.'

'Absolutely correct, my friend. Salt of the earth, Andy. Solid as a bloody rock.'

'And he presumably holds you in similar esteem – and he wouldn't like to see your reputation impugned by something that happened forty years ago when you were a youngster and perhaps had to choose between turning a blind eye to something and seeing a promising career go down the tubes. And anyway, he's coming up to retirement, so he doesn't have much to lose. See, I can't prove *anything*. But I can think of one or two papers – even TV programmes . . .'

Charlie came down from the windowsill. 'We're not in a café now, brother. I could knock your bloody head off.'

'Sure. I bet you know all the ways of working suspects over in the cells without leaving a mark. But you've got to remember, when I get up, I'll be back on the case. You can take a lot of bruises and broken bones and ruptured spleens, for love.'

Charlie Howe's expression didn't change. 'And what's Anne gonner do, exactly?'

Lol told him about the proposed statement on exorcism and responsibility, as outlined by Frannie Bliss.

Charlie sniffed. 'Not a chance. You been led up the garden path, brother. No chief constable – certainly not this one – would put his name to something that could get him in bother with the Church. They don't need that kind of conflict. En't like you get one of these every day or even every year, is it? The Chief'll tell Anne if she wants to say that stuff, she can get out there and say it herself.'

'You think she wouldn't?'

Charlie finally went over and collapsed into his recliner. 'You want the truth, I think she would. The truth – bloody hell, you got me going, now. Have a drink?'

'No, thanks. I was up all night. I'm already running on reserve.'

'You want more truth? I don't think it'd do Anne any more good, long-term, than it would for Merrily. A detective with a big mouth has a limited career span. In the Service, anyway. Might get a job on there.' He pointed the toe of his shoe at the TV screen. 'And I thought she'd got over all that. All right.' He sat up. 'I'll talk to her.'

'Thanks.'

'Don't think this is a victory for you, brother. I en't finished with *you*, yet. And I'm not saying she'll take any notice. But I'll talk to her.'

Lol said, 'Any chance you could make it a priority thing?'

'I'll see if she's free tonight.' Charlie stood up, went over to the phone. 'I en't finished with you, though, I surely bloody en't.' He didn't need to look up the number. 'DCI,' he said into the phone. 'Aye, this is her ole man, if you don't know the voice.' He waited, then he said, 'Colin, how you doing, boy? *Where* is she? Really? What time would that be, then? Aye, I know *that*, boy, but where can I find her *now?*' He blew some air down his nose. 'All right. Thank you, boy.'

'Not there?'

'Gone off tying up the ends of the Stock case,' Charlie said. 'As you might expect.'

'The ends?'

'And there'll be at least one TV crew up there filming, for the news. She's agreed to do interviews early this afternoon, on site.'

'She'll use that as the opportunity, won't she?'

'She might,' Charlie conceded. 'You going back there?'

Lol nodded.

'Might follow you,' Charlie said.


She'd wondered, half-hopefully, if by day - especially on a day like this – it might look innocuous, even friendly. She'd half expected to feel, on arriving here, faintly stupid.

Never before having been asked to exorcize a field.

So it came as a shock, the deadness of it: the yellowness of the grass on what was supposed to be deep loam, the black alleys of poles with their crosspieces looking like some battlefield arrangement from the First World War, so that you expected to encounter occasional corpses leaning against the poles, tatters of uniforms and flesh hanging from grey bones.

But there was only Al.

She didn't see him at first. He was sitting immobile between two distant poles, a white thing like a chalk megalith.

'Stay here,' Simon said. 'He'll be in some kind of trance. Not that we'd disturb him – a Romany shaman could go into trance between checkouts at Tesco. At their spiritual-healing sessions, it's pandemonium, everybody talking and laughing, drums, violins – it's the way they are. I just suspect – call me an old reactionary – that we shouldn't necessarily become involved with his current ambience.'

'Stay at this end, then?'

'I think so.'

Merrily looked up at the sky through an irregular network of wires. How long to noon?' She'd come out without her watch.

Simon looked at his, then took it off. 'Fifty-one minutes.'

He laid the watch on the parched grass near the base of a pole. Stood there in his dog-collar and his ruined jeans, with his fair hair looking almost white and as dead as the grass, and his hands on his hips.

'Over to you,' he said. '*Drukerimaskri.*'

# FORTY-SIX

# Every Evil Haunting and Phantasm

Charlie Howe clearly knew the TV cameraman – grey-haired bloke crouching near the sign saying KNIGHT'S FROME, getting the church into shot. The old Jaguar pulled in next to him and Charlie leaned out of the window, bawling out, 'Jim!'

Lol brought the Astra up behind the Jag, as the cameraman turned in irritation, then saw who it was and grinned, lowering his camera. 'Knew they'd never be able to manage without you, Charlie. Come to take over the inquiry, is it?'

Charlie poked a finger out of the window. 'Now don't you go saying that to Anne, boy.'

Jim said he wasn't that brave, and they laughed, and then Charlie said, 'Talking of whom, you seen that girl at all?'

Lol spotted a slender woman walking through the churchyard, about two hundred yards away. He thought it was Sally Boswell, with someone else, a child it looked like from where he was.

He got out of the car as the cameraman said, 'Nobody here yet, Charlie, only me, shooting wallpaper till the reporter shows. What you doing with yourself now?'

'Creating the new Hereford, most of the time,' Charlie told him. 'So Anne's due when?'

'Two o'clock, outside the pub. That's what I was told.'

Lol ran past them, towards the churchyard.

Sally wore a faded yellow dress and a straw sunhat, and it wasn't a child with her but Isabel St John in her wheelchair. Isabel looked defiant. Her crimson top began just above her nipples.

'Laurence.' Sally pulled off her hat; her misty hair was pushed back over her ears and her skin was pale as moth wings. She tucked the hat under an arm, drew a tissue from her sleeve and blew her nose. 'Hay fever. Isn't it ridiculous? Haven't suffered in years.'

Lol thought she'd been crying.

Isabel glanced back, almost disparagingly, at the church. 'Been trying to do our bit, isn't it?'

'Supportive prayer,' Sally said. 'Though I'm afraid I don't particularly feel any closer to the Deity in there.'

Isabel raised her eyes. 'Should've said. Out here's all right.' A Red Admiral butterfly landed on an arm of her wheelchair and stayed there, as though it had been sprayed with lacquer.

'Where's Al?' Lol said. The air seemed hushed and heavy, not only around the church but over the whole valley. He wasn't aware of any birds singing. He could see Charlie Howe walking towards them, but couldn't hear his steps.

'Al?' said Sally. 'Don't you *know*?'

'Al's with Simon,' Isabel said. 'And your lady. Chasing the gorgeous, pouting Rebekah. Dredging her up from the slime.' Her voice had gone harsh with distress. 'Didn't you know?'

'Now? Today?'

'For noon.'

'They're doing it *now*?'

Sally put a hand on his arm. Her fingers felt like lace. 'Don't interfere, Laurence. It does have to be done, I'm afraid. Al and I quarrelled over it. I didn't want . . .' She half turned away. 'He believes he has no choice. He believes he's responsible for her. That's all there is to it.'

'What about Merrily? Who's she res—'

'You want to concentrate more on your music, Lol,' Isabel said. 'Form a new band. Employ Simon, get him out of this crappy job.' The butterfly still hadn't moved. Isabel looked as if she wanted to swat it. 'Nobody needs this in their lives. We can deal with it, if we have to, when we're dead.'

'Where are they?' Lol said.

'Leave it,' Sally told him. 'Whatever has to happen will happen.'

'While we get to wait on the shore.' Isabel put on a pair of very dark sunglasses. 'Keep the bloody home fires burning.'

The butterfly finally took off, fluttered to a nearby grave. Lol said, 'Why do they need Merrily? Why couldn't they have done this in the first place? I can't believe Simon was scared.'

'What do *you* know, Lol?' Isabel said with venom. 'What do you know of what he's been through over the years? You think it isn't a terrible bloody burden for a priest to be psychic?'

'I'm sure it is. But if he thinks Merrily can come in and shoulder it—'

'Nobody can shoulder it. He has to face it on his own.'

'Then why do they need Merrily? Is it because Rebekah will only come to a woman?'

'Stop it,' Sally said. 'Both of them are Christians. Neither of them is part of the tradition. If anything happens to anyone . . .' She opened her bag, took out a parchment-coloured, egg-shaped label and handed it to Lol. 'I found this when I came back.'

He recognized it at once. It was what you saw when you peered down the soundhole of a well-loved guitar, with the sacred name 'Boswell' printed quite small.

Sally said, 'It's the price you pay. For preserving the balance. What you borrow must be repaid, if not in itself then . . . in kind. Sometimes with interest.'

Below the name was an inner oval in which the serial number of each instrument would be stamped. In this space was hand-printed:

My love
Don't burn
the vardo


The hop-frames were constructed from now-faded creosoted poles, ten to fifteen feet high and leaning inwards. The crosspieces of some were fixed below the top, forming two actual crosses, joined. Merrily took this as significant, and she and Simon each stood under a cross, close to the entrance of the alley.

Al Boswell sat at the far end, seventy or eighty yards away. His head was bowed.

Dead bines hung limp from several frames.

With the airline bag at her feet, Merrily laid the Lord's Prayer on the still, already humid air.

When she'd finished, there was a strange silence in the yard that seemed close to absolute. No birds was what it meant, she decided – there seemed to be nothing here for them to feed on. The hop-yard and adjacent fields were almost in a bowl of earth, the landscape curving up to wooded hills, only the highest ridge of the Malverns visible.

And only one building, the one with the witch's-hat tower. *Should I say it came out of the kiln on the smoke of Rebekah's cremation? Was it scattered with her ashes?*

*What* came out? What was at the core of this? As Simon had pointed out, there was no agreed ritual for this situation.

Merrily glanced up the alley towards Al Boswell. His hands were raised now, in supplication, and he seemed to be chanting, though she couldn't hear anything – was Al's consciousness down there in the Lower World, home of the ancestors and the dead, bargaining with his father, the *chovihano*, for the soul of Rebekah? What was he offering? What did he expect to pay? She felt scared for him because he came from a culture which was, in essence, unbending.

She also felt an agitation and a tension emanating like cold steam from Simon St John. She banished it, closed her eyes and tried to concentrate on her breathing without changing its rhythm.

In her hands she held a slim prayer book. Into her mind came the image of Rebekah in her sleeveless white blouse. No earrings – the girl wouldn't have wanted to look like a gypsy for the picture editor at *Tit Bits*. Poor kid. Poor Rebekah: brazen hussy of '63, blinded by her own sexuality. *As if she'd like to seize the whole world in her teeth.*

Eating the world . . . and suddenly choking. Merrily sensed how dense and dark the flesh-smelling smoke from the kiln would have been, made noxious by all the psychic bacteria that fed on the detritus of violent death. Remnants here, too, of Conrad Lake, his greed, his ultimately murderous cruelty.

This was about separating Rebekah's soul from all of that and guiding it to the light.

Merrily opened her eyes, consulted the book and said quietly, 'Remember not, Lord, our offences, nor the offences of our fore-fathers, and do not condemn us for our sins . . . Lord have mercy.'

'*Lord have mercy,*' Simon echoed from across the alley.

'Christ have mercy.'

'*Christ have mercy.*'

She visualized Rebekah Smith in the kiln, doubled up, the beautiful features blotched and reddened and distended by coughing and retching and wheezing.

'Heavenly father.'

'*Have mercy on her!*'

. . . While the sulphur rolls burned blue and the few remaining hop-cones yellowed on their loft.

'Jesus, redeemer of the world . . .'

'*Have mercy on her.*'

Rebekah screaming inside as the fumes took her.

*I watched her heaving and shivering and struggling for breath . . .*

Merrily broke off from the litany. The air felt dense and weighted. She suddenly felt desperately tired, and she was scared to close her eyes again in case she fell asleep on her feet.

'Oh Christ,' Simon murmured.

She looked across at him. He was aglow with sweat. He said, 'You've brought someone with you, haven't you?' He had his eyes closed now, his fists clenched. 'You're carrying the weight of some-one.'

Merrily began to pant.

'Bleeding,' Simon said. 'She's bleeding.'

Merrily whispered, 'Jesus, redeemer of the world, have mercy on her.'

*Her.* Rebekah, in her white blouse.

*Her.* Layla Riddock in her black kimono.

'Have mercy on them,' Simon cried out.

Sweat dripped down Merrily's cheeks.

'Holy Spirit, comforter . . .'

'Have mercy on them.'

'Holy Trinity, one God . . .'

'Have mercy on them.'

'From all evil . . .'

'Deliver her . . .'

It all came out in a rush now, and they were working together, a unit. '*From anger, hatred and malice . . . From all the deceits of the world, the flesh and the devil . . . Good Lord, deliver them.*'

The cotton alb was fused to Merrily's skin. If she had an aura, it felt like liquid, like oil. The air was very close. There seemed to be a different atmosphere here between the poles, a separate density of air. Between the wires, the sun was like a hole in the sky.

'Lamb of God, you take away the sins of the world.'

'Have mercy on her,' Simon said.

'Yes,' Merrily said.

She felt that Rebekah was very near, but resistant to the idea of being guided towards the Second Death. It came to her suddenly that Layla had somehow been sent as an intermediary. Allan Henry: '*Layla, love, excuse me, but these ladies would like to know if you have much contact with the dead.*'

She prayed for guidance, but she couldn't see the blue or the gold, and her pectoral cross felt as heavy as an anvil.

The cross? Was the cross preventing—?

She touched it. *Please, God, what shall I do?* The cross felt cold. She longed to give herself away, as she had in church on the night of the coin, in true and total submission, so that her life-energy, her living spirit, might be used as a vessel of transformation for the tortured essence of Rebekah Smith: a sacrifice.

She turned to Simon, but he seemed a long way away. She closed her eyes, was aware of an intense pressure in her chest, as though she was about to have a heart attack.

She let the prayer book fall and used both hands to slip the chain and the cross up and over her head.

Simon had both arms around the pole with the wooden cross at the top, hugging it, like a sailor who'd roped himself to the mast in a storm. His body seemed to be in spasm. She was aware of a foetid fog between them.

She heard a cry from the end of the alley—

'*Oh, Mother of God!*'

—Which had become like a tunnel now, a tunnel through the middle of the day, and then there was a wrenching sensation from above, as though the crosspiece linking her pole with Simon's pole was under sudden, severe stress.

*Don't look.*

But, of course, she had to.

Her body was held inert by damp dread, but her eyes followed the leaden, loaded creaking to the cross pole. From it, hanging like a lagged cistern between her and Simon St John, the corpse of Gerard Stock was turning slowly, tongue protruding, white and furry, between the rosebud, spittled lips.

Merrily sobbed and sank slowly to her knees.

Flaunting him.

*Failure.*

Too strong for them.

Too strong for *her*.

Stock swung from side to side like a swaddled pendulum. '*Don't really know what the fuck you're doing. Waste of time, Merrily. Heard you were a political appointment.*'

Merrily's hands fumbled at the airline bag, closed on the flask of holy water.

'Begone!' she sobbed in pain and fear and ultimate despair. 'Begone from this place, every evil haunting and phantasm. Be banished, every delusion and deceit of Satan. In the name of the living God, in the name of the Holy God, in the name of the God of all creation—'

How empty it sounded, how hollow. She was on her knees with the flask of holy water, and she couldn't get the bloody top off.

She would have fallen forward then, into her own shadow, but there wasn't one.

It must be noon.

He'd gone, of course he had. He was never there. Nothing dangled from the crosspiece. There was only Simon, with his face in his hands.

Merrily came to her feet.

'Mine,' Simon croaked.

'What?'

'My projection.' His face was grey-sheened. 'Projection of defeat.'

Merrily leaned against the pole, nothing to say. There was no fog, no Stock, and the air in the alley was the same air that lay heavy on the whole of the Frome Valley. She swallowed; it hurt.

When did it ever go right? When did it ever work? Through the overhead wires, the midday sun was splashing its brash, soulless light over the whole of the sky.

Go out losing. What better way? Nothing to look back on, no foundation for thoughts of what might have been.

Sodden with weariness, she put away the flask, picked up her airline bag.

Simon didn't move. Merrily heard a crumbly rustling that her tired mind dispiritingly translated into brittle hop-cones fragmenting on mummified bines.

'Almighty God,' Simon said numbly, gazing beyond her. 'Please don't do this.'

# FORTY-SEVEN

# Ghost Eyes

The first sound Merrily was aware of was the vibrating of the wires overhead.

It wasn't much; if there'd been a breeze, it would have sounded natural. If these had been electric wires, it would have seemed normal. It was a thin sound, with an almost human frailty, a keening, that somehow didn't belong to summer. The rustling overlaid it, as if all the wires were entwined with dried bines. This other sound belonged to winter. It sang of mourning, loss, lamentation.

The sounds came not from their alley, but the one adjacent to it and, as Merrily went to stand at its entrance, she noticed that it seemed oriented directly on the tower of the kiln, the poles bending at almost the same angle as the point of its cowl.

Merrily stood there with sweat drying on her face, edging past the fear stage to the part where she knew she was dreaming but it didn't matter.

She waited. She would not move. She fought to regulate her breathing.

For here was the Lady of the Bines, approaching down the abandoned hop-corridor, drifting from frame to frame, and the sky was white and blinding, and the Lady moved like a shiver.

Simon St John came up behind Merrily.

'What am I seeing, Simon?'

He didn't reply. She could hear his rapid breathing.

'Whose projection now?' she said, surprised that she could speak at all. 'Whose projection is this?'

She blinked several times, but it was still there: this slender white woman, pale and naked and garlanded with shrivelled hops.

Merrily put on her cross. *Christ be with me, Christ within me . . .*

The bine, thick with yellowed cones, was pulled up between the legs, over the glistening stomach and between the breasts. Wound around and around the neck, covering the lower face, petals gummed to the sweat on the cheeks.

*Christ behind me, Christ before me . . .*

The head was bent, as though she was watching her feet, wondering where they were taking her. She was not weaving, as Lol had described *his* apparition, but almost slithering through the parched grass and the weeds. And she couldn't be real or else why was she affecting the wires?

When she was maybe ten yards away, the head came up.

Merrily went rigid.

The Lady swayed. Her eyes were fully open but hardened, like a painted doll's, under a thickly smeared lacquer of abstraction. They were a corpse's eyes, a ghost's eyes. The end of the bine was stuffed into her mouth, brittle cones crushed between her teeth, and those petals pasted to her cheeks – grotesque, like one of the foliate faces you found on church walls.

She put out her arms, not to Merrily but to Simon, but he stepped away.

'Stay back. For Christ's sake, don't touch her. Keep a space.'

The woman's hands clawed at the air, as though there was something between them that she could seize. Her breath was irregular and came in convulsions, her body arching, parched petals dropping from her lips like flakes of dead skin.

'Don't go within a foot of her,' Simon rasped.

'It's all right,' Merrily said softly.

And she reached for the clawing hands, and waited for the cold electricity to come coursing up her arms all the way to her heart.

## FORTY-EIGHT

# Love First

*Noon: the dead moment in time. All the energy of the day sucked in. Sometimes, for a fraction of an instant, you can almost see it, like a photograph turned negative. Everything still. Everything – the road, the fields, the sky – belonging to the dead.*

But these people clustered in the base of the bowl under the midday sun, they were not the dead.

The severely beautiful elderly woman, weeping, and the sharp-faced, white-haired man with an arm around her and the plump woman in a wheelchair and the leather-faced, crew-cut man demanding an ambulance – surely *somebody* had a bloody mobile phone. And Lol, standing apart from the others, looking thoughtful.

And the pale, naked woman under the hop-frame, lying with the padded airline bag under her head. Not even *she* was dead.

*Keep her here? Would that contain it? For how long? How long?*

Merrily looked up at the sun.

Simon St John understood. 'Get back. Please. Just a couple of yards, please.' Simon was OK, he was in the clear – the woman was not dead, had not been dead when she walked under the wires. Simon was all right with this. Wasn't he?

'Yes,' the woman agreed irritably, 'Just keep back. I'm all right. I'll *be all right*.' She coughed, her head thrown back over the airline bag, a bubble of saliva and a half-masticated hop-petal in a corner of her slack mouth. 'I'll be with you in . . . just give me . . . give me a moment . . . give me a bloody *minute*.'

Merrily looked up at Simon. He nodded towards the woman.

The hop-bine was still curled around her legs, yellowed petals crumbled into her pubic hair.

Simon said, 'You know her?'

'Oh, yes.' Merrily knelt down, was immediately enclosed in a dense aura of sweat and hops. 'Annie, listen to me – were you in the kiln? Were you in the kiln, just now?'

'Cordon it off!' The eyes were still blurred. 'We . . . need the fire service. There's probably—'

'Yes,' Merrily said.

'Gases. An escape of gases.'

'Or sulphur.'

'I don't . . . I got out of there, but I must have lost . . . Put somebody on the door. Don't let anybody go back in there. It may be . . . I think I lost consciousness, just for a moment. You—' She seemed to register Merrily for the first time. 'What the hell are *you*—?'

'I'm going back to the village,' Charlie said. 'We need an ambulance.'

'Don't be ridiculous.' Annie Howe tried to sit up. 'That's—'

'Who's he?' Simon demanded. The woman in the wheelchair had made it from the path, breathing hard from her struggle across the baked ground. Simon was holding her hand.

'Her father,' Merrily told him. 'Charlie, she's right. Forget the ambulance. But—' She met his eyes, his copper's eyes now, hard as nuts. 'There's something else we need to do, and we need to do it now. I'm not kidding, Charlie, we've got a problem here, you must be able to see that.'

'And possibly a solution,' Simon St John said.

'Dad?' Annie Howe struggling to sit up. 'What the hell are *you*—?'

'Stay where you are, girl,' Charlie said softly. 'Everything's all right.' He looked down at Merrily. 'She been attacked?'

'Not in the way you think, no. In the way *I* think – do you know what I'm saying?'

'I don't know, Merrily, her clothes . . .'

Lol was there. 'I think it's pretty obvious she took them off herself, Charlie. The things we saw strewn across . . .?'

'I'll fetch them' Sally Boswell said.

Merrily came to her feet. 'Charlie, I swear to God. I swear to you that this is not some scam. She was in the kiln just now – on her own. The wrong place at the wrong time. Charlie, it all comes down to that place.'

'I was simply—' Annie shook her ash-blonde head in irritation '—taking a final look round before we handed the keys back to . . .' She looked vague for a moment. 'Before we handed over the keys to S – Stock's solicitors. Is there some water? If I can just have some water . . .'

Merrily said, 'Charlie, I don't have time to explain. You have got to— Please trust me.'

'Look,' Annie Howe said, 'where's the fucking car?' She finally sat up. 'Get these people—'

'Stay where you are, Anne.' Charlie's jaw was working from side to side. 'You're naked, girl.'

'*What* are you—?' Annie Howe rose up suddenly, and Charlie Howe stepped to one side so that Annie was in the full sun.

There was a moment of silence, and then she started to scream, her head tossed back, eyes squeezed shut against the blast of light. Her spine arched in a spasm, her white breasts thrust towards the sun, her mouth opening into a big, hungry smile, as if—

In the instant that the screaming turned to laughter, Merrily was down by Annie's side, both hands on her burning forehead. The eyes opened once, a flaring of panic and outrage under the sweat-soaked white-blonde hair.

It wasn't all sweat, though. The top must finally have come the flask inside, because the airline bag, where Annie's head had la was soaked now with holy water.

'*Rebekah*,' Merrily said calmly, somewhere deep inside he '*Listen to me.*'

For an instant, hugging the Lady of the Bines, in all her absorbing their coarse, racking sobs, she found the core – the core found her. The coin spun in the air and stayed i caught in a confluence of sunbeams, and kept on spinn new copper.

She could *do* this.

St Paul said: *Put love first.*

That simple: bypassing fear and revulsion, the heaving aside of a great concrete slab of personal resentment, ignoring even the stunning irony.

Behind her, Simon St John stood quietly, made the sign of the cross in the air above them.

*Love is patient. Love is kind and envies no one. Love is never boastful, nor conceited. Love keeps no score of wrongs. There is no limit to its faith, its hope and its endurance.*

Merrily felt her hands becoming very warm, warmer than the skin beneath. She was in a void, an emptiness that was infinitely vast and yet also movingly intimate. She didn't understand. She didn't have to understand. At some point, the words came automatically, from the final verse of the old Celtic anthemic prayer.

> *Let them not run from the love that you offer*
> *But hold them safe from the forces of evil*
> *On each of their dyings shed your light . . .*

# 1

# Love Lightly?

'Two,' Prof Levin said over the phone. 'Let me get this right. You're showing me two songs?'

Tomorrow, the legendary producer was returning home for a few days. Tom Storey's slow disembowelling of the blues, he said, was making everyone close to clinically depressed; they needed a break. This was costly, sure, but if Storey had any real need to worry about expense he'd be recording at Knight's Frome.

Lol sat on one of the packing cases in the kitchen. It was almost dark. The sky was lime green in the north, and there were great banks of cloud. A storm was coming on and it was very humid.

'I suppose, if I was being honest,' he admitted, because this was a night for complete honesty, 'I'd have to say the last verse of the first one needs rewriting. And I might have to dump the second one altogether, on account of it . . . Maybe it wasn't my place to write it, not really.'

There was a long silence.

Prof said, 'So, basically, just half a song, correct?'

'Hopefully. I'm really sorry, Prof.' And he was. He *should* feel ashamed. He had a lot of work to do.

'It's that bloody Boswell guitar,' Prof said. 'I knew it would be cursed.'

'Oh, no,' Lol said quickly. 'No curse. I don't think so. Probably no curse after all.'

No need, surely, for the burning of the Boswell *vardo* to become any kind of issue – although Al had told Lol that maybe tomorrow, maybe the day after, he would not be *over*-surprised to wake up in the Lower World with a whole lot of explaining to do. He insisted he was taking nothing for granted; he would be grateful for each fresh day with Sally and the ponies and Stanley the donkey. He was grateful, too, obviously, to the *drukerimaskri* – if he'd *had* to borrow a place in which to be found dead, he hadn't particularly wanted to borrow it from Adam Lake.

So, Lol wondered, had he actually encountered Rebekah as he sat in the hop-yard under the midday sun? Had he, in fact, journeyed to the Lower World?

These were not questions that a *gaujo* had any right to ask, Al had said sternly. But, well, if the little priest *had* managed to retrieve the Romany soul of poor Rebekah, he would not deny having performed a little essential groundwork.

Al smiled: gypsies lied.

'I've been thinking about you, Lol,' he'd said finally, leaning on the fence around his paddock, watching Stanley browse the buttercups. 'You and this thing about the Frome. This rootlessness, this having no home? As you may have gathered, we Romanies prefer to see this as a benefit – no estates, no cities, no cathedrals.'

'But I'm a *gaujo*,' Lol pointed out.

'In which case—' Al kept on smiling '—consider it the first stage in your personal development.'

Walking away, in the sunset, Lol had observed Sally coming down from the museum to meet Al. She wore a long, white dress, embroidered around the bosom, wide and flouncy at the hem, and at least forty years out of fashion.

Prof said, 'The other thing – and I want the truth here, Laurence, no placatory bullshit – has that insane bastard been near the place?'

'Who?'

'*Who?* Stock, of course! The impossible creep who claims he's being haunted out of his home. If you recall, around the time I was suggesting you should be thinking about producing at least *four* fresh songs, I also gave express instructions that Stock should not be admitted to the premises while I was gone, yes?'

Lol sighed. 'You don't read the papers much, do you, Prof . . . when you're working?'

'I don't read the papers at all. I don't read the mail. I don't read menus, either, because when I'm working, with my stomach the way it is these days, I don't even eat. No, I don't read the sodding papers.'

'Evidently not,' Lol agreed.

He moved through the silent studio, where the Boswell guitar, in all her quiet beauty, sat on the stand, where the preliminary – and possibly final – tape of *The Cure of Souls* still occupied the deck.

After a lot of noise, it was very quiet now.

A thousand questions still echoing; just a few answers.

Gomer Parry had brought Jane and Eirion across to Prof's, and Eirion's dad's secretary had arrived in the BMW – she'd come up to Hereford by train with a spare set of keys to pick up the car from the police station where it had been accommodated overnight. And to collect Eirion. Jane had considered her options for a while before getting in the car with them. 'Can't let the poor dab face this alone.'

This was after the police had been and gone: Frannie Bliss, with DS Mumford. DCI Howe had left, it was presumed, with her father. 'She'll deny any of it happened,' Merrily had said to Lol afterwards, as they waved the kids away to Pembrokeshire. 'Especially to herself. She'll have had someone tell the press she was called away on another case, and she'll never talk about it, not even to her dad. And she'll hate me worse than ever. But that's the price you pay.'

Lol said, 'What would have happened to her, if you hadn't—'

Merrily had just shrugged, and Lol had conjured, then dismissed, nebulous images of a hungry, promiscuous Annie Howe darkening into corruption.

Like her old man?

'You think?' Merrily had asked him.

'I don't really know. He went out of his way to tell you about Allan Henry and the corruption he *wasn't* involved in. I just . . . don't know.'

'He told me you were going to blackmail him,' Merrily said, 'to keep Annie off my back.'

'You see? He *told* you that. It doesn't fit with him having something to hide, does it? I bet he does, though.'

'Oh yeah,' Merrily said. 'No doubt at all. *Would* you have?'

'Blackmailed him? I never even thought of it that way. I've never done anything like that before.' He'd blushed. 'Maybe.'

'I don't deserve it,' Merrily said. 'I don't deserve any of you . . . Sophie . . . Jane – don't ever tell her I said that! I just . . . flounder about from one irrational scenario to another, making a balls of things, coming to false conclusions – appealing to God, apologizing to God . . . being terrified of coming one day to reject God. I mean, before all this began I was supposed to recruit a back-up team. I don't know where to start. Simon—'

'Forget Simon,' Lol said. 'Like you don't have enough problems.'

'He came through today, though.'

'You don't know what he's like tonight.'

'I do have a situation he could help with. If he'd be willing to talk to someone with the same kind of . . . sensitivity problem.'

'Amy Shelbone?'

'Either she represses it and it goes on causing trouble. Or she gets advice from the wrong kind of people and becomes something monstrous. She won't get sent to a detention centre, but she might get put into the psychiatric system – and who's that going to help? Not Amy, and certainly not any other patients she comes into contact with.'

'Psychiatric medicine doesn't allow for people like that,' Lol said. 'No use talking to Simon, though. He'll only say he'd screw her up even more. How about I talk to Isabel and *she* talks to Simon?'

'Would he talk to the Shelbones, too, do you think? As a psychic and a clergyman?'

'But not in those jeans,' Lol had said.

Merrily had yawned and asked if it was OK to go up to her cell in Prof's cottage and lie down for a while.

There was no need to show her to the room; she knew the way. And, anyway, Prof had rung then.

It was evening now, with a premature darkening of the sky. Probably the coming of the long-forecast storm. Lol sat down in the booth with the Boswell, fingered the opening chords of the River Frome song. He needed to sleep; didn't think he'd be able to.

He thought about the Boswell Romany philosophy: live lightly. And love lightly? He couldn't love lightly, didn't think Al Boswell could either. He found himself wondering, not for the first time, what would have happened if Al and Sally hadn't found them in the hop-yard last night. Decided he wasn't going to think about that ever again.

Or about Gerard Stock hanging in his cell.

'Why did he have to kill himself?' Merrily had said. 'So many things nobody will ever know. *Everyone* said he wasn't the suicide type.'

'Circumstances can change the kind of person you are,' Lol said. 'Wolverhampton?'

'Experience. I . . .' He'd hesitated. 'Suppose he had a . . . prison visitor . . .?'

Merrily had said, 'Huw Owen uses the term "visitor" to describe the appearance of a relative or close friend – a comfort thing, usually.'

'Maybe I mean burglar. Maybe that's not logical. Where would it find female energy in the remand centre?'

'If there's one thing I've learned in the past year,' Merrily said, 'it's that human logic doesn't often come into it. But . . . there might be absolutely no paranormal context to Stock's death. I mean, *I* might have to operate on the basis that the Unseen permeates everything, but society functions well enough – if a little colourlessly – without it.'

Lol padded up the steps, along the minstrel's gallery and into his loft, as the first thunder sounded from the west. He took off his round, brass-rimmed glasses and popped them into their case on the plywood onion box serving as his bedside table.

A vivid mauve light filled the skylight above him. It was open a little, and the loft was filled with the rich caramel smell of ripened hay from the meadow.

Lol felt inexplicably upset.

Well, perhaps not *that* inexplicably.

He let himself fall back on to the camp bed. But it wasn't there.

He came down on hay. He looked up at the blurred purple square of the skylight. Huh? Was he so overtired he'd climbed up to the wrong loft?

He reached for his glasses on the onion box.

A hand closed around his wrist.

With so little sleep in two days, they'd both been beyond exhaustion, but this had somehow made it both more intense and more nebulous. Maybe the fatigue was responsible, also, for that sense of been-here-before, if only in dreams, and Lol had been afraid to sleep in case this should turn out to be another one.

It was the storm that awoke him, creamy lightning in the skylight, and he jumped up to close it against the inevitable rain, climbing on the camp bed, which she'd folded up before spreading the hay and straw and the duvet on top of it.

She said she'd dreamed of Stock. The carcass turning slowly, from side to side.

'You see what you get sleeping with me,' Merrily said.

They made love again, under the thunder, and then she lay on her back, and the rain began to hit the skylight in long, slow drops, as if each one had been calculated.

# 2

# Strung Up

Mid-morning, Merrily went back to the vicarage, and then she planned to go and visit the Shelbones – or try to. Lol wanted to go with her, and then thought no: *love lightly. Don't seek to possess.*

He went into the studio to think about creating a new song before Prof arrived back. Any new song; he knew it wasn't going to be a problem. The sky was washed clean. The Boswell guitar felt like a living thing.

It was around eleven-thirty when DI Frannie Bliss phoned from Leominster.

'Hope you don't think I lied to yer about that press statement, Lol, but it's not happened, has it? And now the lovely Snow Maiden's gone on a few days' leave. Which was unexpected.'

'It's God, Frannie. God looks after key personnel.'

'You didn't talk to anybody yourself, then?'

'Never really got chance, in the end.'

'Ah well . . .' Pause. 'Merrily wouldn't be there, would she?'

'Gone to work. I mean . . . she's . . . at work. Presumably.'

'Only, with the boss skiving off, the PM report on Stock's arrived on *my* desk, with no little controversy.'

'We were talking about Stock earlier.'

'A lot of people are talking about Stock again this morning.'

'It's what he would've wanted. We were still trying to think why he did it – hanged himself.'

'It's a mystery,' Frannie Bliss said. 'And not the only one.'

'Can I give Merrily a message?'

Bliss thought about it, sighed. 'Bugger it,' he said. 'This is tormenting me a bit. Stock strung himself up with his shirt, right?'

'That's what we heard.'

'The PM report says the severe ligature marks found on his neck are what you might call inconsistent with that. According to the Home Office pathologist and the forensics lab, we should be looking for a length of rusty wire, maybe seven or eight millimetres thick, probably multi-stranded. There was no sign of any such wire in Stock's cell. We can be fairly sure he did not bring any in with him. And it was certainly not around his neck when he was cut down. Needless to say, the Remand Centre is being searched, no doubt, even as we speak.'

'Strange.'

'It is, isn't it? There was also an impression on the side of his neck strongly suggestive of a hook being attached to the wire. One of my lads, who was a farmer's boy, had an idea what this might be.'

Lol said, 'You're talking about hop-wire, aren't you?'

# Closing Credits

For technical assistance with hops, kilns, furnaces, gypsies, exorcism etc., thanks to:

Krys and Geoff 'Chovihano' Boswell (no relation), Paul Gibbons, Tony Heavens and Lynn, Mike Kreciala, Jeannine McMullen, Colin Osborne, Tony Priddle, John Pudge, Lisle Ryder, Tony Wargent and Trudy Williams.

Jani Sue Muhlestein gave me a timely reminder about Simon St John, whose rather gruelling earlier history is chronicled in *December*.

Once again, my wife, Carol, edited the manuscript with stunning perception, and pulled back the novel from the brink of the abyss with two perfectly tailored ideas. Thanks, too, to my editor at Pan-Mac, Peter Lavery, scourge of the staccato sentence, for the ultra-sensitive fine-tune, and to my agent, Andrew Hewson, who solved that delicate final problem. (*'Look, she's a 37-year-old woman . . .!'*)

If I bent the facts about the hop industry in the Frome Valley, no blame should be attached to *A Pocketful of Hops*, produced and published by The Bromyard Local History Society or Richard Filmer's *Hops and Hop Picking* (Shire). On Romanies, Patrick 'Jasper' Lee's *We Borrow the Earth* (Thorsons) was an inspiration, as were Jean-Paul Clebert's seminal *Gypsies* and the haunting and evocative *A Time from the World* by Rowena Farre and Raymond Buckland's *Gypsy Witchcraft and Magic*. I'm still not sure know how much of a threat a *mulo* is to a *gaujo*, but my advice is: don't chance it.

Martin Israel's profound and unflinchingly direct book, *Exorcism*, is published by the SPCK.

All the characters are entirely imaginary, and no councillors or officials, bent or clean, in the story have any connection with the members or staff of the existing Herefordshire Council. The Barnchurch Trading Estate is not, we must all hope, on anyone's planning schedule. And while West Mercia Police may have had their problems over the years, none, to my knowledge, have been in relation to the Frome Valley, where Knight's Frome may be difficult to find and nobody remembers the Emperor.

Finally – *that* website. There is, as yet, no Hereford Deliverance site, and anyone with problems of that nature is advised to log on to Worcester's: www.cofe–worcester.org.uk/deliverance